MINUET

Notes from Boston #4

A. M. Leibowitz

Supposed Crimes LLC • Matthews, North Carolina

Published in the United States.

ISBN: 978-1-944591-61-8

www.supposedcrimes.com

This book is typeset in Goudy Old Style.

Content Note

This story is not meant to be representative of the full range of experiences of polyamorous relationships or aromantic, pansexual, bisexual, and transgender characters. Nor does it represent every person with any other identity. Each person's life is their own. That said, my hope is that readers may find themselves on the pages in some way. In any case, whether you feel kinship with the characters or not, you are not alone. Whatever your journey, you have my support.

This novel contains discussion of sensitive topics such as gender dysphoria, child abuse, relationship violence, addiction, and sexual assault. There are no graphic descriptions of any of those subjects, but the conversation is open and honest between characters. This is not a sad or dark story. It's about the blossoming love between people and creating a happy, fulfilled life even amidst challenges. However, readers know themselves and how much or little they are able to take in.

Content Note

This story is not meant to be representative of the full range of experiences of polyamorous relationships or aromantic, pansexual, bisexual, and transgender characters. Nor does it represent every person with any other identity. Each person's life is their own. That said, my hope is that readers may find themselves on the pages in some way. In any case, whether you feel kinship with the characters or not, you are not alone. Whatever your journey, you have my support.

This novel contains discussion of sensitive topics such as gender dysphoria, child abuse, relationship violence, addiction, and sexual assault. There are no graphic descriptions of any of those subjects, but the conversation is open and honest between characters. This is not a sad or dark story. It's about the blossoming love between people and creating a happy, fulfilled life even amidst challenges. However, readers know themselves and how much or little they are able to take in.

The future is no more uncertain than the present.
~Walt Whitman

Thanks

First and foremost, thank you to my excellent and supportive beta readers. Both of them have stuck with me, and this series, from the beginning. I cannot say enough good things about them.

Bree, you are a treasure. I don't know how I'd have made it this far without your unwavering support. You are a fine writer yourself, and I am so grateful to have had you in my corner for so many years and over so many novels. May you reach your own goals and find the kind of generous care you've given me.

Debbie, I don't even know what to say. You have been my writerly rock for so long as well as being a dear friend. You know you've hit gold when the same conversation can involve a random funny story about family life, a nerdy discussion about music and books, and a deep baring of the soul. I have so much respect for you, and I am eternally grateful for the help you've given me in shaping this series.

Of course, my family deserves lots of thanks, hugs, and chocolate peanut blossom cookies in exchange for putting up with my endless ranting about the writing of this novel. It's taken over a year of typing, deleting, hair-pulling, and yelling to get it to its final stages. I suppose I should wish you all luck getting through my next manuscript.

Thank you to my publisher, who for some reason keeps taking chances on me and allowing me to keep on sending her things. Hopefully one of these days, I'll be able to extend in return the kind of grace and care I've received.

Much love and thanks to everyone who worked on this novel to turn it into something good. I hope to have a chance to work with you all again in the future.

Last but definitely not least, thank you to all my dear readers who have waited patiently for each new book in this series. I hope that this final installment delivers everything you wished for. This is the end of the road for these characters as we send them off into the sunset. But it's not the end of all things, and I hope you'll stay tuned for whatever adventures come next.

Much love to you all. Onward and upward!

Part One: Theme

CHAPTER ONE

THE FIRST thing Mack Whitman did when Sage opened the door was aim a punch at his face.

He'd have landed it too, if Amelia hadn't launched herself at him from behind and grabbed his arms just in time. He squirmed, but she didn't let go, so he angled his head to glare at her.

"You don't want the cops involved," she murmured.

He nodded, and she finally let go. Mack clenched his hands at his sides, still itching to have at Sage. Realistically, Sage probably could've taken him. Mack was five-foot-nine and might have weighed a hundred forty soaking wet. Sage wasn't much taller, but he had a good thirty pounds on Mack, mostly muscle. He'd definitely been working out lately.

The look on his face made Mack's rage meter climb again. Smug, taunting. Nothing out of the ordinary there. Mack wanted to smack the expression off his face while calling him a dozen nasty names. The only thing stopping him was Amelia's hand on his back.

"To what do I owe the pleasure?" Sage folded his arms.

"To your continued stalking of Jamie, you sick fuck," Mack spat. He leaned forward far enough that Amelia tightened her grip on his shirt.

"That's a good one. Listen, I have company, so you can come back later." Sage went to shut the door.

Mack stuck out his foot, blocking it. "Not until we get this settled. Don't you dare fucking lie to me, Sage. Did you know Jamie's real messed up because of you? It's not some game."

Jamie. The way he looked the last time Mack saw him, blacked out on his bed, came to his mind. At least a third of Mack's rage wasn't directed at Sage; it was aimed at himself. He'd seen the signs Jamie was bingeing again, but he'd ignored them. Everything had seemed so good when Jamie started seeing Cian. Then the damn flowers arrived from Sage, and it had all gone to shit in a single afternoon. Mack wasn't going to stand by and let a menace like Sage destroy someone Mack thought of as a brother.

"And how do you think I feel?" Sage, being Sage. Another non-shocker. "He's the one who left me, not the other way around. Eight years, and you'd think he could at least talk it through first."

"Eight years of you fucking with him," Mack growled. "Don't even try it, you asshole. Every one of us saw what you did."

A muffled voice came from somewhere in the apartment. Sage's tone changed to sweetness as he called over his shoulder, "Be right there, honey." Turning back to Mack and Amelia, he said, "You see? I've got someone here. Now, why would I want to bother with my worthless ex when I've got him?"

"How dare you!" Mack tried to break free from Amelia again. "Jamie's worth a thousand of you, you bag of rotting, pus-covered—"

Amelia, still clutching Mack's shirt, peered around him. "Sage, I'm tired, okay? I want to go home. Mack's like a rabid dog right now, and it's exhausting. So you listen to me." She let go of Mack and stood next to him, hands on hips. "This is the one and only time I'm gonna say it. Stay the fuck away from Jamie. You won't like the consequences otherwise."

Sage laughed. He eyed her up and down, making Mack's blood boil. "Oh, sweetie. What are you going to do if I don't?"

"Nothing that'll land me in jail. But I'm not alone, you know. Jamie's got friends now, see, and they're not as nice as I am. You ever meet his buddy Nate?" She raised her hand as high as she could reach. "He's 'bout six-five and built like a football player."

Mack wisely didn't laugh. Nate was hardly the type to take anyone out. What was he going to do, sing opera at Sage? The most damage he'd do would be shattering Sage's eardrums with a high, sustained note. He was intimidating on first sight, though. Amelia had exaggerated by a couple inches, but Nate was a giant compared to Jamie.

"You do anything, and I'll call the cops myself." Sage tried to stare Amelia down.

"Not saying he'll put a hand on you," she replied. Still calm, still focused. "I'm saying we know what you're capable of. You'll hurt Jamie and then claim you never touched him. And I'm saying you're gonna regret that. You'll have to go through all of us to get to him."

"Mm-hm. You keep right on thinking you can stop me from doing whatever I want."

Amelia sighed dramatically and shook her head. "I didn't want to have to do this, but you're not the only one who knows things that may or may not be used against you. Are we clear?"

"What's that supposed to mean?"

"It means," Amelia said, leaning closer, "that Jamie doesn't have any more secrets you can pretend you're keeping for him. You, on the other hand..." She tilted her head. "I'll ask again. Are we clear?"

Sage swallowed visibly. "Fine. You have my word, I won't contact Jamie again."

"Oh, hell, no. Not good enough," Mack said.

Amelia smiled meanly. "Get your new man out here."

"What? No!"

Too late. The beefcake who had spoken from the other room emerged, looked at the doorway, and raised an eyebrow. "Sage, what's going on?"

"Nothing, baby. I'll just be a sec."

Amelia beckoned Mr. Muscles with one finger. Obediently, he came over. Well-trained puppy. "You," she said. "Are you his boyfriend, his personal trainer, or just a fuck toy?"

The man's eyes popped. "Uh..."

"Good answer," Amelia told him. "Listen, Sage here has kind of a problem with leaving his ex alone. Do us a favor and make sure he does the right thing, hm?"

Mr. Muscles looked sideways at Sage. "O-okay."

Amelia reached up and patted his cheek. "You seem like a decent guy." She pulled a paper and pen out of her purse and scrawled something on it. Handing it to Mr. Muscles, she said, "Here. My number, just in case you need some help enforcing the no-contacting-your-ex rule. Or in case your interest in men isn't exclusive." She looked him up and down, winked, and then turned back to Sage. "You think long and hard"—she giggled; Mr. Muscles snorted—"about what I said. And stay the hell away from Jamie."

She whirled around, grabbed Mack's hand, and yanked. Too startled to do anything else, Mack followed her. He heard the click of the door and angry voices on the other side. With a quick glance back, Amelia took off down the stairs.

Outside, they leaned against the building. Amelia was shaking, and Mack reached for her. He felt her heaving breaths as she tried to calm down. Mack was grateful every day that he could count on her. If he'd gone to Sage's apartment alone, he'd either be unconscious or sitting in the back of a cop car.

"You okay?" he asked.

She pulled back to look at him. "Yeah. You?"

"Fine, now." He exhaled forcefully. "More than I can say for Jamie."

"God." Amelia shook her head. "Sage is the very worst. What the fuck happened to him?"

"He's always been this way. Ever since I've known him."

Amelia bit her lip. Mack regretted saying it. She had a soft spot for him, or she'd had one when they were kids. Always wanted to believe the best in people. She'd held onto hope that Sage might change or get help or something, but what he'd done to Jamie made it clear it would never happen. Tonight might have been the first time she realized what Mack had known for years.

"Why?" she asked. "Why did Jamie put up with him for so long?" She looked up at Mack, and now her hurt and anger showed. "Why did we?"

"We did it for Jamie's sake." That was mostly true.

He pulled her close again. There was no guarantee Sage would leave Jamie alone, but Mack suspected he wasn't going to keep trying now that Mr. Muscles was about to discover all his carefully constructed lies.

"Come on," Mack murmured. "That was intense. We should check on Jamie and then maybe go over to yours for a while, hm?"

"Yeah." Amelia wiped her eyes. "I'd like that."

They'd taken the T to Sage's apartment, and the next train didn't leave for nearly an hour. That gave Mack and Amelia time to sit in South Station with a couple cups of decaf in front of them. Mack didn't touch his; he was still too worked up from their confrontation with Sage.

He would've like to say he didn't see it coming, couldn't have predicted it, didn't know Sage was capable. Except he had known.

Sage had been obsessed with Jamie from day one.

When Jamie showed up at their school, Mack had him pegged as one of the rich kids. Most of his well-off classmates came from old money, families who generation after generation bought the best education and the best jobs. Mack thought Jamie was one of the ones whose parents had clawed their way into it. He seemed the type, soft-spoken and not quite fitting in, a little too pretty with his neatly styled hair and brand-name clothes. Turned out Jamie had a vastly different story, but Mack couldn't have known.

Jamie was living with his aunt and uncle at the time after years of being homeless and several months on the streets. It took ages before Mack could put it all together, and even now he wasn't sure he knew everything. Jamie still kept some of his life hidden behind closed doors. Only through careful observation had Mack discovered various interconnected bits and pieces.

Before learning where Jamie came from, Mack had planned to stay far away. Not like Sage, but then, he really was upper class. He had his own reasons for hanging out with people like Mack and Amelia. Mack warned him off, but Sage ignored that advice and latched onto Jamie, even after they all knew the truth about his past. It was Sage's personal mission to get his attention. When he wanted to, Sage could turn the charm up to a hundred. Took two more years before Jamie finally cracked. Two years in which Mack wished he'd been able to somehow convince Jamie not to do it, wished he'd told Jamie the truth about what Sage was doing.

Amelia tapped Mack's wrist. "You're thinking too hard."

Mack let her take his hand, but he looked away, staring at the long line at the McDonald's counter. He wasn't angry with her for trying or for how much she'd once cared about Sage. She'd known him longer than either of them knew Mack. She hadn't even questioned Mack when he'd called her to say he'd taken the day off and needed her to accompany him. He couldn't ask her to do any more than she already had.

So he lied about what was on his mind. "I'm wondering if Jamie will be awake when we get back, that's all."

"You're worried about him." She gently turned Mack's head so he was looking at her. How did she know him so well? "He will be okay. He's with the others. I meant what I said. He'll eventually realize he's not alone anymore."

She didn't mean that he'd wake up and see their friends, though that was probably true too. Jamie clung hard to Sage, even now, buying into his lies about who really cared about him. At some point, Jamie was going to have to learn how to be his whole, real self. Mack wasn't going to be the one to tell him that.

An incoming text startled Mack, and he took out his phone. Their friend Marlie. *Jamie knows where you went.*

"Fuck," Mack muttered.

Amelia's mouth dropped open, and she grabbed Mack's arm. "Is Jamie—"

"He's fine." Mack stuffed his phone back in his pocket without answering the text. "That was Marlie. Someone, maybe her, told him what we were doing."

"Oh, shit."

"Right. He's bound to be pissed as hell, if he's in any shape to react."

"Should we go back there?"

"Yeah." Mack looked up at the clock. Still quite a while until boarding. "I need some stuff before we go to yours anyway. Might be better to make it quick."

She nodded and went back to sipping her coffee. Mack still hadn't had his. He really needed a cigarette, but he was trying—again—to quit. Amelia never said a word against him for it, but he knew she was happier when he was off the smokes. They all had their vices, and if Mack was the sort to overanalyze it, he'd probably wonder if they'd inherited some tendency from their family trees.

He successfully managed his craving, at least for the time being. They tossed out their trash, including Mack's still-full cup of coffee. Amelia eyed him, but she said nothing. By the time they were through, someone else had taken over their table. It was just as well. The electronic schedule finally listed their train as boarding. Amelia looped her arm through Mack's as they made their way out of the station to the tracks.

Back at the apartment, there were only a few people left. Marlie was still there, and Cian, Jamie's boyfriend. Neither of them were a surprise. Their friend Izzy, on the other hand, was. His fiancé, Nate, lived with Mack and Jamie, but Nate didn't seem to be around.

The first thing Marlie said when the door opened was, "He's sleeping. Don't wake him."

Mack nodded. "We came to check, but we're going back to Amelia's." He didn't add that he thought Jamie would want some space. Marlie probably already knew that.

Izzy acknowledged Mack with a nod. He merely looked tired, but Cian was an absolute wreck. Mack had only met him briefly a handful of times, but he had the impression Cian was generally the sort to take things in stride. Now he looked awful. His eyes were red-rimmed, and he was curled in on himself. Mack wished he'd done something sooner, the minute he saw Jamie was heading for trouble.

"He needs more help than we can give him," Marlie said.

For a minute, Mack thought she meant Cian, but then he realized she was still on the subject of Jamie. "I know," he said.

Marlie fixed him with her fierce gaze, and it said everything. She was telling Mack silently that taking off to see Sage wasn't going to fix anything and that he should've picked up on the signs sooner. The worst part was that Mack had, but he guaranteed he had a lot more experience with someone like Jamie than Marlie did. Mack might have forced Jamie's hand sooner rather than later, but the outcome wouldn't have been any different.

Mack nodded at her and ducked into his bedroom. He left the door open, and he could hear Amelia talking quietly with Marlie. He didn't catch enough of it to know if she was filling Marlie in on the details of their visit with Sage, but he suspected not. He zipped his bag and brought it out to the living room.

Izzy looked up. "Thank you," he said. "For what you did. He won't say it, so I will."

Eight months ago, Izzy had been there when Jamie left the asshole for good. He'd been the one on call, working at the time as an EMT. Izzy had thought Sage hit Jamie. He couldn't have known that would be entirely unlike him. Sage mostly liked to leave the kind of marks no one could see. It was pure luck he'd managed to cause some physical damage, probably only thanks to Jamie's ongoing challenges with eating properly. Jamie had been dehydrated and underfed, which turned anything Sage did into a risk.

Mack responded with the tilt of his chin. Amelia and Mack said goodnight to the others and left the apartment. Jamie had enough people there if he needed anything, but Mack still felt guilty leaving. He wasn't doing it to brush off the situation or anyone keeping vigil. If Jamie was still so out of it, he and Mack wouldn't be able to deal with what Sage had done or with how Mack addressed it. Mack wasn't going to do any good sitting there waiting for him to come around.

The drive to Amelia's was quick, and they took her car. He

followed her up the stairs to her apartment, admiring the view from behind. He was more than ready to reconnect with her after the day he'd had. He wanted her in his arms, under him and on top of him and around him. It was the best way he knew to release all the built-up tension from his worry over Jamie and his anger at Sage. Amelia knew how to soothe him like no one else.

Inside, she only waited until he'd set his bag down and she'd put her purse on the table by the door. Years of practice and trust and mutual understanding meant she knew exactly what he needed. She put her arms around his neck and drew him into a long, heated kiss. Mack's chest loosened.

He slid his hand to cup her soft, round ass. Amelia had a great physique. Unlike Mack, she was thick and athletic, muscular under her curves from her work as a personal trainer. She used every bit of her full-figured body to her advantage when she and Mack were together. After a few heated minutes of grinding against each other, Amelia led Mack into her bedroom.

Watching her strip down, Mack knew what he needed tonight. He had to have her inside him, taking care of him. They didn't do it often, but he trusted her entirely to give him the release he craved. Naked, he went to the drawer and pulled out the strap-on. Amelia accepted it. She drew Mack into another long, sensual kiss.

Mack put himself in Amelia's capable hands, guiding her while submitting fully to her. This was exactly what he wanted, their lovemaking born from years of understanding and respect. They lay on their sides, and she entered him that way, wrapping herself around him. There was incredible freedom in the way he melted into her arms.

He urged her faster, her hand on his hip and his between his legs. All other thoughts were driven out of his head by the intensity with which she pounded into him. She could've gone harder if he'd been on his knees or his back, but he wanted the sense of being protected he had in this position. He let go, her lips warm and sweet on his neck and her fingers tightening as his spine stiffened. Relief came in brutal waves until he had nothing left to give but a long, stuttering cry.

Amelia carefully withdrew, and Mack collapsed onto his back. His limbs were quivering. Once he'd recovered, he would take pleasure in bringing Amelia to the same heights. For the moment, he needed to breathe. As she always did on these occasions, she draped herself over him and ran her hands along his sweaty skin, following them with her lips.

She lapped at the places where his spunk had landed, taking it on her tongue and sharing it with him when they kissed. It turned her on, and Mack loved that about her—loved that she never hesitated to show him what she liked. He'd met women who enjoyed sex as much as he did, but none besides Amelia who took such delight and fascination in the glorious mess of it all.

The thought amused him, and he chuckled. When he opened his eyes, Amelia was smiling down at him. There was something Mack found poetic about celebrating their reconnection.

"I want to write a new song," he blurted.

Amelia's laughter was like water for his soul. "About how much you like being fucked by me?"

Mack touched her hair, her cheek, her neck. "Yeah."

"I love that." She kissed him. "My turn?"

"God, yes. Tell me what you want."

"Your tongue on my clit and your fingers inside me."

"Anything for you."

Mack rolled over, and his body hummed with the pleasure of making her toes curl and her back arch.

CHAPTER TWO

AMELIA'S BOOTS weren't made for walking; they were steel-toed and made for kicking someone's ass through his teeth. She'd once trained rigorously until she was finally strong enough to take on the man who'd spent the better part of her childhood using her as boxing practice. She wasn't sorry that she'd broken his nose when he grabbed her hair and tried to haul her around like he was used to doing. He'd threatened to call the police, but she had no fear of that happening. He wouldn't like it if the cops discovered all the shit he'd stolen. She had ample proof.

Her sperm donor left her alone for good after that. She didn't know and didn't care where he was now. She'd heard through the grapevine a few months back that he was out of jail after the accident he caused out on the Cape. Misdemeanor motor vehicle homicide, they said. Took out a pregnant woman. Amelia wasn't worried he'd come find her, not with his license suspended for fifteen years.

Which was why, when Mack called her at the end of the summer, she'd agreed to go see Sage. She had power over him, and he damn well knew it. No one was ever again going to control her or someone she cared about. Even Jamie didn't know Amelia was sitting on the truth about Sage. After everything that had happened, she probably owed Jamie the real story. If she'd had any idea things had gotten so bad, she'd have taken care of it in a blink. Mack hadn't told her Jamie was self-destructing, nor had he shared the part Sage played in it.

She would've liked to say it was their stubborn refusal to acknowledge their feelings, but that wasn't it. This one was on Jamie for his belief he'd be burdening someone else with his problems. Amelia could get behind that; she'd done it herself for years. The difference was, she went after the source instead of trying to pretend he didn't exist. She understood why Jamie didn't do the same, but she wished he'd told her or anyone else.

It was all water under the bridge. After his collapse, Jamie went to some day program in Springfield. Last Amelia heard, he was doing better, getting therapy and being cared for by Cian's other partners—his family. Jamie still deserved an explanation, but Amelia wanted to do it in a way that wouldn't set him back. If she told him what really happened with Sage and the band, and that it was never Jamie's fault in the first place, it might wreck his progress. Mack, on the other hand, was never going to be allowed in on that secret. He didn't blame Jamie at all, but he also didn't know the whole story. If anyone was going to be destroyed by the truth, Mack would be the one.

For now, Amelia was content to grab her things and head over to Marlie's. She'd kicked the men out of the house for the night, and even though she had her nine-month-old son, it would still be quiet. She would put him to bed, and then the adults could talk in peace.

Amelia had never experienced the types of relationships with women she had now, with their ever-growing group. She'd been "one of the boys," aside from Cassie and a handful of undefined relationships. Some of the women she'd pseudo-dated were cool with a casual, temporary arrangement. Others...not so much. She couldn't blame them. Without understanding the unspoken agreement she had with Mack, they would've seen her as someone jerking them around.

Amelia wasn't interested in anything with the women whose inner circle she now found herself in. Marlie was hella cool for a straight woman, and she was a connecter. She planned out these nights once a month where they were free from the men. Sometimes they went out, but other times, when the guys had plans, they went to Marlie's so she could be home with Aidan. Amelia might've complained, but he was an angel and usually slept through the whole thing.

By the time Amelia arrived, everyone else was there. Tonight it was Marlie, Nia—Andre's girlfriend—Gemma and Cassie from the Creepy Crullers, and Cassie's girlfriend, Laura. There were a handful of others who occasionally joined them, depending on who was free. Marlie welcomed Amelia in and took her jacket then offered her a drink.

There was a stack of unopened mail on a table next to the couch, a package balanced neatly on top. Marlie picked up the whole pile and deposited it in the dining room before putting a coaster down and disappearing into the kitchen to fetch Amelia's water. When she returned, Amelia couldn't resist, even knowing it was a bit rude.

"What's in the package?"

"Oh, that?" Marlie settled herself on the floor. "My new vibrator."

Amelia was glad she hadn't yet taken a sip of water, or she'd have sprayed it all over poor Laura next to her. "I'm sorry. You said that so casually."

"It's not like it's some big deal. Sheesh. I'd have thought you of all people wouldn't be weird about it."

"I'm not weird about it!" Amelia laughed. "I'm surprised is all. You don't strike me as the type to be open about that kind of stuff."

Marlie nodded. "I wouldn't have been before the whole thing with Andre and Trevor."

"Thought we weren't talking about them tonight," Nia said. "None of our men are allowed."

"We're not talking about them," Amelia told her. "We're talking about vibrators. Or something."

"Anyway," Marlie continued, raising her voice slightly. "It's my first one."

"Seriously?" Amelia gaped at her, thinking about her own collection in her bedside drawer.

Marlie shrugged. "Never needed one." She blushed. "After the baby...well, it's not the same. I've been having trouble feeling...inspired. I thought I'd try this."

It made sense, though Amelia was still surprised and amused. "Don't know what I'd do without mine."

"Spend more time at Mack's?" Gemma suggested. Nia shot her a glare.

"Ha, ha. No," Amelia answered. "Sometimes I'd rather just be on my own, you know? Not have to worry about anyone else."

They were quiet for a minute before Cassie spoke. "When was the first time you figured out masturbation?"

"Thirteen," Gemma said. "This girl at school told me about sneaking a sex positions book her parents had so she could look at the dongs. I found out my parents had the same book."

"I was in high school," Laura admitted. "I didn't get any tingly feels from boys, so I thought something was wrong. Finally figured out I was going after the wrong gender."

"I think I was about five or six and realized I could use my Barbie's feet." When everyone else just stared at Amelia, she shrugged. "It's not like I really understood it until I was a lot older."

"We should have one of those sex toy parties," Gemma suggested.

"Oh, God. No." Amelia groaned. "Those are for repressed middle-class Jesus types giggling over how naughty it is." She had the sense to feel embarrassed when Marlie's face fell.

"That was me. I grew up in that way. Like Laura, I thought something was wrong, but it's because I *did* like getting off. I would do it and then feel so guilty, like everyone at my church youth group was going to know just by looking at me. Any time we prayed silently to confess our sins to God, that's the one I used. I asked God to make me stop wanting to." Marlie's voice broke.

"Holy shit," Amelia said. "I'm sorry."

Laura handed Marlie a tissue. "So how did you overcome it? I eventually just had to tell my religious family to go fuck themselves. Haven't spoken to them in years."

Marlie wiped her eyes. "I had sex with Trevor. It was the summer we were both eighteen, and..." She trailed off, looking at Nia to see if she was going to affirm the no-menfolk rule; she didn't. "It was a relief, actually. The world didn't end."

"I take it you never read smut or watched porn, either," Amelia said.

"No, I did." Marlie blushed again. "I read a ton of fan fiction. No porn."

"None?" Now even Nia's eyebrows rose.

"I've seen it now. I don't like it that much. I don't know. All those skinny women with big boobs, and the noises they make!" Marlie did a fantastic impression of the breathy, high-pitched sounds, which sent a fit of giggles around the room.

"You ever try watching the gay ones?" Gemma asked.

"Oh, hell no," Marlie replied. "I live with men who are having sex together. I don't want to watch them, and I don't want to watch anyone who reminds me of them. It feels...inappropriate, like I'd be intruding on something intimate for them."

"Would it be?" Amelia asked. She and Mack had only invited in a third person a couple times, and she wasn't sure how she felt. Watching the others was intense and sexy, but participating hadn't been as good as she'd hoped.

Marlie shrugged. "It's not like I've asked them, but they're private people. Everything is separate. Their relationship with each other, and their relationships with Nia and me." She swallowed visibly. "And Trevor's relationship with Jamie."

Amelia studied her for a moment in the quiet that followed. "You know, it wouldn't hurt to talk to them about how you're feeling."

"Maybe," Marlie agreed, her cheeks turning pink once more.

"What about you all?" Gemma turned to the others. "Straight or gay porn?"

Cassie waved her hand. "Hello, lesbian here. No, I do not want to watch guys getting it on."

Laura bumped her shoulder. "I kind of like some of it, but I have to be in the right mood. Porn dicks are weirdly fascinating."

"I avoid it like the plague," Amelia put in.

"What? Why?" Gemma's expression was incredulous. "I figured if any of us was into it, it'd be you."

"I used to like it now and again, but then I accidentally stumbled on some with—" She cut herself off. Without knowing who was already aware of Jamie's history, she didn't want to reveal anything.

"Oh, you can't leave us hanging!" Nia nudged her with her toe.

"I'll bet I know." Gemma smirked at her. "Tell them."

Amelia groaned. "Fine. I accidentally saw some with Jamie in it."

"Our Jamie?" Cassie squeaked.

"Who else? I really did not need to see it."

"Jamie did porn?" Nia seemed confused.

"Yeah," Marlie confirmed. "I've never watched, but Trevor said he was in a web series ages ago."

"Why's that such a big deal?" Nia asked Amelia.

"It's weird is all. I don't need to see my friends naked. Or not like that, anyway."

"Not that I would tell him this, but"—Gemma leaned in—

"Jamie's pretty hot."

"Oh, yeah." Marlie grinned. "He's a cutie."

"You guys!" Amelia buried her face in her hands. "This is super embarrassing. I've known Jamie since we were fifteen. Also, he's extremely very gay, so back off!"

The others were laughing, and eventually Amelia joined in. She hadn't meant to see Jamie's videos at all, but Mack had watched the series, and she'd caught some of it a time or two. Jamie and Mack had never been into each other, but Amelia could see why Mack enjoyed it. That in itself was enough to make her feel awkward.

"Was it really that bad?" Gemma asked.

Bad? No. Jamie was skilled. "Uh..."

"Now you have to tell us, or we'll go looking for it ourselves," Nia prodded.

"Oh, my God."

"Spill it, sister."

Amelia sighed. "It was this web series that was more like erotic romance. But part of the selling point for Jamie is that he's, uh, very...blessed."

"Meaning...?"

"He has a giant dong, okay? Like, massive. Probably painful."

"Oh. Oh, God." Cassie broke out in fits of laughter. "I'll bet that makes things real interesting with his boyfriend."

Laura laughed so hard she flopped over. "I've heard short guys often make up for it in other ways. Guess that rumor might be true."

Amelia gasped. "Wait, you guys aren't going to hassle Jamie about this, are you?"

Collectively, the entire rest of the group stared at Amelia. Gemma finally spoke. "No, of course not. Why would we do that?"

"It's happened before." Amelia hesitated. "He's had people do crotch checks on him and stuff. I guess people feel entitled to his body because they've seen it naked."

"That's horrifying," Laura said.

Marlie had gone quiet again, and Amelia met her gaze. She had no idea what Marlie was thinking, but now she wished she hadn't said anything, especially given that Jamie and Trevor occasionally slept together. The size of Jamie's dick really didn't matter, though Amelia feared Marlie would think that was a factor in why he and Trevor had gotten together.

"Hey," Amelia said quietly. "I'm sorry."

"Now you know why I can't seem to get in the mood and why I bought a damn vibrator," she muttered. Louder, she said, "It's been a little rough lately, with him gone and so little news about how he's doing."

Amelia nodded. "I know what you mean." She squeezed Marlie's hand and leaned in. "Call me later, okay? We'll talk."

"Okay, enough of the sads. I brought a game," Gemma announced. She pulled a box out of her bag. "Gotta do something to get our minds off all this other shit. All this talk about vibrators and huge dicks, you all had better bring your A-game dirty minds to this, you got it?"

Chapter Three

MACK SIPPED his water and let the buzz of conversation in Grand Slam wash over him. He didn't know what had made him decide to go. Originally, he'd tried to drag Amelia there, but she had plans with some of their other friends for a women's night in. Knowing them, it wouldn't be what most people associated with that sort of thing. It probably wouldn't involve alcohol, though, out of sensitivity to Amelia. Like Mack, she didn't touch it; unlike him, she never had. She wasn't one for tempting fate the way he was.

Good for her, though. Mack appreciated that he wasn't the center of her universe. It always weirded him out a bit when his friends got all coupled up and wrapped their existence around the next time they'd see their partners. That sort of thing never made much sense to him. Mack had a life; Amelia had a life. It didn't always include each other.

In any case, he would hear about her night at some point, at least the parts of it she didn't deem off-limits. It had been that way since high school, confiding everything to one another. Like the time they lay on his bed talking and ended up both coming out. She'd told him about sharing a sleeping bag with a girl at a friend's birthday party and fooling around after lights out. He'd told her about his sorry-ass attempt at sucking off the captain of the soccer team when he was supposed to have been tutoring Mack in math.

Astoundingly, Rafael had been a hell of a tutor, in more ways than one. Mack had managed to pull his grade up to a B that term, and he'd kept to Bs and Cs the rest of the year without help. A senior when Mack was a freshman, Rafael was the first out bisexual guy Mack had ever known. He'd made no secret of it, and besides giving Mack a decent education in blow jobs, he'd also taught him about being proud of who he was in spite of what others might say. Maybe it wasn't so surprising for a guy who'd spent all four years on the Homecoming Court and was voted "most likely to succeed."

He'd done so, spectacularly. Mack was now sitting in the bar Rafael owned with his long-term partners. In the semi-dark, waiting for that night's show, Mack tried to clear his head so he could focus on the entertainment. Instead, he kept circling back to why he was there.

Nate and Trevor had talked him into coming, just the three of them, and Mack knew why. They all missed Jamie. He was in Springfield for nearly a month at an intensive outpatient program. His bingeing had gotten beyond his control, especially after the shit Sage pulled. The most recent blackout had been the last straw. Mack was glad Jamie'd gotten help, but it didn't take away the weirdness of being alone in the apartment.

Nate had been all right. He mostly lived with Izzy now, their wedding only a few months away. Trevor too, for that matter. He really didn't live with Mack and Jamie anymore—he'd moved in with his boyfriend and girlfriend nearly a year ago, right before their baby was born. Mack and Jamie had been looking for a new roommate or two. Fine, Jamie had been more serious about it than Mack, but he'd been distracted all summer with too many other things. There was Sage's stalking, some fucked-up situation with Trevor, and of course, Cian—more or less Jamie's boyfriend.

Which was why Mack and the others were there. They'd come to support Cian as much as to ease the temporary loss of Jamie. Cian was an Irish dancer, and even Mack had to admit he was hot on stage. Mack was strictly hands-off his friend's man, though, and he didn't think Cian was much of a casual hook-up kind of guy. He was pretty intense at close range, and nearly as protective of Jamie as Mack was.

Not that Jamie was really the jealous sort, but there were lines Mack didn't cross. Jamie was more like a brother. Sharing a partner with him felt nearly as weird to Mack as trying to get with Jamie had. They'd tried once and only once, after years of knowing each other. Another time Sage had behaved like a jackass, in public no less. The kiss Mack and Jamie shared back at Mack's apartment had been...gross. That was the only word for how bad it had been. There was nothing behind it except some kind of strange desperation, and it hadn't worked on either of them. It might've been funny if it hadn't all been Sage's fucking fault. Again.

At any rate, neither Mack nor most of his friends were the strictly monogamous type, aside from Nate and Izzy. Mack liked that about their group. It meant he didn't need to worry about anyone pulling the bullshit Sage always had, talking one way and acting another. Sage would never consent to an open relationship, but he felt perfectly free to cheat on Jamie any time someone he liked better wiggled his ass in Sage's general direction.

Mack glanced at Trevor, who was trying to look relaxed but obviously wasn't. He kept tapping his fingers on the table until Nate swatted him. Mack choked back a laugh. They were nearly as bad as Mack and Jamie, although with the added bonus that they really had sort of been into each other at some point. Mack wasn't entirely clear on their exact history, other than that they'd been fuck buddies or some such and Nate had thought it would turn into more. Nate wouldn't tell anyone the details. Mack thought he should ask one of these days anyway, given what happened between Trevor and Jamie. No way was Mack going to let anyone yank Jamie around again.

He huffed. Not his job. Jamie had already accused Mack once of treating him like a baby, and Mack wasn't in a hurry to have that conversation a second time. And there he was, back to dwelling on how much he missed having Jamie around. Mack folded his arms and turned away from the others to cover for himself.

When Nate squeezed his shoulder, Mack knew he was out of luck on hiding anything. Trevor blew out his breath forcefully and leaned back. Nate let go of Mack.

"We might as well say it," Nate told them.

"Yeah," Trevor agreed. "It's not the same without Jay."

Mack gritted his teeth. He hated that Trevor used the pet name; it annoyed him every damn time, despite the fact that Mack had called him that for years. He said nothing about it, internally repeating that it was not his issue. If Jamie didn't like it, he could tell Trevor so himself.

"He'll be back soon." Mack intended to come off as soothing or something, but instead even he heard how curt he sounded.

Trevor eyed him. "Well, you would know, I guess."

"What's that supposed to mean?"

"Nothing." Trevor's shoulders slumped. "We're all on edge. Maybe we should, you know, just cool it."

Nate looked back and forth between them and then burst out laughing. "Oh, shit. The two of you are horrible. Seriously? Are you gonna keep fighting over Jamie like a pair of toddlers, or do you think you could act like grown-ass men for seven minutes?"

"What?" Trevor snapped. Mack would've agreed with him, except he was too irritated, both that Nate had figured it out and that he and Trevor had a temporary common enemy.

"Look," Nate said. "Every last one of us knew something was up between you and Jamie." He poked Trevor in the chest. "I thought so last winter but didn't want to pry. And you." He flicked Mack's arm. "You're acting the same way my brother did the first time I introduced him to Izzy. I thought he was going to take him out back and interrogate him using secret government tactics."

Mack glared at him. "What would you know about anything?"

"Ooh, look who's gone all defensive. Must've hit a nerve there. Can we just put this aside and have a good time? I want to see Cian dance and then make sure he's doing all right. That would be a hell of a lot easier if the two of you chilled the fuck out."

Trevor had the good sense to look defeated, so Mack gave in as well. Nate was right. They weren't here to figure out who had more claim on Jamie. Mack eyed Trevor, who had gone back to drumming his fingers. What was it that bothered Mack so much? He didn't have the same level of annoyance with Cian. In fact, he had none at all.

The discomfort was unfamiliar. Mack had never considered himself the type to have issues with who anyone had in their bed. He and Amelia both hooked up with other people, and he didn't even really consider her his girlfriend. The others sometimes referred to her that way, but she wasn't. He disliked calling her a "friend with benefits" too, as though there were no benefits to their relationship besides sex. They were close, though, intimate in a way he wasn't with anyone else. Except Jamie.

He didn't have sex with Jamie, but their friendship had lasted a dozen years and through every kind of hell. Trevor obviously couldn't say the same. There it was—the thing he couldn't stand about Trevor. Jamie had a friend, someone he confided in the way he'd always done with Mack. Cian remained solidly in the Boyfriend Zone, where Mack could compartmentalize him. He was the one who got Jamie's dreamy gazes and lovesick sighs. Trevor, though...it wasn't so tidy with him. Sure, Jamie had eventually acknowledged they'd fucked, but it was a lot more complicated than that, and something different from what Jamie had with either Mack or Cian. Mack hated it.

He was still on edge when the emcee announced Cian. Mack took a few cleansing breaths and leaned back. Watching Cian would take his mind off thinking about Trevor. Within a minute, he was absorbed in the rhythm and the movement. Cian's musicians were incredible. Mack's ears perked up, wondering if he could find a way to imitate some of their sound. He typically didn't care for it, but they were electrifying tonight.

Mack shifted so he could see them better. The fiddler was really into his performance, his foot stomping in rhythm with the dancers as he played. It didn't hurt that he was hot. Mack focused on him, picking out the folk melody and noting the complex embellishments. There was no way he could quite reproduce the sound, but he might be able to weave the melody into a song.

The whole performance was so mesmerizing that Mack lost track of time. The crowd loved it too, hooting and cheering louder than they ever did for anyone else. Cian and his troupe were favorites, and they always left everyone wanting more. Mack looked over to see that Nate and Trevor had been equally transported by the music and dance. He supposed it was the one thing he would give Trevor—he got it, the way music was a release.

Afterward, the chatter began again. The live entertainment was done. Mack wondered if Cian would stick around for long. Bars weren't the best places for him to have a conversation; even with his hearing aids in, he couldn't follow along with all the background noise. Neither Mack nor the others knew enough ASL to communicate more than a handful of awkward sentences. Still, Cian would at least stop by. He wasn't oblivious to the reason they were all there, but he would be gracious about it.

When Cian slid into a chair next to Mack, it startled him. Even more surprising was that he'd brought one of the others with him. The fiddler, Mack realized. He was slim, like Mack, but more muscular rather than skinny and a little broader. His dark hair was thick and straight, cut so it was shorter in back and a bit longer in front, styled to look nicely androgynous. He'd changed out of what he'd worn on stage, down to a plain blue T-shirt and a pair of well-worn jeans. Somehow, he made them look classy.

Cian interrupted Mack's intake report. "This is Jomari. He's my most excellent fiddler."

Jomari grinned. "Nice to meet you." He had a great voice, a high baritone that was smooth as silk. Mack was already warming up, and the temperature rose higher still when Jomari turned his gaze on Mack. He lifted both one eyebrow and the corner of his mouth. Even with his attempt at looking casually amused, Mack didn't miss it when his eyes traveled downward and then back up, flickering with interest.

Nate and Trevor didn't miss it either, and they exchanged a significant glance. Nate tipped his head when he caught Cian's attention, and some subtle understanding passed between them. It clicked. Mack was no fool; this was as intentional as everyone's showing up to check in with Cian.

More interesting still was how Jomari rendered Nate's and Trevor's pleasantries into ASL for Cian. Not, perhaps, as smoothly as Jamie would've, but certainly well enough for the brief exchange.

"I have to go," Cian said. "You know how it is in this place." He gestured to his hearing aids. The unspoken *without Jamie* hung in the air. Jomari clearly could've assisted their communication, but it made a convenient cover.

Mack licked his lips. "How about you?" he asked Jomari. "Feel like sticking around for a bit?"

"I could do that." The hinting smile again.

Nate stood and pulled Cian into a hug. Cian wasn't overly affectionate with Jamie's friends, but he didn't hesitate to lean into Nate for a moment. Trevor rose to his feet as well, and he clasped Cian's hand. A different kind of understanding flowed between them, this time about Jamie.

Mack didn't quite follow the saga of their connection. He and Amelia weren't exclusive, but they also weren't a couple. He wasn't entirely sure how he would feel being close friends with other people she hooked up with. He thought he'd rather keep things as they were, with neither of them bringing someone home to meet the other. Cian and Trevor didn't seem to have a whole lot of trouble with that, at least not so far. In fairness, they were both in Jamie-limbo while he was in recovery, but there still didn't seem to be any hard feelings.

Cian headed out, and shortly after, the late-night entertainment started. They were a band Mack had seen a few times before, and they were decent if not remarkable. Trevor got up to go take a piss, and Nate stretched out his long legs under the table. He yawned and looked like he ought to go home and sleep for a couple days.

"You all right?" Mack asked.

"Just tired." He rolled his eyes. "You can stop worrying, mother. I work three jobs. I'm allowed to be exhausted." He nudged Mack's boot with his toes. "But thanks for checking in."

Nate probably was fine, and it wasn't Mack's job to intrude. He, too, was at loose ends without Jamie to fuss over. Nate was right to be incredulous about Mack's concern, since Mack didn't generally play helicopter roommate with him. That had been Trevor's job until they briefly had a falling out over Nate's monumental stupidity. He'd outed Trevor in a comment on one of those blogs known for its asshole writer, effectively killing Trevor's career as a Christian singer. Not that Trevor was deeply invested in the first place, but it was still a dick move on Nate's part, acting out of jealousy.

"Just doing my job," Mack said, trying to make light of it.

Nate laughed. "Yes, dear." He turned serious and leaned in, speaking low into Mack's ear. "I just got my latest test back. I hit undetectable."

"What? Nate, that's terrific." Mack clapped him on the shoulder.

"Been consistent with my meds since spring." Nate grinned and held up his glass. "So now, I'm celebrating." For a moment, he looked wistful. "Even if I wish Jamie were here for the good news too."

Tonight was the closest Nate ever got to admitting how much he'd grown to care about the others. Mack was in the same position, for that matter, talking with Nate about his health. It was hard to believe it hadn't even been a year since Nate's HIV diagnosis, but he was generally doing well. The hard part had been making sure he could pay for his meds. Nate didn't need Mack worrying. He had Izzy to see to him, and from what he'd just said, that was working out all right.

There wasn't time for more conversation. The band started another song, and they were loud enough it was hard to hear. Nate tapped Mack's shoulder and motioned he was going to the bar area, away from the stage where it was somewhat quieter. Mack nodded and watched him go.

He was left alone with Jomari. Being abandoned with a sexy

stranger wasn't a bad thing. Mack could work with that as long as it wasn't too awkward for Jomari. He brushed Jomari's hand with the back of his own. There were dozens of ways to make his interest clear; he only had to pick one.

Before Mack could say anything, Jomari asked, "You want to go dance?" He practically had to shout it in Mack's ear. God, these fools were loud.

"I don't really—" Mack caught the heated, flirtatious look in Jomari's eyes. "Yeah, all right." It beat sitting there wishing the band would turn down the volume so they could talk.

There were a lot of people in the small area, which meant they were closer than they might have been otherwise. Mack couldn't have said later what happened, exactly. One minute they were simply dancing, and the next they were fully in each other's personal space. All around them, there were people pressing in, forcing them into tight contact.

It wasn't any hardship. The heat and the rhythm of the other bodies swelled as the band switched to a slower, sensual song. Maybe this was exactly what Mack needed to get his mind off everything—a crowded bar, ear-shattering music, and a sexy dance partner. He sank into the beat, letting his worries fade.

Mack didn't object when Jomari angled so they were close enough to kiss. Around them, others were doing the same, moved by the music and the dim lights and the heat. This was why Mack loved Grand Slam—people of all sorts just enjoying the moment. He pressed his mouth to Jomari's, pleased at the enthusiastic way he responded. It was just the one, and then they were back to dancing.

They kissed again, and some of the song's lyrics registered in Mack's brain. He almost choked while still attached to Jomari's lips, pulling away and trying to make it seem like teasing rather than shock and amusement. Mack wondered what Trevor was thinking or if he'd even noticed that this band was doing a very slinky cover of his old "worship" song.

Jomari caught it too, and he grinned at Mack. He put his mouth right up to Mack's ear and said, "I've always loved this song. These guys practically make me feel like the singer is giving *me* a blowie."

Mack snorted, laughed, and then met Jomari's heated gaze. Now was absolutely not the time to have Trevor on his brain. Mack dragged Jomari into another kiss, trailing his lips and tongue over his jaw and up to his ear.

"You want to go enjoy this somewhere quieter?"

"Hell, yeah."

In a flash, they were in a darkened hallway, back near the single dressing room, kissing and groping. There were definite advantages to being in one of the bar's regular bands. No one would question Mack's presence, and no one was likely to bother them for a long while. He and Jomari made good use of the space, pressed up against the wall and getting familiar with each other.

Jomari had something on under his shirt, and Mack's fingers brushed the edge, leaving him curious. When Mack tried to slide his hand up Jomari's shirt, Jomari politely but assertively reassigned it to his ass. It wasn't a disappointment—Jomari's ass was quite fine— though it was a bit of a surprise. They were positioned so Mack's crotch was pressed up against Jomari's hip. It hardly took anything to get Mack's core temperature to rise.

Mack would've been perfectly fine to keep making out. He hadn't had a session like this in weeks—days—fine, that morning with Amelia, but who was counting? Jomari was hot and as into it as Mack was, so no problems there. Until he started trying to talk.

"Oh—there's something—uh—I should tell you." Jomari groaned when Mack nibbled on his neck. "God, that feels great."

"Yeah," Mack mumbled into his warm, bronze skin. Mm, he smelled nice, too. Nothing extra, just soap and heat.

"It's just—ungh—I didn't think we'd—God, yes—get to this part so soon." Jomari grabbed the back of Mack's head and dragged their mouths together, moaning into the kiss. He broke it off. "Oh, fuck yeah...I thought we'd"—more kissing—"hang out first."

"We can stop any time."

Another groan. "N-no, this is..." He sounded about three seconds from losing it, but somehow he managed to keep speaking. "Cian said you'd be cool, but...shit."

"Hm?" Mack kissed Jomari's jaw and pulled away far enough to look in his eyes. "Cool about what?" He'd already worked out that this was a set-up. The part of his brain not occupied with wanting to peel off Jomari's clothes wondered what Cian could possibly have said about him.

"Stop for a sec." Jomari pushed gently, and Mack backed off. They both stood there, panting.

"You okay? I hope I didn't misread things. We don't have to do this." Mack touched Jomari's arm.

"No! No, I mean, it's fine. The making out. Is fine. I like it.

Uh…" His laugh was more like a tense little giggle.

Mack's eyes popped. "Wait…you've done this before, right?" He definitely would've handled things differently if he'd known.

"Oh! Oh. Yes. Yes, I have. I've had sex. Lots. All the sex. With, uh, men. And women! And those couple of genderqueer people back in college…" Jomari covered his face. "I'm babbling. Oh, God."

Mack settled against the wall. "It's no big deal," he said. "I'm not mad. That was really good."

Jomari fidgeted. "It's just…okay. Is this too weird? I know Amelia from the orchestra. She's kind of your girlfriend, right? Cian said you're…open."

"Not exactly. Close enough," Mack amended when Jomari raised an eyebrow. "We see other people, yeah."

"And…she's, uh, never mentioned me?"

"Not that I'm aware. Why?"

"We kind of…" He muttered something Mack didn't catch.

"What was that again?"

"Hooked up. A few weeks ago, maybe a month? Dunno."

Amelia hadn't said anything. Not that she always had to tell Mack the details, but she certainly hadn't mentioned getting with someone she had such regular contact with. Mack tried to shake it off. None of his business, not really. He wasn't her keeper or even her boyfriend. It was weird, though, on multiple levels. Mack's brain train derailed, taking him back to what he'd been thinking about earlier—how he wasn't sure whether he could be friends with Amelia's hookups.

On the other hand, Jomari was hot. And right there, willing. Mack's semi-rational thoughts were rapidly being displaced by his more primal ones.

"Nah, she never said so. Doesn't matter. Unless it bothers you? We still don't have to do this." If he left Jomari an out, he wouldn't have to dwell on the other details.

"I want to. But…really? Not a word?"

"Why should she? I don't own her. Now you're kind of concerning me. Did something happen?" Mack snorted. "We're not talking, like, secret baby level shit here, are we?" He cringed, recalling that was exactly how Trevor ended up with both Andre and Marlie. He coughed. "You didn't get my—Amelia pregnant, did you?"

"That would be, uh, not at all possible." Jomari chuckled, and this time there was genuine amusement there. "I'm trans."

"Oh! Ha. Okay, well, that's cool. No secret babies, then. I think we're fine."

Jomari let out another breathy laugh. "Cian was definitely right that you're cool."

"About what? Your being trans, or your hooking up with my—Amelia?"

"Both, I guess? Yeah, both."

It was really sexy when Jomari bit his lip like that. Did he know what he was doing? The tiny, knowing smile indicated he did—or that he'd read Mack's reaction to it. Their fate was sealed, unless Jomari chose to back out now.

"Mm. Cian's great, but I don't really want to think about him now. Did you, like, want to go back to making out, or are we kinda done here?"

"Making out is good. That is, if you still want to. You don't have to. Want to. Make out. Uh...shit. Kiss me?"

Mack laughed and pushed off the wall. "You talk entirely too fucking much, dude."

Jomari made what looked like an attempt at a seductive face. "Maybe you should shut me up, then."

"Gladly."

CHAPTER FOUR

EARLY IN the morning, Mack woke and rolled over. He froze when his arm brushed something, and it took him a minute to remember. Jomari had stayed. No one ever stayed, other than Amelia.

Contrary to what Mack had led his roommates to believe, he didn't hook up all that often, at least not anymore. He sometimes invited people—mostly men—back to the apartment, but all parties were clear on how it was going to go. He rarely had casual sex with women, which he understood. Not a lot of women wanted to go home with a random stranger. There were a couple of regulars, a Bio-Queen from Grand Slam and one of the servers, but generally not anyone unfamiliar. Not alone, anyway. More often than not, the women were part of a different-gender couple.

He'd been a lot of people's first. It no longer surprised Mack how many were looking for someone willing to help them experiment. He went into every encounter fully aware, and it suited him fine. At any rate, he didn't sleep over, and people didn't stay at his place. End of story.

But Jomari had slept there. It had been a fantastic night, if exhausting. First hand jobs at Grand Slam, then back to Mack's apartment for the rest of the night. Holy heaven, hell, and everything in between, Jomari was great between the sheets. His presence filled the emptiness where three roommates had once been, but with the added bonus of mutual satisfaction. In contrast with Jomari's chatty nervous energy the night before, he was indeed experienced and capable—several times over.

Mack withdrew his elbow and lay there unmoving, waiting to see if Jomari stirred. When his breathing was still soft and steady after five minutes, Mack deemed it safe to get up. He shifted slowly so as not to disturb his bed-mate's slumber.

No such luck. The minute one of Mack's legs dangled off the bed, his bare foot almost touching the floor, Jomari turned onto his back. Stifling a groan, Mack slid his leg back under the covers. He wanted to be annoyed, but it was too warm and cozy under there. Not to mention the still mostly naked and very sexy man wriggling closer.

"Yeah," Jomari murmured as he tucked himself up against Mack. "Feels good."

Shit, he was a cuddler. Mack could deal with a guy who changed his mind and asked for a phone number or a second date. Or the guy from Starbucks last spring who hadn't been all that great, insisted on fucking on the damn living room floor, and then had the nerve to demand Mack buy him dinner after. Mack drew the line at cuddling in bed.

Except now Jomari was inching his leg over Mack's, and he was getting dangerously close to Mack's morning wood. Dear God above, this guy was a sex-before-coffee type. That was simply not acceptable. Mack slid away a bit.

"Look," he began, but he yawned.

Jomari's laughter was gentle. "I guess that answers my question. You want me to just go?"

"Go?" Mack blinked. Yes, he supposed Jomari should do that. He'd forgotten why, until he felt toes on his calf. Right, the whole cuddling thing.

"Yeah. You said last night you don't usually have people stay. I can get my stuff and be out of your hair in, like, ten minutes."

"Oh. Yes, that."

More laughter, and now Mack really was reacting to it. He liked the sound of Jomari's voice. And his beautiful brown eyes, his silky dark hair, his lean muscles...damn it, there was no way Mack was going to be up for anything before he'd had caffeine, though he wished he could.

"So, want to do this again some time?" Jomari asked as he swung his legs over the side of the bed. Mack silently prayed for him to stand up so he could admire that perfect ass.

"I..." Mack trailed off, torn between wanting to say yes and knowing he ought to say no.

Jomari finally stood, but he turned to face Mack far too soon. Except the front view was as good as the rear, so Mack wasn't exactly disappointed. Nice, firm abs, neatly shorn pubes that showed off his guy pussy—as Jomari called it—and a tiny tattoo above his left hip: a daisy. Mack almost sighed when Jomari slipped on his underwear and jeans. Hell, he even made adjusting his packer sexy. Mack had to wipe his chin to make sure he hadn't actually drooled.

"I get it," Jomari said, the words muffled by the T-shirt he was pulling over his head to cover the tight tank he'd kept on in bed. "You don't purchase the merchandise. I don't either, but I'll admit I prefer if I've at least been inside the store before."

"That...is an incredibly weird metaphor. What?"

"Cian said you like to keep it casual. I'm not really looking for a relationship with a man right now, but for some obvious reasons, randomly picking a guy up in a bar is not my thing, present company aside. I took a risk with you because Cian said you were all right, and I trust him. It's nice to have a semi-regular partner, but if you'd rather not meet up again, I'm not going to be pissed."

"Okay." That should've been fine with Mack. And it was, really, but he'd had a good time the night before. Another go at it wouldn't be a bad idea. "And if I do want to?"

Jomari shrugged. "'K. I'll leave my number on the way out."

"Don't you want breakfast? You've stayed this long."

"You didn't seem interested." Jomari lay down next to Mack and touched his thigh, a naughty smile playing on his lips.

"Not that kind of breakfast. I mean the kind you eat. Food! I meant food." Mack hadn't been this flustered since the time he caught Jamie and Cian literally with their pants down at Jamie's cousin's wedding.

"I'm good. Unless you really want me to stick around." He inched his fingers higher.

Mack wanted to tell him yes, to stay and eat and then get naked again. Instead he settled for a casual, "Either way."

Jomari sat up and looked at Mack, thoughtful. "I'm gonna go. But I'll give you my number like I said. The rest is up to you."

He stood, the bed bouncing a little as he did. With one last mischievous smile, he was out of the bedroom. Mack stretched his legs, listening for the sound of the apartment door opening and closing. He gave himself a couple of half-hearted tugs, deciding coffee and a nice, long shower were in order. He had nowhere to be until the band's rehearsal and then his shift at Legal later on, so there was plenty of time.

When he rose from the bed, Mack spotted a thin, silver chain on the nightstand. He picked it up. A crucifix. Must've been Jomari's, as Mack didn't own one and neither did Amelia. He held it in his palm and curled his fingers around it. A promise, he decided. He would have to see Jomari again to return it, and who knew where that could lead? Mack grinned as he dragged on a pair of ratty sweatpants. Reliving last night's adventures suddenly took on a whole new appeal.

Rehearsing with the band wasn't the same without Jamie. Cassie had found them a temporary replacement drummer, some buddy of her girlfriend's, but he wasn't anywhere near as good. He had the technical skill to keep up, but he didn't have Jamie's heart. It left Mack flustered and annoyed. They had a gig on Saturday, and Mack wasn't sure they'd be in shape to appear.

Not that the Creepy Crullers were fantastic to begin with. Their sound could best be described as the musical equivalent of a face only a mother could love. All four members had other jobs and responsibilities, which meant they weren't investing the kind of time they needed in order to become something better. Until losing Jamie, it hadn't mattered all that much to Mack. He liked being part of a small-time band that played for fun and a little side cash.

Only now, minus their stellar drummer, did Mack realize how much of himself Jamie had given to the band. Out of all of them, he was the one who probably could have gone somewhere with it. Mack knew Jamie stole away to practice, even though he'd tried to hide it. It didn't make sense, aside from the way Jamie was secretive about everything. He lived as though his entire existence was something to apologize for. It wasn't until after he'd gone that Mack recognized Jamie's fear he might be imposing on everyone to ask for even something simple, like time and space to practice.

Mack's enthusiasm had vanished. Without Jamie, it was like having all the sunshine blotted out. That sounded terribly cheesy even to Mack, but it was the truth. He set down his guitar with a heavy sigh.

"Five minute break," he said.

Cassie, the bassist, chatted with the fill-in guy—Dirk or Derek or something. Mack watched them for a few minutes. The man's very presence irritated Mack, and he wanted to tell him to get lost. Except they needed him, and Mack knew it. He turned to Gemma, who stepped out from behind her keyboard to approach him.

Keeping her good ear toward Mack, she leaned in close and murmured, "It's not the same, is it?"

"Not even a little."

"He's okay, you know. Cian's partners are looking out for him, and they keep us in the loop. Got a text yesterday that he's been able to have meals with them for almost a week straight."

Mack's eyebrows rose. That was a huge step. Jamie barely tolerated meals with his roommates anymore, let alone people he hardly knew.

"That's good," he said.

"I'm sure it helps that he's been doing some of the cooking. They're making freezer meals for when Nell has the baby."

"Soon, right? I mean, maybe before Jamie comes home?"

Cian had three other partners besides Jamie. They were a family unit, and Cian didn't live with them, nor was he the father of the soon-to-be-born baby. Mack had only briefly met them because he'd gone to Gemma's wedding, and they were her friends. She'd married Jamie's cousin over the summer.

"Baby's due any day," Gemma confirmed. Her cheeks reddened. "Speaking of that..."

Mack choked a little. "You're pregnant already?"

"No, but we're trying."

"O-okay," Mack stammered. He wasn't sure why Gemma was letting him in on this information. "Really? You've only been married, what, two months?"

"We've been together for years, Mack." She rolled her eyes but then turned serious. "I thought you should know. Because of the band."

Right. The band she probably wouldn't want to be part of once she and Brandon had kids. It seemed like was all his friends were getting tamed these days, between weddings and engagements and parenting. Mack hadn't counted the official total, but it was still "everyone" in his mind.

"Sure. I get it," he said. He didn't. He'd never seen the appeal.

Gemma looked like she wanted to say more, but Cassie and her friend were back and ready to start again. Mack took a deep breath and picked up his guitar.

"Let's do 'Luck of the Draw' from the top," he said.

The drummer—Diedrich, that was it—gave them a beat. It felt weak to Mack, but he also knew his focus was off. He needed something to concentrate on other than the lack of Jamie's distinctive style. He closed his eyes but snapped them open again when the first image that came to mind was a very naked Jomari in a position that wouldn't improve Mack's focus.

On second thought, it was a mental picture worth saving for later as inspiration, and it had gotten his mind off less pleasant things. He turned his attention to the song, riding the good vibes still left from his wild night. Out of the corner of his eye, he caught Gemma and Cassie exchanging a meaningful look, but he ignored them. They would just have to keep up. Mack had a feeling nothing was going to hold him down today.

CHAPTER FIVE

AMELIA BID goodbye to her Saturday morning light aerobics class. This was one of her favorite groups. All of them were cancer survivors. She liked offering classes for people who had experiences in common—it made most of them less self-conscious. She knew what it was like to be judged on the external alone. She'd met few who didn't draw conclusions about her on sight, let alone who believed she was a former athlete turned personal trainer.

The rest of her morning would be spent with her clients. Mostly regulars, but in the mix was a new one. Cian had called her earlier in the week about bringing in his younger sister for some strength training. They were first on the list, and she'd booked a double slot. The combination of an injury and a stubborn teenager meant she'd need extra time for some creative thinking. She grabbed her clipboard and went to wait in the lobby.

Amelia waved Cian over as soon as he appeared at the main entrance. He grinned at her cheerfully, but the teenage girl with him looked like she would rather be anywhere else. Amelia had her work cut out for her. Fortunately, she had plenty of experience with sullen clients.

"Hey," she greeted them when they stopped in front of her. Cadence's gaze flickered over Amelia briefly, but it was long enough to register a small degree of surprise. Amelia would parse it later.

"This is Cadence," Cian said. "My sister." He had a light Irish accent Amelia found appealing.

"Right, yes. You mentioned. And she had an injury, right?"

Cian motioned to his hearing aids. "Can we talk somewhere quieter?"

"Sure."

Amelia led them into one of the small rooms lined with mats. Some days, it was used for tiny tots classes, but it was empty at the moment. She turned to face Cian and Cadence.

"Okay, Cadence, why don't we spare your brother from having to be the middle man here. Tell me what you're looking for."

Cadence eyed Cian, who nodded at her with a distinct air of you'd-better-tell-her. With a sigh that sounded half exasperated and half grateful, she looked away from him. "I hurt my knee before our last performance. I did some physical therapy and stuff, and I did the performance, but I guess I re-injured it. I haven't been able to dance in class yet."

"I think we can work with that. You're looking to build up muscle tone, right?"

"Yeah, I guess." Cadence shrugged and then crossed her arms.

Her posture told Amelia she wasn't getting anything more at the moment. Amelia had seen all this before. A lot of people were intimidated by the idea of working out, especially in such a public place. Just because Amelia had confidence in her body didn't mean everyone did. It was why she'd chosen to work at a women's gym.

"Whatever it costs—" Cian began, but Amelia cut him off.

"Let's not worry about the future until I've had a chance to work with Cadence today. If I think it'll work out, we'll talk details then."

"You're a lifesaver." Cian kissed her cheek. He turned to Cadence, started signing something to her, then glanced at Amelia and spoke aloud. "I'll leave you to talk, yeah? Gonna go grab a coffee around the corner."

Amelia watched him go, wondering how he was doing these days. Was fussing over his sister, and taking charge of her rehabilitation, a function of his role as her dance teacher? Or was he trying to keep his mind and his time occupied so he wouldn't text every five minutes to check on Jamie's progress? They weren't close enough for Amelia to ask those questions, so instead, she stared at his retreating back.

As soon as he'd gone, Cadence turned to Amelia. "I didn't even want to do this. He's making me."

"Which part?"

"All of it."

"'All' covers a pretty wide territory here. Is he making you go back to dancing? Or making you get in shape? Or making you come see me specifically?"

Cadence glowered. "Yes." Her shoulders slumped, and her face relaxed more into sadness than anger. She sighed so dramatically that Amelia had to bite the inside of her lips to keep from laughing. "I lied to him. There's nothing wrong with my knee. I don't know if I want to dance anymore. I used to love it, but..."

Amelia beckoned to Cadence. "Come on. Let's go sit somewhere and talk about it. I'm happy to help you, but I think we need to be on the same page here. Okay?"

Cadence nodded, and Amelia led her into a small room with a few tables and some vending machines. No one was in there. They sat at one of the tables, and Amelia offered to get Cadence a snack.

When they both had something to eat, Amelia said, "Let's start with what you said about dancing. That's perfectly natural—lots of people decide a sport isn't for them. But I have a feeling there's more to this story. Want to talk about it?"

"I used to love it," Cadence said. She picked up a pretzel twist, but she didn't eat it. She looped it on her finger and stared at it.

"Did something happen to change it?"

"There was this girl in my class. She's been there forever, I mean since Cian started teaching. She goes to my school too, and she's a real bih—a jerk." Cadence peeked up at Amelia, who carefully kept her face neutral. "Cian teaches us ASL in class, and she's good at it, so she learned how to call me all sorts of names without the teachers knowing. If they catch her, she just says it doesn't mean anything. Since they don't know ASL, they believe her."

"And they don't believe you when you explain it?"

Cadence shook her head. "Not at all. She acts one way with them and another way with me. I stopped bothering after I told one teacher I knew what she'd said because my brother is deaf. She told me I shouldn't give her a reason to pick on me."

"Cian still allows this girl in class?" Amelia couldn't imagine him doing something like that, but she truly didn't know him well enough. It lowered her opinion of him.

"No. He spoke to her last year, and she promised to be nicer, but she wasn't. So he told her she couldn't do the summer show and not to come back this year either. I guess she found some other studio that does competitive stuff, and even though she only just started there, she's been even worse than last year about it. She keeps making fun of us for not being 'real' dancers because we don't compete."

"And you agree with her." Amelia knew she'd hit it dead on when Cadence winced.

She looked away for a moment, and when she turned back, her expression was full of fire. "He's done it! He's a fu—freaking professional dancer. He says it's for our own good that he doesn't push us that way, that he just wants us to have fun. But how bad could it really be? Maybe he's not good enough after all." She sat back with a huff.

Amelia didn't know how to answer that. Cadence might not've seen him dance; most of his performances were in gay bars and clubs. Cian was fantastic, but Cadence very well might not know it firsthand. Amelia still sensed there was more to it than Cadence was letting on.

"So why let him drag you here to see me? Didn't you know I'd have to evaluate you and make recommendations?"

"I was hoping I could..." She flushed.

"Lie to him? I mean, I'd love to know how you were planning on getting out of it."

"I would've made him drop me off and then gone somewhere else." She fidgeted and peered up at Amelia through her curtain of bangs. "You'd have told him."

"Well, yeah. Hon, training isn't free. He can't pay me so you can go hang out in the cafe around the corner."

Cadence's face darkened. "Is that what you think of me?" She stood and gestured down at herself. "That I'd rather be eating a bagel with all that fattening cream cheese than getting in my daily workout?"

Amelia stared at her for a moment before rising. "Seriously? You thought I was going to judge you?" She swept her hand down her body. At Cadence's non-response, Amelia continued. "This is why I do what I do. A lot of people think they are too fat or too sick or too disabled to be allowed to play sports or dance or just plain have some fun. I've heard it all, from every kind of person. You know Cian's boyfriend Jamie?"

Cadence nodded. "Yeah."

"I don't know if you know much about what happened with

him, though I can't really say much."

She shrugged. "He told me he has an eating disorder. It's not really a secret from our family or anything."

"Right, okay. Well, Jamie's one of my very best friends, and when he comes home, he wants me to help him listen to his body a little better. If I can help him, surely I'm not going to judge you about anything."

Cadence sniffled and wiped her eyes. "I was good at dancing," she said. "Really good. I didn't tell Cian, but I went to another studio to see if I could do it. And they were...mean. They said I could only go there if I lost weight. Like, a lot. I don't want to be stuck with my brother just because someone else said I'm too fat."

"Like the girl at your school," Amelia said. "God, people are so vile. So, what do you want to do?"

"Well, maybe do what you said you could do for Jamie. See if I can learn to listen to my body, I guess?" She sniffled again. "Maybe figure out how dance can go back to being fun. And...tell Cian the truth."

"I think we can do that." Amelia smiled at her. "I have a few ideas for you. We'll pick what's best for you and hopefully have a good time with it. Today, how about we just play around a bit? There's a games room here. After that, if you want, I'll help you talk to Cian when he gets back. Okay?"

Cadence graced Amelia with her first real smile of the day. "Yeah. Let's do it."

When Amelia finally reached the end of her day, she was surprised to see a text from Jomari. They'd gone out once—or rather gone to bed once. It had been while riding the emotional high of a summer concert, and they'd gone back to Amelia's to enjoy the rest of the night. It wasn't exactly like they were dating, though they were friends, casually speaking.

His text was asking if she'd be interested in catching up over dinner. The new season for their orchestra had started, but they'd both been too busy after rehearsals for more than a brief conversation on the way to their cars. It sounded like a nice way to wrap things up after a long day, so Amelia texted a hasty **sure** before gathering her things.

She couldn't help letting her mind go there. Jomari was not only gorgeous but the sex had been great. Wild, different from other people she'd been with. The man had some serious stamina, and he was damn creative. Amelia chalked that last bit up to being a professional artist. Jomari not only played the violin, he was learning to make instruments. It wouldn't bother her one bit if he'd really only texted her to see if she was up for another night together.

Negotiating the terms in person sounded much better than doing it via text, so she was happy to see his response to her: **Great!**

She smiled, pausing in the foyer of the gym. **Where and when?**

Cafe Velocity about an hour?

Good choice. See you then.

Amelia put her phone away. Nate worked there, but he wouldn't be in on a Saturday evening. She wouldn't have to worry about running into a friend and it being all awkward. Not because Nate would assume she was there on a date—which she wasn't, and he wouldn't care—but because she felt weird being served by someone she knew.

On the off chance "catching up" meant more than eating bagels and talking about Mahler's second symphony, Amelia took extra care in the shower. She used the expensive gel she reserved for special occasions. Mack didn't count—he couldn't care less what soap Amelia used. Jomari, she suspected, might appreciate it more, though she couldn't have said why.

She dried her hair and tried three separate outfits before settling on galaxy-print leggings and a flowing purple blouse. Getting her hair, clothes, and makeup right was always the fun part of going out. Whether Jomari cared or not was anyone's guess, but Amelia liked to make herself feel good after a long day at work. She was pretty and she knew it.

At last she was ready. Just in case, she packed a small bag with a few items she might need. She'd leave it in the car, but it didn't hurt to be prepared for any situation. One last glance in the mirror satisfied her that she looked her best, and then she was out the door.

Jomari was waiting for Amelia when she arrived. He looked good, as always. Casual, just a soft green T-shirt, faded jeans, and a black hoodie. For some reason, he didn't have his cross necklace on. She'd never seen him without it. Amelia wasn't religious herself, but she knew Jomari's family was Catholic, and she was fairly sure he still believed. She'd never asked outright, but there were subtle cues.

She only realized she must've looked less than thrilled to see him when he stepped closer, a puzzled expression on his face.

Amelia pulled herself together and smiled.

"Everything okay?" Jomari asked.

"Oh, sure. Got sidetracked for a second." She leaned in and air-kissed his cheek, not wanting to spoil her lipstick or get it on him.

His cheek-kiss landed its mark. "Good. You hungry?"

"I could eat." She laughed. "Make that, I am starving. I haven't had a break since taking an early lunch."

They put their orders in and then took a table by the window. Outside, a few people passed the cafe. Someone opened an umbrella just as the first few thick drops struck the glass. There was a flash of lightning in the distance, and a moment later, rain pelted the sidewalk.

"Glad we're in here and not out in that," Jomari remarked.

"Me too. And I'm glad we don't have rehearsal today either. I'm not up for a wet walk from the train."

Jomari nodded. "Speaking of that, did you get the notes Tre'Ana sent us?"

"Ugh, don't remind me. I can't believe she's adding another piece to the program. As if we didn't have enough already!"

They carried on talking about their conductor and the upcoming concert until their food was ready. When they sat back down, Jomari didn't pick up his sandwich right away. Instead, he cleared his throat.

"So...I'm thinking you want to know why I asked you to meet up."

Amelia had been, but she played it cool. "We haven't had a lot of time to talk since summer."

He chuckled and leaned in to whisper, "You mean since we spent the night screwing like bunnies?"

"That too."

"You should know that I, uh, went home with Mack the other night. Your friend."

"I know who Mack is!" Amelia laughed, covering—she hoped—her surprise. Though now she thought about it, was it really so shocking? The guys had gone out to see Cian at the bar. Jomari was Cian's fiddler and his friend. Jamie was away, and Mack had been lonely. She couldn't be sure whose idea it was, but it did make some sense they'd try to set Mack up. Of course, they probably didn't know it wouldn't go anywhere but the bedroom.

"It's not weird for you?" Jomari still hadn't touched his

sandwich, and now he fidgeted with his cup.

"Not really. I don't think our one night together gives me some kind of claim on you, does it?"

"Well, no, I guess not." Was that disappointment in his voice?

Amelia reached out and put her hand on his. "Mack and I are best friends. Yeah, we have sex sometimes, but that's the relationship we've always had. We're all adults, and obviously we're capable of having a grown-up discussion about it. Unless there's a problem on your end we need to talk about, I'm good."

She was, really, even if she needed a minute to process. She and Mack had never hooked up with the same person before, that she knew of. Guilt crept in; they wouldn't even be in this position if she'd done what she always did and told Mack about her night with Jomari. She wasn't sure why she'd wanted to keep it to herself.

Jomari shook his head. "I'm okay with everything. Just figured it was better to do what you said, have a grown-up discussion."

"And we did. So, tell me about how your day went?"

"Well...that would be the other reason I asked you here."

"Oh?"

"You know how I'm in this Irish folk band? Um...see...we lost our flute player, and..." He bit his lip, and Amelia thought it was both adorable and hot. He'd had no hesitation when it came to finding out what would send electric thrills through her body, but he could barely ask her to do him a favor with the band.

"You'd like me to fill in until you find a replacement?"

"Um. Yes?" He turned on a charming grin, and she giggled.

"I'm not that great at playing by ear or improvising. I mean, I could learn, but I can't start out that way."

Jomari sat up a little straighter, all business. "I can give you some sheet music. You'll get the hang of it, I promise. And it really is only for a little while. It pays okay," he added.

"Good to know. Sure, I'll do it."

Now the big things were out of the way, Jomari picked up his sandwich. Amelia tested her soup, which was cool enough not to burn her mouth. Something still felt off, and she could tell Jomari wasn't paying much attention to his food. She reached out her free hand and put it on his.

"Tell me for real," she said. "How are you doing?"

He set his sandwich on the plate and picked at the crust. "I still don't have a doctor." He looked up at her. "I've been out of my prescription since the end of July."

Not long, then, but still a problem. Jomari was a casualty of the Lighthouse closing. He'd been going there, and he was supposed to have been referred along with a number of other people enrolled in their program. But the Lighthouse had closed, and he'd been one of the few on the waiting list who hadn't been transferred to a new primary care doctor.

"So, no leads on a good primary?"

Jomari withdrew his hand from hers. "No. The problem is, Dr. Joyce knew me. Now not only do I have to find a doctor, but I have to deal with proving again that yes, I really do need to be on T, and yes, I really do need ongoing care specifically fit for me." He glared at the sandwich instead of meeting Amelia's gaze.

"I could ask around, if you want," Amelia offered. "I know a few people who might help out."

"Yeah?"

"Sure." She chuckled. "I was about to try to explain to you this really complicated friend circle I've got going on these days, thanks to Mack, but it could take a while."

Jomari laughed too. "Oh, believe me, I know. Didn't we end up with crossed wires when we both tried to set up friends last spring?"

"Right, yeah. Only we accidentally got Cian and Jamie together. Or they thought we did, anyway."

"Seems to have worked out for them."

"For Kevin and Jason, too. Did you know Kev got a job out on the west coast, and Jason's decided to move with him?"

Jomari's mouth fell open. "No, Kevin didn't say a word. I'll have to talk to him next time he's in at Grandad's shop. Good for them!"

"I feel like I accomplished something." Amelia finished her soup. "Anyway, I'm sorry about all the shit you're dealing with right now. I'll see what I can do."

"Thanks."

The rain had slowed, and people were leaving the cafe. Everything felt soft and relaxed. Simply being around Jomari made Amelia feel good, and she enjoyed the lazy bloom of arousal from being near him. Jomari stood, and Amelia followed. She didn't want their time together to end, so she brushed his arm with her hand.

"You know, we could keep hanging out or something," she offered. "Maybe you'd like some company right now."

Jomari hesitated for only a moment before replying, "Okay. Your apartment? Otherwise, we have to go to my parents' house, and my sister is there, probably with her friends, and—"

Amelia had forgotten Jomari still lived with his family. "No problem. I live alone, and I'm not too far from here."

"Cool. I remember where you live." He blushed. "I wish I could move out, but everything is so complicated right now."

"No problem at all. I totally get it. See you in a few minutes?"

"Yeah."

The young woman at the cash register called, "Have a nice day!" as the two of them headed out, and Amelia gave her a wave. Jomari's hand brushed hers, catching her off-guard in the way it didn't feel unintentional. She brushed back, and he twined their fingers, only letting go once they reached their cars.

Jomari followed Amelia in his own car back to her apartment. She knew they weren't really going to "hang out," given how things had gone the last time she'd invited him to her place. They'd ended up celebrating their concert naked in her bed, and she had no problem with a repeat performance.

Amelia's first confirmation Jomari was on the same page was the fact that he'd brought his gym bag in with him. Her second was that the minute the door closed, he stepped a little closer and tilted his head.

"We don't have to..." he began, but she put a finger to his lips.

"I asked you back here with the fully informed view that it might go this way. You okay with that?"

"Oh, yeah."

And with that, he closed in, and a moment later they were enjoying a mutually satisfactory kiss up against the wall. It had begun to drizzle again on the drive to her apartment, showering them on their way in. Amelia's temptation was to get Jomari out of his slightly rain-damp clothes and into her bed as soon as possible, but he seemed to be in no real hurry to break the kiss.

That is, until his lips traveled from her mouth down her neck, his fingers toying with the top button on her blouse. He paused only long enough to get her consent to unbutton, and then she was gasping at the gentle pressure of his hand around the bare flesh of her left breast. Maybe she wasn't in a rush to go anywhere after all. The idea of having each other right there in her entryway made a very sexy mental image, causing her to let out a breathless groan.

Jomari kissed his way back up her neck and along her jaw until his lips were right by her ear. "Yeah?" he murmured.

"Yes," she hissed.

He wrapped one arm around her waist, holding her close, then walked his fingers down her belly to the top of her leggings. She squirmed, but not out of discomfort—Amelia loved being tickled, especially when she was aroused. It heightened the sensations and made her feel playful. She helped Jomari by shimmying out of her leggings and sliding the blouse and her bra off. Jomari backed up enough to shed his hoodie, though he left his T-shirt on. He still had on his jeans too, and Amelia put her hand on the waistband.

"How do you want to do this?" she asked.

"I've got my other cock in my bag," he said, tilting his chin at the duffel on the floor where he'd dropped it when they came in. "But, uh, I'm kind of..." His cheeks darkened. "Screw it. I'm having this amazing fantasy of finger-fucking you right here and then getting you on your knees."

Amelia snorted a laugh. "Well, get your pants off, then, mister. I'm game—that same fantasy's been on my mind since we walked in."

The minute Jomari's jeans, underwear, and stand-to-pee lay in a heap behind him, they were back to kissing. His hands were soft and warm where he ran them up and down her sides. Everywhere he touched her sent sparks of desire through her. She was done waiting; she grasped his wrist and directed his hand between her legs. He let out a long, shaky breath as he touched her.

She rode his fingers, their kisses becoming more shallow until they disappeared into her open-mouthed panting. Amelia was close, just a little more. She needed it. Jomari's hand jerked, and Amelia let out a whining huff as her whole body stiffened. She arched her back, feeling like lighting raced down her limbs and out through her fingers and toes.

Sweaty and still gasping, she put her hand on Jomari's forearm to stop him from moving against her sensitive flesh. It had been over so fast, Amelia barely had time to enjoy it. Fortunately, they had the rest of the night to take it slower. She kissed Jomari, and he backed up to let her push off the wall.

"Your turn?" she asked, curling her lips into an enticing smile. "I believe you said you'd like me to suck you off."

She circled so he had to turn to face her, and she nudged him up to the wall where she'd just been. Amelia didn't waste any time sinking down to her knees and drawing Jomari's dick between her lips. She liked doing this with him, in part because she could let him come in her mouth. When he'd had his other packer, he'd loved when she blew it as foreplay. For now, she licked and sucked the natural flesh of his pre-installed cock, enjoying the way he ran his fingers through her hair and tugged a little whenever it felt especially good.

"God...shit...ah." He jerked, and she felt his orgasm throb against her tongue as he exhaled forcefully.

She gave him one last playful lick before rising and kissing him. What she'd intended to be a quick peck turned into Jomari drawing her close and sliding his tongue between her lips. After several minutes, the two of them finally separated, and Amelia patted Jomari's cheek.

"You want some water?" she asked.

"Yeah, thanks."

On the way to the kitchen, she peered over her shoulder to give him a smoldering look. He grinned and winked back. Water first, and then they could decide if they were ready for round two yet. This was going to be a fun night.

Chapter Six

Jomari emerged into wakefulness, blinking to clear the sleep from his eyes. He glanced over at Amelia, who was sound asleep. It was still mostly dark, with some patchy gray light beginning to filter into the bedroom. That meant it was fairly early. With another sideways look at Amelia, Jomari slowly leaned over the side of the bed and fished in his jeans for his phone.

Sure enough, only six. He didn't have to be up yet, but he wasn't going to be able to settle back down. He'd had plenty of good quality sleep, and he was an early riser as it was. With great care, he slipped out from under the covers and began picking up his things. He paused and watched Amelia for a moment then set his clothes back down. If he took everything, she might think he'd left.

Instead, he grabbed his gym bag with his change of clothes and a few toiletries. He didn't think Amelia would mind if he borrowed her shampoo and soap. They'd now spent the night together twice, so he figured he'd earned at least a few privileges when staying at her apartment. Besides, she wasn't really the type to get mad about that anyway. He'd dated a woman once who'd had such an attitude about having her boyfriend "steal" her shampoo. That relationship had lasted roughly a minute and a half.

Jomari stood in the bedroom doorway, his gaze on Amelia. He smiled. Sure, the sex was fantastic. Amelia was creative, and she never made a big deal of it if something didn't feel comfortable.

Funny as hell, too. The first time she asked if she could touch his prosthetic dick, she'd offered to use her "slinky voice" any time she needed permission—and then demonstrated.

He hated comparing her to anyone else, but it made him think of the night he'd spent with Mack. They were different but somehow similar. Maybe that wasn't a surprise, given how long the two of them had been friends. The thought sent a whisper of envy through Jomari. He was only beginning to know them both, but they'd had half a lifetime together first.

He tore himself away from the bedroom and went to shower. He laughed softly when he saw the sticky note on the mirror, telling him where to find towels and confirming that it was fine to use whatever else he found in there.

In the shower, he stood under the spray and had a long, lazy piss before sliding his hand down to stroke himself while reliving the previous night. He shivered out an orgasm then soaped up with something that smelled divine, like grapefruit with a hint of tropical flowers. It only occurred to him he'd been in there a while when he heard the tap on the door.

"Yeah?" he called, grateful he'd finished jerking off before Amelia knocked.

"You want some breakfast? I'm making a little something before I go to work."

"Sure, thanks!"

He'd forgotten Amelia wouldn't be off today and they couldn't make plans. Grandad was old-fashioned, so the shop was still closed on Sundays. Amelia's gym wasn't, though, and she worked every other weekend. He felt only a little guilty about having kept her up the previous night. She certainly hadn't complained or asked him to leave.

A short time later, he was out of the shower and sitting in her kitchenette with a steaming plate of eggs and a bowl of fruit-topped yogurt in front of him. He wanted to ask if Amelia had any bacon, but he knew perfectly well she didn't. She wasn't a vegetarian, but she didn't eat any meat other than chicken. Today was not the day to try convincing her of its crispy goodness.

She slid into a chair across from him and waved her fork. "Eat, before those eggs get cold," she scolded.

Jomari laughed. "You sound like my mother."

Amelia cringed. "Oh, hell no. I don't play those kinds of games." She put up a hand. "Not that there's anything wrong with it, of course."

Blushing, Jomari refused to look at her when he snagged the pepper. He probably put too much on, but he didn't exactly want to think about Amelia and his mother in the same context.

He changed the subject so he could meet her gaze again. "What've you got going on today?"

"Work, mostly. Then dinner with a friend. Marlie. I think maybe you've met her? Or her boyfriend? Big blond guy."

"Oh!" Jomari knew who she meant. That guy had been there the night Jomari hooked up with Mack. His face heated up again. Great. Yet another subject he didn't want to bring up. Except there was one detail Amelia didn't know. "Yeah, he was there in the bar last weekend. Speaking of that..."

"Oh, god. You're not gonna ask me for any more favors about the band, are you?"

"No." Jomari laughed, but it was half-hearted. "I thought you should probably know that I told Mack you and I...you know."

"'You know'? Are we in middle school?" Amelia huffed. "Sorry. So Mack knows you and I fucked, and I know you and he did. All cleared up now. Good?"

"Yeah." Jomari coughed artificially. "I mean, good."

"Great. So, changing the subject, when are rehearsals for the other stuff?"

Jomari suppressed a sigh. Was Amelia upset with him? Or just annoyed that he'd brought Mack up for the second time? He didn't have a good read on her. He'd thought she was open-minded, but sometimes he didn't pick up on the cues correctly. He shrugged it off and followed her into the next conversation.

"It depends," he told her. "We have a bunch of people to schedule around, but usually we try to practice on Saturday afternoons. That seems to get everyone most weeks."

"Okay. That might be rough with my work schedule, but I may be able to flex my hours a little. I don't work every weekend anyway."

"Awesome!" Jomari left the previous tension behind. "This is gonna be so fun. You'll like the others."

"Cool." She smiled now, looking much more relaxed herself. "I'm a little nervous, but Cian's a sweetheart, and I'm sure he'll forgive my screw-ups in the beginning."

"He will. Don't worry."

Amelia glanced at the clock. "I gotta go soon." She stood and circled the table to put a hand on Jomari's shoulder. "But…" She looked like she was steeling herself for something. "You wanna do this again?"

"God, yeah." Jomari stood too. He put a hand on Amelia's cheek. "I had a good time last night." He leaned in and kissed her lightly.

"Me too," she said, and her smile made his stomach do complicated gymnastics.

He retreated to the bedroom to finish packing his bag, and his grin remained stubbornly in place the whole time.

By the time Jomari went to work Monday morning, he'd long since left his happy bubble from his night with Amelia. He entered the shop and tried to set it aside for the sake of his duties, but his head still wasn't clear on a whole lot of things.

The shop was longer than it was wide, a storefront in between an indie bookstore and a bagel place. The customer area was out front, and the work space was behind a curtain. That was where Jomari was now. He jumped a little so he could sit on the workbench. Grandad had been a luthier since long before Jomari was born, and now Jomari was honored to be learning the art himself. All of Jomari's jobs revolved around his violin in one way or another—the shop, the orchestra, and being part of Cian's music and dance troupe. It was vastly different from his parents.

They both worked for an insurance company. Mee was an actuary, and Da was a claims adjuster. They'd always supported both their children in their artistic pursuits, though. Jomari's sister, Hazel, played piano and trumpet, but not professionally. She was following their parents' footsteps into the wonderful world of financial mathematics.

Grandad handed him a violin along with a set of strings and the small parts he would need. "JoJo, finish this up, would you?"

Jomari's name might've changed, but not the nickname Grandad still used. It worked. Jomari had chosen his name carefully, something to reflect both his Filipino and Irish roots as well as his family's devout Catholicism. He'd kept part of the name his mother chose for him when he was born, honoring the bond they shared.

Despite their religious background, Jomari had never once worried about coming out to his family. He remembered vividly sitting at the top of the stairs with Hazel, listening to Mee and Da talking. They overheard their parents' hushed conversations and their quiet agreement with marriage equality before the law changed. Jomari, as a preteen, had already been wrestling with his budding identity. One night, he'd had a strange sense, almost a vision, that some of what they were saying might apply to him. He hadn't fully absorbed the meaning, but the image stuck with him.

It took another almost six years before he was ready to come out. Right away, his mother joined the local Asian and Pacific Islander chapter of PFLAG, and she'd been his biggest supporter, aside from Grandad. His father had been slower to warm. Not because he struggled to accept his son as a man but because they'd lost some closeness during Jomari's teen years. They both joked that the Red Sox single-handedly saved their relationship. Jomari had a lot in common with his mother, but not much with his father—aside from their mutual love of the game. During the most intense part of their struggle to build a new, adult relationship, Jomari took Da to a game. A simple gesture became a way to connect.

While Grandad began staining a cello, Jomari put strings on the violin. He was quiet this time, not filling Grandad in on all the happenings in his life. There was too much to think about. He'd never been with more than one person at a time, even casually, and it was definitely new having them also know each other. Somehow, he'd managed to find his way into a group of friends with a spider web of relationships among them, and now he was a bit tangled up in it too.

This wasn't at all anything Jomari had expected. He'd always seen relationships as being fairly easily defined. Maybe not as strict as the Church dictated, but still within those parameters. A situation like the one he was now in didn't come with a set of prayers for guidance. Neither Mack nor Amelia was religious, and though Mack had remarked he'd grown up in a church, he wasn't Catholic. It wasn't as if Jomari could ask either of them. He paused in his work, watching Grandad and feeling for the silver crucifix he never took off.

It wasn't there.

Jomari tried to suppress a gasp. The absence of the cool metal against his fingertips felt enormous. He couldn't recall why he'd removed it or where he'd left it.

Grandad straightened his back and peered at Jomari over his glasses. "What's the matter, JoJo?"

"I—nothing." Jomari tried to go back to putting the strings on, but he stopped. "I lost my crucifix, that's all."

Setting down his brush, Grandad stepped closer. He looked Jomari up and down and nodded. "It'll turn up, God willing. Any idea where you left it?"

"Uh..." There were only a few places. He was more frustrated with himself that he hadn't even noticed it was gone until now. If the chain had broken, it could be anywhere. If not... "Maybe." He didn't really want to explain to Grandad that he might have left it at Mack's or Amelia's and what he'd been doing that might've made him take it off.

"Well, then, you'll start by looking there." Way to be Captain Obvious, but Jomari knew Grandad meant well.

No matter how hard Jomari tried to set aside thoughts of Mack and Amelia, the loss of his crucifix—which he was now convinced one of them had—made it impossible. He was mildly annoyed, too. If one of them had kept it, why hadn't they said anything?

Stringing instruments wasn't complicated or difficult work, so it gave Jomari the opportunity to let himself be distracted. He could forgive Amelia if she had his crucifix. She probably didn't realize yet. Mack, though, was another story. Jomari paused in laying the D-string against the fingerboard. Maybe he'd done it because he wanted to see Jomari again. The idea made him flush. He'd left his number with Mack, but at the lack of a follow-up phone call, he'd assumed it was a one-off, nothing more than picking each other up in a bar.

Jomari had been with far fewer men than people of other genders, and Mack was one of only two who weren't trans. The last man he'd been with had only lasted a few months. It had been long-distance, someone he'd met while with Grandad for a workshop in Worcester. Any time they got together, the guy told Jomari he was "boring" in bed. It got old; Jomari knew he wasn't, and his boyfriend's issues seemed deeper than terrible sex anyway. Jomari wasn't especially interested in another relationship with a man. But Mack...

Grandad interrupted his thoughts. "Your mother asked me to come have supper tonight. You gonna be around, lad?"

"I should be. I've got rehearsal afterward, but I'll be home for a bit."

Jomari handed over another finished instrument, and Grandad hung it on the rack with the others. He'd built the display himself, with slots for the cellos and double basses on the bottom and the violins and violas hanging above them, suspended by their scrolls. Jomari could competently play all of them, though he only rarely did anymore.

Grandad didn't make acoustic guitars, but he did fix them on occasion. There were a few in back, waiting to be repaired. One of the violists from the orchestra, Kevin, had left his bow to be re-haired. He would be in later to pick it up. Good thing because Jomari wanted all the gossip about how Kev and Jason were doing and when they were moving to the other side of the country.

"JoJo!" Grandad called from behind the curtain that separated the display from the work area.

Realizing he'd been staring at the finished instruments for far too long, Jomari answered, "Yeah?"

"Come in here and help me with this wood, will you?"

Jomari stepped away from the display and pushed aside the curtain. He inhaled the fragrance of the fresh wood and the polish, and he relaxed. Nothing better to clear his head than his work. Squaring his shoulders, he began stacking the wood with Grandad at his side.

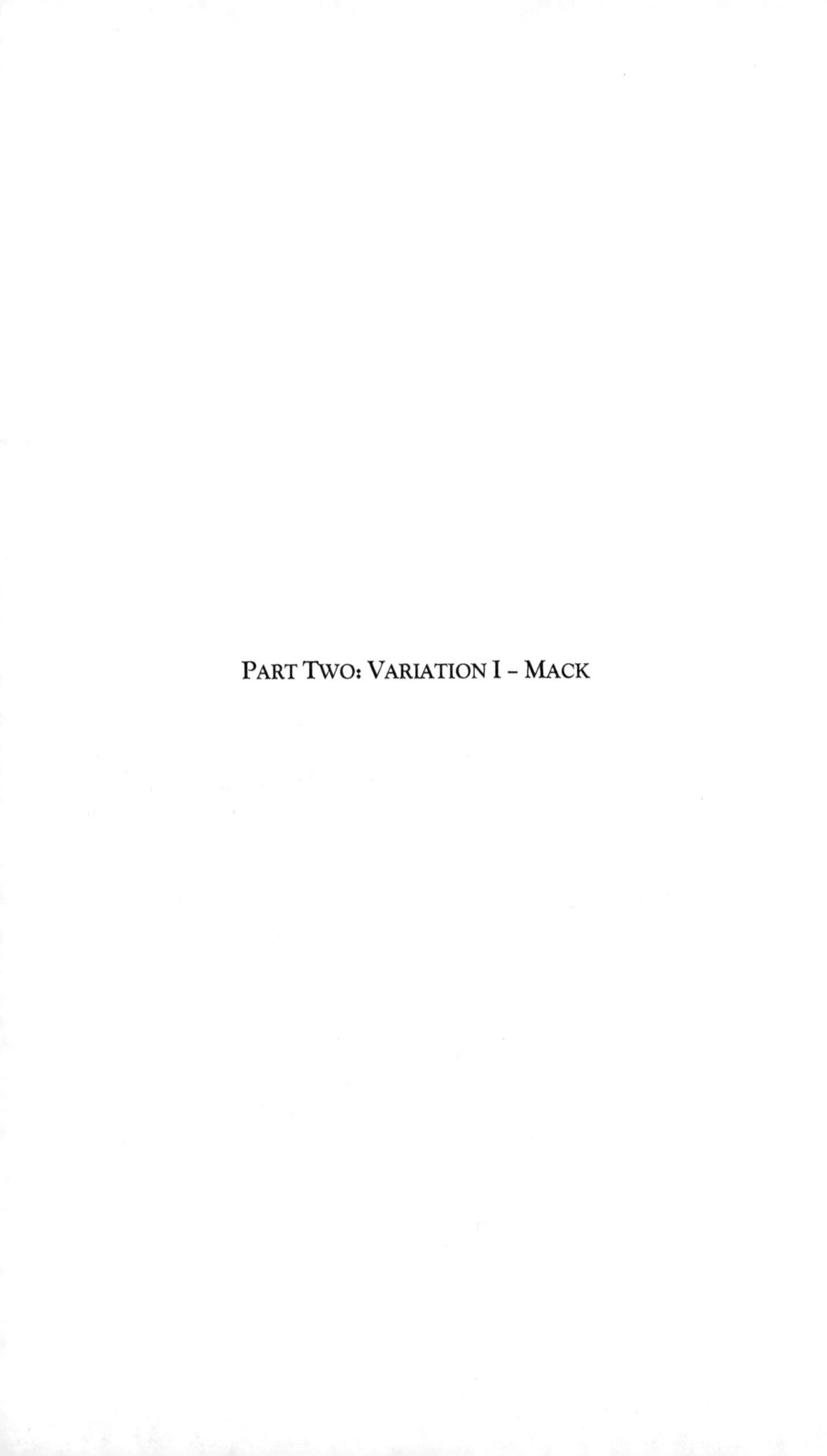

Part Two: Variation I – Mack

Chapter Seven

MACK DEFINITELY didn't want to be awake. He groaned and buried his face in his pillow, cursing both the sun and his own foolishness. He'd stayed up far too late, entertaining the jerkface from Starbucks despite knowing better. The lingering goodwill from an unusually productive rehearsal the previous day had evaporated, replaced by the sting of regret. He'd bought the guy a pizza afterward, which got him out of the apartment. But it was still a poor life choice, and not one Mack planned to make again.

A restless sleep and waking too early left him groggy and disoriented. He was brought out of his barely-functional state by his phone buzzing on the bedside table.

He reached for it and mumbled, "Hello?"

"Hey, sport." Dad's voice was soft, like always.

Mack hauled himself up and tried to clear his fuzzy head. Hearing from Dad always produced a cocktail of impending doom and aching pity. Once again, he regretted giving up his smokes because if he ever needed one, it was now.

"Hey, Dad." Mack didn't ask what was up. There weren't too many reasons for the phone call, so there was no need.

"You stopping by any time soon?" Now there was a hopeful note in Dad's tone. Good; nothing drastic had happened, or he'd have sounded worse.

"Did you need me to?" The joys of being an only child of a chronically ill parent and her sole caregiver. There was no one else to turn to, no one to go in Mack's place just this once.

"It would be nice if you could." Dad *ahem*'d. "You know, if you have the time."

A lump formed in Mack's throat. He ran his fingers through his hair and tugged. *Not now. Please not now.* He didn't want to reveal his grief to Dad, who already had enough to worry about. Mack swallowed several times, vainly trying to stem his emotions.

"Uh-hm. Yeah, o-okay." He'd held it together, mostly. "Later, all right? I gotta get a few things done here first." It wasn't a lie, but it wasn't the truth either.

"Sure, sure." A pause. "You're a good kid, Mackenzie. I'm proud of you, sport." Dad was speaking to him in that odd way he had, as though Mack had gone back to being six.

It nearly broke him. "Okay, Dad. See you soon." Mack ended the call before his father could reply. He'd reached his limit on reining in his pain.

He didn't want to see her. There was a time, a few years ago, when Mom still knew who he was. She might've been too drunk for a coherent conversation some of the time, but at least Mack wasn't the son she forgot she had. Back then, she'd still been able to hug him and tell him she loved him, even if he wasn't sure she meant it.

When Mack was little Dad always assured him Mom loved him. Maybe she did, but she loved being wasted more. Dad said last time Mack visited that she was drinking less than she had been. Possibly now that she couldn't recall the details of her life, she didn't need to drink to scrub them out. He shuddered; if things had been different, he could easily have ended up the same way, only without someone like Dad to look after him.

Mack stood and stretched. He needed coffee and a long, hot shower before facing his parents. For a split second, he wondered if Amelia would go with him so they could do this together the way they had with Sage. He dismissed the idea. Mom wasn't her responsibility. She didn't need to be burdened with any of this, not with her own family history. Later, he could call her and let her come over to take care of him in some other way. Not sex—she would make him hot tea and wrap him in a blanket and let him lay his head in her lap while they watched some God-awful, decades-old movie and he tried not to cry himself to sleep again.

It was an acceptable plan. Mack grabbed his least ratty jeans and a blue T-shirt Jamie had bought him once, complaining Mack's wardrobe was too depressing. For a moment, Mack held out the shirt, contemplating putting it back on the grounds it would only make him feel worse. He pictured Jamie rolling his eyes and making it clear he thought Mack was being purposefully stupid. For the first time since waking, Mack smiled. A shirt wasn't as good as having Jamie there, but it would do. He kept it after all and headed for the bathroom.

In between navigating through traffic, Mack spent the entire forty-minute drive on 93 rehearsing what he was going to say to his parents. There were a lot of off-limits topics with Dad. He could probably have said almost anything to Mom and she wouldn't remember it later, but he didn't want to upset her in the moment.

Work, the band, and Amelia were safe, as long as he didn't get detailed about the venues he played or the exact nature of his relationship with her. Roommates were all right if Mack kept to bland statements about their jobs. If Mack stuck to his list, he could have a nice-but-slightly-strained visit.

If Mom was lucid enough.

He ignored the niggle and pulled up next to their trailer. It looked like it always did, the way Dad kept up the external appearance. Come to think of it, the inside was always clean too. Dad did like to give the impression everything was fine. Mack killed the engine and sat there, not wanting to get out but also not wanting to turn around and drive home.

Home. Most people got to think of their childhood house as "home" in some sense. Not Mack. Home was where he didn't have to help Dad clean up broken glass or spilled wine or fresh bodily fluids, both treating it as if this was a normal, everyday occurrence in other people's houses too. It was where he could breathe and let go of pretending he'd only started the band as a hobby and not a way to escape. Home was a place where he didn't have to reassure anyone he would someday settle down with a nine-to-five job, a sweet, perky wife, and a minivan to shuttle around his kids. Well, he had the van down, anyway, albeit with most of the seats removed.

Before Mack had made up his mind to finally open the door, Dad appeared on the steps to the trailer. He waved and came down to the van. Mack rolled down the window.

"Before you come in, I should tell you—"

Mack cut him off, knowing what was coming next. "It's fine. I get it."

Mom wasn't getting any better. If that's what Dad expected, he would remain disappointed. It was like this every time. Dad warned Mack that Mom was in a state, as though Mack had somehow caught her on a bad day and the rest of the time she was fine. They both knew better, but sometimes it was easier to go along with it. The only time Mack had argued, Dad had told him to get out and hadn't called for over a month.

Together they made their way inside. Mack smelled whatever Dad had used to clean mingled with a faint, lingering stench of piss and body odor. Mack was puzzled. Mom's dementia made her confused, paranoid, and forgetful, but it rarely made her incapable of basic grooming or toileting. He wondered now if she was getting worse and if Dad was ready to admit he needed more help caring for her.

Mack almost scoffed out loud. *Caring for her.* Dad had been doing it in one way or another for decades. What held Mack in check from commenting was the understanding it could've been him too if he'd stayed on her path.

There wasn't any need to ask about it. Dad gripped Mack's arm before they stepped into the living room and filled in the blanks.

"She's convinced someone's trying to poison her through the shower head," he murmured. "I talked her down for today, but..."

Mack nodded, shrugging off Dad's hand. He looked to the other end of the living room, where the television was on at a low volume. Mom sat in front of it in her plush chair. She'd had it a few years, a gift from Mack after his first paid gig with the Crullers. Not that she would recall it was her son who gave it to her or how proud she'd been. Or the way her enthusiasm had given way to another bout of despair over her losses. Maybe it was better she didn't know who he was after all.

He stepped around so he was in front of her. She was humming softly while she gazed at the television. It was tuned to some cooking show, which gave Mack another pang. Mom hadn't cooked for anyone in at least ten years, not since the last time she'd ended up with her hand singed from grasping the handle on a cast iron pan. She'd been too out of it to feel a thing.

"Hey, Mom."

She glanced down to where Mack was now kneeling. "Hello there." She smiled, and for a moment Mack thought she recognized him. "Are you here to fix the shower?"

Mack sucked in a breath and looked up at Dad, who shook his head. Dad's whole countenance reflected sadness, but underneath was a kind of calm strength. Mack remembered that Dad had spent the better part of three decades watching the woman he loved destroy herself. The only thing keeping Mack from losing it right there was knowing it wouldn't help Dad.

He turned back to Mom. "No, I came by for a visit."

"Oh, are you Shirley's son, the one from the book club?"

Mack almost asked her what book club she was talking about but caught himself in time. "No, I don't think I know a Shirley."

Mom smiled, and something about it was eerie. "Shirley was the one who told me about how all the town's water went bad. She started a book club." Her expression turned thoughtful. "I do remember she said she had a grown son, though. Not you?"

"No. Not me." Mack swallowed. "I'm your son."

For a fraction of a second, Mack was sure she was going to argue. She tilted her head, peering at Mack over the top of her glasses. "Well, then. If that's so, surely you can do something about the damn shower."

There wasn't a category for Mack's reaction. He wanted to laugh, cry, and hit something all at the same time. Mom believed him this time, which was possibly an improvement. She might try to fill in the gaps in her memory by making up the details of his birth or childhood, but he could endure a fairy tale about himself as a boy. He might even be able to convince her he'd fixed whatever she thought was wrong with the shower.

"Okay, Mom. I'll look at it. Did you want to have lunch first?"

Mom frowned. "Was I supposed to make something? I think we have some cold cuts." She twisted to look back at Dad. "Isn't that right?"

"In the fridge, yeah." He motioned to Mack. "You can, uh, have a look at the shower while I get the food out."

Mack stood and followed Dad out to the kitchen. Silently, they began putting things on the table. Mack wondered if this was a good time to finally have a conversation with Dad regarding what they were going to do about Mom. All of them deserved better than this tense, lonely attempt at family life.

"Hey, Dad?"

"Yes, sport?"

"Do you think we could talk about Mom?"

Dad shrugged one shoulder. "What's there to talk about?

You've seen how she is."

"I know. It's just..." Mack trailed off, unsure how to bring up the idea of Dad getting someone to help him.

Putting a hand on Mack's shoulder and squeezing gently, Dad said, "I'm real glad you're here today. I think it's helped her perk up a little, you know?"

The subject was closed for another day. Mack sighed. "Yeah. Yeah, I think it did."

Mack dumped his keys on the table by the door and shed his sweatshirt on his way to the couch. He tossed it onto a chair then pulled out his phone. He opened his "favorites" and hit Amelia's number at the top of the list. She answered almost immediately.

"Hey, you. What's up?" She sounded unusually cheerful, which made Mack smile despite his mood.

The lightness quickly dissipated. He swallowed heavily before replying. "Not much. Went to see my parents this afternoon." He did his best to make it sound casual, even knowing Amelia would see right through him.

"Oh, babe. You hanging in there?"

"Yeah." He ran his fingers through his long hair. "You want to come by? We have the place to ourselves."

There was a long, awkward pause. "I can't tonight."

"You— Why not?" Mack gripped the phone, trying not to flip out. Amelia didn't belong to him, and he had no right to expect her to drop everything when he called. Still, this wasn't like her.

"I'm going out with a friend." Another pause. "Jomari, from the orchestra."

So not any old friend. Specifically a friend she was having sex with or at least had done so in the past. Mack could live with that, most of the time. Tonight, though, it hit him right in the gut. He needed her after the kind of day he'd had, and she was with someone else. Someone he'd also fucked. It wasn't even the sex, though. He wanted to watch shitty movies and hear her commentary on the terrible plots and bad acting. He wanted her to keep him from dwelling on things he couldn't change. But as her longtime best friend, he also didn't want to stand in the way of something that made her sound so happy.

"Okay," he told her, trying not to let his disappointment show.

"I'm sorry." He voice was softer now. "I didn't know you would need me."

"It's fine. Have fun. I'll probably go out later anyway."

"Are you sure?" Now Mack detected a low-key thread of worry.

"I'm not going to do anything stupid." He opted for a bit of humor. "Maybe I'll see if that barista gets off work soon." He wouldn't, not after the night before, but she didn't need to know that.

"The one who thought floor sex was hot?" Amelia laughed. "Only you, Mack. Do try not to injure your back this time."

"I'll be okay. Talk to you in the morning?"

"For sure. I'll even bring you cinnamon rolls for breakfast. Night, babe."

He ended the call and sat there with the phone in his hand, running through the possibilities. He already hadn't been in any shape to go out, and even less so with the nagging frustration that Amelia was with someone else. If Jamie had been home, they could've done something together. But he wasn't, and Mack was at a loss.

It wasn't as though he didn't have friends. There was the band and Amelia and Jamie. He had their other roommates too, though Trevor had moved out months ago and Nate was on his way out soon. Mack didn't need more than a few close friends. That is, until a night like tonight when he craved a distraction.

He considered Trevor—everyone was always welcome at his house. But Mack didn't feel up to hanging out with a nine-month-old, and he wasn't in the mood to explain what was going on. Marlie would've asked, since Mack wasn't in the habit of calling Trevor to spend time together.

Nate was an option. He and Izzy probably wouldn't get too nosy. Before he could change his mind, Mack scrolled until he found Nate's number and hit it.

"Hey-o," Nate said when he picked up.

"Hey. It's Mack."

"Oh, dude! How are you?"

"Been better." That damn lump in his throat was back. "Listen, I could use something to do tonight. What are you up to?"

"Nothing much. What did you have in mind?"

"No specifics. Needing company is all." Once again, Mack tried to cover the slight warble in his voice.

Nate snorted. "Company, right. I'm not having sex with you if that's why you called."

"You know what? Fuck you. I'm hanging up now." Mack pulled the phone away from his ear. He'd forgotten Nate's filter was thin.

"Wait! Sorry, man. You sounded kind of rough, so I was joking around. Izzy's at work until midnight, but you can come hang out for a while. I'll show you what he got us." There was an undercurrent of excitement in his tone that cheered Mack a little.

He chuckled in spite of himself. "I thought you said we weren't having sex."

"Fuck off, dude!" Nate was laughing now too. "You like gaming at all?"

"Yeah, a bit. You got something good?"

"Only an Xbox One and a couple of games even I haven't tried yet."

"You and Izzy are into gaming?" This was a side of him Mack hadn't known about.

"I am. Izzy fakes it pretty well for me, though. You need to unwind and get your mind off shit? This'll do it."

"Sounds perfect to me. I'll be there in a half hour or so."

They ended the call and Mack sat back for a few minutes with his eyes closed. Nate would shake him out of his melancholy for a little while. With any luck, it would be enough to get through another night.

Chapter Eight

Mack had the night off, and he was in a mood. *The* mood. The itch hit him forcefully in a way it hadn't in a long time. Mack hadn't touched a drop of alcohol in over five years. Not that he hadn't wanted to or come close in all that time. But he'd had Jamie then. Countless nights that first year, when Jamie and Amelia were there every time he gave in. And when he was finally sober, Jamie was there for him again.

Jamie wasn't there now, wouldn't be back for a few more days, and the combination of the gaping hole he'd left and Mack's internal buzzing brought back a whole lot of buried desires. He wanted something to take the edge off. He hadn't seen Amelia in days, he still missed Jamie, and he was keyed up.

At first, he tried funneling the feeling into writing a new song. The lyrics wouldn't come, and he couldn't settle down enough to focus. He bounced off the couch and wandered into the kitchen, where he poured himself a glass of water. Standing by the sink, he paused. If he wanted, he could have something stronger. He could cave, and no one would know.

A memory surfaced of his mother, standing in exactly the same position he was now. She was at the sink, not with a glass of water but with a carrot and a knife, making dinner. Singing. Probably already halfway to drunk. The knife slipped, and—

Mack's hand shook, sloshing water over the edge of the glass.

The cold splash woke him up. He remembered what Jamie had said before he left, about not wanting to become his mother. Mack understood. He gulped the water, the cool liquid sliding down his burning throat. It wasn't enough, but he would have to live with that.

A warm body. That's what he needed. It would've been plenty easy to head over to Grand Slam. Mack was reasonably confident his occasional hookup, the Bio-Queen, was performing that night. She went by Candie Gram, and she was hot, funny as hell, and nowhere near as old as her stage name and makeup implied. They didn't fuck while she was in drag.

He didn't relish the long train ride, though, and he needed to stay away from anywhere he might be tempted to drink. Besides, he didn't think Candie was who he had in mind. Everything with her was over a bit too fast, which was fine if that's what he was chasing. But she always finished too soon, and she didn't do any kind of oral, neither giving nor receiving. Too bad, since that left out two of Mack's favorite activities.

A nameless, faceless guy from an app wouldn't do either; he always preferred the fun of flirting first and the subtle—or not—cues that the night would end well for everyone. The thrill for Mack was higher when all parties were in on it from the start, though he did like some variety. For the most part, he stuck to his regulars with someone new in the mix on occasion. He'd tumbled with Nate's friend Del a couple of times and once with one of Nate's exes. Piero, the androgynous one with the pretty, sad eyes. That had been a mistake.

Mack rarely regretted a hookup, but there were a handful of times. Several when he was too drunk to enjoy it, back in those days. The one that he'd tried to forget right after by downing as many shots as he could and nearly wrapping his car around a utility pole at two in the morning. That one had gotten him his one and only DUI and a wake-up call. And then there was Piero.

He hadn't meant to get with a friend's former partner. In fact, he hadn't remembered Piero at all—Nate only brought him over once before crushing his heart. For some reason, Piero had been at one of the Creepy Crullers' gigs. Mack thought he was about to have a good time with one of their fans. In fairness, they'd never really had sex. Mack had Piero's pants down around his ankles and was about to blow his mind when the poor guy lost it and started sobbing instead. His confession of chasing down Mack's band to make Nate jealous only half made sense, but it was enough to convince Mack to keep it zipped. He still had Piero's number, not that he was planning to use it.

Tonight, he wanted someone to absorb his restless energy. Someone who wouldn't be here and gone in less time than it would've taken Mack to just use his own hand. Someone like...

His gaze landed on the silver cross still sitting on his bedside table. He had to return it anyway; maybe he could make it worth both their while. He had a brief stab of discomfort. Jomari had been out with Amelia, and Mack wasn't sure what that meant. On the other hand, he figured there was a mighty good reason she kept going back to the guy, and Mack might as well enjoy himself.

If he was lucky, Jomari might spend the night again. Mack quickly shook that idea off. Just because he didn't need to work the next morning didn't mean Jomari had the day off. It was the middle of the week, and most people had jobs with more reasonable hours than Mack's. Maybe Jomari wouldn't want to come over at all.

Only one way to find out. Mack picked up the cross, which was sitting on top of the paper Jomari had left with his number.

An hour and a half later, Jomari rolled off Mack, panting, his light bronze skin glistening with sweat. Mack stretched then placed his hands behind his head. He closed his eyes, wanting to imprint every detail of their hot, loud fuck into his brain. God, Jomari was a stud.

"Hey."

The soft word made Mack open one eye to squint at Jomari. He could've done without any talking. Why ruin the moment? Mack thought it sounded stupid to suggest he'd come harder than ever before in his life, but he had to admit, it had been powerful. All he wanted was to bask in it, not have a conversation. Especially not the one he suspected was on the horizon.

"Hm?" He intentionally made it sound sleepier than he felt in hopes of deferring some mushy nonsense about where their relationship was going.

"What are we doing here?"

Oh, God. And there it was. "I dunno," Mack mumbled. He sighed and rolled to face Jomari. "Dozing off after a spectacular fuck? At least, I was trying to."

To Mack's surprise, Jomari laughed. "No, I meant whether we're planning to go again or if I should leave."

Now Mack's eyes popped wide open. He propped himself on

his elbow. "Gotta admit, that's not what I was expecting."

"I realized that as soon as I said it. Sometimes my mouth gets ahead of my brain." Jomari snickered. "Sorry. Anyway, about my question..."

"You can stay." Mack hid his relief behind a chuckle at Jomari's raised eyebrow. It would've been too hard to explain his need for company; he didn't think they were that close friends yet. It warmed him to think maybe they could be, though. He sat up. "You hungry?"

The predatory gleam in Jomari's eye and his wicked grin made Mack glad he'd phrased it that way. Jomari stretched and sat up as well, leaning in for a kiss that went on a lot longer than Mack had planned.

When they ended it, Jomari said, "I could eat." He winked at Mack and bounced out of the bed. "Lemme clean up first."

He didn't cover anything up on his way out. Mack made a noise halfway between a grunt and a sigh as he watched Jomari's delicious ass exit the bedroom. It was fine even encased in the tight briefs he had on to keep his cock in place while they fucked. No way was Mack ready for round two yet, but he was going to enjoy every second of the anticipation.

The water turned on in the bathroom, and Mack rolled over to snuggle the pillow, half dozing until he heard it stop. Eventually, he stood and stretched. He took his own turn in the bathroom and then purposefully didn't put underwear on when he left to join Jomari in the kitchen. His heart ached only a little that the reason he could be so free was Jamie being away.

Jomari was rummaging in the fridge. He set a couple of containers on the counter along with a pitcher of filtered water. Mack came up behind him and set a hand on his arm. When Jomari turned his head to beam at him, Mack ran his hand down until he reached Jomari's left butt cheek, which he gave a gentle squeeze.

"What's in these?" Jomari asked, tapping a finger on one of the containers.

"Leftovers." He swallowed. "Amelia and I cooked last week, and I pulled it out of the freezer this morning."

"Ah." Jomari didn't look upset at the reference to Amelia, but it was hard to tell.

"Does it bother you? That she and I are...whatever we are?"

"Should it?" Jomari shook his head. "Don't answer that. I was being rude. No, it doesn't bother me. She knows about this. Does it bother you that she and I have been together?"

"She's not my girlfriend. Already told you that."

Jomari sighed. "Right, but you have something going on between you. I assume trust is part of it."

"We don't talk about every single hookup we have." Mack moved away from Jomari. In a literal sense, what he'd said was the truth. He'd conveniently left out the part where talking about their hookups was a regular feature of their foreplay until Jomari came along.

"Uh huh. That's not what—" He stopped himself, and Mack watched as the last traces of sex flush drained from his cheeks. "I mean—"

Frowning, Mack crossed his arms and said, "Yeah, tell me. What did you mean?"

"She and I—we—" He cringed visibly. "We've gone out a couple times since the night you and I...at the bar..."

So that's what this was about. Mack wasn't sure if he was disappointed or not. Or if he should be. Amelia had only mentioned the one time, but he'd figured there might be more even if she hadn't said so. It made him feel guilty for times like tonight, which he might not have shared with her, either. Their relationship was more than calling each other every so often for a roll in bed, and they were usually open about everything. Fucking the same guy was a new one for both of them, and he wasn't sure what the etiquette was.

"It's cool," he finally said. "Like I told you, we're not a couple. She's free to do what she likes. That's our agreement."

"And what about you?" Jomari approached Mack, the containers on the counter forgotten. "Are you free to do what you like?" He put his hand on Mack's chest and toyed with the hairs there.

"Yeah." Distracted, Mack groaned when Jomari rolled his nipple.

"Mm. And what is it you like?" Jomari leaned in to kiss Mack's jaw.

"That," Mack barely managed to say. "I like that."

"How about this?" Jomari's hand wandered down, but he didn't put it on Mack's dick.

"Yes."

Jomari kept it up, touching Mack everywhere and making him light up like Boston Harbor at night. Each time, Jomari rewarded

Mack's "yes" with a shiver-inducing brush of his fingers. By the time he was finished, he'd reduced Mack to a weak-kneed, pliant mess.

"Want to take this back to bed?" Jomari's voice was smooth and sexy, and it made Mack tremble.

"What about the food?"

"It can wait." Jomari pulled away to give Mack his cat-that-ate-the-canary grin. "Suddenly, it's not leftovers I'm hungry for."

Mack groaned. "Holy Mother of God on a popsicle."

Laughing, Jomari spun away from him, grabbing his hand on the way. They raced down the hallway and back into the bedroom, landing in a tangle on Mack's bed. Every other thought flew from Mack's mind as Jomari went down on him.

It only took a few minutes of feeling that fantastic before Mack couldn't stand not having his hands and mouth similarly occupied. His whole body sang, and he wanted Jomari to feel every thrill to the same degree. He had to know all the ways Jomari wanted to be touched. Gently he nudged Jomari until he raised his eyes.

"I need to know what else you like that we haven't done yet."

Jomari pulled off. "Uh-uh. You first, and then I'll show you."

Happy to comply, Mack agreed, tipping his head back and writhing against the sheets when Jomari got back to business.

When Mack woke, it was still dark. The curtains fluttered in a breeze from the open window, letting in the amber glow of a street lamp. He rolled slightly to pick up his phone and check the time. Only 2:30. Mack closed his eyes again, willing sleep to return.

After several minutes, he concluded it wasn't going to happen. He turned his head to look at Jomari, tucked up on the other side of the bed. No cuddling this time, so Mack was fairly sure he could extract himself without incident. He slid out of bed and dragged on a pair of briefs and a T-shirt. Not a peep from Jomari.

Mack tiptoed out of the bedroom, pulling the door shut. In the living room, he flopped onto the couch. He didn't feel much like flipping channels—not that there was much on at this time of night— or scrolling through Netflix for something. His thoughts were too jumbled to concentrate on anything.

He didn't recall the details of the dream he'd been having nor what woke him, only vague images and a lingering restlessness. The nagging itch from earlier was mostly gone, thanks to mind-blowing sex and Jomari's willingness to stay. Mack appreciated that he hadn't asked why or demanded some kind of define-the-relationship talk. His presence was enough to keep the demons at bay for the time being, and it didn't need to be any more complicated than that.

A different kind of urge hit Mack. He needed to write. In the drawer under the lamp, he kept a small notebook for jotting things down. He had one in every room, including the bathroom, just in case the mood struck. Now he pulled out the one in the living room and opened to a blank page.

For a few minutes, he stared at the empty lines. He still wanted to write a song for Amelia, a hymn for her curves and her muscles and how good her skin tasted and her hair smelled. He smiled, recalling how she'd suggested he write about the way she fucked him. He wanted to; as far as he was aware, a song about being pegged by a woman wasn't common.

He also wanted to write one for Jamie. It would make Jamie blush all the way to the roots of his hair, but Mack was going to do it anyway. There weren't nearly enough songs about the kind of friendship the two of them had. Thinking about it made Mack snort. If any of the other guys knew how hopelessly poetic he was about his friendships, they'd probably laugh themselves sick.

Or they'd tell him he was harboring romantic feelings. Mack got tired on a regular basis of explaining why he and Amelia weren't a couple. They were close friends, and they had sex regularly. Why couldn't that be respected as enough? Mack didn't scoff at Nate and Izzy, the most intensely romantic pair he knew. Nor at Trevor, who went starry-eyed any time he talked about one of his partners. Mack didn't even make fun of Jamie when Cian sent him flowers.

Mack sighed. They all thought he was nothing more than a player, looking for the next fuck toy. They accepted his hookups, but he knew they all thought the same things about him: Commitment-phobe. Heartbreaker. Immature. Asshole. None of those were true at all, nor was he unhappy. He had real relationships already. So what if they didn't happen to include hearts and flowers and long walks by the Harbor? Instead, he had friends who knew the things he tucked away deeply from the public eye. Friends who accompanied him on a mission to threaten anyone who harmed another one of them. People who gladly shared his bed without demanding something he couldn't give.

All of that was why he never discussed his past with anyone but Jamie and Amelia. They'd have blamed Mack's mother or maybe his father. Possibly both. He couldn't explain that his mother's pain—

and her ways of coping—were not the cause, nor were his father's desperate attempts to save her. His childhood had been equal measures heartache and joy, a strange balance he'd misunderstood until it nearly wrecked him.

If not his parents, they'd have blamed the incident that made him quit drinking. His mind wandered to the five-year token he usually kept on him. It wasn't open for conversation. He never wanted to experience that loss of control again, in any sense. As lucky as he was to be alive, it wasn't what made him who he was. Cheesy though it might be, Mack wanted to be defined by how much he cared about his friends—not by being the star of his own romance novel.

A breeze filtered in, and Mack shivered. He got up to close the window then returned to the couch. He wasn't going to touch any songs about two of the people he loved most in the world. Instead, his thoughts drifted to Jomari. He shivered again, not from the cold this time.

Jomari was sensual and confident. He knew what he liked, and he wasn't afraid to tell Mack exactly what that was. Sex with him was so different than with Amelia, but it brought out a lot of the same feelings of being cared for and protected. It wasn't a matter of how aggressive or how soft the sex was. He'd done it both ways with both of them. It was more a sense that they were honoring who he was as a person, as a man.

Mack turned back to the page in his lap and began scribbling. That was it—he wanted to capture the essence of being his own man. Something that went against the garbage of guarding his heart and independence and control. The strength he felt when his partners topped him and the gentleness when he made love to them. The way being claimed made him feel masculine or the way claiming them made him feel feminine. The vulnerability of letting his friends in on his deepest fears and the near-holiness of being trusted with theirs.

Saint Brigid's poodle in a dress, he was sappy. And he didn't care one bit as the words flowed out onto the page. He lost track of the time, filling the notebook with the precious treasures pouring from his soul. It wasn't until he heard the flush of the toilet that he looked up.

Jomari strode into the living room. His undershirt was off, but he'd put the silver cross back around his neck, the only thing he had on. He looked good, soft and innocent despite his nakedness. They'd been inside each other mere hours earlier, but somehow it made Mack feel more trusted to be allowed this view of him without his binder or his tight A-shirt. Mack smiled and patted the couch.

Jomari sat. "Whatcha doing?"

"Writing a song." Mack thought about it for a moment. Once the words were on the page, they didn't feel as fragile as glass. He could share them after they'd been inked. He held the notebook out to Jomari and watched as his eyes flicked over the lyrics.

"Hey, this is really good."

Accepting the notebook back, Mack nodded his thanks. "So this is what I do when it's after three a.m. and I can't sleep."

"I can think of other things we could do." Jomari winked.

Mack laughed. "Maybe in a bit. Unless you have to get up for work or something."

"Nope. Shop doesn't open until ten. I'm good as long as I'm there by nine."

"Shop?" Mack had never asked what Jomari did for a living other than playing fiddle with Cian's musicians.

"My grandfather's business. He's a luthier, and I'm his apprentice."

Mack blinked. "I have no idea what that is."

"A violin maker. Any acoustic string, really, but we specialize in making and repairing violins." Jomari smiled. "What about you? Is the band your only job?"

"Oh, are we at that stage now? Where we can ask all the personal details?"

Jomari snorted. "I guess. We are friends, right?"

"Sure, yeah. All right, if you must know, I work at Legal Seafood in the kitchen."

Jomari's eyes widened. "You're a chef?"

"Uh...no." Mack's face heated. "I wash dishes."

"But do you want to be? I mean...I don't know. You mentioned cooking with Amelia, but maybe that didn't mean anything."

Mack didn't speak for a while. He'd never considered doing anything but getting by every day. Legal was a way to make ends meet. He liked the location where he worked; it was well-managed and the staff was nice. But that's all it was, a job. A way to pay the bills and something with enough freedom he could still play with the band.

He licked his lips. "I've never thought much about what I wanted."

"Hm," was all Jomari said in response.

Enough was enough. Mack had a hot man on his couch who he'd specifically invited over for sex, not baring his soul. He reached over and put a hand on Jomari's thigh.

"I'm a moment to moment kind of guy," he said. "Right now, this is what I want."

"Fine by me."

Mack kissed him, and within minutes Jomari was pulling Mack's clothes off and tossing them aside. Jomari straddled Mack's leg, riding him as his hand wrapped around Mack's cock. Mack toyed with Jomari's ass, motivated by the sexy moans he made. It didn't take long before Jomari stuttered that he was about to come, just as Mack let go with a huff of relief, his eyes pinched shut and his mouth agape.

They lay there panting for a couple of minutes. Mack's head began to clear, but the sex-fog was replaced by pleasurable sleepiness. If he wasn't careful, he'd doze off right there with Jomari half on top of him. Mack grunted, causing Jomari to shift.

"Back to bed?" Mack suggested.

"I could sleep."

Jomari extracted himself, and Mack stood as well. Mack paused in the bathroom to clean up then returned to the bedroom. They lay down, and to his surprise—but not, this time, to his dismay—Jomari curled against his side. The cuddling wasn't so bad after all, Mack decided.

Chapter Nine

Mack had spent the entire morning cleaning, a thing he despised to his core. He missed having Trevor around to pick up after everyone. Sometimes Mack wondered how Trevor survived having a baby, but he had the impression Andre and Marlie were the tidy types too. Every time he was at their house, it had the polished veneer of a magazine cover. He couldn't decide if they did that for their friends' benefit or if that was how they existed all the time.

Focus. He had to focus. He'd tried distracting himself by practicing the two new songs he'd written, one each for Amelia and Jomari. His rhythm was off, and he kept losing his place in the lyrics sheet. He had to face facts—he wouldn't be able to calm down until Jamie walked through the front door.

With the floors gleaming nearly to the point of requiring sunglasses and the bathroom so clean a person could eat directly off the surfaces, Mack had nothing left to do but the dishes. He put in his earbuds, turned up the music, and threw himself into scrubbing last night's dinner out of the Dutch oven while singing along to Queen's "Don't Stop Me Now," first on his "tell no one you like this" playlist. It would ruin his image.

The result of drowning out all other sound was that he missed it when the door opened. A hand on his back made him fling the soapy sponge over his shoulder onto the table. Mack whirled around, yanking out his earbuds and hitting pause on the way. There was Jamie, a little thinner and a lot more worn than he'd been when he left but with a distinct new sparkle in his eyes and poorly disguised amusement all over his face.

Mack didn't care; he grabbed Jamie and held on, inhaling the familiar scent of his hair gel and body wash. Jamie's laughter was a gentle vibration against Mack's chest as he returned the embrace. Mack didn't want to let go, at least not until he had himself under control and had been assured it wasn't a complex hallucination. Weeks' worth of emptiness and worry were replaced with relief. Jamie was okay; he was here, in Mack's arms, solid and real.

Jamie released Mack, making it awkward for Mack to still be clinging to Jamie. He let go and backed up, keeping his hands on Jamie's shoulders. He looked mostly the same as he always did. Thick, brown hair, neatly gelled, slightly longer than it had been. Fair skin, a bit paler than usual but still with a nice, pink glow in his cheeks, unless that was a little makeup. Warm brown eyes, lined with liquid black. Piercings nearly everywhere. He had on tight blue jeans and a sea-green henley, a gold chain peeking out from where the buttons were undone.

Jamie grinned. He seemed tired, but Mack felt the joy radiating from him. He was happy to be home, and Mack was glad to have him back. Life without one of the two best friends he'd ever known was hardly worth enduring.

"Looking good, Jamie," Mack told him.

On closer inspection, he saw the new piercing in the left shell of Jamie's ear: a semicolon. Mack's gaze flicked to his own version—a tattoo inside his right forearm. It was a heart made from the bass and treble clefs, the dots on the "C" turned into a semicolon. When Mack raised his eyes again, he remembered why Jamie had all the other piercings. His stomach tightened.

Jamie caught on that Mack was inspecting him. "What?"

"This is new." Mack gently touched Jamie's ear. "Shit, I'm sorry."

"About what?" Jamie frowned.

"Did you and Cian—" Mack couldn't say it.

"Oh! No, nothing like that." Sliding into a chair, Jamie tapped the table. "Come sit, and I'll fill you in."

Mack plunked down kitty-corner to Jamie. "So everything is okay?"

"More than." Jamie chewed his lip. "At least, it is now. When I was first there, it was hard. I wanted to come home. I wanted you or

Trevor or Cian to get me and tell me I didn't have to go back." He twisted his fingers together. "I wanted to call Sage."

"That son of a llama-riding—never mind. I'll be quiet."

That seemed to relax Jamie a little, and he half-smiled. "Every day, I felt like I wasn't going to make it. I thought constantly about finding a way to—to binge. By the end of the first six days, I was so ashamed all I wanted was…" He looked right at Mack. "…to die. I didn't have a plan or anything, but I wished I could sleep and never wake up. Everything felt pointless."

Mack understood, and he knew Jamie was aware of it. They both acknowledged the shared pain before Mack said, "Go on."

"My therapist at the center added the extra week because neither of us thought I'd be ready after only three. Eventually I got through it, though. I learned how to cook and helped make stuff for after the baby came." His eyes lit up. "She's adorable, by the way."

Chuckling, Mack said, "I'll take your word for it."

"At the end, my therapist suggested the new piercing. I told her why I have the other ones, and she said to think of it like I was 'breaking up' with my eating disorder. I didn't want to at first. I mean, remember all the times I got one after breaking up with Sage and then went right back to him? She told me that's going to happen, in a way, with this. I'll have times like now, where I feel good about my recovery, and times of relapse and having to get up and try again. So this is a way to acknowledge it."

"That makes sense, yeah."

"There's more to it." Jamie continued, "She thought it might be time for me to recognize that it's okay to celebrate the good parts of breaking up. I was convinced for a long time that I deserved the pain. I deserved to eat until I almost made myself sick or to go back to Sage to let him abuse me. But that's not right. I owe it to myself to make my body feel good with food, not bad, and I am allowed to have someone like Cian."

Mack wasn't used to Jamie being so open with him. Their relationship, like a lot of Mack's friendships, was based more on what was between the lines. As much as he'd known Jamie felt this way, he'd never spoken the words out loud before. Mack didn't know what to say. He wanted to reach out to Jamie and offer some kind of reassurance or wise words or any of the other things he'd done before, but all of those reactions seemed flat and bordering on inappropriate.

Before he could formulate an answer, Jamie said, "Enough

about me. How are you doing?"

Mack considered what to say. Jamie'd only just come home, and Mack didn't want to dump everything on him about his parents or the way things had become complicated with Amelia. He wasn't ready to talk about Jomari, either. Or about the fact that he'd had a couple of bad days lately when he'd almost risked his sobriety. He opted for casual and shrugged one shoulder.

"Not too bad. Quit smoking again. Wrote a couple new songs."

"You did?" Jamie grinned. "It's been forever since we've had new material. Something must've happened while I was away."

"Uh…" Mack hesitated, since some of his recent sexual encounters had inspired both songs. He deflected. "I thought it was about time. But damn, we need you. Diedrich is all right—that's Cassie's friend who filled in for you—but it's not the same."

"It's nice to be missed."

Mack set a couple of glasses of water on the table. "You hungry? Um. Wait. Is that the wrong thing to ask?"

"It's okay." Jamie's lips curved into a soft, mildly amused smile, but it was quickly replaced by a more serious expression. "It's complicated. I'm supposed to keep to a set schedule, to make sure I eat stuff that's good for me. I can't shop unless I go with someone or have you check the bags when I get home. It's easiest if things are kept to measured portions, but I can manage without. I have to slowly retrain my body to eat intuitively, but it takes work first." He looked away and then returned his gaze to Mack's. "I'm sorry. I don't mean to burden you with all this."

Mack put a hand on his wrist. "It's not a burden. We'll do whatever you need."

"I might have to keep my door open for a while so I don't try to hide shit in there." He snorted. "Gonna make jerking off kind of a pain."

"Like I haven't seen it before," Mack answered, and suddenly they were both laughing. When they'd calmed down, Mack asked, "So Nell had the baby. What about Cian? Things good with you two?"

"Yeah." Jamie swallowed visibly. "Cian's still there. He thought I'd want to come home so you and I could hang out. I'll see him tomorrow." He fidgeted, tapping his fingers then running them around the rim of his glass. Mack felt the brush of Jamie's jiggling knee.

"Everything okay?"

"I'm fine," Jamie answered, too quickly. He sighed. "I want to see him. I want him." His cheeks reddened. "We haven't had sex since before— I'm not sure I can. I shouldn't be talking to you about this." He gulped some water.

Jamie was probably right. Mack wasn't the type of person people came to with their intimate problems. He sometimes dropped advice for other stuff, but only when he knew his friends were acting out of being clueless. Otherwise, he wasn't the sort to offer a sympathetic shoulder.

"Are you not allowed?"

"Oh, no. We are." Jamie sat up straighter. "We'll work it out. Listen to me. I said I wasn't going to make it all about me, and here I just did it again. Tell me about those songs you wrote, okay?"

Mack grinned and then let it fade into a wicked smirk. Might as well cover his mild embarrassment with humor. "Which one do you want first? The one about getting pegged by a girlfriend or the one about blow jobs?"

Jamie swatted him. "Tell me you didn't rewrite Trevor's mess of a 'worship' song."

"Of course not!" Mack put on a fake offended look.

"Wait, you seriously wrote two songs about sex? What the hell have you been up to since I've been away?" He held up a hand. "No, don't tell me, especially if it's that asshole from Starbucks. Just show me the songs."

Mack laughed as he stood to retrieve the notebook from the living room. "Wait and see," he called over his shoulder, earning another laugh. The sound was music to his ears.

Chapter Ten

JAMIE WAS in the shower, and Mack had finished getting dressed and was tying his hair on top of his head. They planned to ride in to work together, since their shifts lined up. While he was twisting the hair tie, his phone buzzed. He glanced at it on the dresser. Trevor. He ignored it. Trevor could leave a voicemail; there wasn't time for a conversation before they had to leave.

Just as Mack shoved his phone into the pocket of his black work trousers, it went off again. He sighed and pulled it back out. Trevor, for the second time. He frowned at it and answered.

"Yeah?"

"Mack, thank God. I can't reach Jamie."

Saint Paul's pet pony, couldn't everyone leave Jamie alone for five? Mack swallowed a rude remark and said, "He's fine. Showering for work. I'll have him call you in the car if it's that important you check up on him."

"No, I mean...uh...I was trying to reach him first. It's fine, I can tell you."

"Tell me what?"

"Joyce—Andre's Grams—died this morning. At home, like she wanted."

Oh. Mack sat on his bed. It wasn't entirely surprising. She'd been having heart trouble for ages, and that was why the Lighthouse—her baby, her decades' worth of charity work—had closed. Mack hadn't known her, but Jamie had. She'd helped him when he'd come to her so sick with the flu he'd almost died after escaping his mother's abusive ex. Mack felt guilty finding out before Jamie did and then terrible for having that be his first thought.

"You there?" Trevor's voice sounded tinny where it emitted from Mack's hand in his lap. He'd forgotten he was on the phone.

"Uh...yeah. Still here. What happened?"

"Probably a heart attack. She'd been getting worse—congestive heart failure, I think, something about her having long-term complications of being sick as a kid? I dunno. Marlie had all these medical details 'cause she's into that, but it makes no damn sense to me."

It made sense to Mack, but he thought it was ironic that a woman who dedicated her life and medical career to getting help for people like his mother would die of something Mom was at risk for.

"Do you guys need anything?" A canned, standard response. Mack didn't know what else to say.

"I need to tell Jamie myself. Can you have him call me?"

"Yeah, no problem. Let me know when stuff is going on, okay?"

"I will. Gotta go."

Trevor ended the call, and Mack sat there staring at his phone for a long time. It hardly seemed fair. Joyce had helped so many people over the course of her lifetime. Mack heard the water shut off, and he thought about how if it weren't for Joyce, Jamie wouldn't be toweling off in the next room. Mack never even would've met him.

And Nate. Would he have denied anything was wrong? Failed to get tested? He'd fallen through the cracks on his health insurance at the time and needed help figuring out how to get things in order. Joyce hadn't done any of that personally, but she'd known people who could help. Her network was extensive, built up after more than forty years.

Mack stood slowly. There was no way to pretend to Jamie that everything was fine, so he went and knocked on the bathroom door. "Jay?"

"Be right out!"

"Trevor called. You need to call him back ASAP."

The bathroom door opened. "Trevor?" Jamie looked confused. "He called you?"

Mack scrubbed the side of his face. "You were in the shower. He couldn't reach you."

Jamie rolled his eyes. "Jesus. Even Trevor's acting like I'm a baby who can't take care of myself." He peered at Mack. "You look like shit. What's wrong?"

"Call. Trevor. Now."

Mack stalked off. He needed some air. A cig would've been nice right about then. He couldn't stand there talking to Jamie and not tell him what was going on, but he'd agreed to let Trevor do it. He stood by the apartment door, hand on the knob, half expecting Jamie to have followed him. Instead, he heard Jamie on the phone, his anguished cry piercing Mack's heart. Mack rested his forehead against the door.

He didn't turn around at the footsteps behind him. "Trevor told you?"

"Yeah."

Mack faced Jamie, folding him into his arms and letting him sob on Mack's shoulder.

The theater where Nate, Amelia, and Jomari all performed was more than half full. Joyce's family had already had her Homegoing, which had been closed to the public and for relatives only. Now they were having a public memorial because she'd affected so many lives in their community.

Mack supposed he shouldn't have been surprised the local news there as well. He shook off a reporter who was asking everyone if they would like to make any commentary on camera. He was probably the last person they should be asking, though he wondered if Jamie had agreed to be interviewed. Now he thought about it, he wondered if they should speak to Andre or his family before talking to the press, regardless of how they were going to report on the service.

He finally spotted people he knew. All his roommates—current and former—were clustered with their significant others toward the front, near the taped-off area reserved for them. Andre kept fidgeting with his suit jacket, tugging the sleeves down, and pushing his glasses up even though they didn't appear to be slipping. Trevor put a hand on his back, but Andre shrugged it off.

"Hey," Mack said.

Andre stopped messing with his clothes long enough to shake the hand Mack extended. He pulled Mack in for a brief, distracted hug.

"Thanks for coming." He sounded wooden, as if he'd planned a handful of answers he could interchange depending on who he was talking to.

Mack felt out of place. In his entire life, he'd only attended a few funerals, all family, mostly people he didn't know well, like great-uncles. Even when it was people he'd been closer to, it never felt any less awkward. He understood how Andre felt in his formal clothes, as if something didn't fit quite right.

The light streaming in from the hallway behind them disappeared as the auditorium doors closed. Andre motioned for their small group to cluster closer to him.

"You should know something before we start." He glanced at Trevor, who nodded. "Marlie, Nia, and Trev are already aware. This isn't just a memorial service."

"Go on," Nate said, leaning in.

"It's going to take months or years, but we weren't finished dissolving the Lighthouse when Grams died. And she left us a sizable chunk of money in addition to the funds still tied up in the Lighthouse. There are a crapload of rules and regs attached to distribution of funds after a charity dissolves, not to mention issues with the small endowment we had. Lemme tell you, it is a legal nightmare. But..." Andre hesitated and again looked at Trevor. "If we decide not to dissolve after all, then we don't have to redistribute."

Jamie's jaw dropped, and everyone else just stared. Mack didn't know a whole lot about any of it—running a non-profit or what one did when the founder died—but he understood how complicated things were for Andre.

Trevor put an arm around Andre. "Go, do what you need to. We're here, and we'll figure it out later."

Andre kissed him and then Nia and slipped around them toward the stage. He looked like climbing the stairs was taking every ounce of strength. Trevor shuffled everyone else toward their rows of seats. Mack slid in next to Jamie, followed by Amelia and Jomari. Up on the stage, there were five people seated in chairs to the left of the podium. A woman stood on the stage, level with the podium but several feet away. Andre crossed to the podium and stood at the microphone.

Once he was in place, people fell silent. Andre waited until all the talking had faded into a few random coughs and faint rustling before he began talking. The woman interpreted everything in ASL.

"Good afternoon. My name is Andre Cole, and today we're honoring the life of my grandmother, Joyce Bridges."

He spoke movingly about Joyce and her long years working to protect families, help those in need, and provide access to care for people who might otherwise have fallen through the cracks. By the time he wrapped up his speech, Mack heard sniffles and outright crying all around the auditorium behind him. To his left, Jamie wiped at his eyes, and Cian grasped his hand. Amelia leaned her head on Mack, and he wrapped his arm around her, surprised when he brushed against Jomari's sleeve. He ignored how weird that felt in favor of concentrating on Andre.

He introduced his parents, who came up together to say more about Joyce. Following them, Andre's sisters each separately spoke. Mack had assumed the man on the end of the row of chairs was married to one of them. He knew one of Andre's sisters was a lesbian, and the other was married to a man, but Mack had only met all of them once. He thought Amelia might know them a bit better, but he wasn't sure. Except the man continued to sit there, so Mack was confused about his role in everything.

Andre returned to the podium. "Grams knew she was never going to stop us from letting her people honor her life. We kept her Homegoing small, like she wanted. But this is for all of you to pay your respects too. So we've set up different ways to do that. There are several rooms here paying tribute to her life. You are welcome to explore those at your leisure. There's a quiet space set up as a chapel for silent prayer and reflection. And shortly, we'll open the stage here for anyone to speak briefly about how she touched your life. Feel free to come and go as you like. First, however, I'm going to invite Monty St. James to tell you about one last way my grandmother has blessed our community."

The man in the last chair rose and came forward. He was a tall and broad with warm brown skin and long locs pulled back in a ponytail. He wore a dove gray suit, and when he turned, the earring in his left ear caught the light and gleamed. He stood beside Andre.

"Monty St. James is a lawyer with six years' experience working in the non-profit sector. He has helped charitable organizations both begin and close their doors gracefully. He holds degrees in business and healthcare administration. At one time, Monty was served by my grandmother's organization, but I'll let him tell you about that." Andre stepped back, taking the seat Monty had formerly occupied.

"Thank you," Monty said. "When I was thirteen, my parents both died within a few weeks of each other. I won't go into detail about that. The only thing you need to know is that I was without a home or family—or so I thought. I was placed in the system even though my older brother was by then an adult and could have taken me in. He had a stable job and a home. We will never know for sure whether it was his race or his sexual orientation—or some combination of both—which led to him being denied custody of me.

"For a year and a half, Curtis tried to fight the system on his own. Eventually, someone gave him Joyce's contact information. With her help, he was able to take me in. Because of her, I finished school and graduated from college."

He continued speaking, but Mack missed some of it. He was too busy making the connection with Curtis the bouncer from Grand Slam, someone he'd known for years. Curtis had told bits and pieces of the story, but Mack had never met his brother. Now that he knew who Monty was, the family resemblance was undeniable, and he couldn't see how he'd missed it before. The initial surprise having worn off, Mack returned his attention to what Monty was saying.

"...figuring out what to do with the sizable gift she left as well as the remnants of the organization. It is currently not operating, in limbo as we redistribute the money. However, it is my goal to eventually reopen the Lighthouse's doors with renewed purpose. No child should ever have to go through what I and countless others have. And no person or family, especially the LGBTQIA-plus community, should be without access to necessary food, shelter, and healthcare due to lack of funds."

There was a collective gasp, followed by silence and then thunderous applause. Mack sat back, stunned. So that was what Andre had been trying to tell them. Monty was either taking over the charity or searching for someone else who could. No wonder Andre was nervous and stressed. Complicated didn't even begin to cover it.

Monty was saying there would be opportunity for people to give money in Joyce's name in order to help finance reopening. He stressed that this was a long process but that everything would be transparent for shareholders. Some programs, such as housing for homeless youth, would continue to operate during reorganization. Others would need more time.

When he finished, Andre returned to open the microphone and send people out to pay their respects in other ways. Mack didn't move. He wasn't sure how everyone else was taking this news, but by the energy around him, they were all equally surprised. Since Mack's investment in the process was far less than the others—aside from how it had affected his friendship circle—he didn't know what to make of it. He trusted Monty, even without knowing him, because he trusted Curtis and how highly he spoke of his brother. And he trusted Andre, who would fill them in when his heart was in it.

Eventually, Mack rose and followed the others. There was a reception set up in the atrium, and he wanted to browse the displays along with his friends. As he walked back up the theater aisle, he reflected that he wished he'd known Joyce better; she'd clearly been one hell of a woman.

Chapter Eleven

They didn't discuss the Lighthouse project again, in part because they hadn't had a chance to get together more than two or three at a time. As the weeks ground on toward Thanksgiving, Mack's work and rehearsal schedules kept him from seeing anyone except the band. Outside that, even seeing Jamie—who lived in the same place—was hit or miss.

When Mack finally had an evening to himself, he made plans to see Amelia. If there was one person he missed spending a few hours with, it was her. She agreed to stop over after work. He spent the afternoon actually cleaning, rather than shoving everything aside for later. Trevor would've been proud.

Mack knew something was off the moment Amelia walked in the door. She was pale and seemed like she'd had a long day, though he couldn't discern the cause. He'd never been any good at picking up on anything more specific than her general mood.

"I'm really sorry," she said, preventing Mack from having to ask. He appreciated her directness. "I feel like crap."

"You're sick? Do you need to go home?" Mack realized a half second too late he might've sounded rude. "Or you just need some TLC?"

Amelia flopped onto the couch. "Same old shit. I got my period."

"Oh." It didn't bother Mack, but he also didn't have much of a clue when it came to what she needed. The only thing he understood was that she'd dealt with the problem for years and been dismissed as it being "normal for some women." Mack thought that was probably bullshit, and he'd said so on more than one occasion, but Amelia had waved him off. He supposed he didn't have enough experience to know anyway.

"You know how it is. I'd have stayed home, but last time you called me—" She stopped short of mentioning Mack's visit with his parents and how she hadn't been available afterward. It was an eternal sore spot.

"Tea?" he offered, shifting the conversation away from potentially touchy issues.

"Yeah, that'd be great."

Mack went to put the kettle on. He couldn't stand microwaved water, even though it—probably—didn't really taste any different. One of the things he refused to take shortcuts on. Over time, he'd slowly been accumulating various kitchen gadgets, including an electric kettle. He glanced over his shoulder. Amelia was pulling a blanket up around herself. Quickly, he finished up and brought her the tea and the sugar bowl.

Amelia wrapped her fingers around the mug and sighed. "I really am sorry. I know we had plans, but I think all I can manage is a movie or something."

"It's fine." Mack had figured on a quiet night anyway. He flipped on the television and was about to find something to watch when Amelia's phone went off.

"Hello?" She paused, listening. "Uh huh." Pause. "No, I'm at Mack's." Pause. "I think it's fine. We're just watching a movie." Pause. "Hang on." She muted the phone.

Mack raised an eyebrow at her. "Who is that?"

"Jomari. He asked to see me. He's having a rough time tonight. Can he come over and hang out with us? I mean, since we're just watching movies."

"What's up?" Mack frowned.

Amelia looked like she might not answer, but then she said, "He's got his period too, and he's dysphoric. Doesn't want to sit at home with his family hovering."

Mack considered. It was maybe weird, or maybe not, but she was right. They weren't exactly busy. If Mack had been to his parents' place again, he'd have said no. But this was an ordinary night, and he didn't have an excuse.

He shrugged one shoulder. "Might as well, I guess."

"Cool, thanks." Amelia unmuted the phone. "Okay, Mack said to come over. See you soon. Bye." She slid her phone onto the coffee table and sighed. "This is all fallout from the clinic closing."

The Lighthouse, which now maybe wasn't fully closing after all. Mack wasn't quite following the connection, though. "What do you mean?"

"Joyce referred most of her patients, but she hadn't gotten to everyone before the doors shut. She was even still working through the list from home. Jomari hasn't had access to his T in months. Denver's trying to help him get an appointment to where she goes, but there's a waiting list. It was something like an average of three to four months. He's got an appointment scheduled, but it's not for a while yet."

Now it made sense. Joyce's program covered patients up until age twenty-five. Denver, now in her early thirties, had aged out years ago, plus she was a co-owner of a business and had more healthcare options. Jomari was still young enough to have been at the Lighthouse clinic, and he'd somehow fallen through the cracks.

"That sucks," Mack remarked.

Amelia sipped her tea then nodded. "I think he just needs a shoulder right now."

Mack turned on a cheesy comedy while they waited for Jomari to arrive. By the time he did, Mack was torn on how he felt about having the two of them in the same place at the same time. There were a lot of unspoken agreements among them, and he didn't know what the official etiquette was for creating a fourth dynamic out of three separate friends-with-benefits arrangements.

At first, it seemed okay. They lined up on the couch with Amelia in the middle. At some point, the other two gravitated closer. Jomari had his head on Amelia's shoulder, and she was running her hand through his thick, dark hair. He shifted a little to smile at her, and Mack felt the now far too familiar itch burn in his skin.

Instead of dealing with it, he left them to sit on the sofa and finish the movie without him. He sat at the kitchen table with this notebook, half pretending to write songs so they would think he was busy and not ignoring them. He wasn't sure how successful he was, especially when Amelia kept turning around to give him puzzled frowns.

Being in a different room didn't stop him from seeing them out of the corner of his eye, nor did it prevent them from occasionally interrupting to ask him to bring them something. This was far too weird. Mack couldn't exactly blame them. He'd agreed to it, after all. Not that Amelia had given him much of a choice. He thought he'd have looked like a dickhead if he'd said no.

The comedy ended, and Amelia turned on some bizarre space show the two of them apparently liked and Mack didn't follow. For some reason, this episode was making both of them full-on cry. By that point, he recognized himself as a third wheel; he'd had enough. He huffed as he tossed Jomari the tissue box from the bathroom, causing Amelia to roll her eyes.

"Try a little sympathy, Mack," she snipped.

So Mack brought them the last pint of coconut milk ice cream—Jomari couldn't have dairy—in the freezer and then called Trevor. He took the phone into his bedroom and shut the door. "Trevor? It's Mack."

"Hey, man. What's up? You sound...funny. Everything okay?"

"Yeah...no." He lowered his voice. "I've got two people cuddling on my couch, crying at some TV show that *isn't even fucking sad*, and sharing a pint of cookie dough fake ice cream. I am about to lose my entire shit here. Get me out!"

To Mack's annoyance, Trevor laughed. "What the hell is fake ice cream? And where's Jamie?"

"It's for people who are lactose intolerant or something. Jamie's working and then going back to Cian's. I am all alone, and I can't take this any longer!"

"Okay, man. Whatever. You can help me do the shopping for Turkey Day. Are you guys coming, by the way?"

"I gotta ask the others. I didn't know there was gonna be a thing. Who cares about that right now? I'm desperate. You want me to pick you up?"

"Sure. That'd be great."

"You're not bringing your kid with you, right? He's great and all, but I don't think I could take it."

"Relax. He's staying home with Andre. Nia's coming over in a bit so they can spend time with him."

"Good. I'll be there in ten."

Mack grabbed his keys and stalked out of the bedroom. He had just reached the door when Amelia paused the show. She wriggled around to face him.

"Where're you off to?"

"Helping Trevor with the Thanksgiving shopping." He gritted his teeth and took a couple of calming breaths. "Did you need anything?"

Amelia exchanged a look with Jomari. "Can you bring back some gummy bears? Ooh, wait, no. Some of those sour worms."

"Yes! Good call," Jomari told her, and she grinned at him.

"Thanks, babe!" Amelia called just as Mack shut the apartment door.

He leaned against the outside for a moment before shoving off of it and making his way to the parking lot. A few minutes later, he pulled into Trevor's driveway. He was in a bad enough mood he was tempted to just honk, but out of respect for Andre and the baby, he got out and knocked. Trevor opened the door, pulling on his jacket as he stepped out. He called a quick goodbye to Andre and shut the door.

The ride to Stop & Shop was silent, and Mack was convinced Trevor could feel the waves of irritation rolling off him as they drove. Mack wasn't even sure which part bothered him more—that Amelia and Jomari were bonding or that he would've been stuck watching it if it hadn't been for Trevor and his shopping.

Trevor interrupted Mack's irritable thoughts. "Want to tell me what has you so mad?"

"No," Mack grumbled. He thought better of it when Trevor raised his eyebrows and glanced at Mack like he didn't quite believe him. "Fine. Apparently, the two of them both have their periods, and when they're not ignoring me while they get cozy on the couch, they're acting like I'm an unsympathetic ass just because I went and sat in the other room."

Trevor snickered. "Are they right?"

"Probably. Yes." Mack hunched over the steering wheel, scowling out the windshield.

"Have you ever been genuinely sympathetic? I mean, with Amelia?"

Mack threw a sideways glare at Trevor. "She deals with it fine herself! It's not like I think it's gross or weird or some shit, but what am I supposed to do about it other than make her tea and bring her a blanket? Which I did, before you ask."

Trevor shrugged one shoulder as they turned into the Stop & Shop parking lot. "I wasn't specifically talking about this situation, but you could try asking her what she wants instead of assuming, for starters."

"Oh, like you know so much about this," Mack muttered. He wanted to add a dig about how everyone knew Trevor wasn't exactly an open book himself, but he kept his mouth shut as he parked the van.

"Maybe I do, actually." Trevor unbuckled. "You ready to go in, or do you need a minute?"

"I'm fine." Getting out meant Mack could wiggle out of this conversation.

Once inside, they worked their way through the grocery list in order of the store's aisles. Trevor was organized, with everything stored in a checklist in his phone. To Mack's dismay, he even stopped in the period supplies aisle. There was apparently no escape from the subject, even inside the store. Trevor browsed the display for a moment then grabbed a purple box of tampons and a package from a row with a numbering system Mack didn't follow. He tossed both into the cart.

"You need any?" Trevor asked.

"I'm good—wait. What? No." Mack held up his hands. "What would I do with them?"

"I meant for the others, man. Jeez. Isn't that why you brought it up in the car?"

"They didn't ask."

Trevor made a what-the-hell face. "You...you have two people staying with you who menstruate, and one of them has been your bed buddy for years. And it didn't occur to you they might need stuff while they're at your place?"

"Whoa, there. I asked, and they didn't mention it. Also, 'menstruate'? What is this, middle school health class? How do *you* know Marlie needs anything?"

"Because I've known her forever, and I pay attention. Also, I'm a grown-ass man who knows how to ask what pads my girlfriend wants when I see there's none under the sink." Trevor tapped his phone and turned it around for Mack. "See? She texted me a photo." He wrinkled his nose. "No wonder they said you're unsympathetic. How is it that you're way more experienced at dating than I am, but I'm the one telling you about this?"

"Because you're...domesticated. Or something. Anyway, like I said, Amelia and Jomari didn't ask me for any."

"So you don't have any idea what brand, then."

Mack glowered at him. "Of course I do." He pretended to browse then picked up a box with pink-wrapped pads inside.

Trevor peered at it when Mack tossed it into the cart. "They use the same kind?"

"What? I mean, yeah. Why not?"

"Marlie likes the kind without the little extra tab thingies. I'd have thought Jomari might have a preference for those too, or something different." Trevor frowned. He looked at Mack for a long time. "Look, I'm all for normalizing a pair of dudes discussing this like it's about shampoo. I have a kid who someday might date someone who bleeds, and I want it not to be awkward. But is all this drama really about periods?"

It wasn't, and now Mack was caught out. He no longer cared that Trevor would know Mack didn't have a clue what to buy. He plucked the package out of the cart and set it on the shelf. "You've been living with Marlie too long," he muttered.

Trevor laughed. "Maybe. Or you. How often did you rip into me on something you thought I was being dense about? Come on. Let's see what else is on the list."

"The others didn't ask for this shit," Mack waved at the shelves, "but they did ask for those sour gummy worms."

"Oh, Night Crawlers? Good call," Trevor echoed Jomari. "Marlie loves those when she's on her period. C'mon, I'll show you where they are."

They strolled up and down the aisles, Trevor continuing to stop occasionally to throw something in the cart: diapers, pureed peas, turkey stuffing, four cans of cream of mushroom soup, cranberry sauce. In the candy aisle, Trevor tossed Mack a large bag of Night Crawlers. Mack eyed it, wondering what the others saw in them. He would rather have eaten the mushroom soup straight out of the can.

Trevor eyed Mack and then grabbed a bag of some kind of chocolate. "Dark chocolate almond bark," he said. "I promise we'll leave enough for Amelia and Jomari, but I'm gonna make you try it first." He threw it on top of the diapers.

They stood in front of the display case with all the turkeys, debating on whole or breast-only. Trevor argued that no one liked the dark meat; Mack said breast-only was dry as fuck if it wasn't prepared well, and he wasn't convinced Trevor was up for the job. They argued good-naturedly for a bit longer before Trevor relented and put a 16-pound turkey in the cart.

"So...about Thanksgiving." Trevor headed for the checkout.

"What about it? You said something about us coming over. Are you guys hosting a big dinner?"

"Yeah. Andre's mom isn't up for it this year, and I think his sisters aren't either. They're both spending the holiday with their spouses' families. My folks are taking a cruise, and Marlie's are going to see her sister. We thought we'd have Andre's parents in, maybe ask you guys to come over too."

"Okay. I still have to ask. Amelia..." He trailed off and shrugged, shoving his free hand in his pocket. He didn't know what the plan was, not with Jomari to factor in.

"What about Jamie?"

Mack glanced at Trevor, who looked hopeful. "I'll ask."

"I mean, he might be going over to Cian's, I guess."

"He hasn't said." Mack stopped walking. "Are you two..."

"Nah. He's back to watching Aidan, but he doesn't stick around after I get home." Trevor let his breath out in a huff. "He stays when Marlie's there, though."

"Give him time." It was the only response Mack could come up with. He hadn't talked to Jamie about it himself yet, but he supposed he would need to if they were going over for Thanksgiving. Wonderful; another one for the "strained conversations I'd rather not have" list.

"I know. I'm not upset that he wants to only be with Cian right now. I miss him, that's all." Trevor tapped his fingers on the cart handle.

Mack frowned, but he didn't say anything. It was tense enough between them over Jamie as it was, to the point Mack was shocked Trevor was talking about it to him. They paid for the groceries and headed for Mack's van. Once they'd loaded it up, Mack went to start the van, but Trevor put a hand on his arm.

"Wait."

"What?"

"I'm not letting you go home without talking about what the hell that was back there. You were really pissed off when you came to see me. You're calm now, but if you go back home, you're gonna get right back into that mess all over again."

He was right, and Mack knew it. He turned over the engine. "Look, it's freezing out here. I'll drive you back, and I'll explain on the way."

"Fair enough."

Mack waited until they were out on the road to say, "It's fucking weird, having both of them together. It's not like it hasn't happened before, but not like this. I don't know. It felt like they were doing this bonding thing, and I wasn't part of that."

"I get it," Trevor said.

"Do you? Because your family looks different."

"What is it you wanted? To have Amelia to yourself? You've said she's not your girlfriend. So why does it matter?"

"I don't know!" But he did know. He had a very clear idea why it bothered him so much. Mack slammed his palm against the steering wheel. "She and I...we're both fucking Jomari. We all know, but we've never hung out just the three of us."

Trevor seemed to contemplate that. "Yeah, I'd say that's different from my family. It really bothers you, huh?"

"Not that. It's..." Mack didn't know how to explain the way he'd seen the tender gestures between Amelia and Jomari. Sure, she would do the same for him, but it didn't look or feel identical for some reason Mack couldn't pinpoint. "I guess they've been getting to be closer since she started playing with Cian's band."

"Makes sense. Spending more time together. But you think there's more going on?"

"I don't know," Mack admitted. "Up until now, I wouldn't have thought so. She always said she was mostly into women. She doesn't date men, and she made that clear to me. I didn't care. But now here she is, and I can't really tell what's going on. She's already cancelled plans with me so they could go out."

"Ah." Trevor was quiet a moment. "People change, you know. Until Andre, I thought I only loved Marlie and the couple times I fooled around with guys were, like, just sex. Then after Andre, I thought maybe Marlie was my exception and I mostly wanted guys. Now I'm not sure, but it doesn't matter because this works for us. Jamie's only into men, but I know he's fucked women on camera and enjoyed it. He said Cian can't separate love and sex, he's got a high drive for both, and he doesn't care about gender at all. Maybe Amelia's needs have changed."

"Maybe."

It wasn't only about whether or not her relationship with Jomari was changing. It was why. Why now, after years of things being the same? What made him different from everyone else? Mack hated the feeling she'd finally had enough and was choosing someone who might be able to give her what he couldn't. But why would she have told him their kind of relationship was enough if it wasn't? She knew who he was and that he made no apology for it. Was it like Trevor said, and she was changing, or had she been dishonest?

"Listen," Trevor said as they pulled into his driveway. "Why don't you invite Jomari for Thanksgiving?"

"What? Why?"

"It might be easier if it's not the three of you having to figure this out alone, that's all." Trevor unbuckled, but he didn't move. "Talk to them. The only way I made it work with Andre and Marlie is by telling them both the truth. And the only way I didn't fuck it up with Jamie was by telling them I needed him in my life too." He curled his fingers into a fist. "If only we could work that out."

Mack didn't reply. Jamie was still a sore spot for both of them. He helped Trevor unload the groceries and put things away. They had some time for him to think about inviting Jomari, but he wasn't sure he was going to.

"Thanks for your help," Trevor said. "Hey, you feeling better?"

"Maybe." Mack accepted the Night Crawlers from Trevor. "I should get these to the others."

"Good luck."

Back in the van, Mack looked at the package on the passenger seat. For once, Trevor was right, but tonight he didn't have the right words. Instead, he would bring the sour gummies as a peace offering and sit with them this time, even if it meant he had to watch confusing science fiction shows. He pulled out onto the road and headed for home.

Chapter Twelve

Mack finally had a chance to talk to Jamie in between their shifts. Trevor giving him the task of asking about Thanksgiving struck Mack as immature and annoying. Why couldn't he just do it himself? Whatever. Mack managed to corner Jamie before he left for work.

"About Thanksgiving," he began.

"I'm not going to Trevor's, if that's what you're talking about." Jamie gelled his hair and washed his hands.

"Yeah, it was. Why not?"

Jamie put tiny black studs in his ears. "Because it's not good for my recovery." He sighed and turned around. "It's a whole holiday based on eating a shit-ton, and I can't manage that yet."

"But this is our friends. And how is it any better that you still work in a restaurant?"

"It's not just the food, and you know it. It's all the expectations and the pressure to prove I'm fine in front of everyone. Cian's promised me a quiet day together, and we'll go see his partners in the evening after they get home. This is what I need."

"Who's pressuring you? This is us, Jamie. Your friends. We're not going to do anything to hurt you, not like—" He cut himself off before he mentioned Sage's name.

"You just fucking did." Jamie shoved past Mack out of the bathroom.

"Wait! God, I'm sorry. It's just that I..."

Jamie whirled around. "You just what, Mack? Tried to compare yourself to my asshole ex so you'd look better?" He glared at Mack, breathing hard, lips pursed. He looked like he was about to drop it, do the same thing he always did and clam up. But then he straightened his spine and began speaking again.

"My therapist says I need to practice telling people what's really on my mind. So this is me, telling you no. I'm not going to Trevor's because right now, it's too hard. I can't be around him with all those people there, pretending that I'm not maybe going to pick at my food because I'm too stressed to eat but then pray to whatever gods exist that I won't come home and raid our cupboards. I still want him, but I have to talk to him about it just the two of us. Which I was going to do tomorrow, when I'm there to watch Aidan, and which you'd have known if you'd fucking asked me instead of getting caught up in Trevor's insecurity. I don't need you to protect me from Trevor any more than I needed you to protect me from Sage."

"Hells and damnation, I'm gonna rip that asshole's throat out for what he did to you," Mack muttered.

"You have to stop blaming Sage for my problems. He is not responsible for my eating disorder." Jamie's shoulders sagged, and his face lost its tension. "And neither are you."

He'd hit it squarely. "But—"

"No," Jamie said firmly. "I was bingeing before I met either you or Sage. Maybe that's how I coped with what Sage did to me this summer, but it didn't start with him."

This was all new information, something Jamie had never shared. Mack's head spun. "When did— No, never mind. You don't owe me that."

Jamie blew out a noisy breath. "No, I fucking don't. But I'll tell you anyway because it's you. I started when I lived with Brandon, after all the shit my mother and I went through. I didn't start because of Sage. That's just when you first caught me at it. He kept me from doing it on and off for years. Know why it didn't work?"

"Because Sage is an acid-breathing hell-troll?" Mack guessed.

A low snarl escaped Jamie's throat before he relaxed a fraction and shook his head. "No. It didn't work because he was putting a bandage on it, not helping me solve what was causing it. That wasn't his job, and it's not your job to fix me or keep tabs on me. My recovery is mine to own. Let me do it my way. Please."

"Jamie, I—" Mack choked up. He swallowed hard, not wanting

to let Jamie see how it affected him. "I love you. You know that, right?"

"Yeah, I do. Even if you suck at showing it sometimes."

Jamie stepped closer and pulled Mack into a hug. Mack felt the slight tremor and heard Jamie's soft sniffle. He didn't let go for a long time, not until he was sure his own emotions were under control.

"We're good?" Mack asked.

"We are. Unless you try to play go-between again." Jamie gave him a pointed look.

"Nope. You can talk to Trevor yourself from now on."

"Good." Jamie finally cracked a smile. "Now, let me out of here. I gotta work."

In the end, Mack and Amelia went to an awkward Thanksgiving dinner at Trevor's. Except for Marlie, Andre, and the baby, the only other guests were Andre's parents. Selfishly, Mack was glad not to endure it alone. Jomari was with his family, and he and Amelia both seemed to feel there were rules about not bringing your fuck buddy home to meet Mom and Dad.

They ducked out early and went back to Mack's to work out their mutual tension. She didn't stay long. If he were a betting man, he'd put money on Amelia leaving his place to go see either Jomari or Denver from the bar. Mack had found out Amelia'd been casually sleeping with her for a few months. He tried not to care, both about Amelia going elsewhere and about all the things she hadn't been telling him lately. Instead of moping, he spent the rest of the day working out new lyrics in his notebook.

He'd lied to his father when he called, saying he had to work. The same dance they did every year. Mack wasn't sure if Dad even realized half the time it wasn't true and the other half he only worked the few hours the restaurant was open. He would visit them on the weekend, days not so wrapped in his memories of the holiday.

His mind wandered from the notebook open in his lap back to his childhood. A time when Mom wasn't drunk all the time, only when everything was too painful for her. Thanksgiving was one of the worst. Mack wasn't stupid; he could do the math. She'd found out she was having him then, before she was married to Dad. His entire childhood, he had known his birth derailed all her plans. She didn't ever say it to him when she was sober, but he'd heard it as often when she was drunk as he'd heard the soft strains of Bach.

He couldn't listen to it now. It made him remember Mom at every Thanksgiving, drunk and sprawled on the sofa, a nearly-empty bottle and a glass on the coffee table. Crying, with the sound of the classical guitar in the background. And Dad, picking Mack up with a soft, *C'mon, sport* as he carried him away from her.

And the mornings after, when she remained in her dark bedroom while Dad kept Mack quiet. Dad was home then since he worked in one of the schools as a custodian. Mack wondered now whether he took that job to make sure he was always at their trailer when Mack was. Mom wouldn't have hurt him on purpose, but her carelessness might've.

Mack blew out a long, slow breath. Some things weren't worth dwelling on. He turned back to his notebook, but the words ran together. The band had only played a couple of gigs since Jamie got back, with only two more scheduled so far. Mack was having a hard time caring. When they first put the band together, it had just been for fun. Then they'd started playing for pay, which was mostly due to Sage's parents' influence.

Now, though, despite their growing popularity and how they'd finally started to sound halfway decent, Mack didn't have the same commitment he once did. The others, too. Gemma had already said she didn't know how much longer she'd be able to continue. Jamie had enough to deal with. Mack didn't know how Cassie felt, but then he never did have a good read on her.

Instead of trying to write the lyrics to a new song, he scrawled a couple of random lines. He stared at the page until the letters blurred. He huffed and closed the notebook. No sense wasting his time on bad poetry. Tossing the notebook onto the couch, he retreated to his room. Maybe everything would look better in the morning.

Mack chose to visit his parents when he knew he only had a short time before he had to work. He couldn't count on Amelia to be available afterward, given the last couple of times. He was on his own and made plans accordingly.

The first thing that struck him was the pile of garbage bags outside the trailer. Dad was normally so fastidious. He never wanted anyone to think their home was less than perfect. The only time Mack ever saw him angry was the day he overheard a couple kids at the school where he worked referring to a classmate as "trailer trash." He'd ranted about it for hours, scrubbing everything in sight the entire time until it gleamed. Mack never had the heart to point out his own overcompensation.

Dad didn't meet him outside the trailer either, also strange. Mack killed the engine and sat for almost five minutes before he confirmed Dad wasn't coming out. He exited the van and slammed the door. Still nothing. Puzzled, Mack climbed up the wooden steps. At least the row of flower pots was still there, cleaned out and waiting until spring for new plants.

Slowly, Mack opened the door and stared in shock. There were more garbage bags inside, albeit neatly lined up in the living room. He could smell the all-purpose cleaner Dad used. Mom was sitting in her usual spot, apparently oblivious to whatever scouring and purging Dad was doing. More game shows on the television. The volume was up, which probably explained why Dad hadn't heard Mack arrive.

Mack tensed, wondering how upset Dad would be that he came in unannounced. He might feel it violated the unspoken code between them, the pretense that Mom was "having a bad day." There were no more good days; all of that was behind them. But nothing about this day felt like the usual visit anyway, so Mack decided to go look for Dad.

He was in the second bedroom, the one that had once been Mack's and now was filled with years' worth of stuff his parents hadn't wanted to throw away. It was virtually empty save a bed, desk, some plastic bins, and another set of garbage bags. Fewer this time, Mack noted.

Dad looked up when Mack knocked on the door. "Hey, sport." He paused to rub the side of his nose.

Mack didn't bristle at the old nickname. "Dad, what's all this?" He gestured around the room, but he meant the trailer at large.

"Bit of tidying up. Needed to be done, you know?" His voice was cheerful but strained.

"Need a hand?"

"I'm almost done." Dad put the lid on the last bin. "Those bags there?" He pointed, and Mack nodded. "Think you can drop 'em off for donation when you go?"

"Sure." Mack helped Dad lift the bin onto another one.

Dad stood with his hands on his hips, surveying the room. He turned to Mack. "You see Mom when you came in? She seem okay?"

Mack shrugged. "Same as usual, I guess. Television's too loud, though. Is that why you didn't hear me come in?"

"Yes. Listen, I know you probably want to visit with her a bit" —he flinched at Mack's snort— "but maybe we should talk first."

"Kitchen?"

"Yeah. Coffee?"

"I'm good."

They left the bedroom, and Mack settled in at the kitchen table. He concentrated on the gray Formica top. They'd had this table forever, might even have belonged to Mack's grandparents. Dad ignored what he'd said and set a steaming cup of coffee in front of him before sitting kitty-corner to him.

Dad thumped the table softly with his hand. "Mom's not doing so well."

"Today?"

"Any day." Dad sighed. "I'm cleaning out your old room. I know you took a lot of it with you, but your mother's old stuff was in there, and I wanted to find it. That's what's in those bins. If I can get her to remember…"

Mack shook his head, but he kept quiet. Mom wasn't going to remember. He had no idea whether what was messed up in her brain was from the alcohol or some other kind of dementia, but it wouldn't do any good to try—again—to convince Dad.

"What's all the other stuff?" he asked.

"Old junk, stuff we got from our parents, that kind of thing. Anything worth saving, I did. There's a whole pile of clothing no one wears anymore. 'Bout time we thought about throwing out what we don't need and rescuing what we do."

"Yeah?" There was more. Mack was sure there was more.

"I mean, you never know how much time you have left for that kind of sorting, and I'd hate for you to have to—" He cut off abruptly, and Mack's stomach knotted.

"Dad." He put his hand on top of his father's.

"Cancer," Dad said, lifting one shoulder.

"I—damn. She has enough problems." Mack had to admit that he was surprised but not too much. Mom's body was probably a mess. The same mess, he reminded himself, that his could've been in another thirty years. If he made it that long.

"No." Dad shook his head. "Not Mom."

Mack stared at Dad. Those were real words, but they registered the same as if his father had started speaking in an alien language. His heart sped up almost to the edge of panic.

"What?" he finally managed.

"Stomach cancer. It's early yet," Dad said. "Stage II. Odds are better than I'd thought."

The way he said it sounded like he was resigned already to their being bad. A dozen different thoughts warred for Mack's attention. How long? What were they doing about it? What was Dad going to do about Mom?

"You never said you were feeling sick last time I was here."

Dad shrugged. "I wasn't. I'd gone in for a follow-up for the ulcers, and they caught the cancer."

"Ulcers? Jesus, Dad. When were you going to tell me any of this?"

"I'm handling it. Just have to put things in order, that's all."

"So the cleaning..." Mack prompted, if only to give his brain a chance to catch up.

"Right. Gotta get it all done before treatment." He ran a hand down his face, his way of stalling. "I can't take care of Mom by myself. Louisa, you remember her from a few trailers down?" At Mack's singular nod, he continued, "Well, she used to work for the visiting nurses. She's got me connected to see if they'll come around and whatnot. Help me out too while I'm in treatment."

Still in denial, then. Dad sounded like that's all they needed, someone to check in on them and lend a hand for a while. He had more realistic—if tinged with pessimism—feelings about his own prognosis than about Mom's. Mack's hands shook with the tension of holding back what he really wanted to say.

"What do you need from me?"

"Nothing right now, sport." Dad stood. "I have something to show you."

Mack followed him back into the spare room. Dad got down on the floor to pull something out from under the bed. When he stood back up stiffly, he suddenly seemed years older to Mack. And then Mack noticed what he'd slid from beneath the bed.

The leather case was cracked, and the hinges squeaked when he opened it. Inside lay Mom's old acoustic guitar. They'd long since given away her mandolin and her father's banjo. Mack had always assumed this was gone too. He had no idea where Dad had stored it until now because he knew for sure it wasn't under his bed when he was a kid.

Dad closed it. "Needs some fixing. Think you can do it?"

No, Mack didn't think so. But he didn't tell Dad that. "Yeah, maybe."

"Good. It's yours, then." He latched it and set it at Mack's feet.

"I don't want your mother to see this, so I'm going to put it by the door under a bunch of other stuff you're taking with you."

Mack understood. Few things triggered her memory now, but seeing the guitar probably would. He picked it up and followed Dad, who now had the donation bags in hand, out of the bedroom. They piled it up by the door and then re-entered the living room.

Mom barely registered their presence. She shushed them and waved to the television. So Mack sat with her and watched game shows, his skin itching the whole time with the need to be out of there. At last he was able to say goodbye.

Dad held onto him for a long time before helping him carry everything to the van. Once Mack was on the gravel road, he turned to see his father waving, still on the porch. Some things would never change, including the way Dad said goodbye.

Mack 's vision was blurred with tears the whole drive home. He was grateful he had work instead of having to sit around thinking about the guitar now lying on his back seat.

Chapter Thirteen

By the first weekend in December, Nate's boxes were all packed and lined up against the wall of his room. Mack had fully expected him to move out sooner, but they'd never found a replacement for him, and he didn't seem to be in a hurry anyway. He'd considered briefly waiting until after the wedding, but it made more sense for him to leave when the lease was up. It was only a couple months before he and Izzy got married.

Nate and Izzy each took one box and said goodnight to Mack and Jamie. They'd be back for the rest over the next couple of weeks. Jamie turned to Mack, looking as though he had something on his mind. Mack couldn't read his expression to figure out whether it would be good news or bad.

"I—" Jamie began but stopped. After a long hesitation, he said, "I'm moving out too."

"What? But—you—you can't!" Mack gaped at him, panic rising in his throat. He hadn't even had a chance to talk to Jamie about anything yet. Or consciously had chosen not to.

"Don't do this, please."

"Why? Why now?"

Jamie's shoulders sagged. "The lease is almost up. We've lived here for a long time. Trevor's been gone for a year, and now Nate's moving out. We didn't find anyone else anyway, and Cian's asked me to live with him. I said yes."

"Just like that? You've only been dating since summer, and...and..."

So softly Mack almost missed it, Jamie said, "Sage never asked."

As much as it hurt to admit it, Mack knew part of what had held him and Jamie together was Sage's refusal to commit. Mack had wanted to believe Jamie was like him, that it hadn't mattered if Sage thought of them as a real couple. Trevor, too, was safe because Jamie wasn't interested in living with his growing family. But Cian...he was Jamie's anchor. It made every kind of sense, no matter how hard it was for Mack to accept it.

He walked to the window and placed his hand on the glass, looking down at the strip of parking lot behind the building. What would he do now? He couldn't afford the rent alone, and he didn't have any other roommate prospects lined up. It made no difference that those weren't real reasons, that he had time to work it out, that he could ask for help. Jamie was leaving, and that was all his brain could process.

Letting out a long, slow breath, Mack turned back around and sucked in a distressed response in favor of dismissal. "If this is what makes you happy."

Jamie shook his head. "It's not about being happy. I already told you that." He swallowed visibly. "I don't think 'happy' is a thing that will ever apply to me, not the way it does for other people."

"I don't understand." Or maybe he did, but he needed to know what the words meant to Jamie.

"I can learn to be content, and I can have good things in my life. I'm definitely happier than I was. But..." He fiddled with his lip piercing. "I'll never be 'cured.' The rest of my life will be spent managing my recovery." He gave Mack a pointed look. "Surely you get that?"

Mack's hand went automatically to his pocket, to his five-year coin. He did get it, and part of him suspected Jamie was right. It wasn't the same thing, though; Jamie's struggles were not born from addiction, and he couldn't work on them in the same way.

"Yeah," he finally said. "I do."

"You gonna be all right?"

Instead of acknowledging his fears, Mack said, "What about your job watching Aidan?"

"Cian's lease was up a couple months ago. He paid to stay for a little while longer. We'll be splitting the difference in a place of our own. I can drive to Trevor's, and I can still take the train to my other job. I might not have it much longer anyway."

That was news. "Why not?"

"Got a call from my former producer to do another web series."

"What?" Mack's mouth dropped open and he needed a moment to get his shock under control. "Are you sure that's a good idea? And is Cian okay with this?"

"Yes, and yes. It's not strictly porn, like the other one. It's a comedy-drama. But even if it were, Cian is one hundred percent fine with that. He called my work art." Jamie laughed quietly. "I think the director is making more of my skills than I deserve. They're not exactly what I was memorable for."

"Oh, no, I think your...uh...*skills* are exactly what you're remembered for." Mack chuckled in spite of himself.

Jamie groaned, but a faint smile still played on his lips. "All the sex is simulated, and there isn't as much anyway. No one is going to see my package."

Now Mack laughed out loud, some of the tension dissipating for the moment. "Your poor fans will be so disappointed."

"Right? Well, they'll adjust." He turned serious again. "Listen, I do want to make sure you're okay. I kind of sprang this on you. Cian asked at Thanksgiving." He blushed. "In bed, after."

"Jesus," Mack said. "I did not need that information."

Jamie's casual shrug made it clear he didn't care. "Maybe you can finally move in with Amelia. You've only been joking about it forever."

How could Mack explain that he'd never wanted to, that it was exactly that, a joke? They were not suited to living in the same space. Mack needed his own place, preferably with friends he wasn't also fucking.

"I don't know."

"Or you can stay here. There are single bedroom units, like where Mrs. Phelps lives."

"Who?"

"Mrs. Crotchety in two-B." Jamie rolled his eyes. "You really need to learn people's names. I called the rental office already, and you can pay to finish out the month here until you find a place. Nate and I both agreed we'll pitch in, now that he's caught up on what he still owed us from last year when we covered his share."

Mack nodded. He had until after Christmas to find somewhere, then. He could manage that, at least in a physical sense.

Jamie gripped his shoulder, an unfamiliar gesture. Mack wasn't used to Jamie being so decisive, so in control of his actions. It pinched Mack's heart. The landscapes of all his friendships were changing, and he didn't know what to do with it.

He watched Jamie walk away, into his room with the door shut. That was it, then. Another friend whose life was settled and at peace. As much as Mack was glad they'd all found their joy, he couldn't help the sense of loss that clung to him and left a bitter tang in his throat. Where was his joy, and how would he find it?

His mind was still on it a few minutes later when Jamie emerged with his bag. He said goodnight to Mack and left the apartment. It felt too big and too empty without him, even though he hadn't even packed his things yet. Mack stood in the same spot he'd been when Jamie made his announcement. The familiar, unpleasant itch was back.

He moved then, wanting something to curb the intensity. If one of the constants in his life wasn't there, maybe the other would be. He picked up his phone to call Amelia.

When she answered, he could tell she was distracted. "Hey. What's up?"

"I—are you free tonight?"

There was a pause so long Mack was afraid they'd been cut off, but then she said, "Not exactly."

"What's that supposed to mean?"

"It means what I said. I'm not at home, but...hang on." The sound was muffled, like she was talking to someone. "We could come over, if you need."

"'We'?"

"Jomari and I."

It hit Mack with a jolt. He'd known the two of them were getting close, but he'd convinced himself it was more like his relationship with the two of them. Now he was sure there was something different going on. They were together, out somewhere. On what sounded like a date. Looking back, the clues were all there, if he'd cared to see them.

He didn't want to be their third wheel. He'd been there and done that already, and it had been awkward and frustrating. "Nah, it's fine. You guys have fun."

"You sure?" Now Amelia sounded puzzled and concerned. "Did something happen with your mom? I know you were supposed to see her, but you never said if you did."

"No... I talked to Jamie." He didn't want to give her the news about his father over the phone. For some reason, he didn't want Jomari to know either.

"Oh." Another uncomfortable pause. "So he told you."

She'd known? "That he's moving out, yeah."

"Oh! Uh...right, yes. That." She covered the phone again; there was more muffled talking. "You all right?"

"I'm fine. I'll fill you in when I see you. Maybe tomorrow?" He tried to hide his distress from her, though he had no idea how successful he was.

"Sure. I'm free after work." Her voice softened. "You, me, a bad lesbian rom-com, and some ice cream?"

He managed a weak chuckle. "Perfect."

He ended the call and flopped onto the couch, putting his head in his hands. Both Amelia and Jamie had been keeping secrets from him, believing—independently of each other—that he couldn't handle the truth. From the way Amelia sounded, they'd discussed something, or several things, without him. Never mind that he hadn't told them everything either. Instead, he focused on his anger. At them, at their betrayal, at the universe. Who knew anymore where the blame lay?

He was alone for the night with only his muddled thoughts to keep him company. He looked at the acoustic guitar his father had given him, now sitting in a corner of the living room. He made to reach for his notebook and then changed his mind. There were no songs to write that could capture the pain. No amount of poetry would touch the vast emptiness in Mack's soul.

It sounded stupid and overwrought, and he knew it. Mack couldn't help it. He needed something to get his mind off it. There was a commuter train in about a half hour. If he hurried, he could walk to the station. Grabbing his keys on the way out, he walked to the station, muttering about the fresh air to clear his head.

The long commute and the walk to the bar should've been enough to make him reconsider. Every point along the way was another missed opportunity to change his mind and do something else instead. Half a dozen times, he'd told himself Jamie's announcement wasn't enough to get so upset over. Every time, he'd grown more agitated.

He stood outside Grand Slam, hands in his coat pockets. Inside, it would be warm and inviting. It wasn't drag night, so he wouldn't see Candie. He might see the server he sometimes hooked up with, or he might find someone else. He told himself that was the only reason to go there. It was all lies, from the refreshing walk to the company of a warm body. Those weren't the reasons he was going to Grand Slam.

He knew what he wanted, but he hoped that Denver or Jack would be there to talk him off the ledge. They had standing orders to give him water or a soft drink but never anything stronger than a Coke. It was why he'd chosen Grand Slam and not another bar. Anywhere else, he'd have gotten shitfaced without anyone there to catch him. This way, he'd stay sober and maybe find company with someone hot and sweet...

His mind wandered to Jomari and hooking up all those months ago. He didn't really want anyone except him or Amelia at the moment, someone who understood him. A random stranger was all right when he was in a good mood, but not now. He pulled his hand out of his pocket to open the outer door but was stopped by flirtatious giggling behind him.

He looked back and stifled a groan. This was the last thing he needed. Sage, with a date. Not the beefcake they'd caught him with at his apartment. A new guy, tall and lean with his loose curls gelled within an inch of their life. He had a handful of freckles across his nose, giving him an innocent look, but Mack could tell by the crinkles at the corners of his eyes that he was older than Sage. The guy was hotter than a sidewalk in hell, of course. The two of them together radiated sexiness.

That was the one thing about Sage. He was incredibly good-looking, in a refined, aristocratic way. He had great genes, aside from his parents both being even bigger assholes than Sage. Beauty ran in their family. It was no wonder he could attract men like flies, but keeping them depended on being a better human being than Sage was capable of.

Mack was about to turn around again and ignore them, on the off chance they were too focused on each other to notice him. Sage wasn't allowed in Grand Slam anymore, so they weren't going where Mack was. Boylston Street had other places available to them. Before he managed to duck out of sight, Sage's gaze locked on his.

"Well, look what the dog dug up in the yard," he drawled.

"Fuck you too," Mack said.

"Aw, is that any way to greet an old friend?"

"We're not—" Mack started.

"Oh, is this the guy you were telling me about?" Freckles—the nickname Mack gave him in his head—interrupted.

"Naw, that was my ex. This is one of his lowlife minions, though."

"Nice as it is to see you, and meet your new plaything, I'm going inside. Where you can't come." Mack stepped closer to the door.

Sage grabbed his sleeve. "Wait. I'm sorry. I—" He looked over at Freckles. "How's Jamie? I heard he wasn't doing so well."

"Oh. My. God." Mack yanked his arm away, wishing he had the guts to punch the fake sympathy right out of him. "You are a real piece of work. I don't buy a second of your 'concerned friend' bullshit. I don't owe you anything when it comes to Jamie."

Sage's pretty face contorted with anger. "Protecting him, like always. Tell me, does he know what you and I did?"

Mack clenched his jaw. Sage was baiting him, and he knew it, but he couldn't help himself. Of course he hadn't told Jamie. It would've killed Jamie at the time, and now, five years later, there was no reason anymore. Sage should've been out of their lives. Only here he was, standing on the sidewalk outside the one place Mack still thought of as safe.

"You spiteful, maggot-crusted, rotting bag of testicles," Mack hissed. "Get the fuck away from me."

Sage didn't, not right away. He leaned in and whispered, "Do you still think about me every time another man has his cock up your ass? I'll bet you do."

Mack swallowed. He hadn't anymore, although admittedly, Jomari was the first man he'd allowed to top him since. He didn't count Amelia. Now the memories threatened to eat him in one gulp.

Sage backed up. "I'm not surprised you can't tell me anything. You're alone tonight. All your loser friends ditched you, huh? Looks like you finally got what you deserve." He returned to Freckles' side. "Let's go. That dickhead's done messing with me."

Mack tracked their progress up the street until they disappeared. His heart thundered. How could he or Amelia ever have had any sympathy for him? He was right, though. Mack was by himself, and maybe it was even his own fault.

Maybe Jamie had been right to wait until the last minute to tell him he was moving out...moving on. Amelia must've known that he would react badly if she'd told him they were done with the kind of relationship they'd always had. And Sage wasn't far off the truth too. He knew he'd won, bringing up what had happened between them. He'd left his mark.

Mack wanted to permanently erase the memories Sage had dragged up with a single, soul-piercing comment. He had alternatives—surely there was a meeting somewhere, or he could've dug up the phone numbers of anyone who might've been able to help. His sponsor, who he hadn't called in ages. He hesitated outside Grand Slam, knowing if he went where nobody knew him, they wouldn't stop him. Denver or Jack would. But a small part of him knew there was a chance they wouldn't be there or be available, and that's what he was counting on.

And then he was inside the doors, past Curtis—the bouncer—making his way to the bar. He didn't recognize the young woman, which meant she wouldn't know him either, his past firmly hidden. He tried to seem casual when ordering the first drink he'd touched in more than five years, but his belly rocked with nerves. Like riding a bike, he told her what he wanted with practiced ease, hoping she couldn't hear the tremor in his voice or the last traces of pleading silently with her to say no.

She set the shot glass on the bar in front of him and turned away to take care of someone else. Mack gazed at it, trying to read his fortune in the tiny whorls of the dark amber liquid. He ran his index finger around the rim. Who knew that more than five years' worth of sobriety would steal his courage? There'd been a time when he wouldn't even have tasted it, just swallowed it and chased it with more.

This had been a terrible idea. He both wanted what was in the glass and was repulsed by it. The dueling sensations made the memories surge forward of the last time he'd touched a drink. His fingers trembled where they rested, and his chest tightened. He barely remembered what had happened, but his body certainly recalled the sensations.

It was after going to see Sage. Jamie wouldn't play with him that day and delivered an unexpected ultimatum, so he'd quit the band. The fuckwad had made a big scene and publicly dumped Jamie at a rehearsal before walking out on all of them. Mack wanted to know what the hell had happened.

Later, Mack had been in the place he'd called home at the time—his parents' trailer. By then he hadn't needed to swipe from Mom's supply anymore. Instead, he had his own hidden stash. He remembered the rage he'd tried to quell with cheap whiskey. The liquid burned a little going down, but as the first rush hit him, it brought a dark relief. It also brought on the courage to confront

Sage.

Instead of doing what he should have, Mack had chased him to his apartment. They'd been meant to talk, but Mack was already halfway to hammered. Instead of answers, he'd ended up with Sage's tongue in his mouth, frantically trying to undo each other's belts, getting off on their mutual fury. Just like old times, both before and after Sage'd mesmerized Jamie.

Until Mack started to sober up and realized what he was doing. It was never meant to go that far. Mack hadn't wanted to betray Jamie again. Sage didn't care. Didn't listen to Mack's protests or his pleas not to hurt someone they both supposedly loved. Didn't let up until Mack swore he would stop getting between Sage and his prize. Threatened to ruin the band the whole time he was ruining Mack. His last words were that Mack couldn't love anyone, and Sage was going to take from him the one thing he had left to give.

Afterward, the only way Mack could make the pain go away was to find the nearest place to get shitfaced. Hitting the utility pole was a bonus; he'd wanted to die. He barely remembered anything after that, only finally registering what had happened when he was in a holding cell.

In the present, Mack gasped for air, choking on the flood of distilled panic. He'd been transported by the memories, trying to wash away the image of Sage's haughty sneer as he reminded Mack of everything. The way he'd spun Mack around and pinned him face-first to the wall and—

Now here he was again, submerged in his own anguish and trying to soak himself in shots of...he couldn't remember now what he'd ordered or how many he'd had, even though another one sat in front of him, weeping sweat down the sides of the glass. Life was happening around him, but he was numb and barely aware of it. His brain was fixated on the details of what had happened: the sharp tang of blood where he'd bitten his tongue, Sage's hot breath against his ear, the bruising pinch of fingers on his neck and hip...

"...any idea how much he's had?" That was Jack's voice, breaking through Mack's haze.

The young woman who had been serving him sounded nervous and apologetic. "Maybe five or six? I didn't know not to give it to him."

"Including that one?" Jack sounded frustrated.

"No," the bartender said, her voice more hushed now. "Before that one."

Jack exchanged a few more words with her. Mack vaguely heard him call for Denver, and then they were both magically beside him. He was too out of it to make sense of their conversation.

"Hey." Denver's hand was on his back. He looked up.

"Who can we call for you?" Jack asked.

"No one. There's no one. Nobody, nobody, nobody."

"Give me your phone."

"I've got it." Denver pulled it out of Mack's jeans and handed it to Jack.

"I'm going to call someone." Jack was less hesitant this time. "Tell me who."

As foggy as he was, Mack tried to push through it to think of someone. He didn't want any of the people who were the current source of his pain. "Nate," he mumbled. "Call Nate."

And then he was sobbing, and Denver was helping him off the stool and up the back staircase. Mack lost track of time, curled up in Rafael's office on his couch. The next thing he was aware of was Nate kneeling beside him.

"We've got you," Nate said.

We? Mack blinked and looked up to see Izzy. The two of them lifted Mack and supported him between them. Words tumbled from Mack's mouth, incoherent babble about Jamie and Amelia and all the other miserable messes Mack had made. He wasn't fully aware of anything he was saying until Nate spoke.

"Sage? What's that asshole got to do with anything?"

Mack clammed up then. What Sage had done to him was a secret he would take to his grave. It would destroy Jamie if he knew the truth, and even sloshed Mack knew enough to protect his best friend.

"I'm sorry...I'm sorry..."

"C'mon," Izzy said. "Let's get you out of here. We can talk in the morning."

No, Mack decided. There was nothing to talk about. Not with Nate or Izzy or maybe anyone at all. That was his last thought before the rest of the night became a blank.

PART THREE: VARIATION II – AMELIA

Chapter Fourteen

It had been two weeks since Mack's meltdown. Amelia was pretty sure Mack had been drinking in the interim. It wasn't as if being dragged home drunk by his ex-roommate's fiancé was enough to humiliate him into stopping. Amelia knew him; once he started, he wouldn't quit on his own. So she was there with Jamie to make sure he did what he needed, especially with Christmas looming.

They sat in the living room, not speaking. Occasional noises drifted from Mack's room where he was cleaning. Better to leave him to it. He would have to come out at some point, and they would talk to him then. Amelia heard him talking to himself angrily, which meant he was nearing the end of his rant. He would run out of words, and then he'd come out. She nodded, causing Jamie to look over at her with his eyebrows raised in question. She sighed.

"Sorry. Just calculating how much longer."

"Ah."

They went silent again, and Amelia had a good, long look at Jamie while he stared out the window. He'd always been attractive, but today even more. His hair was longer, almost shaggy, but it was stick-straight and very fine, so he was able to tame it smooth. He always wore a little eyeliner, but she was almost positive he had on more makeup than that. It was really pretty, but she wasn't sure if she should say so.

He must've felt her eyes on him because he looked over again. "What?"

"You look nice."

"Thanks."

Jamie turned his gaze to the hallway, as if he could use x-ray vision to peer into the bedroom. His fingers twitched, and Amelia felt a sympathetic jolt of tension in her arm. Yes, she understood the itchy feeling of wanting to do something but not being able to yet. She couldn't stand this isolating silence and awkward non-conversation.

"He fucking needs help," she muttered.

Jamie turned his whole body toward her this time, and now she saw the tension in his neck muscles too. "What would you even know about it?"

Amelia gaped at him. "What's that supposed to mean?"

"Only that you have no idea what it takes, every day, to keep yourself in check." He shook his head. "I know what he's going through."

"And I don't?" Amelia hissed, trying to keep her voice down.

"You made a choice that you weren't ever going to take that risk," Jamie murmured, low.

"I make the same choice day after day, year after year."

Jamie scoffed, but he didn't respond this time.

Amelia balled her hands into fists. Jamie thought she was judging, but nothing she'd said came from a place of seeing herself as better than Mack for never letting down her guard. No, her need for tight control was exactly why Mack was trashing his room under the guise of "cleaning."

"You blame me too, don't you?" she asked.

"What?" Jamie frowned. "No. I have no idea what you're talking about."

"You think if I hadn't been so selfish, he wouldn't have—" She cut herself off, not able to finish the sentence without losing it entirely.

Jamie's soft sigh broke her out of her worried thoughts. "That's not it at all. We didn't do this. And we can't fix it." He didn't have to add *just like you couldn't fix me*, but it hung there between them anyway.

"I..." She paused. "We?"

"It's my fault too. We all dumped our shit on him, and we expected him to be able to take it."

"I didn't show up when he needed me."

"Yeah? Well, neither did the rest of us."

"Except Nate. And Izzy."

"Izzy's a contender for sainthood, so he doesn't count."

Amelia chuckled. "True."

After a beat, Jamie said, "Nate, not so much."

"Maybe Izzy's rubbed off on him."

They looked at each other and muffled their laughter just as a burst of swearing erupted from the other room. There was a crash, then silence.

"I believe Mack's done 'cleaning,'" Amelia whispered, and Jamie nodded.

Mack emerged. When they'd finished dealing with the shit they all needed to get out, Amelia would go in there and straighten up the damage Mack had done in his search for whatever he'd been looking for. She kept her gaze on him as he walked into the living room. He leaned against the wall, arms folded.

"You were waiting for me," he said.

"No kidding," Amelia muttered, and Jamie elbowed her harder than necessary.

"Go on," Mack told them. "Say what you need to, and then get the fuck out of my apartment."

Amelia tried to catch Jamie's eye, but he wouldn't look at her. He wouldn't look at Mack, either. She braced herself for Mack's reaction and said, "Why'd you do it?"

"Why not? It's not like you care anyway. You're busy 'having a life.'" He used air quotes, making Amelia wince. He continued, "And by that I mean fucking your new toy."

That was the last straw. She stood, pulling herself up to her full five-foot-two. "I sincerely hope you mean my vibrator because if you're referring to Jomari, he might like to know what you said before he decides to share your bed again."

Mack's jaw twitched like he was grinding his teeth. "Maybe you should tell him."

Amelia was more than ready to have a go at Mack, and she knew with her physical strength and in his state, she could easily take him. She held herself, though, calming down when Jamie stood beside her.

"Mack," he said quietly. "Come sit down."

Mack's shoulders slumped, and he obediently went to the couch. He sat, and Jamie settled in beside him. He gave Amelia a pointed look, and after a moment's hesitation, she sat on Mack's other side.

"You fucked up, dude," Jamie said, but he put a hand on Mack's leg. "So did we."

"But..."

"But nothing. We weren't there. I'm sorry."

"No." Mack shook his head vigorously. "You needed me more, and I couldn't be what you wanted."

"Why? Why do you always think that?"

Mack turned to look at Jamie. "It's the truth."

"No." Jamie looked like he might say more, but he closed his mouth.

Amelia swallowed. She'd sat on what she knew, and Mack deserved her honesty. Not yet, though. She wanted to see how it played out with Jamie first.

"Sage—"

"Don't go there, Mack," Jamie warned. "This isn't the time."

"I tried to keep him away from you." Mack's words were barely audible.

Jamie threw up his hands. "Is that what this is about? Because you can stop any time. We both know what a dickhead Sage is, and you didn't make all that happen. I'm away from him for good. Why is he even part of this?"

"Because I failed. Because I never told you the truth." Mack leaned back against the couch. "I..." He gasped, and Amelia heard the way he was holding back a sob. "Before. After. The whole time, I—"

"The whole time he was in the band, the two of you were fucking? Yeah, I know."

Now Amelia drew in air sharply. Jamie knew? She'd held onto her precious cargo for years, keeping Mack's secret, but Jamie knew.

"How—?" She cut herself off. Maybe it was better if Jamie didn't realize.

Too late. He leaned around Mack and glared at her. "You knew too, but you never said anything."

"It's not like you did either." She crossed her arms.

Jamie ignored her. "Yeah, I knew."

"We stopped," Mack said. "When he quit."

"You mean when I caught him cheating on me with one of my costars? After months of begging me in jealous fits to stop filming, telling me if I didn't he'd leave the band? I remember that." Jamie stood up. He paced then turned to look at Mack and Amelia. "I thought he would stop chasing me once the two of you were together, but he didn't. He kept saying you couldn't give him what he wanted." Jamie swiped at his eyes, smudging his makeup. "You know how he finally got me?"

Mack looked up at him. "How?"

"He bought me a winter coat." Jamie laughed without humor. "A fucking jacket. Not even anything precious or special or fancy. I needed a new one, and I wouldn't ask Brandon's family. He told me no one should be without one, and he took me shopping. The whole time, I kept expecting he would do what he always did—flatter me, tell me how hot I'd look in the clothes we passed in the store along the way. I wondered if there were gonna be strings attached, like I'd have to agree to go out with him.

"But the only thing he did was buy the coat. He said it was shit, what happened to me, and he told me no one deserved that." Jamie sniffled. "You know, he never once asked for the money back. A week later, when I got my next paycheck, I told him I'd give him a little at a time until I'd paid it off. He refused, and he stopped asking me out too. Instead, he would pull me aside, check in with me and ask if I was doing okay, if I needed anything.

"That spring, we were packing up my drums, and..." Jamie was outright crying now, mascara-streaked tears running down his cheeks. "I saw him differently, this side of him he never showed anyone else. I...stopped him. And I kissed him. We ended up getting off in the back of the recording studio while everyone else was loading my drums into Mack's van."

Amelia exchanged a glance with Mack and saw he was as surprised as she was. The whole time, she'd thought Sage wore Jamie down until he said yes. Judging from Mack's raised eyebrows, he'd thought the same.

"I had no idea," Mack confirmed. "I'm sorry."

Jamie drew his wrist across his eyes then looked at it in disgust where he'd smeared his eyeliner. "He knew exactly what he was doing. It was never about me or what I needed. He was manipulating the whole thing. You weren't wrong to try keeping him from me. You just did it in the wrongest, most fucked up way possible."

"I know." Mack's eyes glistened. "Jamie, that night—the one when I almost died—I went to him. Wanted to beg him to stay. I didn't know you'd kicked him out. I—we—" Mack shook, and

Amelia grasped his hand. "I wasn't gonna ever tell you. Thought it would break you. But now...He raped me, Jay. He thought he could take whatever he wanted from anyone he wanted."

"God, Mack."

"Fuck." Amelia put her arms around Mack. He'd told her he and Sage "had sex," that he'd gone to apologize because it was his fault Sage left the band. Jamie said it was his fault, that he'd made Sage pick between the band and whoever he was cheating on Jamie with. Sage had told her he'd gotten a better job—which was true, but it was his parents who bribed his way in. So many years gone by, so many lies.

She began, "You told me—"

"That I'd agree to it. I know. I did, at first, but then he—" Mack's chest heaved. "It came back. All of it. I thought I was better. Stronger. That night, after Sage, I wanted to die and didn't. This time...I couldn't do it. My mom—you—everyone. I wanted it to go the fuck away, wanted to get wasted enough to forget."

He leaned into Amelia, sobbing. Jamie came and sat on his other side again, and they held him. Amelia sniffled. It was her fault too, for not telling anyone what she knew. Maybe she should've said something, kept Mack from going to see him. Kept Sage from hurting him.

"I'm sorry," she whispered into his hair. "I'm so, so sorry."

Mack's sobs subsided, and he sat up, rubbing his eyes. "For what?"

"For not being honest with both of you sooner. I knew what he was like and what he and his parents did." She ran a hand over her face. "I knew he was playing both of you, trying to get a wedge in between you so he could take anything he barely had legal claim to when you split up. Except you never did, and he's been pissed off about it ever since. I should've said something."

Mack shook his head. "No. He told me he'd ruin us. If I hadn't agreed to what he wanted—"

"It's not your fault," Jamie interrupted. "And it's not like I didn't know about the two of you. He kept saying you couldn't love him the way I did."

Mack whipped his head around to stare at Jamie. "What?"

"Yeah. When we were alone, he would say shit like how no one ever loved him the way I did. He cheated on me every single chance he got—including with you—but he said it wasn't the same." Jamie sighed. "But he also told me the reverse, that no one would ever love me like he did, and his 'love' nearly killed me."

"You know what he said when he—" Mack curled his hand into a fist, and the corners of his mouth tightened. "When he raped me. I'm gonna stop pretending that didn't happen. He said if all I could give him was sex, then that's what he was gonna take away from me, my chance to have sex without thinking about him and the way he hurt me. The first time I fucked someone afterward, after I got sober, it was a giant 'fuck you' to Sage. He couldn't take that from me."

"Me," Amelia said softly. "You told me I was the first one after you did your time and got clean." His trust in her with his body was more courageous than she'd known.

Mack nodded. "You were, yeah."

She brushed at her eyes. "God. There's not even a word for him." She peered around at Jamie. "I'm sorry, but it's true. He is not worth dog shit scraped off your shoe."

"No, I agree," Jamie said. "Even a few months ago, I'd have argued. Said there was still something in him worth saving. But he doesn't want to be saved." He sat up straight. "I'm happier now. I have to work at it, but I know what it's like to have real love, not the kind Sage pretends to give. He's unhappy, and he wants everyone else to be too." Jamie paused and squeezed Mack's hand. "I'm glad you told us, but why now? What has he got to do with any of what happened?"

"I saw him," Mack said. "Out with yet another new man. He pulled that fake-sympathy shit he always does then asked about you. When I wouldn't tell him, he wanted to know if I still thought about him. I told him to fuck off, and he laughed and said it looked like I finally got what I deserved."

"Oh, babe." Amelia rested her head on his shoulder.

They fell quiet, all of them lost in thought. Mack was the first to break the silence. He reached into his pocket and pulled out his five-year coin. He rolled it between his fingers, his hands shaking.

"I was looking for this. Before, I mean, in my room."

Jamie frowned. "You always keep it on you."

"Not that night. I left it. Tossed it aside. It rolled under the bookshelf." He glanced at Amelia, guilt all over his face. "I made a mess."

"I know," she said and put her hand on his. She didn't think he was talking about the shelf.

Mack looked again at the coin, and his expression morphed

into rage and pain. He hurled the coin, and it hit the wall, leaving a mark where it bounced off before landing on the floor and rolling under the television. Mack put his head in his hands.

"I made a mess," he repeated.

Jamie grasped his hand. "So now you start over. Like I did."

"Go to meetings again, you mean."

"It's what worked for you before. And call your sponsor. Please?"

Amelia sat back and watched them. She wasn't part of this moment. Jamie was right that she didn't have their experience. She'd poured all her energy into winning, into having the upper hand. Her enemy was seen—the other team on the field; her father; Sage. This wasn't an enemy with a face, and she couldn't battle it for either of them.

She thought about Jomari and the relationship they'd begun to build. She needed some time to breathe, to think about what it was she wanted. Like Mack, she'd been sure she'd conquered her demons, especially after she'd taken out the person who'd done her the most harm.

"I need some space," she murmured. "I'm sorry."

Mack looked over at her. "I know. I'm sorry too. And I didn't mean what I said."

"Yeah, you did, and you need to think about why. But I understand." She kissed his cheek as proof. "I'm gonna go and let you two sort some things out." She stood. "I'll come by another time to help you pick up in your room."

Jamie turned his attention to her. "I'm probably the last person you want to hear this from, but...you gotta deal with all that anger. Get some help for yourself, okay? It's good to talk to someone who isn't involved. We've all been through a lot."

Amelia sighed. "I'll think about it."

She headed for the door, and the others watched her go. Outside the apartment, she leaned against the opposite wall to gather her thoughts. She needed a friend more than she needed a lover, and she was pretty sure she knew exactly who to call. She waited until she'd dashed down the stairs and out to her car before pulling out her phone.

"Hey, Marlie? Are you free for lunch?"

Chapter Fifteen

Amelia met Marlie outside the cafe where Nate worked. The guys were always so weird about not wanting to go there, but Amelia had no such qualms. She went there all the time, and Nate never seemed to mind seeing her.

A light snow was falling, and on an ordinary day, combined with the inviting multi-colored lights on the cafe and the surrounding shops, it would've put her in a festive mood. Not now, though. She shivered and pulled her scarf up to cover her mouth. She could've waited inside, but Nate was working, and she wasn't in the mood to be alone with him.

Fortunately, Marlie appeared just as Amelia began stamping her feet to keep warm. Inside, Nate waved at them in greeting then took their orders when they came to the counter. He handed Amelia the water she asked for and told them he'd bring everything else out when it was done, so the women found a table near the back.

Marlie was fidgety, and Amelia wondered if she felt awkward being there. Like Amelia with Mack and Jamie, Marlie had known Trevor and Nate for years. Unlike with Mack, Marlie had been entirely in the dark about Trevor's bisexuality until a couple of years ago. Amelia was never sure what happened—aside from Marlie getting pregnant and having to figure out what kind of relationship to have with Trevor. Things had been awkward and messy for a while, but sometime after Aidan was born, they all seemed to settle down.

Until recently, which might've been why she was antsy. Marlie had left Aidan home with the men. As far as Amelia could tell, Trevor and Andre were both doting daddies. Jamie, too, for that matter, now that he'd gone back to babysitting for them. But his relationship with Trevor was different. Amelia didn't have head space for it at the moment.

"So," Marlie said, but she left the word hanging.

"So..." Amelia sighed. "We're lifting that rule about not talking about our men, right? Because that's currently a lot of my problem."

Marlie rolled her eyes and laughed. "I think that rule got made so we'd talk about the rest of our lives too. We have jobs and kids—some of us—and other stuff going on that doesn't revolve around them. Plus, some of our friends are in relationships with other women. But honestly, who else are we going to talk to when one of them is being a stubborn jackass?" She smiled, but then she turned serious. "We bottle it in. My mother told me that I should never, ever talk about my relationship problems with anyone but my husband. I mean, leaving aside the fact that she assumed I'd have a husband at all, she believed if you talk about it, everyone will begin to believe your spouse is a terrible person and they'll stop liking them."

"That's...weird?" Amelia couldn't fathom that. Then again, she hadn't had a mother to coach her on it.

"Tell me about it. It took every ounce of courage for me to talk to Nia when I got scared about being in a polyamorous relationship." Marlie shrugged. "My parents are very conservative. Mom had a list of Bible verses for 'marital adversity' in her nightstand drawer. Not sure what that says about her and Dad, though they have always seemed happy to me. My home was pretty peaceful growing up. Maybe it worked for them."

"Maybe." Or maybe Marlie's mother did the whole bottling thing Marlie mentioned. "Anyway, I'm glad that's not off the table because I have a whopper of a problem. And the massive headache to go with it."

"You want something?" Marlie fished in her purse and laughed when she came up with a bottle of children's Motrin. "Um...possibly not this." She put it back and retrieved a couple of other bottles. "You have options. I always keep a stash of over-the-counter meds."

"Oh my god, thank you." Amelia accepted a couple of tablets and swallowed them with a sip of her water.

Nate stopped by with their orders and set everything down. "Here you go."

"Thanks," Marlie said, smiling up at him. That answered Amelia's question; Nate was definitely not the source of her tension, and she already looked more relaxed.

"Let me know if you need anything else." He touched Amelia's shoulder briefly on his way past.

As soon as Nate was gone, Marlie said, "So now tell me what's been going on that sparked the headache. I gather this has to do at least a bit with Mack?"

"You heard, then."

"That he's drinking again? Yeah. There aren't really too many secrets among us at this point, at least not when it comes to current events." Marlie reached across the table and took Amelia's hand. "Are you doing okay?"

"Not really." Amelia withdrew her hand and rubbed her temples. "It's a lot right now."

She didn't know where to start, whether it should be with her worries about Mack or whatever it was she felt for Jomari or today's mini-intervention with Jamie. She felt bad for leaving them, and then she felt bad for thinking either of them was too fragile to handle it.

Marlie stepped in before Amelia could decide. "It's okay for you to need somewhere to unload all this. You're trying to do the right thing, and you don't want to let him down. But you also can't take all his problems on yourself."

"That's not exactly it." Amelia closed her eyes. "Jamie said I couldn't understand because I've never been where they are."

"Understand? Maybe not. Empathize? Of course you can."

"Maybe he's right, though. I swore I would never turn out like my father, and I never took a chance on so much as smoking weed. But..."

She trailed off and thought about what else Jamie had said, for her to get help too. Did she need it? She loved pushing herself physically, but she never took it too far or overused it, not since she built herself up to get away from her father. She'd spent a lot of time learning to respect herself and her body, and her entire job was teaching others to do the same. It had taken her years to reach this point, though not without a price.

"But?" Marlie prompted.

"But Jamie also said I should think about seeing someone about my anger. A therapist, he meant. I haven't seen a counselor since high school."

"It might help." Marlie shrugged. "Some people believe everyone could benefit from spending some time in therapy. I'm more of the mind that there isn't one single way to become a better version of yourself. Only you can make that decision."

"I don't know."

"I can give you a couple of names from when I volunteered at the Lighthouse. Up to you." Marlie dumped more sugar in her tea than Amelia wanted to think about before she continued. "For now, you feel like talking about what happened?"

Amelia tried to keep herself under control, but she finally slumped, shaking. "Jamie and I went to see Mack today. As far as I know, Jamie's still with him now. He didn't think Mack should be alone after we talked. I couldn't stay. It—it was too much."

"I don't blame you."

"I need to clear my head. I can be there for Mack as his friend, but I don't know if we can go back to the kind of relationship we had yet. I told them both I wanted space."

"I have an idea." Marlie bit her lip. "Um, do you have a passport, by any chance?"

"I do," Amelia confirmed. "Got one a few years ago for a trip I never took." Marlie didn't need all the gory details of finding out her father had killed a pregnant woman in a DUI, leading to Amelia wanting to get as far away as possible. Mack had talked her out of it, of course, and she hadn't really had the money anyway. "Why?"

"Okay, well...I have this cousin. Misty?"

Amelia frowned. "Okay." She didn't add a sarcastic "and so..." but she was pretty sure Marlie heard it because she rolled her eyes again.

"Misty lives in England. She met her wife when they both went to college in New York. Anyway, they got married, but it took a bunch of years before Misty could move there to live. They finally have a cute little house." Marlie pulled out her phone and showed Amelia. "So she said I could come and visit, and if my friends wanted to come along, they could." Marlie giggled. "I think she sort of meant Trevor and Andre but didn't know exactly how to group them together."

Amelia scrolled through the pictures. The house was indeed

adorable, exactly the sort of place Amelia wanted someday. She passed the phone back. "So are you and the guys going?"

"No way am I taking them on my vacation." Marlie laughed. "I asked Nia if she wanted to go, and now I'm asking you."

"When?"

"We'd leave a couple weeks before Nate and Izzy's wedding. This airline only has flights to and from Boston on certain days, so it makes it a bit tricky for planning. But we'll have about six days there. I'm sorry it's a bit short notice—less than two months away."

"Right before their wedding? Shouldn't we be here to help?"

"Oh, lord, no," Marlie answered. "They've got Jagathi, since she's been doing some wedding planning on the side. And I don't know about you, but I want nothing to do with any of them while they attempt this thing."

"Fair enough." Amelia considered the offer. She'd never been to England, and a trip where she wouldn't have to pay for a hotel sounded pretty nice. Plus a queer-friendly household and some fun? She was definitely in, as long as she could get her vacation days approved. "Where is this place, exactly?"

"We-ell," Marlie said, and she chewed her lip again. "It's kind of out of the way. So if you were thinking we'd, like, pop over to London for the day...nope. Not a problem for me or Nia. We figure we've seen enough of city life living here, and I've been to London before. You okay with that?"

"Fine by me. They have kids? And speaking of, what are you going to do with yours?"

"Trevor, Andre, and Jamie can handle one small child among the three of them while I'm gone. They have a grand total of four sets of doting grandparents, too—Jamie just took Aidan to meet his mom, and as predicted, she melted. They'll manage just fine. As for Misty and Dawn—"

"Their names are Misty and Dawn?" Amelia pursed her lips in a poor attempt not to laugh.

"Get it out of your system now," Marlie said. "They've heard it all before."

Amelia let loose and laughed until her eyes watered. Eventually, she calmed down, though she still giggled every so often at the couple whose combined names sounded like either Pokémon fan fiction or one of Jamie's costars. Or both. "Okay. Carry on," she said to Marlie.

"*Anyway*, no, they don't have kids. They're both in their early thirties, and I'm not sure whether they want them. I've never asked." She leaned forward. "What do you say?"

"I say let's go for it. I could use a vacation." What she would do in the meantime was anyone's guess, but she would manage somehow. She always did.

They ate in companionable quiet for a few minutes. The food was always good at Cafe Velocity, which explained why it was so busy every time Amelia was in there. Her mind wandered to Jamie's suggestion. Not that she didn't think he might be right, but she was building her support network. There was an Employee Assistance Program at work, and she thought it might be worth taking advantage of those resources.

She set down her half-eaten sandwich. "We talked about me, but you seemed when you got here like you had something on your mind too. Want to share?"

Marlie leaned in. "I talked to Trevor like you suggested." Her pale cheeks turned a nice shade of pink.

"Ooh, sounds like something happened with that." Amelia grinned.

She was about to ask, but Nate showed up to top off their coffee. "Here you go. Anything else?"

"No, but thanks, Nate." Marlie smiled up at him like she had before, but this time, Amelia almost laughed. Marlie had the *please-leave-us-the-fuck-alone* charm turned up full-volume, expert level.

Nate got the hint. He flashed them a grin and retreated. He peeked once over his shoulder, but Marlie's arched eyebrows sent the message loud and clear that he should stay away.

Once he was out of earshot, Amelia said, "Tell me everything."

"You sure you want to know?" Marlie giggled, full of nervous energy.

"Only if you want to tell me, of course." Amelia sure hoped Marlie was in the mood to confess it all. Not that she would pressure her, but what was the point of asking if they weren't going to talk about it?

"Okay. Well, I put on my big girl panties and told Trevor how I'd been feeling. All of it—how I couldn't get in the mood and that I was having all these thoughts about being good enough for him. I even told him about how I avoid anything with guys having sex, including books, because it felt intrusive and I was scared I'd start thinking inappropriately about him and Andre."

"What did he say?"

Marlie sipped her coffee, clearly thinking about how she wanted to respond. "He listened and said he understood. Then he said he needed some time to process it. Which is a big deal—usually he comes off like he hasn't really paid attention, and then he does something stupid because he's bottled up all his feelings about it." She rolled her eyes, but she was smiling.

"That's fair. Did he ever get back to you?"

"Yes. And it was...not what I expected." The nervousness was back. Marlie fiddled with her napkin.

"O-kaaaay," Amelia replied. She wondered where this was going.

"He came back to me later and asked if it was okay to discuss it with Andre and Jamie. I said sure, but I didn't know what would happen. As it turns out, a lot."

Amelia couldn't decide if she wanted to demand Marlie stop dragging it out. She held in her eager reply and instead told Marlie, "Another big step for him, huh?"

"For sure. Well, it turns out he sort of had two very different discussions. With Andre, it was more about working through these patches of jealousy we all get from time to time. So that was good, and I think it helped them, too. Trevor's been avoiding talking about Nia because he didn't want Andre to feel responsible for Trevor's feelings. Anyway, then I guess he talked to Jamie, and that was..." She trailed off.

"That was what?"

"The whole thing was Jamie's idea, really. But I mean, Trevor was okay with it, and I was kind of nervous, but it all worked out, and—" Marlie stopped abruptly. "Um. I should probably explain."

Amelia laughed. "I'm a little lost, yeah."

Marlie glanced around then leaned even closer. "Jamie suggested I might like if we could all make love together."

"A threesome?"

"I guess? Kind of? I always thought of that as, like, all three people want to be together. But Jamie's gay, and I'm not really into him that way. So he meant sharing Trevor. I could see what it was like between them, but I'd get to participate."

"So did you?"

Marlie nodded. "At first, I was scared it would feel like I was fetishizing them. Like I wasn't supposed to find it sexy watching them kissing and touching. But Jamie really kind of...took charge, I guess. I've never seen him like that, and Trevor said later he's usually more passive. It was like he was directing, the way he told Trevor what to do and how to help me relax and get into it."

"Makes sense, given how Jamie's been on film. Then what happened?"

"It was good," Marlie said with a one-shoulder shrug. "Trevor made me feel really special, and I could tell Jamie was doing the same for him." She giggled. "Oh, and Jamie definitely is *blessed*, as you put it. Trevor's on the smaller side, which I like—and apparently so does Jamie—but God, Jamie's really beautiful. Anyway, it was amazing. The guys thought so too and asked if sometime we could do that again. Not all the time. Both of us want Trevor to ourselves usually. But I'd be okay with it."

"Good for you guys!" Amelia said. "I can offer you a couple other things to try alone too. If Trevor's into taking it, you might get a strap-on, for example."

Marlie's cheeks reddened again. "I don't know if he is or not. That, uh, wasn't part of what he and Jamie did with me there, anyway. But I can ask." She stared into her empty mug and wouldn't meet Amelia's gaze. "Being with Trevor and Jamie like that helped me understand better what was getting in my way."

Amelia reached out and put a hand on Marlie's arm. "You feel like talking about it?"

"Jamie thought this would be easier on me, since I'm not interested in him."

"Okay..." Amelia was beginning to understand, but she needed Marlie to say it. "Meaning?"

"I think..." Marlie closed her eyes and kept them shut when she said, "I'm starting to have feelings for Andre."

Amelia gave Marlie's arm a reassuring squeeze before withdrawing her hand. "That's only natural. He's Aidan's other dad, and he lives with you. He's a good man." She smiled. "Handsome, too. I don't blame you a bit."

"The problem is, I don't think he feels the same. And I don't think Trevor feels that way about Nia. We're already talking about her moving in soon, which is fine with me. I love her to bits, though it's more sisterly, seeing as we're both straight. It all feels complicated and hard right now." She sniffled. "I don't know if what I feel for Andre is love for how good a father he is or what Jamie called 'queer platonic' love—even though I'm really not queer, or at least don't call myself that. Or maybe it's something else. I just don't know."

"Talk to them again," Amelia urged. "All of them. You have to work it out, or all your relationships are at risk." Amelia had the good sense to feel mildly ashamed for not having done the same. She'd wanted to protect Mack from being hurt that she was spending so much time with Jomari, only her failure to talk to him had done the very thing she'd tried to avoid.

"I will," Marlie promised. "Trevor and I have a real date this weekend, and I can tell him then." She giggled despite her still-teary eyes. "Trevor shocked me that he actually talked to the others, so maybe there's hope for me after all."

Amelia laughed. "There's always hope." She picked up her sandwich again, wishing she believed her own words.

CHAPTER SIXTEEN

AMELIA GAVE in after a week of lying in bed with her phone, willing herself not to call Mack. She'd told him she needed space, and she'd left Jamie to deal with things. It wasn't fair of her, and she knew it, but she was still angry.

It wasn't all directed at Mack. She was white-hot with renewed fury at Sage. She'd put up with him for years, believing he needed healing every bit as much as she or Mack or Jamie. Of course, she thought that ought to be done away from the people he was hurting—chiefly Mack and Jamie. Still, she'd hoped. What Mack told her obliterated any shred of empathy she had left.

She held her phone, favorite contacts list open, practicing in her head what she was going to say when Mack answered. With a deep, cleansing breath, she touched his number. She put it on speaker and set the phone in her lap; her hands were shaking too hard to hold it.

"Hey." Mack sounded tired.

"Hi, you." Amelia sniffled and then immediately lost it. Every last word she'd planned out left her brain. "I'm sorry I didn't call," she said through her tears.

"Oh, babe. No. I..." Mack sounded like he was crying too. "I'm so sorry. I fucked up, baby."

For a while, they stayed on the line, crying together. She wasn't ready to forgive him yet, but she was going to do the one thing for him she never had. She wiped her eyes and breathed slowly until she was under control.

"Yeah, you did," she said. "But I could've done better too. I..." She swallowed and then forced herself to say it. "I'll go with you on Christmas. You shouldn't do it alone."

"N-no, you don't have to. I mean, I know it's not your thing—"

"Mack." She couldn't keep the irritated edge out of her tone. "You have asked me every year for probably the last ten to go with you. And now I've said I will, but you're all 'No, don't.' What gives?"

"I...it's..." His voice shook. "Please."

Mack was at a loss for words? Something was wrong. "Tell me, hon. What happened?"

"My parents..." He was silent for a few seconds. "It's bad."

"How bad?" Amelia hadn't seen either of them in years. Mack's mother had finally ended up spending most of her time either sleeping or drinking, and Amelia couldn't handle being around her. Mack went alone to see them, and she consoled him afterward. Except this last time, she reminded herself.

Mack said, "Dad has cancer. And Mom..." He sighed. "Dad claims she's not drinking, but that's not possible. She'd be in the hospital if she tried to quit like that. I don't know what Dad's been doing. She's got some kind of dementia, and not only from being wasted all the time. He won't do anything. Says the neighbor's gonna look after her while he's getting chemo. It's so goddamn ridiculous, but I don't know what else to do. I can't—" He sounded like he was hyperventilating.

"Sh. Hon, it's okay. I'm gonna go with you, all right? We'll get through this."

"Okay." Amelia heard Mack's breathing slow down.

"Good. After that, we'll help you move if you want."

"Thanks. The manager says there's a single bedroom unit open, and I can sign a new lease in January." He chuckled. "I guess Mrs. Phelps put in a good word for me."

"The nosy lady from 2B?" Amelia giggled. "Actually, Jamie says she's really nice. Did you know she once left a note for Trevor on his windshield because she thought he and Andre were so sweet together?"

Mack laughed. "No, I never heard that story."

They were quiet again, and Amelia wished they were together and not on the phone. But she knew the separation was good for them both. Mack had to stop relying on her comfort to dull his hurt, and she had to stop providing it. Physical contact wasn't the only way to be his friend, and it was time she did things a little differently.

"Hey," she said, breaking the spell.

"Yeah?"

"I'm here, all right? Call me if you need to. Just not for sex right now."

"I know. So I'll see you on Christmas?"

"I'll be there."

They ended the call, but Amelia still held her phone. She had another one to make, another apology to deliver, this time in person. She hit the number before she could change her mind.

"Hello?"

"Hey, Jamie. Can you meet up with me this week?"

Amelia took her lunch break to go see Jamie. He was still avoiding anywhere he would have to make complicated food-related decisions, and it was too cold to sit outdoors. Instead, they met at the library and sat in the empty community room used for children's programs.

Jamie looked really good. He'd done an enviable job of smokey eyes, and his nails gleamed with gunmetal-colored polish that matched his shirt. He had a small stack of books that he set on the long table. Amelia wasn't sure if they were for him or for Cian. She glanced at the titles: two novels, a biography, and one that was about drum techniques. The last one was clearly Jamie's.

"Hey." He gave her a hug before pulling out a red plastic chair and dropping into it. He seemed tired but otherwise all right.

Amelia sat across from him. "Thanks for coming."

"Sure. What's up?"

"I'm sorry," she said. "For everything. A lot of this is my fault for not talking to you or Mack."

Jamie looked at his hands, flicking his nails against each other until Amelia reached over to stop him. He looked up. "Why didn't you?"

That was hard to explain. She'd told herself it would kill Jamie to know the truth, and now it made her uncomfortable how she'd seen him as breakable. Her sympathy toward Sage and belief that Jamie would leave on his own complicated her decision to keep it all to herself.

"Sage made a promise when he quit that he would ruin the band and everyone in it. He has the means—he would've made sure none of you could use your songs again." She shook her head at Jamie's horrified expression. "No, he doesn't have the rights to them, but that was his plan. His intent was to drive a wedge between you and Mack and pressure you both to sell out." She sighed heavily. "He's had this dream of owning a record label, and he wanted something to start with. His parents already did some vaguely shady things to get that going."

"What does that have to do with...oh." Jamie nodded as it dawned on him. "You didn't want to help him." He scowled. "Did you really think we were that fragile?"

"Yes," Amelia admitted. "You went back to him no matter how much he hurt you."

Jamie huffed. "You probably weren't completely wrong, but you should've said something to one of us."

"I know."

"Does he still have any kind of control when it comes to the band?" Jamie was fidgeting again, and Amelia wondered where this was going.

"Not that I know of. He's a manipulative ass, and he was planning to use what happened with Mack against you. But he didn't actually have any more power than we all gave him."

"Good." Jamie hesitated then said, "Please don't think this is because of what Mack did, not back then and not now."

"Think what is?"

"I'm quitting the band. After New Year's. We're playing at Grand Slam, but then that's it. I don't even think Mack's in shape for it, but we'll make it happen since we've been booked for months. We've barely rehearsed, and we haven't had new stuff in a couple months. None of that is why either. I'm only telling you because I don't think I'm the only one burned out."

"I get it."

She did, when she thought about it. Gemma and Brandon were trying to have a baby. Cassie and Laura were starting their own catering business. Jamie had a new job with Spider Industries starting soon. Mack was the only one left who didn't have something to move on with. Amelia winced. Mack already felt as if everyone had abandoned him. She hoped this wouldn't push him farther away.

"I think we could do an occasional gig, but none of us are

invested. If we were, we wouldn't be mostly known for being terrible." He laughed softly.

Amelia smiled, but she couldn't find much humor even in Jamie's scathing but accurate statement. "You have to do what's right for yourself. But..." She trailed off, thinking about how much drumming meant to Jamie. He'd always said it got him through the worst of everything.

"I'm not giving up music," he said. "I fill in sometimes with Cian's musicians, and I play more with Trevor and Andre just for fun. Last time I was with Cian's people, Jomari said you guys need percussion ringers with the orchestra. That would be a fun way to do something different."

"It's pretty cool," Amelia agreed. "And yeah, sometimes we need, like, eight people back there."

Jamie pulled a piece of paper from a stack in the middle of the table. There were baskets of markers, crayons, and pencils beside the stack. He grabbed a pencil and started doodling while they talked.

"I mean, someday, I want to figure out what it is I want to do. I'm not sure I want to work in a restaurant forever, you know? It's a good job, and I like the people, but...I don't know. I've never had the chance to dream." He peered up at Amelia. "You know?"

"Yeah." Another way she'd had some things easier than her friends. A full scholarship to play soccer and a few good connections meant she now had the kind of job she wanted. "How are you doing otherwise?"

"Okay," Jamie said. He put down the pencil and pulled the markers closer to fill in the outline he'd made with color. "My doctor, um, gave me some meds. For anxiety. It helps. I-I mean," he stammered, "it's not...it isn't—" He was tripping over his words, something he only did when he was tense or upset. "It...fucking...isn't..." He snarled, set down the marker, and switched to ASL, even though Amelia couldn't understand his signing. "Permanent," he finally spit out.

"Oh." Amelia put her hand on his. "It's fine."

Jamie took a minute to calm himself down. "All this shit with Mack is a lot. It was bad, the last time I went to talk to my therapist. I almost started bingeing again. What Mack told us—"

"See? This is why I never said anything."

Jamie glared at her. "Not the cheating. The other—" He was shaking, so Amelia took his hand. She rubbed slow circles with her thumb until he relaxed. "I told myself what Sage did to me didn't count as—as rape." He whispered the word like it was torture to speak it any louder. "It was, though, or at least he didn't always care if I said yes. It wasn't—not like what Mack said. N-not v-violent or...or..."

"You don't have to say any more if you don't want to."

Withdrawing his hand, Jamie said, "I told my therapist. I couldn't deal with it, everything kind of rushing at me like that."

"And I left you with him because I thought—I thought you guys didn't want me there. Because of what you said. That I don't really know what it's like." The truth was harder to face, that she'd been angry and embarrassed on top of her worry. "I'm sorry."

Jamie shoved the markers away and crumpled his drawing before Amelia could see what it was. Some things, she supposed, needed to remain private, even a drawing on library scrap paper.

"I was pissed at you, yeah. But Mack and I needed to get right with each other. I love him like a brother."

"Are you worried about telling him you're quitting the band?"

"Not really, no. His heart's not in it anymore, and I think it'll be a relief. But we'll need to let him rant about it, I think." He pulled out his phone. "I gotta go. My shift starts soon."

"Okay. I've got an appointment in a bit anyway." They both stood. "Thanks for meeting me."

"Mack says you're going with him on Christmas."

"Yeah. What about you? Any plans?"

Now Jamie's whole face lit up when he smiled. "I'm spending Christmas Eve with Cian's parents and siblings. They're Catholic, but instead of Mass, they'll be coming to Trevor's church for the family service. Then we're gonna go have a late dinner with them. On Christmas Day, we'll be with Cian's partners and the new baby."

Amelia laughed. Jamie was endlessly fascinated by infants, and she never truly understood why. It was beautiful, though, the way he glowed when he talked about them. He liked kids in general, to the point where Amelia wondered why he'd never thought about a job working with them. More power to him; she preferred keeping a bit of distance.

They pulled on their coats, and Jamie took his hat out of his pocket. Amelia grinned. It was red and white candy striped, and he had a matching scarf. Very festive. When he hugged her goodbye, a little of his holiday cheer made magic in her heart, leaving her thinking maybe they'd be okay after all.

Amelia had a late-day appointment with Cadence. At first, they'd met weekly to work on goals. Cadence was a natural with strength training and enjoyed that best, so Amelia coached her on it. Their meetings had grown farther apart as the school year progressed, but she was keeping up and doing well on her own now. Amelia had reduced their sessions to once a month to catch up and set new goals.

They sat in the room with the vending machine afterward, showered, changed, and sipping hot drinks. The only thing they'd done today was a light workout and some stretching. Cadence had said she was tired, so Amelia hadn't pushed. Now that they were relaxed and in chat mode, she was curious about the change in routine.

"Tell me what's new," she said, blowing across her coffee to cool it.

Cadence stirred her cocoa. "Well, I..." She paused, then grinned. "I joined the swim team at school."

"Oh, yeah?"

"I love it! I was nervous at first. But I figure if I can get up on a stage and perform, then I can put on a freaking bathing suit and give it a try. Guess what?"

"What?"

"It's a co-ed team. There are literally kids of every single size. It's a small school, so no one cares that much what you look like as long as you can swim well." Cadence sighed happily. "And that bi—uh, I mean jerk—who was so mean to me? Her parents decided to pull her out and send her to public school anyway. I don't know or care why. I'm just happy to be rid of her finally!"

Amelia laughed along with her. "Well, that's great news. But no wonder you're tired if you just came from swim practice."

"Yep. I mean, I will get back to coming in more regular when the season is over in February if that's okay. I'm pretty worn out after practices every day plus meets."

"No problem. The stretches we did today will be great for keeping yourself from getting stiff or sore." Amelia sat back with her cup and sipped, peering at Cadence. "What else is new?"

"So, you know all that stuff we've been talking about with, like, listening to my body?" Cadence's cheeks turned a brilliant shade of pink. "It's kind of helped with...other things too."

Amelia sat up straighter. "Do tell."

"I like girls," Cadence blurted. "I mean, like-like. Not friends-like. 'Cause I'm, you know, gay and stuff." She covered her face and peered at Amelia, but she was smiling.

"Awesome!" Amelia held out her hand for a fist-bump. "Welcome to Team Sappho."

"'Team Sappho'?" Cadence giggled. "What's that mean?"

"Ladies who like ladies, basically."

Cadence gaped at her. "Wait...you're queer too?"

"Yep, I sure am. Bisexual." Amelia smiled. "Does your family know?"

"Yeah, and, like...okay. So you know how Cian's bi, and my baby sibling Caleigh says they don't have a gender, and Cathleen will tell literally anyone and everyone that she's asexual and aromantic? Well, I feel like I should've figured out this whole gay shi—thing a lot sooner. I mean, Cian says he knew when he was twelve, and Cathleen's only eleven. Caleigh's not even nine! Ugh. I don't know. I just feel...old."

Amelia stifled a laugh. "Everyone goes at their own pace. A lot like what I've been trying to teach you here."

"I know. It's just...a lot of people at school knew about themselves too. It's not like I have no gay friends. Plus, like half my family is super queer! How did I miss it?" She shook her head, her damp curls swaying. "I didn't have any crushes even, not until this year, and not that much."

"Our friend Nate is like that," Amelia said. "He says he would get a crush, so he'd start dating the person and try to do what he called 'typical dating stuff.' But he wouldn't be into it. Not until he met Izzy." She smiled, thinking about them. "Those guys are some serious relationship goals, if you're into that kind of thing."

Cadence sighed dreamily. "Maybe someday I'll meet someone like that." Her mouth turned down. "But maybe it's more thinking about Mom and Dad and if they'll be sad if none of us does the whole 'traditional marriage' thing." She made air quotes.

"Have they said so?"

"No way. Mom was super excited for me, like you were, and Dad was cool too." She shifted in her seat. "Even at my Catholic school it's no big deal. So I don't know what I'm so worried about."

"We take in a lot of bad messages, even if our families love us. Just keep being your awesome self, okay?" Amelia reached over to put her hand on top of Cadence's and gave it a squeeze. "And if you want to talk more, I'm here."

"Cool." Cadence finished her cocoa. "I gotta go. Cian's picking me up so I can have dinner with him and Jamie at their place. Mom and Dad are each taking the others to their stuff tonight, so Cian said I could come over. I can't wait. They promised me card games and movies."

"Sounds great. I'll let you or Cian call me when you're ready for another session."

They stood, and Amelia offered Cadence a hug. They met Cian in the foyer, and Cadence grabbed him in a full-body hug. He laughed and peered around her at Amelia.

"Guess it went well."

"Sure did." Amelia didn't know how else to tell him she appreciated everything he'd done, not just for Cadence but for Jamie. The best she could do was to offer one of the only signs she knew: *thank you.*

He smiled and repeated it back to her, *you're welcome.* Somehow, she thought he understood exactly what she'd meant.

Chapter Seventeen

Mack drove when they went to see his parents. Amelia had considered traveling separately, but she knew deep down that was for the sake of leaving herself an out. She couldn't do that to Mack. He was counting on her to be the strong one this time.

They pulled onto the little patch of gravel that served as a driveway outside the trailer. The string of Christmas lights, wrapped perfectly around the railing, was at odds with what she'd expected. It had been years since she'd been there, and she'd forgotten how obsessed Mack's father was with a tidy home.

Amelia unbuckled, but she continued to sit until Mack looked over at her. He slowly unfastened his own belt and seemingly even more slowly reached for the door handle. He paused.

"It's not gonna be like the last time you were here. Dad's only just gotten home from his surgery, and Mom..."

Amelia put a hand on his arm. "I've got you, okay?" She maintained eye contact until he nodded.

They climbed out of the van, and Amelia reached for Mack's hand on the way. He squeezed her fingers once but let go after that. He'd never told his parents what sort of relationship they had, and Amelia understood that he didn't want to give his parents the impression there was more going on.

Inside, Amelia caught the faint post-operation odors: antiseptic, surgical drains, sweat. Someone had gone to the trouble to keep the trailer clean and the smells to a minimum. There otherwise wasn't any evidence of Mr. Whitman's surgery. The interior was as sparse and tidy as the exterior. There was a small artificial tree strung with blue and white lights. It was decorated with a few ornaments, about half of which looked like Mack had probably made them in school. The rest were ordinary, the matching sort one might find in boxes on the two dollar shelf at Walmart.

A woman Amelia didn't know greeted them in the entryway and took their coats to hang on a rack behind her. She kissed Mack's cheek. "Hello, dear. Your father's on his way out." She turned to Amelia and extended her hand. "I'm Louisa Hedlund, one of the neighbors, in to help out after Rod's surgery."

Amelia shook her hand, too stunned to do anything else. She glanced at Mack, but he didn't seem surprised. At that moment, Mr. Whitman came out, helped by a young man who looked college-age or even still in high school. Amelia wasn't a good judge of ages.

"This is my son Johnny," Louisa told them. "He's home from college for his winter break."

"Hey," Johnny said with a single, small wave.

Amelia looked Mack's father over. He was worn and pale, appearing much older than Amelia remembered from the last time she'd been there. His hair had been thinning then, and now he had a decent-sized bald spot. He'd lost weight too, and his clothes were baggy where they shouldn't have been. Still, he was as warm as always. He held out his hands to take Amelia's between them.

"Hello, Amelia. It's been too long." He smiled, his eyes crinkling at the corners. "I was so glad when Mack said he was bringing you."

"Thank you."

Mr. Whitman turned to Mack. "Merry Christmas, sport."

Mack shifted, and Amelia sensed he was trying to keep himself under control as he carefully hugged his father. "Merry Christmas, Dad." He handed Louisa the loaf of braided holiday bread he'd made that afternoon. "Brought something with us for dinner."

"Excellent," she said. Why don't we go put this in the kitchen?"

Amelia followed the others around the dividing wall, sneaking a peek into the living room on the way past. She assumed the woman sitting in the armchair facing the television was Mack's mom. Amelia couldn't see her face, just her elbows on the armrests.

She hadn't even stirred when they came in. Amelia shivered.

It was warm in the kitchen area, and the small meal Louisa had made smelled delicious. Pork roast with potatoes and homemade gravy and a tossed garden salad. Amelia felt bad that everyone had gone to this much trouble, especially one of the neighbors. She looked to Mack, but he was silently working side by side with Louisa to plate everything up.

Amelia waited until they'd set five plates at the table to pull Mack aside. She whispered, "Isn't your mom going to eat with us?"

Mack tensed, and his expression said it all—they were better off if she didn't and if no one mentioned it again. He did do the courtesy of whispering back, "Dad would usually make her, but Louisa will bring her something later."

The rest of them sat down at the table. At first, the silence, occasionally broken by polite exchanges or the clink of utensils against the plates, was eerie. It was no wonder Mack struggled to find it in him to spend holidays with his parents. He'd told her once that his compromise was being with them on Christmas and telling them he had to work most other holidays. Sometimes he even intentionally traded shifts or signed up for a holiday in order to bolster his lie.

Amelia was able to mostly sit quietly and enjoy her dinner—the roast was really good—while Mack and Louisa did what little talking occurred. In fact, once Louisa decided to talk, she kept the conversation going on her own. It turned out Johnny was studying to be a nurse, and he had an older brother, Jimmy, who'd joined the Air Force. Louisa sounded proud of her sons. She didn't mention a husband or wife, so Amelia assumed she was a single parent.

Mr. Whitman didn't eat the same meal as the others. He was still only tolerating a light diet, so Louisa had made something for him as well. He didn't seem to be interested in it, moving it creatively around his plate. Eventually, he set his fork down. Amelia supposed he wouldn't have been very hungry, although she didn't know what having part of one's stomach removed entailed. At some point, he remembered Amelia was there and turned his attention to her rather than his plate.

"It's been so long since we've seen you," he remarked. "How have you been? What's new for you?"

She set down her napkin and cleared her throat, trying to find something other than one of the subjects she knew wouldn't go over well. That left Jomari, Jamie, most of their friends, and her own father out of the lineup.

"Um...well, I work at Body Balance. The women's gym?" It came out as a question, though Amelia had no idea if Mr. Whitman had ever heard of the local chain.

"Oh! Mm-hm. What do you do there?"

"I'm a personal trainer."

"That's excellent. I'm sure your family is very proud of you."

Either he didn't remember or Mack had never told him anything about her parents. Amelia strained to smile as she said, "I'm sure they are."

Mr. Whitman gave her a puzzled glance, but it passed quickly. "Would either of you like some coffee?"

"No thanks, Dad," Mack said at the same time Amelia said, "Sure."

Mr. Whitman made to get up, and it occurred to Amelia it must've been hard on him to leave all the host duties to Louisa or Johnny. Mack put a hand on his arm to stop him, but Louisa was already up. She rested her hands on Mr. Whitman's shoulders.

"You stay put. I'll get it." She squeezed his shoulder gently and ran her hand along his back as she stepped away.

Amelia tried to catch Mack's eye, but she got Johnny's instead. He shook his head subtly, and she understood. Mack probably had no idea there was anything going on other than a kindly neighbor checking on her friends during a difficult time. She was glad, though, that Mr. Whitman had her, whatever circumstances brought them together.

"So, Amelia," Mr. Whitman began. "How is your family doing?"

Amelia took a swipe at Mack's leg under the table. Apparently, he'd never told anyone. Mack kicked her back, and Amelia relented. What good would it have done, then or now?

"It's just my father, and he's being well cared-for." She opted not to mention exactly where the caring was happening nor exactly what type it was.

"Good, good." He didn't seem to have more to say on the subject, so he focused on Mack. "I should get the gifts while that brews. Then we can take them out to the other room and sit with Mom while she opens hers."

"You'll do no such thing," Louisa said. She tilted her chin at Johnny, who was now standing at the counter and putting food on a divided plastic dish, cafeteria style. "Johnny's fixing a plate for her now, and then we can go to her after we have our coffee."

Louisa served them dessert too, a coconut angel food cake with berry topping. It was nice, and Louisa continued to fill them in on the details of her life—the way she'd been widowed when Johnny was eight and how she'd worked hard to keep the trailer. Amelia caught that Mr. Whitman had been giving her help whenever he could.

"So I'm glad now to be returning the favor." She took Mr. Whitman's hand, and he smiled at her.

Mack's mouth formed a perfect round O. Amelia dug her nails into his thigh, willing him not to reveal that he'd finally caught on. His body went rigid, but then he relaxed. Amelia released her grip.

"Now," Louisa said. "Rod, you mentioned something about presents. Why don't you show Mack and Amelia where they are? I'm sure they'd help you get them while I clean up out here."

Mr. Whitman stood with some difficulty. Amelia moved to one side while Mack went to the other. They helped Mr. Whitman walk down the short hallway and into his bedroom. He sat down on the bed. Mack's shoulders slumped as he breathed out. Amelia put her hand on his back, rubbing slow circles. This whole evening looked like it was exhausting on all sides.

There was a stack of neatly wrapped presents in the corner. Amelia had no doubt Louisa had been responsible for that too. She wondered whether Louisa had done the shopping for them as well. She heard a drawer slide open and glanced over. Mr. Whitman now had a small package in his hands. He stared at it, the silence oozing back into awkward territory.

"Dad?" Mack said, sitting next to him.

Mr. Whitman looked up. He fiddled with the bow on the little box. "I'm sorry I never told you about Louisa," he said.

"Me too." Mack put his hand on his father's arm. "How long?"

Mr. Whitman sighed heavily. "Nine years." He wiped his eyes. "I needed someone who could love me back. You can understand that, right?"

For a second, anger and pain flashed across Mack's face, and Amelia was sure he was going to say something he'd regret. Instead, he ran his hand over his mouth and chin. "I did too, Dad. My whole life."

Mr. Whitman put his hand on top of Mack's. "I know you did, sport. I tried. I really did. I'm sorry I failed you."

"No, Dad. She...she didn't care about either of us." He brushed his own tears away. "You did what you could."

Amelia stood in the doorway, not wanting to intrude on their moment. Side by side, they bore little resemblance, physically, other than both being very lean. Mack looked much more like his mother. But there was something similar in their defeated postures, the way they both carried the weight of their lives on their shoulders.

There were some things Amelia understood, like the way Mack kept a six-foot emotional gap between himself and almost everyone else. She knew it in the same way she never wanted to become her father. The two men in front of her were miles apart in so many ways and yet alike in the way they both tried so hard to protect the ones they loved.

Mr. Whitman stood slowly. "Let's get these to the other room."

Mack and Amelia each took a few. They brought them out with Mr. Whitman shuffling slowly ahead of them. Louisa came from the kitchen to help him into his chair in the living room. Amelia looked to Mack for suggestions where to put them. He pointed to the coffee table, so she carried them over. They sat down on the couch.

Amelia was examining the tags on the gifts while Johnny and Louisa took care of things with Mrs. Whitman. They managed to convince her to turn her chair around, and the television fell mute. Amelia barely managed to hold in her shock. Mrs. Whitman looked like a woman decades older than her actual age must've been. Her hair was almost entirely gray, and she didn't have on any makeup. This was so unlike the person Amelia recalled from the last time she'd been there.

At that time, she'd still been full of life and fun. When she was sober or had only just begun her drinking for the night, she was bubbly and outgoing, fashionable and full of tips about how a woman could look her best. She got less social and more snide the more she drank. Amelia had only ever seen her truly drunk once, and Mack wouldn't let her ever again. She'd blocked the door and screamed at the two of them at the top of her lungs about God's punishment on them for their filth, and it had only been because she'd passed out that they were able to leave.

Now Mrs. Whitman stared at her blankly for a moment and then said, "You look like that girl my kid used to go out with. What was her name?"

"Amelia."

"Yes, that's it. Well, you look like her, except older and more..." She made a curvy-figure with her hands.

Amelia bit back a reply. She wasn't going to antagonize this woman, not today or any other. "That's my name too," she said.

"Oh, is it now. Well, if you know her or my boy, you should tell them to come over more often."

That was as much as she seemed interested in saying. She turned her attention to the gifts on the coffee table, and Amelia sat frozen in her spot. Mack was sitting right next to her, and his own mother didn't know him. Amelia recalled every single instance when his mother had referred to him as a "disappointment" or declared he'd ruined her life because those were the times Mack had escaped to find her. She had once been able to predict with almost uncanny accuracy when Mack would show up at her door. It was lucky for him her father kept strange hours or passed out drunk often enough not to know.

She still resented the way this woman had made Mack's life miserable and how his father hadn't taken him away from her. Instead, he tried to make up for it while still protecting her. Amelia might've been even angrier if Mr. Whitman's affair with Louisa had been while Mack was still at home, but it wasn't.

For the rest of the evening, she endured Mrs. Whitman's odd, blurted remarks and the careful way Mr. Whitman and Louisa moved around each other. At last all the gifts were opened. Mack had a book of musical composition paper, and Amelia had a new pair of earrings. They were pretty as well as being confirmation Louisa had done the shopping.

Mack made the rounds of goodbyes, and Amelia politely said goodnight and waited for him by the door. Johnny offered her a small, sympathetic smile. Louisa came to hand them their coats despite the fact that they could've retrieved them on their own.

She leaned in and said quietly, "I know it's not strictly orthodox. But it works for us. You won't have to worry about your father." She glanced over her shoulder. "Or your mother, for that matter."

"Thank you," Amelia said, knowing Mack meant it but wasn't yet able to say it.

"I'll come by again after New Year's. My band's playing then," Mack said.

"You're a good son." Louisa folded him into a long hug, and Amelia heard them both sniffle.

Mack and Amelia stepped out into the frosty night. All around them, Christmas lights twinkled, and someone was playing the radio loud enough they could hear. Amelia stopped outside the passenger door to listen. When she realized what song it was, she peered through the window to Mack's side of the van, where he was doing the same, his eyebrows raised.

They climbed in, and as soon as the doors were closed, they broke into fits of laughter. The day's tension was broken by the confirmation they'd both heard "Grandma Got Run Over by a Reindeer" coming from the neighbor's trailer.

When they'd calmed down, Mack said, "I guess that was kind of a fitting end for the night."

"Yeah."

"Thanks. For coming with me, I mean."

Amelia shifted so she could face him and leaned in. "Okay?" When he nodded, she kissed him. "Any time you need me, I'm here. Promise."

She sat back in her seat, they buckled up, and without another word about it, they headed for the main road.

New Year's Eve at Grand Slam was packed, as usual. Amelia loved the energy of the bar's First Night celebration. She recalled this was where Andre and Trevor met, and most of her friends had either worked or performed here over the years.

She'd discovered the place right after college. Her hookups during those years had been with people she'd met in women-only bars, but no one she'd stayed with long-term the way she had with Mack. The majority were either only interested in a one-time deal or were put off the minute she mentioned either Mack or her bisexuality. Only one had stuck around for a while, and she'd ended up calling it quits when she met someone else.

In search of a place that might be more open and welcoming to people of all sorts, Amelia had stumbled on Grand Slam when she learned it was owned by someone she vaguely remembered from school. Technically co-owned with his partners, and really, it was Denver who made it feel like home. Rafael was great with the books and the business side, while Denver was the creative genius behind it all. Curtis, their third, was the bouncer.

Amelia now made her way to the bar to say hello—briefly—to Denver and grab a soda. The Creepy Crullers would be on before midnight this time. Denver loved her friends, but she'd booked a different band to ring in the new year. Amelia thought that was probably wise.

"Hey, sweetheart," Denver greeted her. She leaned across the bar for a light kiss. "How you been?"

"Doing okay. Can I get a ginger ale?"

"Anything for you." Denver winked at her, and Amelia laughed.

Denver was what Amelia thought of as classically beautiful. She was tall and lithe, with sleek dark hair and a warm glow in her naturally tan complexion. She had the darkest eyes Amelia had ever seen, so dark her pupils were invisible in the low lighting. She always had flawless makeup, and her clothes were a mix of stylish, professional, and sexy. On reflection, Amelia decided that was an accurate representation of Denver's personality too.

Denver set a glass on the bar in front of Amelia and leaned in. "Is Mack doing okay? He wouldn't talk to me when they were setting up, and Jamie waved me off in favor of hovering like a mother hen."

Amelia sipped her drink while trying to come up with an acceptable response. "He's doing better, I think. Going to meetings seems to help." She shrugged. "Never did a damn thing for my father, but I think he liked his life better when he was drunk and mean." Denver was one of the few people Amelia felt all right saying that to.

"Well, good. About Mack, I mean, not your parental unit."

"He'll talk to you again. He needs time. Jamie took forever before he felt all right around Izzy."

"Speaking of..." Denver switched gears. "They are driving me bananas with all this wedding shit. They asked me to officiate instead of Rafael, seeing as I can and unlike him, I'm also Jewish. But seriously, I'm about to let them have it and tell them I changed my mind. They've been ridiculous about the details. Can't they leave Jagathi to do her freaking job?"

Amelia laughed. "Not if Trevor and Jamie are involved. Those two are the worst. Trevor obsesses about details, and Jamie wants perfection in the style. I have wanted to tell them for ages to let Jamie go first, then give Trevor the specs. But they will not listen."

"Well, whatever. They'd better work it out or I'm telling them to get married somewhere else." She glanced at the people now crowding in at the bar. "I'd better go help Jack and the others. Enjoy your night!"

Amelia carried her glass up to the second level, where most of their friends had congregated to wait for the Crullers. The group was smaller than usual, but she was pleased to see Nia, Marlie, Trevor, and Andre all together. She set her drink on the table and leaned in to offer her friends side hugs.

"Who's got the baby?" she asked Marlie.

"My parents this time." She rolled her eyes. "He's the only reason they tolerate everything else in my life, but at least they're willing to have him."

Nia had a somewhat loopy expression. She said, "It's our first real double date. I'm not counting when those two"—she waved her hand between Trevor and Marlie—"tried to get engaged." She giggled.

"Oh, lordy. How tipsy are you?"

"Too," Nia answered, holding up two fingers. "I mean, one. I only had one!"

Andre nodded. "It's true. She doesn't really drink, and that was potent." He looked sheepish.

"Jeez, guys, get her some water, at least." Amelia grabbed whoever's glass was sitting on the far side of the table.

"Don't!" Trevor exclaimed at the same time Marlie said, "That's not water!"

Amelia stopped and left the glass alone. "Are *any* of these water?"

Andre handed her his glass, and she passed it to Nia with instructions to drink. Fortunately, Nia had the sense to obey. Hopefully the effects would wear off, especially given she hadn't had anything else.

The Crullers were setting up, and that caught Amelia's attention temporarily. When she got bored, she tapped Marlie's arm. "Where's everyone else?"

"Nate and Izzy are coming." She snorted. "Probably literally. I think I interrupted them when I called. Why the hell Nate would answer his phone is beyond me, but whatever."

Amelia laughed. "My guess is to mess with you. And the others?"

"Cian's probably helping them set up."

That made sense. He'd want to be where Jamie was, and it would make it easier to communicate if he waited until Jamie was with him to hang out with the others. Amelia nodded and picked up her ginger ale to take a sip.

She stopped short when Trevor said, "I think your friend...guy...guy-friend?...Jomari was with them too."

Now that definitely didn't make sense. Or it did, but in a way Amelia found grating. He was there to see Mack, of course. Amelia wondered how much he knew about what had happened before Christmas and what role he'd played in Mack's drama. Probably not all that much. To her knowledge, they didn't have quite the same relationship she had with either of them, and Mack might not've been honest about what he'd done or why.

She sighed. Not her problem, but she couldn't help worrying anyway, even though she wasn't sure which one of them she was more concerned about. This whole sort of seeing the same guy was breaking new ground.

They'd never independently shared a partner before. They'd invited someone else into their bedroom a couple times, and not with an ongoing relationship for any of them, just something that had happened spontaneously. Anything else had always felt like a thing that could wreck their friendship, though she couldn't explain why.

Amelia thought about that. Marlie was uncomfortable with the idea of imagining Trevor and Andre together, and she understood now. Marlie and Andre weren't involved, and there was already some low-level tension there. Was it the same thing with Mack and Jomari? Picturing them together...Amelia's belly tightened, and she felt a prickle of desire. Maybe hooking up with the same person gave her permission to entertain the notion. What would it be like to have Jomari between them?

Marlie interrupted Amelia's musing. "You okay?"

"Uh...yeah, sure. Just zoned out for a second there. Oh, look! The band's about to start."

Not that they couldn't talk—the Crullers weren't really worth their undivided attention—but it made a convenient excuse. Marlie looked like she was going to try to continue anyway, but Nate and Izzy showed up and distracted her.

Left alone with her thoughts, Amelia let them flow freely through her mind as the Crullers began their set. Would it even work, being with both of them? She and Mack had a particular style when it came to sex, and it wasn't much like the way she and Jomari were. She wondered if the two of them had yet a third style.

She tried to focus on the song, and when she realized what they were singing about, it didn't help her confused mix of desire and stress. She knew Mack had written it for her, about the intimacy between them. And yet, there he was, with Jomari backstage and not her. Or did she wish Jomari was here by her side, hearing these words while their bodies were pressed in close? It made for a strange tension between what her body wanted and what her heart wanted. Closing her eyes, she pictured both of her partners and let her imagination do the rest of the work. They'd be beautiful together, she thought, though she had no idea how or when to approach it.

That was a conversation for another day, both internally and with the men. She gave herself only until the song finished, and then she resumed conversation with her friends. It was easier than trying to puzzle out her confusion.

CHAPTER EIGHTEEN

AMELIA LAY in bed with Jomari, trying to hold onto the calm she usually felt after good sex. It was difficult; her mind kept wandering to Mack, hoping he was all right. Which only led her to thinking about how she was happy to have Jomari here with her instead of either of them being with Mack. And finally, her brain went right to her mental picture of all three of them together. Guilt crept over her even though she knew she shouldn't allow it, and she was back to worrying about Mack and wondering how much he still blamed her.

He wasn't exactly saying so. He'd admitted to what happened with Sage, and that would've been enough. But then Amelia had seen for herself what was going on with his parents. That was the primary source of her shame. She couldn't shake what it had been like the day they'd spent with them on Christmas. It reminded her she hadn't been there when he needed her. The thought frustrated her because he should've said something, should've told her he needed help.

To kill her worries, she trailed her fingers down the center of Jomari's chest. She loved his body. The human form was endlessly fascinating to her. Carefully, she avoided the looser flesh on his chest; he didn't like being touched there. Instead, she flattened her hand and rubbed slow circles on his belly, delighting in the way it rippled with his sharp inhalation and light laughter.

She paused. "Sorry!"

"No, I like it." He smiled when she peered up at him. "I remember you said you enjoy being tickled."

"I do." She shifted to snuggle in closer. "Mmm. This is nice."

She closed her eyes. He smelled good, like soap and sex and warm skin and some kind of fading fragrance. Cedar and vanilla, she thought, and wondered what sort of cologne it was. He stroked her hair, and she sighed. She wasn't sleepy, but she didn't want to move from the protective cocoon of Jomari's arms, where her worries now faded.

"I got some good news over the holidays," he said.

Amelia shifted so she could see his face better. "Yeah?"

"Grandad promoted me! I'm not an intern anymore. I'm a full employee, with benefits and everything." He grinned.

"No way! That's awesome. Did you start already?"

"Yeah, soon as the shop opened back up after New Year's. And I saw my new doctor, too."

"Want to tell me about it?" Amelia rolled onto her back and felt for Jomari's hand.

He linked their fingers. "I love him. I'm finally back on T, and we talked about some tentative future plans." He squeezed her hand. "I'm still not sure what I want to do, if I want any surgeries, and he reminded me it's all right to take my time."

"He's right." Amelia kissed Jomari's cheek. "I'm really happy for you."

His smile faltered. "I...are you okay with all this?"

She frowned. "Well, it's not really up to me, is it? But if you need me to say it, then yeah, of course I am. Why wouldn't I be?"

He was quiet for a long time. "You've known me like this"—he gestured down himself with his free hand—"since we started seeing each other. Will you be disappointed if it changes?"

"No, not at all. It's your body. That's not what I lo—like about you." She nudged him with her toe, and her heart sped up at her near mistake. Where had that come from?

He raised his eyebrows, but he only said, "Maybe it's not you I'm worried about. I guess I'm...scared."

"Whatever you decide, I'm here. You can always talk to me. Besides, I think it's good to keep communication open." She didn't add that she was burned out from the lack of adult conversation with Mack. They used to talk about everything, but he'd been shutting her out. A pang of jealousy made her shiver when she thought about how he'd turned to Nate and not her when he was hurting and drunk.

"Okay, well, I have a question for you." Jomari broke the spell, and she turned her attention to him.

"Go for it." Anything to get her mind off her troubles.

"I don't think I ever asked how you identify. Like, I know you can't be straight, 'cause you and Denver hook up sometimes. But what do you call yourself?"

"Bisexual," she answered automatically.

"Same. I mean...obviously?"

Amelia snickered. "Right, well, Mack..." She trailed off, cringing. "Sorry."

"Nah, it's fine. What about Mack?"

"He would say he's pansexual. In a practical sense, it's amounted to the same thing. We've both dated people of more than one gender."

"So how did you decide?" Jomari turned onto his side and propped himself on his elbow. Amelia mirrored him.

"I thought I was a lesbian for the longest time. If I'm honest, I still prefer that my casual one-offs be with women. I have an arrangement with Denver for a reason. I'd missed having a woman in my life before she and I started spending time together."

Jomari grinned. "I also thought I was a lesbian. Then I thought I was straight once I knew I was a guy. I don't think T changed me, even though I've heard other guys say they think it did for them. It's more like...I was afraid to look like a straight woman, y'know? So once I felt like I was really *me*, I could let myself enjoy men."

"That makes a lot of sense."

"What made you know you weren't a lesbian?"

"Mack." Amelia swallowed, tamping down the heavy feelings his name brought up. "I'd been saying I was gay at least in part to piss off my father but also because I couldn't imagine ever wanting a man. I was pretty angry back then. When I was fifteen, Mack told me about how he was trying to figure out if he was gay too. He'd thought he was straight until he discovered a guy he was into, and then he wondered if he was gay. I guess he couldn't grasp anything other than those two options. Somehow, talking about it ended with us having sex. It felt right for both of us. We've kind of been doing that ever since."

Jomari was quiet for a bit. "Mack's not really into relationships, is he?"

"No. Or not romantic ones, anyway. For him, it's always been about being a sky's-the-limit kind of person, open to whatever people come into his life. He doesn't spend a lot of time working out his sexuality, just lives in the moment. Not me, though. I'll fight anyone who makes a thing about who I am. I'm out, I'm proud, and I couldn't care less."

Jomari warmed her belly with his laughter again. "Same, but maybe I'm a little less fierce than you?" He put his hand over his face for a moment before peeking out at Amelia. "I babbled about it all over Mack the first time we—" He cut himself off. "I'm sorry."

Amelia sighed. "We shouldn't be afraid to discuss someone we've both fucked. I know it's weird right now, but we can't pretend none of it happened." She shrugged her exposed shoulder. "It's nice to have someone else I can talk to about him. Was it...was it good, that first time?"

"Yeah," Jomari confirmed. "Sex with him is like...like when you're out at a restaurant, and you're eating something so delicious you just have to share it, y'know? He gets so into it, but he's going, 'Oh, my god, this is amazing, you've got to try it.' And then he makes you feel as if the whole world is yours."

"That's it!" Amelia's heart ached with how much she missed being with Mack, even though she knew she was doing the right thing. "That's it exactly."

Jomari ran his hand down her arm. "Mack always makes sure I'm comfortable with what we're doing. But he doesn't make a thing out of it, y'know? You don't either."

"What do you mean?"

"It's the difference between 'I don't know yet what you enjoy' and 'I don't know what trans guys like.' I can't say it any better than that." He chuckled. "Back when I was testing stuff out and hooking up more than I do now, I was with this one guy. It was...kind of blah. The worst part, though, was when I got up to get us some water and came back to find him on his phone, texting some other dude. I was behind him, so he had no idea I could read it when he said he'd just done it with a trans guy and wanted to know if he'd leveled up now."

"Oh, geez!" Amelia stifled her laughter. "That's awful."

"It was definitely not amusing in the moment, but his reaction when he saw I'd seen it was priceless. Especially after I told him he wasn't that good."

"He wasn't a skinny blond dude who works at Starbucks, by

any chance?"

Jomari's expression turned bewildered. "Yeah, actually. Why?"

Amelia turned her face into her pillow to muffle her laughter. "Oh, god. That guy gets around."

Jomari shoved on her shoulder, and she pushed back. They wrestled playfully, laughing until he drew her into a long, heated kiss. Amelia lost herself in it, carried away from every other thought. She didn't hesitate to say yes when Jomari asked if she wanted to make love again.

Cian's band hadn't managed to find a permanent flute player. Amelia didn't mind, though it was a stretch learning a completely different style. She didn't play on every piece, with different songs calling for different instrumentation, which meant she had the opportunity to listen and learn. Not being of Irish heritage herself— that she knew of—it was all new to her.

The first time she'd gone to a rehearsal, it had been a mess. The mandolin player, who also had working knowledge of several other instruments, took pity on her. He sent her to a list of websites with tips on playing Irish trad. It had been more helpful than Amelia had anticipated, but she'd always been relatively quick to pick things up once she had an idea what she needed.

They were in the Dyer Theatre, where they now rehearsed. Typically, they met while Cian was still running one of his dance classes. Once he was finished, he and the other dancers joined them to put the pieces together. Jamie had said he occasionally played, but that seemed only to be when they were using a more contemporary style and needed him. Amelia didn't tend to play those because they called for a more rock style.

The musicians ran through the songs Jomari had sent them. No vocalist on this set either, apparently. There were extensive notes, mostly Cian's and a few of Jomari's, on the characteristics of the dances and how they should be played. Cian always had a vision, and he liked to create a story with his dances. These ranged from fairy tales and legends to modern social causes. Not always, but sometimes he incorporated sign right into the dance. Other times, he had an interpreter. There was always one when they had a vocalist, but on occasion, he had storytellers now as well.

Most of the time, they performed in their regular slot at Grand Slam once a month. When the weather turned warm, they would begin playing some outdoor festivals around the area as well. This time, they were upping the ante a bit. The Dyer Theatre's general manager wanted to capitalize on their popularity as well as Cian's growing dance studio. Right after Nate and Izzy's wedding, they would be playing to a bigger crowd right on this stage.

The other musicians poured their hearts into rehearsal and then took a break to wait for Cian to descend from the upper level where the classrooms were. Amelia hopped down from the stage and parked herself in the middle of the auditorium seats to check her phone for messages. While she scrolled through half a dozen, Jomari slid into the row and sat next to her. She tucked her phone away.

"Hey," she said.

"How are you doing? I know this time we had a lot more to cover."

"Okay. I still feel like I'm not fitting in yet." She shook her head. "I guess I expected you'd find someone else."

"Nah," Jomari said. "Cian likes you. He thinks you bring something fresh."

"Maybe it's the fact that I'm approximately zero percent Irish?"

He laughed. "Hey, you never know, right?"

"True. I don't really know for sure. It's not like that was a big conversation I had with my parents."

She barely remembered her mother, who took off when she was little. Her father wasn't coherent or in a good enough mood to ever ask him. At some point, going through old stuff in her father's apartment, she'd found some names of dead relatives and gone on a fairly fruitless search. It didn't matter to her except for now, when she used it as an excuse for feeling out of place.

"My ethnic heritage was all I ever heard about growing up." Jomari rolled his eyes, but he smiled. "Two pretty different cultures, but that only made life more interesting."

Amelia caught the flash of his silver crucifix. Distracted, she pointed to it and said, "Oh, you found it."

Jomari laughed, but he turned it into a cough. "Mack had it. I, uh, left it there the first time we...yeah."

"So, you're Catholic, then?" Amelia asked. "Or do you wear it as jewelry? I never asked."

"Well, in a sense, you're never really not Catholic exactly," Jomari replied. "It's cultural. For me, on both sides of my family."

"Huh. Our friend Nate said that too." Amelia giggled. "And now he's converting to Judaism."

Jomari laughed again, for real this time, the sound warm and sweet like spring. "That's one way to let it go, I suppose. I really am a practicing Catholic, though."

"How? I mean...um..." Amelia flushed. She didn't grow up with any religion or particularly understand it.

"Explaining the whole thing could take a while. The short version is that our church isn't recognized by the Vatican. It happens more often than you'd think. You do enough things wrong—say, serving Holy Eucharist to non-Catholics or disagreeing with the Church's position publicly—and they don't want you, not even your money. There are a growing number of congregations that won't tolerate the abuses and go rogue."

"Wow. So that's what happened to yours?"

"Yes. It's a long story, which I'll tell you when we have more than five minutes. It's at least partly my family's doing from back when I was in Catholic school."

Amelia gaped at him. "Seriously?"

"Yep. Cian's siblings go to the same school now, and it's way different these days."

"Oh, huh. I didn't know that."

They were being summoned up on stage again, so Jomari stood and offered Amelia a hand. She took it, and he didn't let go right away as they made their way up the aisle. The warm pressure of his fingers threaded with hers gave her comfort and a tiny, unexpected thrill. She looked to where they were joined. It looked and felt right in a way she hadn't experienced perhaps ever.

Too soon, he withdrew his hand. She made to ascend the stage steps, but Jomari's hand on her arm stopped her.

"Um, I was wondering," he said. "Did you want to maybe go-out-with-me-this-weekend?" He spoke so fast she almost missed it.

Her heart sped up. Did she want a real date with him? Not a bite to eat in the cafe as a precursor to sex? Or just plain meeting up for sex? That was a very, very good question. She hesitated but saw she'd waited a fraction of a second too long as Jomari's hopeful expression began to slide into disappointment. He withdrew, backing up a pace.

"Wait," Amelia said. "I'd love to."

His happy grin would be etched into her memory forever, and it gave her energy that carried her all the way through the rest of rehearsal.

CHAPTER NINETEEN

BEFORE THEIR date—which Jomari had said was a surprise but that she should dress warmly—Amelia did a lot of thinking. She had to talk to him about Mack. Not about the fact that they'd both spent the better part of the previous nearly six months partnering up in different configurations. Everyone knew, and no one had much of a problem with their arrangement.

It was other things, like Mack's ongoing struggle with his sobriety. She had talked to him, and seen him, since Christmas, and she had the sense he wasn't back to drinking. She hoped she would know about it if he were, but he'd hidden too much from her lately to be sure. Whether Jomari knew about any of it or not, she had to encourage them to talk to each other before someone, most likely Jomari, got hurt.

Mack had said he wanted to tell Jomari the truth on his own terms, and Amelia respected his wishes. Not much of anything stayed secret in their friend group these days, so Jomari might already have some idea. She wasn't going to take that risk. She didn't want to betray Mack's trust, but she did hope there was an opening in which she could encourage Jomari to speak with him.

They met up near Jomari's house, at a small outdoor ice rink. No wonder he'd told her to dress warmly. Jomari paid the entry and rental fees, and they sat in the small building to lace up. He led her out onto the ice, and they looped around the rink lazily, dodging giggly teenagers and toddlers having their first go at skating.

Properly warmed up, Amelia wanted to skate faster. It had been a while since she'd been on the ice, but she felt prepared. With a wink, she looked back at Jomari and said, "Think you can keep up?"

"Oh, it is on!"

They chased each other around, gaining a following of fellow skaters until they had a whole line. Music pumped through the speakers, some easy listening station playing pop songs from Amelia's childhood. For a couple minutes, she lost track of Jomari among the group of people who had joined their race.

She glanced behind her, but she didn't see him. Facing forward again, she nearly jumped out of her skin when he appeared right in front of her. He laughed and grabbed her hand, twirling her around and away from the other skaters toward the edge of the rink. She plunked onto the raised edge, sitting down with a thump. Jomari came to a stop and sat beside her.

Once she'd caught her breath, she laughed. "Cheater."

He grinned in the same cheeky way she always loved. "Maybe. But I still caught you!"

"Fair enough."

"Want some cocoa?"

She nodded, and they made their way to the tables by the rink. He brought them both steaming cups a few minutes later and set Amelia's in front of her before dropping into the seat across from her. She pulled the lid off her cup and blew on the hot liquid. It smelled wonderful.

"They had flavors," he explained. "That one is caramel, but if you like the mint better, that's what I got."

"No, this is good."

They sat quietly for a bit, watching the other skaters. Stars popped out in the clear sky as it darkened from purple to deep blue. Amelia shivered from the sweat drying under her layers.

Jomari's hand on hers startled her. "You've looked since we got here like you have something on your mind."

Amelia popped the lid back on her cup and sighed. "I don't want to ruin our date talking about heavy stuff."

"Hey," Jomari said. "It's okay. You've listened to me about a whole bunch of my stuff. Let me do the same?"

She nodded. "Okay. I...I can't say a whole lot because I think it's his place to tell you. But there's some things going on with

Mack, and it's maybe more than I can manage on my own." She swallowed around the lump that had formed in her throat. "Talk to him, please? I'm going on my trip in a couple weeks, and I won't be around to distract either of you."

"This sounds big." Jomari squeezed her hand.

"Are you sure it's okay that I discuss him with you? I feel like I'm..." She trailed off, and a tear slid down her cheek. Brushing it away, she continued. "Like I'm somehow messing things up with both of you if I do."

"No," Jomari answered. "It's like you told me before. We should be able to do this, be honest about someone we've both been with."

"All right. Well, I'm worried about him and his family, and that's everything I can say right now. Mostly because he should've told you, but also because I'm maybe a bit upset with him for how much he's been keeping from all of us."

"I'll see what I can do. No promises, but I'll do my best." Jomari sipped his cocoa, looking thoughtful. "How did you and Mack meet? You said you knew him in high school, but it seems like there's a story there."

Amelia didn't answer right away. She didn't know how soon it was appropriate to tell Jomari the truth about her own family, let alone Mack's. Eventually, she settled on saying, "We went to school together from the time we were little."

It didn't fool him. "You took a pretty long time to answer that," he remarked. "That doesn't seem like something you'd have to think real hard about. I mean, you don't have to tell me, but I'm curious."

Drawing in a deep breath, Amelia braced herself. "Our parents were—are—all alcoholics. Mine, Mack's, and Sage's."

"Sage," Jomari said slowly. "Why do I know that name?"

"Jamie's ex. You know, the jerk." She didn't even hide the bitterness in her tone now.

"Oh, him." The muscle in his jaw twitched, but he didn't say anything else. He didn't need to.

"In seventh grade, the school counselor got this brilliant idea we should all be in a group together to 'work through our issues.' They tried to sell us on it being a social skills thing. We figured out the truth pretty fast. The whole point of the group was that we'd been labeled as at-risk by our teachers."

"Wow. That sounds harsh."

"In some ways, yeah. Nobody considered whether they ought to do something about our home situations, really. None of us fit the mold of the sad, lonely kid with horrible parents. As if anyone except kids on TV ever does. There were two other kids in the group, another girl and a boy, and it was the same story for all of us. I was popular but starting fights all the time. The other girl's parents were broke constantly, and she was selling her body so they could eat. Mack was struggling in a lot of ways by the time we were in high school. I don't remember about the last kid, but Sage..." She paused. "He was very charismatic and persuasive. It caused all of us trouble." That was as much as she could say at the moment without breaking Mack's trust about his mother or Sage's hand in pushing all of them over the edge.

Amelia didn't look at Jomari, but she heard him shift. She didn't know whether what she'd said made him uncomfortable. It wasn't that she didn't want to talk about it. More like she didn't know how. Those years were a strange time in her life, full of figuring things out. She'd blamed her father—and his beatings—for a lot of things, but she wasn't sure he deserved all of them.

"Did it work, this group?" Jomari's hesitant question snapped her back to the present.

"Yes and no." Amelia sighed. She knew he was really asking because he wanted to know about Mack and what it meant for his current problems, but she wasn't going to cave. "I can't tell you more about Mack because I think he should give you details. For me? I put my energy into learning how to fight my abusive father instead of my classmates."

"So that's how you became a personal trainer."

"Sort of, yeah." She wasn't ready to tell Jomari about breaking her father's nose. "I joined the soccer team and got into working out. Got me a full ride to college and my dream job, at least for now. Anyway, I don't know what happened to the last two kids from our group. I haven't seen them since the end of middle school."

"Funny that three of you turned out to be queer," Jomari remarked.

"Yeah. I thought for a long time maybe my father's minister was right and it could be caused by having shitty parents. I also thought that's why my father acted how he did."

"Oh?" Jomari's eyebrows rose.

"My father..." She took a deep breath and let it out bit by bit.

"He was a former boxer, and let's just say he had a well-practiced right cross. I hated even the thought of dating guys because of him, even though I was secretly fascinated by them. I only told a few friends at school. Telling my father I was a lesbian was one of the few times he didn't beat me. He asked if I was doing it for attention, to get guys turned on. Instead of using me as a punching bag, he put a lock on my door so I couldn't sneak boys in." She snorted. "Mack kept it a secret from everyone but me that he'd been messing around with a boy, someone a few years older. Sage was completely open. He flaunted it because his parents were such assholes, and he wanted their attention. Even bringing his boyfriends on their precious boat didn't make them take notice."

There was a long silence, during which they finished their drinks. Jomari didn't seem like he was upset or angry or avoiding the conversation. It was more like he was contemplating the best reply.

"I'm sorry," he finally said. "For all of that."

"Thank you," Amelia replied. She put her hand on his. "For listening."

"Any time." He stood, wobbling a little on the ice skate's blades. Amelia was grateful that he broke the tension by saying, "Want to skate some more? We have another half hour."

"Definitely."

She let him pull her to her feet. They threw away their cups and stepped carefully back out onto the ice. The sky was fully dark and had clouded over. A few fat snowflakes began to fall, and Ed Sheeran's "Thinking Out Loud" was playing over the speakers. Hand in hand, Amelia and Jomari circled the ice. The crowd had thinned, giving them room to make wider arcs.

As the song finished, Jomari pulled to a stop and faced Amelia. They stood on the ice, the light snow swirling around them. Jomari took the ends of her scarf and tugged her closer until she almost fell against him. They both laughed. Amelia looked up, lost for a moment in his beautiful, dark eyes, captivated by the mischievous sparkle. He was still grinning, but there was something else there too, an intensity she hadn't noticed before. He leaned in, and she realized he was going to kiss her.

They'd kissed before; they'd been in bed together before. So why was her heart galloping, her palms sweating, and heat rushing to her cold cheeks? What could possibly be more special about this than any of the previous times?

When their lips met at last, it was pure magic. And that's when she knew what was different. This kiss broke all her carefully indexed rules. Six months ago, her life was organized—coded, stacked, and filed in tidy bins. There was Mack and work and the occasional good-time-had-by-all with casual dating and a hook-up here and there. Jomari razed her orderly system with a single fit of his mouth to hers against a backdrop of skating and fresh snow. It was like a scene out of one of those sugary rom-coms Jamie was so fond of.

She ended the kiss first. Though her pulse still throbbed in her ears, she tried to stay calm as she backed away. She had to get back to the playfulness of their earlier romp, when her only worry was keeping just ahead of Jomari on the ice. It was her fault anyway, for letting him catch her, in more ways than one.

Jomari cupped her cheek, smiling. Amelia made her best effort to smile back in spite of her mad storm of emotions, all the things she'd tried so hard to keep in check over the last few months. She'd been afraid Mack would hurt Jomari, and now she was the one putting his heart at risk. She breathed slowly until she relaxed then turned her face to brush her lips against his palm.

He dropped his hand and said, "Ready to go?"

"Okay."

"Did you want to—"

Amelia did want to. But she knew this time it would be a bad idea. She had to clear her head, to think about what this meant and what she wanted. "I...can't," she said.

"Oh." Jomari's face fell. Amelia didn't think it was about denying him a place in her bed, not this time.

She put her hand on his arm. "I'm sorry. I need a little time, okay? This was wonderful. But...can we slow down a bit?"

"Of course." Jomari's voice was flat, disappointed. He sighed. "I'm sorry. Take all the time you need, okay? I'm here."

Amelia closed her eyes and nodded. She didn't know if she'd ever be ready for what she sensed he was offering. He took her hand again, and she opened her eyes. They made their way off the ice and back to the building to return their skates. Somehow, it seemed fitting that the song now playing was about heartbreak.

To avoid dealing with any of the muddled mess in her heart, Amelia called Denver a few days after her date with Jomari. She needed to be with a woman not to erase anything but to reassert control over herself. Denver was usually more than happy to meet up, and she didn't disappoint this time either.

She wasn't working, so she stopped by Amelia's apartment. As soon as she was inside, there wasn't much question what they'd be up to. They hastily made their way to the bedroom, shedding every last stitch of clothes and stretching out on the bed together. Denver reached into the drawer where she knew Amelia kept all her toys then lay on her back and smiled up seductively as she handed a vibrator over.

Amelia kissed her, a hard press of their lips. She put out the tip of her tongue to trace the thin ring in Denver's lower lip. Amelia loved it—so sexy. Denver was gorgeous: the spread of her legs and the way her firm, small breasts pushed out when she arched her back. The soft sighs and whisper-moans coming from her mouth reminded Amelia why she'd needed this break from the men.

Denver didn't like having her genitals directly stimulated, so she'd long since taught Amelia the finer arts of muffing. Her fingers were warm and soft where they rested against the back of Amelia's hand. Together, they worked the vibrator, pushing it into the inguinal canal. Amelia enjoyed using her thumbs, too, the way Denver's heated skin felt around them, but this was good as well.

"Oh—oh, God—I'm coming," Denver gasped.

Amelia lowered her mouth to suck gently on Denver's pulse point in her neck just as she came, shuddering and letting out a long, shaking breath. She relaxed against the pillows, sliding her legs down straight. Amelia ran her hands over Denver's curves. After an intense orgasm, she always liked some gentle massage, especially on her belly and thighs. Amelia was happy to oblige.

After several minutes, Denver laughed softly. "That was just what I needed." She rolled onto her side and put her thumb against Amelia's nipple. "You want me to go down on you?"

"Nah, not tonight. Just your hand, please?" When Denver slid her fingers between Amelia's legs, they both sighed, and Amelia said, "Yeah. Like that. The guys try, but they don't quite get the angle and pressure the way you do." She grunted as Denver's motion sent a ripple of need through her.

Denver chuckled. "I feel you on that, sweetie."

Her expert fingers moved with exactly the right rhythm. The whole time, she pressed hot kisses all over Amelia's neck and shoulders. She flicked her tongue against Amelia's nipple, and that did it. Amelia let go, her head back and her hips pushing forward, seeking a last bit of friction as she came, breathing hard. She was quieter than Denver, but she didn't feel any need to make noise. Denver wouldn't expect it. With each other, they could do things differently than with their other partners.

Afterward, they lay holding each other. Denver rested her head on Amelia's chest, and Amelia stroked her hair. They were in a similar boat, though Denver and both her male lovers were in a romantic triad. She had a different relationship with them than Amelia had with Mack. The small voice in the back of Amelia's head suggested she might think more about what she was doing with Jomari, but she silenced it the same way she had for the last several days.

She and Denver were so comfortable with each other that anyone might've thought they were a couple or that they'd been doing this for more than a single year. But Denver was no more Amelia's girlfriend than Mack was her boyfriend. In a similar way, this was an outgrowth of their friendship and mutual need for a woman's touch.

"Mmm, that's nice," Denver said, her voice slow and sleepy. "I don't get this so much with the guys."

"Me neither."

Denver snorted. "I didn't picture Mack as the cuddly type."

Amelia laughed. "He's not, but Jomari is. It's not the same, though."

She realized her mistake the minute Denver shifted to sit up. "Jomari? Hot fiddler Jomari, from Cian's band? What the fuck, lady? Spill it!" Denver gave Amelia a playful shove.

"Yes, yes, and I'm sorry I didn't say anything." Amelia pushed herself up and sat back against the pillows. "I don't know what's going on at this point. We've kind of been seeing each other, mostly having sex, but..."

"Oh, my God. Sweetie, that's amazing! He's such a honey. And hot-t-t!" She drew out the word. "So what's the problem?"

Amelia's cheeks burned. "He's also fucking Mack."

Denver's jaw dropped. It took several tries, opening and closing her mouth, before she finally said, "Well, that's a new one."

"I know! We've never been into the same person before. Mack's made it clear they're not romantically involved, and I think he expects the same from me. I mean, I've never—" She cut herself off. She and Mack had very different reasons for not wanting long-term relationships. Jomari hadn't made Mack question anything because it was how he was wired. Amelia had always told herself it was good enough for her. Being with Jomari had made her rethink everything, and she didn't know how to communicate it to Denver.

"You're really into him," Denver remarked, sounding surprised. "How'd that happen?"

"I don't know," Amelia admitted. "Last weekend, he took me skating in the park, and...he kissed me. Not a 'you're hot, let's do it' kind of kiss. More like..." She trailed off, not yet willing to tell Denver it was a falling-in-love kind of kiss.

Denver's delighted laughter shook the bed. "Oh, my dear. You really are in deep, aren't you?"

"No! I mean...maybe?" Amelia threw an arm over her eyes. "I don't want to go there."

Denver rolled to partially lie on top of Amelia. She gently moved her arm and leaned in to kiss her cheek. "Dollface, you are a beautiful, smart, wonderful woman. You deserve someone like him."

"What about Mack?"

"What about him? You're not his keeper. Don't use him as a wall here."

"Well, then, what about you?"

Denver laughed. "Hon, you know I like doing this with you. But for the love of all things sexy, please don't make me a reason to avoid something so wonderful."

"I need time."

"Of course you do. You're going away soon with Marlie and Nia, right?" When Amelia confirmed, Denver said, "Then use that time wisely. Your friends have your back, and so do I." She giggled and reached underneath Amelia to tweak her back, making Amelia jump a little and snort out a laugh. "Figure out what you want. I'd hate to give this up, and I'm betting Mack would be sorry to lose you too. But we'll deal if you and Jomari want to be exclusive."

Amelia shook her head. "I don't even know if he wants that, and I don't think I do. I'm just not wired that way." She ran a hand down Denver's arm. "I don't know yet what it means for us."

"Then do the hard work of dealing with it, sweetie. We all deserve that, including you." She booped Amelia's nose.

"Yeah." Amelia stroked Denver's glossy hair. "Thanks. You always know how to set me straight."

"Doll, there is not a thing 'straight' about either of us." She leaned down and offered another smoldering kiss. "Food and round two?"

"You got it."

They rose naked from the bed and went to raid the fridge. Denver was right, but Amelia's stomach knotted. Everything felt out of control. She hoped her vacation would give her the chance to find order in the chaos, but she had a bad feeling she might get exactly the reverse.

PART FOUR: VARIATION III – JOMARI

CHAPTER TWENTY

IF THERE was one thing Jomari loved, it was his jobs. He'd always enjoyed playing his violin, from the time he was wee, as Grandad put it. The first time he'd held one, he was three years old. It was itty bitty, brand new and polished until the amber wood shone. Grandad had placed it under his chin and curled his hand around the fingerboard so he felt the cool metal of the strings. It was his earliest memory, and he didn't recall much other than the delight it gave him.

Grandad had started him off learning folk melodies, both American and Irish. The only trouble with that was arriving at school, feeling confident he "knew how to play," and having to re-learn in the classical style taught at his elementary school. Still, he was a quick learner and didn't struggle much. He adapted just fine to switching back and forth depending on where he was playing. He supposed it was a little bit like Mee's bilingual upbringing or his own bicultural identity.

Playing the violin—or the fiddle—brought Jomari through a lot of difficult years. It was less an escape than an oxygen mask. Even now, when he needed room to breathe, he could clear his head with a bit of practice time. The weight of the instrument, the bite of the strings under the pads of his fingers, the motion of the bow, and the high, clear notes all served to relax and open his mind.

Because Jomari was still staying with his family, he didn't need to worry about places to play. No one there minded if he shut himself away in the music room, and no one complained about how long he was in there. As much as he wanted to be out on his own already, he did appreciate the finer points of still living in a house instead of an apartment as well as a remarkably understanding family. Besides, it was already a multigenerational household, with Grandad living there now Grandma was gone.

Jomari took out two sets of music. One was for the orchestra, their repertoire for an upcoming concert. The other was printouts of the music Cian had sent. Currently, both of them made him feel awkward and uncomfortable, which was an unusual state of being. He scowled at the music, tempted to ditch both and play something out of the childhood music books still lined up on the shelf.

Amelia had gone for an extended vacation in England. Something about her friend Marlie having family there. Well, that was just fine for her, but she'd left Jomari hanging. She'd told him something was going on with Mack and to talk to him, but then she'd also backed away from seeing Jomari too.

On their last real date—Jomari did think of it that way, even if he wasn't sure Amelia did anymore—they'd shared this incredible kiss. A toe-curling, make-your-heart-race, explosion of joy like nothing he'd ever felt before. He'd loved many people over the years. With each new relationship, he always felt optimistic, a spark of hope that this might be someone he could stay with. It hadn't worked out that way so far, but his philosophy was that dating was a lot like learning a concerto. Nothing happens overnight, and it takes a lot of mistakes before hitting the right notes.

When he and Amelia had first started spending time together, he'd liked her. She was gorgeous, smart, and fun, not to mention enthusiastic in bed. Since she seemed at the time only interested in something casual, he'd thought of their time together as a placeholder of sorts. It hadn't occurred to him it could be anything else until now. Taking her on a real date had been a tuning note, a way to check if their relationship had the right pitch. Once they kissed on the ice, that was it. He was sure.

Only she didn't seem to be. The moment had been lost in her need for more time. So there she was, finding herself on a trip across the ocean, while Jomari waited for her answer. The most heartbreaking part was if her answer was no, that would be it. He couldn't ask her for more.

Which brought him to his practice. Both sets of music were intimately bound in his love for Amelia. They played together in both places, and he didn't know if he could bear to see her at every rehearsal and know whatever had been between them was gone. He didn't even care that he was being melodramatic. She'd asked for time, not for him to go away forever. The waiting was just so damn hard.

He sighed and tucked his violin under his chin. No rehearsal music today. He went to the bookshelf after all, but he didn't take one of the simple books. Instead, he pulled out Bloch's Sonata No. 1. He'd used it for an audition once, and now he needed the agitated melody to purge the distress inside him. He took a deep breath and began to play, letting his worries melt into the music.

The weekend arrived, warmer enough for an icy drizzle instead of snow. Jomari was more than happy to borrow Da's car rather than take public transit, even though he hated driving through the city. He parked behind the Dyer Theatre and dashed inside, chilled from the frozen droplets pelting his head.

The heavy doors closed behind Jomari, and he was enveloped in an almost painful silence. The opera company that normally rehearsed there was off for the next month, which made sense, seeing as one of their co-directors was getting married. Since they weren't preparing a show, this meant no one but the clerk at the ticket booth and the custodial staff were in the building.

Jomari loved it when they had the place to themselves. It meant Cian's company could rehearse in the auditorium instead of in one of the practice rooms or the smaller recital hall. A lot of groups used the stage, from the small LGBTQ opera company to the orchestra. The scheduling coordinator had her hands full keeping everyone happy.

Shaking the water out of his hair, Jomari tugged on the auditorium door and slipped inside. The theater as a whole was a little stuffy, and it couldn't decide whether to be too hot or too cold. Any given practice session might mean some of both. Today, it felt like someone had cranked the heater to full blast, and Jomari was glad he'd worn layers. He was down to his T-shirt before he had his instrument out. He wondered how the dancers would fare in these conditions and hoped that it was miraculously cooler on stage.

Jomari tuned his violin and experimented with a bit of improvisation as a warm-up before ascending the steps to the stage. The other musicians were in the process of tuning. They had an occasional vocalist, Einin, and she was there that day. She was part of a small Gaelic pop group that had some local success. Jomari had no idea where Cian knew her from.

Einin had one of those high, melodic voices. Cian liked having her because she could sing in both English and Irish. Not that he cared all that much for himself, but audiences loved it. She had chosen the song they were currently working on, a folk song several popular bands had covered. Typical Cian, wanting others to have a say. Jomari—and most of the others—still thought of him as being "in charge" no matter how many times he tried to tell them he wasn't. Their music and dance troupe was his baby, after all, even though he tried hard to make things equitable.

On stage, Jomari spotted Jamie and acknowledged him with a wave, earning a shy smile in return. He now seemed to be a regular fixture with the band. In the past, Cian had occasionally brought him along to watch them rehearse. Jomari was okay with this in theory, though he did like to rib Cian for it. Now that they had use of the theater instead of a cramped dance studio room, it wasn't a big deal if someone had a guest. Today, Jamie was actually part of the band. They'd needed a drummer in a pinch a few months ago, and however he'd done it, Cian had persuaded Jamie to join their fun. He hadn't given up on them yet, which was a good sign.

As soon as they were ready, they began. The song Einin had chosen was lighter and sweeter than Cian usually went for, with a very pop music feel. But he was giving some of the other dancers the spotlight on this one, so it made sense. The song was beautiful, sung first in Irish and then in English.

Jomari started them out in a light duet with the penny whistle player, trying hard not to miss Amelia. He focused only on the music, becoming absorbed in the song as they practiced. Out of the corner of his eye, he caught Jamie and almost did a double take. Jamie joined in on the bodhrán instead of snare or the couple other percussive instruments he usually used. He wasn't doing anything complex, but he was giving them a good, steady rhythm and was focused on what he was doing. Jomari tore his gaze away and concentrated on the song.

When they finished the whole piece, Cian motioned for their attention. He didn't have his hearing aids in, so he signed while one of the other dancers explained what he'd said. He wanted to go over specific transitions. When he was through giving the list, he went to the white board he'd wheeled in and wrote down the spots to work on with his own shorthand for the steps.

They returned to work, going over those spots and then finally running the entire song again. Jomari stole another glance at Jamie during a part where the fiddle dropped out. Einin had switched to singing in English, and a slow blush crept over Jamie's cheeks even while he kept the beat. Jomari tuned into the words, which he hadn't done the first time through, and he almost choked. They were a little naughty with a bit of longing.

He wondered if Cian had read through the lyrics. He must have, in order to choreograph it properly. Jomari glanced over at him, and sure enough, he was watching Jamie with a cheeky smile. Even knowing it was likely to distract him, Cian signed something to him that made Jamie's entire face red. He only faltered for a beat or two, recovering as he gave Cian a clearly amused scowl. The whole scene left Jomari somewhere between exasperated, entertained, and wistful, much like the song he was now almost forgetting to come back in on.

When they were through, Cian made his way over to Jamie. Jomari knew quite a bit of ASL at this point—hard not to with Cian around—so he understood when Cian thanked Jamie and arranged a place to meet after he'd changed out of his dance clothes. With a quick peck on Jamie's cheek, Cian disappeared into the wings.

Jomari returned to the seats to put his violin away. The hesitant tap on his shoulder startled him, and he turned to face Jamie. "Oh, hey."

"Hey."

"What'd you think?" Jomari asked. "You were doing a hell of a job on that bodhrán. Where'd you learn it?"

"YouTube." Jamie grinned.

Jomari laughed. "Seriously?"

"No," Jamie admitted. "Just messing with you. I took some lessons from a friend of Einin's. She's an amazing player. I think at least fifty percent of our time was spent on her explaining the different kinds of sticks and what makes a good drum. But at least I learned the basics, and she'll give me another few lessons if I want."

"Do you? Want to, I mean."

Jamie flopped into a seat next to Jomari's violin case. "Yeah, I do. You know the Creepy Crullers broke up, right?"

Once Jomari had latched his case, he slid his violin over and sat next to Jamie. "I'd heard, but I didn't know it was official."

"First Night was our last gig." Jamie shrugged. "It's okay. I'm ready to move on. I like doing other stuff better these days."

"Helps to have your hot boyfriend in the dance troupe." Jomari elbowed him.

"That too."

"Speaking of all that..." Jomari drew his lip between his teeth, wondering how to bring it up. He finally decided to simply go for it. "How's Mack?"

"You sure don't waste any time," Jamie muttered, but then he relented with a sigh. "You need to talk to him yourself. He's in rough shape right now."

"Yeah, I know. I tried calling him and texting him and even freaking emailing him—who the hell does that anymore?—and he won't answer me."

Jamie didn't respond right away. He looked up at the stage, where Einin and the penny whistle player were talking. Finally he said, "Maybe he doesn't see you the same way he sees us."

"What's that supposed to mean?" Jomari demanded.

"Have you two ever just hung out, like friends do?"

Oh. That was what he'd meant. "Um...no, not that I recall."

"Okay. Then why do you want to see him now?"

Well, there was the million-dollar question. Jomari knew he was clinging to Mack out of the emptiness of missing Amelia, but he certainly wasn't going to tell Jamie that. "Amelia said something was going on with him, and she thinks I should talk to him. Except I can't because he won't answer me."

"Maybe he thinks all you want from him is sex, and he can't give you—or anyone—that right now."

"I didn't think he wanted more of a relationship than that. Amelia said—"

Jamie huffed. "He doesn't. But he needs friends, and if he doesn't see you as one, if he thinks you're an occasional great hookup, then he won't see he needs you." His expression softened. "He does, though. It was different with you. Mack doesn't get those squishy, in love feelings, but he does care. And he was better when he was spending time with you. I think he'll talk to you in a way he won't with me or Amelia."

"If you're sure." Jomari frowned. This was all news to him.

"Give him time." Jamie's posture made it clear that discussion was over. There was obviously something else on his mind, judging by the thoughtful way he tilted his head and studied Jomari. He was quiet for a minute before he said, "Is it okay to ask you something?"

Jomari nodded. "Go for it."

"Okay. Well, uh...how did you...I mean...what made you know you were a guy?"

That was not at all what Jomari had been expecting, although maybe he should have, now he gave it a moment's consideration. "I'm not exactly sure," he said apologetically. "It wasn't any one thing, more like a long time of slowly realizing. I knew for certain by the time I was in high school, but it's pretty fuzzy before that." He paused. "Why?"

"I never really got a chance to think about it before. I was too busy trying to survive. And now..." He fidgeted, glanced at Jomari, and stopped. "I don't feel like a man."

That had to have taken a whole lot for Jamie to say. Jomari put a hand on his shoulder. "How do you feel?"

"Honestly?" Jamie made a face. "I don't know. Mostly not really like anything, or like nothing fits."

"You don't need to know right away. Besides, there's more than two genders."

"I know." Jamie finally cracked a smile. "YouTube."

Jomari chuckled. "Right. Useful for both bodhrán and gender analysis." He looked up to see Cian heading their way and nodded his chin in that direction. "Does he know?"

"Of course he does. But he's always been sure and confident about himself, at least as far as gender. He's been great about it, but he doesn't get it completely, you know?"

"I do."

Jamie stood. "Gotta go. See you next rehearsal?"

"Definitely."

Jomari watched him go, and the open affection between Cian and Jamie made him simultaneously happy and sad. He needed to get himself under control or he'd never get through the next two weeks until he saw Amelia again. He pulled out his phone and stared at it, willing one of the two people he cared about to call him. The phone remained silent and still, and Jomari shoved it back in his pocket. He picked up his violin and trailed up the aisle after his friends.

CHAPTER TWENTY-ONE

JOMARI GAVE up trying to contact Mack, figuring Jamie was right and Mack would either get back to him—or not. It didn't stop him from thinking about it and wondering what was going on, but he didn't have some kind of claim on Mack. He grudgingly admitted Jamie had a point in saying their entire time together was mostly spent in the bedroom. Or the shower. Or bent over the kitchen table...

He definitely needed to get out of his own head.

Work provided a good distraction. All in the same morning, Jomari taught a middle schooler how to replace her own strings, re-haired three bows, and put stain on a brand new viola. He didn't have time to think about anything except customers and their instruments. While he worked mainly in the front, he listened to Grandad whistling along with the radio in the back.

Just before lunch, the bell over the door jangled, and Jomari looked up from filing some work orders. Mack stood in the doorway, a guitar case in hand. Jomari's hands went clammy, and his efforts to appear casual were wasted. He shoved the last of the work orders into the correct folders and stepped out from behind the desk.

"Hey," he said. "What can I do for you?"

Mack fidgeted and looked around. Jomari followed his gaze to the long rack on one wall where they kept the finished instruments. Violins on the top, violas in the middle, and cellos on the bottom with price tags dangling from the pegs. Another rack had bows of various sizes and types. The instruments were arranged with ones made there at O'Brien's on the near end and older refurbished ones toward the far end.

Shifting his guitar to his other hand, Mack said, "This isn't quite what I expected your shop to look like."

"No?"

"You said you make violins. I thought there would be, like, sawdust or half-finished pieces lying around or something."

Jomari chuckled. "Yeah, we do have that. In back." He swept his hand around at the quiet, carpeted space. "This is what our customers see."

"I've never been inside a place like this."

"You've never had one of your instruments repaired?"

Mack shook his head. "Not here. I usually play electric guitar."

"And that?" Jomari nodded at the case in Mack's hand.

Mack ran a hand over his face, but he didn't answer. Jomari studied him. He looked tired and like the world rested on his shoulders. He set the guitar down and shoved his hands into his jacket pockets.

"We need to talk," he said.

"Yeah." Jomari came closer. "But let's start with this, okay? You brought it here for a reason. Guitars aren't usually our specialty, but I can take a look. If you come in back, you can see the sawdust and half-finished instruments." He tried to smile, but at Mack's lack of response, he turned around and motioned for Mack to follow him.

They stepped behind a curtain to the repair room. The crafting bench was through another doorway, but Jomari didn't lead Mack there. Grandad was still whistling, and Jomari heard the sander. Mack wrinkled his nose, and Jomari inhaled the scents of wood and varnish. He moved three instruments from the workbench to make room for Mack's guitar.

Mack set the case there and opened it up. Jomari peered in then ran his hand along the guitar. It was in rough shape, but more from disuse than from being broken. It needed a full new set of nylon strings and likely had some other hidden damage Jomari would need to uncover through examining it. Otherwise, the dark amber instrument was beautiful, meant for classical rather than contemporary playing. This wasn't something Mack was going to use in a regular gig, and it had Jomari curious.

"It's a nice acoustic instrument. Going for a different sound?"

"No, not exactly. It's more of a...hobby." Mack kept his gaze on the guitar.

Jomari's eyebrows went up. "I didn't know you played that kind of music."

Mack shrugged. "Yeah. My mom taught me some. She was almost a professional." There was a tiny tremor in his voice.

"Almost? What happened?" Jomari winced. "Sorry. Me and my big mouth."

"Nah, 's okay. Life happened, I guess." Mack took the guitar out of the case. "When I was a kid, my parents still had a tape deck." He chuckled, but it sounded forced, as though he was recalling something that wasn't actually funny. "Mom had this one, *Parkening Plays Bach*. And..." Mack cleared his throat. "We listened to that tape a lot."

There was definitely a story there, and Jomari's brain screamed at him to press for more. Whatever was on Mack's mind, this was part of what both Jamie and Amelia had alluded to. If Jomari went too fast, pushed too hard, the moment would be gone. He applied the brakes firmly and forced himself to set further questions aside for the time being.

"You'd like us to fix this up so you can play it. I think we can do that."

"What's it need?"

Jomari held out his hand, and Mack passed him the guitar. It was obvious right away that the instrument hadn't been kept properly humidified, judging from the fine cracks in the surface. There was also some damage around the seams and more cracking all along the fret board. While it wasn't Jomari's primary experience, and Mack probably could've gotten better help from a guitar specialist, a lot of the issues were similar to old violins.

He showed Mack what he was talking about. "It's quite a bit of work, but it's manageable." He peered inside. "It's not as bad as I thought when you first opened the case, but it's not necessarily good, either."

"But you can do it?"

"Yes." Jomari might need Grandad's help on this one, but he was confident he could manage. "Hang on a sec. Grandad!"

The whistling and sanding stopped, but the radio remained on. It felt like forever until Grandad emerged from the other room. He looked Mack up and down before stepping closer. There was nothing particularly judgmental in his gaze, only assessing. Jomari knew he was only gathering information, the same process he used with all his customers, but he wondered what Mack was thinking. Grandad could be a bit much sometimes when people first met him. Rather than tensing, though, Mack actually appeared to relax in Grandad's presence. Jomari watched the two of them, intrigued.

Grandad extended his hand. "Welcome! I'm Charlie O'Brien." He turned to Jomari. "No one's out front, unless Johanna's back from her break. Would you mind going and seeing to it while I help your friend here?"

Jomari glanced between the other two, but he said nothing. They seemed all right, and Grandad would be able to give Mack proper estimates on the time frame and cost for the repairs. He couldn't have argued anyway; Grandad would've waved him off. Jomari nodded and stepped out of the workshop.

In front, Johanna was already back, and Jomari was fairly sure Grandad had known it. He had an uncanny ability to pick up on a lot, and he must've had his reasons for wanting to talk to Mack alone. Jomari wondered if it had anything to do with what Mack wasn't saying about the guitar's history.

Since he couldn't work in the other room, and Johanna didn't need his help at the desk, Jomari slipped into the practice room where customers took their new or repaired instruments for a test drive. There was a brand new violin and a cello there already, waiting to have their price tags affixed. Jomari picked up the violin.

He ran his hand over the smooth surface. It was the first one he'd done all on his own, and he was proud of how it turned out. He tucked it under his chin and began to play, calming his restless soul with the strains of Bach.

It took forty-five minutes before Mack emerged with a work slip to present to Johanna. In the meantime, Jomari had played three pieces, helped a nine-year-old fit a viola, and pretended to read while listening to Johanna talk on the phone to someone about a pageant her daughter was in. He was bored, hungry, and positively itching to know what Grandad and Mack had been discussing that whole time.

Mack looked better than when he'd come in, despite the fact that his eyes were red-rimmed. His back was straighter, as if something that had passed between him and Grandad had eased his burden. Even though Jomari's curiosity was piqued, he was also relieved. Grandad treated every instrument as if it had a story to tell, and each time, he drew it out of customers with his gentle warmth and guidance.

Jomari approached Mack with caution. "Everything okay?"

"Sure, yeah. Your grandfather says it'll be done in a couple weeks, I guess."

"Sounds about right. So...I'll see you when you come to pick it up?"

"Or you could come over."

Jomari's mouth went dry, and his stomach flipped. "Yeah, I could do that."

"I'm working the next couple nights, but I'm free after that. Text me?" He smiled ruefully. "I promise I'll answer you this time."

"Yeah. I'll do that."

Johanna handed Mack his copy of the work order, and he waved to Jomari on his way out. Jomari stood staring at the door, knowing full well Johanna was eyeing him. He didn't move until Grandad came out of the back.

"JoJo, why don't you come give me a hand with this?"

Here it came. Either Grandad guessed from the exchange Jomari had with Mack or it had been part of the conversation he'd had himself, but either way, Jomari was in for a Q and A session. He glanced at Johanna, whose body language suggested it was best he obey his grandfather. Jomari ducked behind the curtain.

The guitar was still out on the bench. "This isn't next on the work orders list." That was about as close as Jomari would get to openly defying Grandad. He was a kind and loving man, but he was not to be crossed when it came to his work.

"No, it's not." Grandad's firm tone changed to cheerfulness as he added, "But there's no time like the present for you to learn how to do it."

"I know how to repair a guitar."

"But not *this* guitar," Grandad countered.

"This one isn't any more special than the others. I don't have some deep relationship with it." Jomari scowled.

"You are a stubborn lad. This guitar is indeed very special. There's much more under the surface than you know."

Jomari sighed and turned to the workbench. *Every instrument has a story.* He touched it, willing the guitar to tell him what Mack couldn't, to confess its deepest, darkest secrets. Looking back up at Grandad, Jomari shook his head. He couldn't speak for fear of what might tumble out of his mouth.

Grandad stepped closer and put a hand on Jomari's shoulder. He touched the top of the guitar. "I don't know all its secrets yet, but I know how much this means to your friend."

Jomari swallowed. "Did he tell you anything?"

"Some. It's wise for you to ask about it yourself."

"I will. It's just...complicated."

"Ayuh. That it is. Now, tell me what you think this instrument needs."

Jomari picked it up and braced it against his hip. He pointed out to Grandad all the flaws, but he suggested most of them were on the surface and could easily be corrected with the right types of glue and varnish. The interior had held up well and only needed minor adjustments. Jomari went through the entire list until Grandad stopped him.

"Excellent. You've spotted most of what I saw, but you've missed the most obvious one."

Jomari frowned, but then he flipped the guitar around. Sure enough, there was a long, ugly scratch on the back. It was mainly cosmetic, and it wouldn't affect the sound. He wondered what had caused it. The damage to the front was all from lack of moisture in the wood. The back, though, made no sense.

"This was done on purpose," Grandad said. "See this?" He pointed, and Jomari saw what he meant.

"We won't be able to completely fix it."

"No, but it won't matter. Sometimes an instrument simply has to live with its scars." Grandad patted Jomari's hand where it still rested on the guitar.

Jomari put the guitar back into its case and then pulled up a stool. He thought about both Amelia and Mack and the scars they lived with. Until now, he'd never invited them to show him. He'd assumed asking would be too painful for all of them. And what would he do with the information he learned?

He would do the same thing he did with the violins people trustingly laid in his hands. A repaired instrument wasn't the same as a brand new one. It didn't sound the same. It contained a whole lifetime—or several, as the case might be—of belonging to someone. Jomari wasn't responsible for any of what came before him, and he couldn't change it. All he could do was add his own touch, even when he wasn't convinced it would be enough.

Jomari sighed and looked up at Grandad. "I'm not sure I can do it."

"Of course you can." Grandad peered at him. "There's something you're not telling me."

Naturally Grandad would be able to pick up on Jomari's discomfort. "I don't know how to explain." Or, more accurately, he didn't want to explain. Grandad was great and all, but would he understand this situation? Jomari couldn't answer that question.

"Something to do with your friend?"

"We're not exactly—yeah, kind of, but it's more than that."

"Boy trouble?"

"Sort of." Jomari cringed. There was no way he could tell Grandad what sort of relationship he had with Mack.

"Girl trouble?" Grandad smiled; Jomari snorted, but he finally smiled too.

"It's complicated." Jomari took a deep breath and let it out slowly, making his bangs puff.

"Ayuh, I know a thing or two about that, JoJo." Grandad finished the instrument he was varnishing and pulled up a stool. "About girl trouble and boy trouble and how that gets complicated, as you called it."

Grandad had never made it a secret from Jomari that he'd loved his share of men in his youth, before he met Grandma. Now Jomari thought there might be more to it.

"Go on," he said.

"Now, I don't know what you call it these days. You young folk are always thinking up new ways to name things. Back then, I said I was 'sowing my oats,' as it were. This was before Grandma, you understand."

"I know."

"She never paid any mind to it. Said all she cared about was that we were together, but I know she meant all that was behind me, something dead and buried when we got married. Well, at some point—this must've been when your Da was just starting school—I met a man. His sons were older, closer to your aunties' ages than your Da's. They were in our parish." Grandad sighed. "We spent a lot of time together, more'n we should've. Your Grandma, she tried to be understanding, at least at first. His wife...not as much."

Jomari wanted to ask, and yet he didn't think he wanted the answer. He swallowed, tension making his heart speed up. This wasn't the kind of story Grandad would tell over a turkey dinner, embellishing to the delight of the younger grandchildren. It was private, and Jomari heard the hesitation and sorrow in his voice.

He licked his lips and finally murmured, "What happened, Grandad?"

"Nothing more than a stolen kiss in a hidden alcove of the

church. It shouldn't have happened. Not because of our wives but because of the secrecy. I told Grandma, but to my knowledge, he never told his wife. Avoided me after that until they moved away."

"Was there ever anyone else?"

Grandad shook his head. "I don't know if anything would've come of it anyway, even if his wife had known and approved. After that, I never met anyone else I felt about the way I did for my Colleen." Grandad smiled, but it was sad and longing. "Ah, I do miss her."

Jomari nodded. "Me too, Grandad." He looked down at the guitar still in his hands then up at Grandad. "Why did you tell me that story?"

"Because your 'not exactly' and 'it's complicated' made me think you might be in a similar place."

"It's different. I—she—he—we all know about each other, but I'm not sure if we know how to make it work."

"You'll figure it out."

"Aren't you—I mean, is it weird? I don't know too many people like us. Some of their friends, but those are different too."

Grandad hopped down from the stool. "Every relationship is different, lad. I tell you, you'll find a way." He motioned at the guitar. "A lot like fixing that up. Go on and get started while I sort out the list of work orders."

He shuffled into the next room, and Jomari stared after him for a minute. He'd given his implied approval, but he'd offered no real advice. Jomari was worried, too, that he'd upset Grandad with his questions and bringing up memories of Grandma. That fear lasted all of ten seconds before he heard Grandad's voice from the other room.

"Hurry up, JoJo! The sooner you get done with that, the sooner you'll be on to the next thing. Can't keep our customers waiting!"

With a soft sigh, Jomari turned his attention to the work at hand, both Mack and Amelia still on his mind. He did need to talk to Mack, but he had the feeling Amelia pushing him that direction was her own deflection. Mack wasn't the only person who needed to open up, and the three of them together could use a dose of honesty among them. How to orchestrate it was going to take more planning than Jomari's brain had room for at the moment.

Chapter Twenty-Two

Jomari didn't bring an overnight bag to Mack's apartment. His new one, apparently, though in the same building. It made sense, now Mack lived alone. The layout was similar, but there was only one bedroom instead of three. No roommates to potentially interrupt either, although Jomari had never seen Jamie or Nate at Mack's old place. Something about a rule they had, but Jomari suspected most of it was that both guys were usually with their significant others.

Unlike with Amelia, the meal they shared wasn't a date. It was a bridge, something to have between them so the silences wouldn't feel awkward. Mack was still in process of cooking when Jomari showed up, and the scent of fresh vegetables and spices greeted Jomari on entering.

Mack was wearing an apron unironically. Jomari might've laughed, except one, it made sense, given the food he was preparing, and two, it looked kind of hot on him. Jomari recalled the times Mack had fed him leftovers after an especially vigorous fuck, and his mouth watered thinking about both.

He needed to stop, at least regarding the sex. That wasn't what he was here for. They were only going to talk, and from the sounds of it, this wasn't bedroom-appropriate conversation. Mack had already said he was taking a break for a bit to clear his head, and Jomari was committed to respecting his space.

Just like with Amelia's emotional distance, he thought, and

then wondered where that idea had come from. He shook it off and then realized Mack was speaking and he'd missed whatever it was.

"...start with the seafood, and then go from there," Mack finished. He looked over his shoulder and gave Jomari a quizzical look. "You do eat seafood, right?"

"Of course I do. Sorry, got distracted. What were you saying?"

"That I'm glad to have somebody to make this for. Nate won't eat it now, and Jamie...well, he's a bit picky." Mack had the sense to blush. "I didn't mean it like that. He has foods he won't or can't eat."

Jomari stepped closer, and Mack held out a fork with a scallop. It had been braised in some kind of spicy brown sauce, and it smelled incredible. Jomari let Mack feed it to him, closing his mouth around the bite and letting the flavor rest on his tongue before chewing and swallowing. It was perfection.

"God," Jomari said when he could speak again. "That was amazing."

"Yeah?" Mack grinned. "Okay, we can eat these. The beef pinwheels are roasting, along with the potatoes."

He set the cast iron pan on a hot pad on the table, and the two of them sat across from each other. Jomari had no experience with this and didn't know where to begin. He was anxious to get Mack's side of the story, but he wasn't sure how to ask. So he resorted to what he did know: how to babble like an expert.

"So, I was over at the theatre earlier. Y'know, the Dyer. Anyway, we have this concert next weekend. And I hope you'll think about coming because it's going to be freaking amazing. It's kind of too bad Amelia's missing it...oops." He hadn't meant to say her name, not knowing if it was taboo at the moment.

Mack's laugh was thin. "I'm sure she'll regret having taken a vacation to England in the face of a 'freaking amazing' orchestra concert."

"Oh, yeah, that totally sounds like her."

Now Mack guffawed, and it sounded genuine, so Jomari relaxed. He picked up his shrimp fork—where the heck did Mack get fancy utensils from?—and poked a scallop, stuffing it in his mouth to avoid further missteps in conversation.

Mack hadn't touched the food. Instead, he folded his hands on top of the table and pursed his lips. After a while, he said, "You know why she left, right?"

Jomari had thought it had something to do with himself, her

need for space. Now he wondered if he was mistaken. Would she have talked to Mack about that? Jomari shrugged. "I guess? She and I...we..."

"It has nothing to do with you." Mack put a hand to his hair, but it was tied back, so he lowered it again. "It's my fault. No, that's not right. Makes it sound like she didn't deserve a vacation. But I don't think she'd have gone if I hadn't completely fucked things up."

"Okay," Jomari said slowly. "Meaning?"

Mack stood and went to the sink. He kept his back to Jomari when he said, "You know I'm an alcoholic, right? I told you that."

"In recovery. Yep, I remember. You were explaining to me why you don't drink."

"Did you know," Mack continued, turning around slowly and leaning against the counter, "that I had my first drink when I was ten? Or that I was already addicted by the time I was fourteen?"

"Um, no." Jomari kept his eyes on Mack, hoping his expression was as neutral as he tried to make it. "You didn't say that part."

Mack drummed his fingers against the cupboard behind him. "That guitar I brought in—it was my mother's."

"Yeah?" Jomari wondered how they'd gotten back to the guitar or where this was going, but he forced himself not to race three steps ahead. Whatever story Mack had to tell, Jomari needed to be ready to hear it.

"Yes. She's originally from Nashville. Incredibly talented, playing classical music with her own unique country flair. By the time she was sixteen, she had an offer for a recording contract. She released exactly one album under that label."

"Wow."

Mack nodded. "That's what she wanted to do. Her parents said no. They wanted her to go to college. Said that she needed to grow up first, have a backup plan. She compromised and said she'd study music. So she came here. Maybe her parents were right, and it would've worked out for the best. I don't know. I've never met them to ask."

"What, uh, happened?" Jomari gulped. He was afraid he was pushing, but Mack didn't seem troubled.

"My father worked for the college, on their custodial staff. He's not much older than Mom," Mack assured Jomari. "Mom was feeling rebellious, I guess. They fell in love. At least, he did. I think maybe she liked the idea of Dad more than she liked him. It doesn't matter. Before she graduated, she was pregnant with me.

"Dad still wanted her to pursue her dreams. He promised he would take care of me, and she agreed. He says those were happy times, their quick wedding and planning for the future."

Jomari heard the shadows under the sweetly romantic story of making it against the world. He wondered what had gone wrong. Mack turned around again as though protecting both himself and Jomari from whatever came next.

He went on. "When Mom had me, it was...bad. She nearly died, and so did I. For the first couple years of my life, I was really sick, and so was she. My parents did nothing but take care of me and try to survive. My father got a higher paying job with a school so my mother could be home, since she couldn't work at that time. I don't know if that's exactly when she started drinking. Dad says she was always a bit of a partier, but not bad like it got.

"She never really stopped. My whole life, I've known I was the reason she stopped performing. It doesn't matter that she could've tried again when we were both doing better or when I went to school or at any other point in time. Instead, she chose to drown the life she hated and never wanted." Mack gripped the counter top. "It's not my fault. But as a kid, I didn't know better. I'd caused her pain simply by existing. Her path looked easier, so I followed her down it."

"I'm sorry," Jomari said. "I don't know what else to say."

Mack faced him again. "You don't have to. But you do need to hear the rest."

"There's more?"

"I got sober five years ago. And then, before this Christmas, I botched it all because I went back to believing that would be easier." He finally sat back down at the table with Jomari. "It's not."

"You started drinking again?" Jomari wasn't prepared for the reality of speaking that question out loud. It sounded off-pitch.

"Yeah. I'm getting clean, but I'm not keeping it a secret or pretending it's easy." He rested his hand on the table, but Jomari didn't take it. "The reasons I got sober in the first place matter, and I think I should tell you that too." Mack looked over his shoulder at the kitchen timer. "Food's almost done. Let's eat, and I'll finish explaining. You deserve the whole truth for two reasons."

"And what are those?"

"One, because my feelings about you and Amelia are part of what happened. And two, because I like you." He smiled, and Jomari returned it, though with little enthusiasm. "I don't get the kind of thing between you and her. I don't experience the world like that. But I'm not cold or heartless or afraid of commitment."

"I never thought you were." Jomari thought Mack was about as far from cold as possible, even if he did close himself off.

"Good."

The timer went off, and Jomari helped Mack put the main course on the table. Everything looked and smelled so good, and Jomari wondered again why Mack had never thought of going back to school. It might've been the challenges of the classes, or maybe he didn't want to be a professional at something he loved. Jomari suspected there was more to it, especially after the story about Mack's mother. He didn't want to push his luck by saying anything, though.

While they ate, Mack continued to talk. It was as if he'd kept all those words sealed up in a cave and then suddenly moved the barricade at the entrance. They poured out of him, sometimes shocking and sometimes heartbreaking. He gave Jomari the story of how the Creepy Crullers had formed, how he met Jamie, and what Sage had done to all of them.

It took them all the way through dessert—a sweet and tart berry trifle—for Mack to finish. Jomari was sure he'd never heard Mack speak so much at one time. It was a lot to take in, and he'd never been on the receiving end of so much of someone's pain.

"I hope," Mack said, "that you can forgive me for being such an ass. I would say I hope we can keep meeting up, but I think I need to let you and Amelia sort things out." His smile was sad now.

Was that what Jomari wanted? To work things out with her and stop seeing Mack? It hadn't occurred to him he might be hedging, seeing both of them until he was ready to choose between them. They hadn't offered him the same things. Mack was sex and food and poetry and fun. Amelia was warmth and understanding and quiet talks that turned to lovemaking. How could he possibly pick one over the other?

And therein was his entire problem. He didn't want to, and he didn't think they did either. They were worried about hurting each other and Jomari being caught in the crossfire. He might, after all. His life in no way looked like theirs. Unlike the two of them, Jomari had grown up loved and treasured, respected both for the girl they thought he was and for the man he became.

He knew, suddenly, what it all meant. The weight of it bore down on him. He would need time, a good cry, and some important conversations with the two people he trusted most. But the answer was right there in front of them, and maybe—just maybe—he could help both Mack and Amelia see it.

Tamping down his rising excitement, Jomari grasped Mack's hand on top of the table. "Amelia and I will talk. And then we all will."

Mack's shoulders relaxed. "Yeah. That's probably a good idea."

"After the wedding?"

"Definitely. I'm not sure I'm ready yet, and we're all going to be up to our eyeballs in it soon."

Any lingering tension dissipated, and Jomari snickered. "I am gonna be so glad when I stop hearing Jamie whine about it."

"God, yes. He's been a royal pain in the ass. I've had to hide from Trevor too. Also, I do not want to know what those two are gonna do when they finally make up. I have a feeling Andre, the women, and their kid are gonna be hiding out with the rest of us when that happens."

"Wait, what?"

Mack looked taken aback. "You didn't know about them?"

"Not exactly? I knew they'd had a thing but not that it was still going on. And they're fighting about so much stupid wedding shit right now that I doubt anyone would have a clue."

"Personally, I think they ought to kiss and make up sooner rather than later. The sexual frustration can't be good for planning."

"Whose idea was it to let those two loose on it anyway? I mean, I'm glad it's not my job, but wow."

Mack laughed. "Fair point. Enough about that. You wanna watch a movie? For real, I mean. That's not a proposition."

"Sure."

They flopped onto the couch, and Jomari settled in. A movie would let him stay with Mack while giving his mind a chance to wander. He had a lot to think about, and not one bit of it involved Nate and Izzy's wedding.

Chapter Twenty-Three

Of the two of Jomari's parents, Mee was the easier to approach. She was no-nonsense and a logical, mathematical thinker, but she understood him better. Mee was first generation American-born, and she got what it was like to balance being her own person with her parents' expectations. Jomari also had a sense that growing up in a bilingual home, learning to fit in at school and with family, wasn't too dissimilar from his own challenges.

They sat at the kitchen table, and Mee offered Jomari some cocoa. The homemade kind, with fragrant spices, instead of packaged. It was one of the things his mother knew how to make. She wasn't a good cook. That had always been Da's territory. Hot cocoa, though, was her specialty.

Jomari was quiet while Mee worked at the stove. She talked as she stirred: an anecdote or two about work, a nice restaurant Da had taken her to, something about Hazel going on a music tour with her college wind ensemble in about a month. Homey, ordinary things.

"...and met Hazel's girlfriend," Mee said.

Once again, Jomari had been too distracted to pay a whole lot of attention, but that snapped him back. "Wait, what? Like her friend who is a girl?"

"No." Mee chuckled. She began ladling cocoa into mugs. "Her girlfriend as in the girl she's dating."

"Hazel," Jomari said slowly. "Our Hazel. Is dating a girl? When did that happen?"

Mee set the mugs on the table. "After she went back to school, I guess? She said it sort of surprised her."

"And she didn't tell me." Jomari pouted a little at his cocoa.

Mee patted his hand. "We only met her because we were dropping off a textbook she'd left home. Hazel said it was all right to tell you."

"Okay, but why didn't she at least text me or something? It's not like I'd have been mad!"

"She thought you might be, actually." Mee gave him a knowing look.

Jomari thought about it. Maybe Hazel was right. He supposed he thought of being queer as his thing. He was different from his parents and sister in so many ways. Now here they were, he and Hazel more alike than he'd known, and he wasn't sure how he felt about it.

"That's fair, I guess."

Mee nodded. "She'll talk to you. She said she never thought much about it because she was more concerned with supporting you." Mee held up a hand when Jomari went to protest. "It's not a bad thing. Hazel needed to be on her own to figure herself out. Not every person knows from the time they're eleven." She smiled and touched Jomari's hand.

Jomari returned her smile. "No, I guess not." He turned serious again. "That's kind of why I'm here. There's some things going on, and I–" He looked down, biting his lip to stop the trembling and willing himself not to cry. Again. He'd done what he thought was enough of that, alone in his room.

"Hey." Mee flipped his hand over and laid hers in it. "I'm here. Talk to me."

"I met this woman. She was already sort of involved with someone, and...it's complicated and weird and...and..."

"I'm not following." Mee frowned. "You're seeing a married woman?"

"No, it's not like that. They're not married. This guy isn't even really her boyfriend. Or, uh, mine. Because we both were with him, kind of." Jomari's heart raced, and his hands were sweaty enough he pulled away from Mee so as not to get her clammy. He wiped his palms on his jeans.

"A love triangle?" Mee guessed.

"This is not some angsty teen romance!" Jomari cringed as

soon as he'd finished. "I'm sorry. No, I mean we're all kind of involved, and it's very weird, and..." He swallowed. "What if what we're doing is, y'know, wrong?"

"Oh." Mee sat back, and she had on her thoughtful expression. She was about the least judgmental person Jomari knew, but he was aware she needed time to absorb new ideas. This was going to take a few minutes, if not longer.

They sipped their drinks, and Jomari tamped down his impatience waiting for Mee's words of wisdom. He had no idea what was coming. Mee wasn't strictly traditional, but she was still a good Catholic, deep down. Jomari figured she'd accepted him because she assumed he would form a family much like theirs, regardless of his spouse's gender. The concept of anything outside those boundaries might be unacceptable to her.

Mee closed her eyes, and Jomari watched her take a few deep breaths before she opened them again and met his gaze. He clenched and unclenched his hands under the table.

"Well," she said, "I can't pretend I understand it. I'm not made that way—I think I would get mixed up if I tried to be with anyone but Da, and I really don't want to share him, either. But I'm not sure it's a sin, if that's what you're asking."

"I guess, yeah. But I thought maybe you'd be mad because it's not the same as our family."

"No, it's not." Mee leaned in closer. "Are you sure I'm the one you're worried about?"

Jomari shifted uncomfortably. "I'm going to tell Da eventually."

"That's not what I meant."

Her words pierced him. She was right, of course. He'd known Mee—and Da, once he knew—wouldn't be any less supportive than Grandad had. His family wasn't perfect, and he had his share of relatives who would have something to say about the whole thing. Probably some who would never be allowed to know about what kinds of relationships Jomari had. But Mee, Da, Hazel, and Grandad had stood by him his whole life. Not much was going to change that unless he hurt them directly.

His own fears, however, were another matter.

Before Mack and Amelia, Jomari would've said his life was uncomplicated. He thought maybe one day, he would settle down. He pictured a wife, or possibly a husband, maybe a kid in some far-distant future. What his parents had. Being with Mack and Amelia made him question if those were his dreams or the ones he thought he was supposed to have.

"This isn't what I imagined I'd be doing," he finally admitted. And then he really did cry.

Mee moved so she could hold him while he grieved the loss of what he'd always thought he would have. It wasn't Mee who wanted him to live a picket fence life. That's what he'd believed in for himself. It had made him feel safe at a time when his whole world was tilting on its axis. Now he was in love with one person, and cared deeply for another, who had never known nor wanted any of that. How could Jomari choose between two people he felt so strongly about and the dream that had seen him through so much?

When his sobs died down to soft hiccups, he sat back. Mee put her hands on the sides of his face and wiped his tears with her thumbs. He closed his eyes, warmed by her gentle touch.

"Life doesn't always go as planned," Mee said. "I thought I was going to be a doctor and marry one of the men my parents suggested. Instead, I fell in love with math—and your father. And look at Hazel. Remember how she was in high school? I doubt anyone would've pictured how she is now."

Jomari smiled at that. He might've come out, but he was never especially rebellious. Hazel had singlehandedly attempted to find every possible way to push their parents' buttons. Here she was, a college junior and an outstanding student, studying to become an accountant.

Mee continued, "You have to decide what you want, not what I want. So it's not what we all imagined. We'll get used to it. But it starts with you. Be okay with who you are and what you want first. The rest will follow." She kissed the top of his head. "Pray about it. That's something you've always been good at."

He hadn't been lately. His prayers had languished, a desire to hide from both God and himself. Maybe it was time to be honest there too.

"Okay," he said. "I think I can do that."

"Good. Do you want to talk more about this?"

"No, but I did want to tell you about something I'm working on with Grandad."

"Ooh, sounds like work is going well, then." Mee stood. "More cocoa?"

"Sure." Jomari held out his mug. When Mee took it, they traded a look of mutual understanding, and Jomari finally felt at peace.

It was more delicate business talking to Da. Jomari lamented the fact that it wasn't yet baseball season, or he might've taken his father to a game. Or not, but telling himself that gave him time to stall. He finally had an opening on a night when Mee had gone to something at the office for one of her coworkers. The two men were on their own.

Jomari helped himself to the soup on the stove. He'd made the bread to go with it, and he waited nervously for Da's assessment. Da wasn't much like Mack, but Jomari had the sense they were both somewhat perfectionistic about their cooking.

Da slowly buttered the bread, and Jomari knew he was prolonging it on purpose. It was a good sign—if he hadn't been in the mood to tease his son, tonight wouldn't have been a good night to begin a difficult conversation with Da. Not to mention he was kind enough not to make fun of something he wasn't willing to eat, so Jomari already understood the bread was fine.

"It has a good texture," Da remarked. "Did you use Grandma's recipe?"

"I did." It was a pain, too, but Jomari didn't complain.

Da took a bite, and Jomari held his breath. "Mm. Yep, exactly like I remember her making."

Jomari relaxed and grinned. "Not bad for my first time."

"Not at all, son." Da picked up his spoon and dipped it into his bowl, stirring slowly. "You sounded like you had something on your mind. What's up?"

"I was thinking about..." Jomari searched for an acceptable topic, something to break the ice and ease into what he was about to say. "...you and Mee. How did you know she was 'the one'?" He made air quotes, causing Da to snort.

"I think it was her passion for math history," Da said. "We met in that class. Even though we were both in the math department, we were on separate tracks and in different years, so our paths hadn't crossed yet."

"So was it, like, a love at first sight kind of thing?" Jomari knew his parents had met in college, but he didn't remember the whole story, if either of them had ever shared it.

Da laughed. "No, not at all. We were set to become more like instant enemies."

"Seriously? That sounds like a bad movie plot. What happened?"

"I made the grave error of asking why we weren't talking about

Einstein in a discussion of the greatest mathematical minds. She stood up, turned around, and gave me a death glare while declaring Einstein didn't count and wasn't a real mathematician anyway. I said if she was so smart, who did she think the best one was. And she proceeded to give me *an entire lecture* on why Agnesi was the single greatest and how not enough people give her the respect she's due, especially as a woman of faith."

"And that's how you knew you liked her?" Jomari stared at his father.

"Uh...no. I was embarrassed at having gone into that class with absolutely no idea about math history whatsoever, and I was mad at her for calling me out in public."

"So then what happened?"

"I went to the library to look up Agnesi." Da smiled. "And your mother was right—she was pretty cool. So I checked out a book about her. On my way out, I ran into Mee with a couple of her friends. At first, she looked like she might walk on by, but then she noticed the book. She said, 'That's a good one. I read it twice.' She apologized for coming on so strong and said she loved math history. I told her I'd only taken the class because I needed the elective and it looked better than the others. She told me to talk to her again at the end of the semester and see if I still felt the same."

"Did you?"

Da chuckled. "No. I thought it was dreadfully boring, actually. But I got talking to your mother, and by the end of the semester, we were friends. It took a bit longer for us both to know we wanted to be together. I asked her for a date on the night she presented her senior thesis. Of course she said yes. Then she stayed with me while I finished my own final year of school."

"That's...actually really sweet."

"And getting married has only given us the chance to argue about the greatest mathematician in the same household." Da winked.

"Is that what being married is like?" Jomari grimaced. He didn't know where that had come from.

Da eyed him with a bit of suspicion. "Not really. Why?"

Now or never. "There's this woman. In my orchestra. We..." He sighed. There wasn't a good way to explain the sort of relationship they'd had up until their ice skating date, so he didn't try. "We've sort of been seeing each other. It was kind of casual, y'know?"

Da nodded. "And you think maybe it's something different from what you've been doing."

Jomari finished his soup before answering, trying to figure out the best response. "I really like her. No, I—I love her. But..."

"You're not sure she feels the same way. Have you told her?"

"It's, um, complicated. There's this guy—"

"Ah. I see."

Jomari set his spoon back in the bowl and leaned forward. He was about to rip this bandage off. "No, you don't. It's not a weird love triangle. We're all seeing each other. I care about them both, and they've been kind of together for years. I don't feel the same way about each of them, but I don't want to lose either of them. And so far, no one has been able to tell me how I can stop that from happening." He sat back and crossed his arms.

Da looked stunned, and he said nothing. In theory, it should've been easier to tell him than Mee. Of the two of them, she was the more religious and had more traditional views about relationships. Da was mostly Catholic in name only, however well he chose to hide that from Grandad. And yet here they were, Da so shocked he couldn't speak. Jomari wondered if this was the last straw between them.

Finally Da spoke. His words were careful, as if he was trying to talk around what he really wanted to say. "You love this woman—"

"Amelia," Jomari said shortly.

"Amelia. And you both have someone else you care about who is a serious part of your lives." Da didn't sound like he quite grasped it, but it was a pretty good summary.

"Yeah, that's about it."

"Have you all ever talked about it?"

"Not together, no. I'm not sure any of us knew what we were doing." Jomari ran a hand through his hair, exasperated as much with himself, Mack, and Amelia as with Da.

"You might want to consider starting there."

"That's it? That's all you're going to say to me about it?" Jomari flung his arms out, not caring that it was a bit dramatic.

"What did you want me to say?" Da sighed heavily. "You know I will support you no matter what, but this is new to me too." He looked away for a moment. When he turned his gaze back to Jomari, his expression was something between worry and sadness. It hurt more than Jomari had anticipated. "I've had a lot of adjusting to do with you. I never thought of myself as closed-minded. I've always voted for things I thought would make us collectively better.

But it was out there in the world, not right in my own house. Things that I thought were just fine for other people but maybe not for my family."

"I'm sorry I'm such a disappointment to you, Da." Jomari didn't hide the edge in his voice.

"You're not. You never have been. I'm incredibly proud of you." Da folded his hands on top of the table. "I worry for you, what your future will bring. Who might hurt you because of who you are or who you love. This adds yet another layer."

Jomari put his hands on top of Da's. "You don't have to protect me anymore from the fourth grade bullies. Or from the administrators who told me I had to use the faculty bathroom because some parents complained."

"I know I don't." Da's hand's twitched with tension. "But can these two people you're involved with keep you safe?"

So that was it. Jomari understood now. "I believe they can, just as much as I can keep them safe."

Da's shoulders slumped. "Then that's all I care about."

He pulled his hands away. It was the best Jomari was going to get right now. At some point, he wanted to be able to bring Amelia and Mack to see his parents. He didn't know Amelia's friends well, but he knew many of them had brought their additional partners home, with varying degrees of success. There wasn't an overnight fix for this. Da needed time, like most people probably would in the same position.

Quietly, they cleaned up from dinner, and Jomari shut himself away in his room. He'd had three different answers from three different people, but no advice. He lay on his bed, wondering what his next steps were, when something occurred to him. He grabbed his phone from the bedside table and scrolled to Hazel's number.

Hey, you. Text me when you get a chance, k?

It was less than an hour until Jomari's phone went off with Hazel's ringtone. She hadn't replied to his text, but now she was calling. Jomari tensed. On reflection, he thought it was probably better not to do this via texts anyway. He'd wear out his thumbs.

"Hello?"

"JoJo! You said to text, but you, like, never do that. So I knew I had to call you. What's up?"

He rolled over onto his stomach and propped himself on his elbows, setting the phone on the pillow and hitting speaker. "Okay, so...I had literally the worst night. It's kind of been a shit week, but...ugh. Whatever."

"Dude, start over," Hazel instructed. "What the heck happened?"

"Da."

"Not this again. I thought you two were okay. You need me to come home and yell at our parents?"

"No! I mean, it's not like before. I just had to explain some stuff about the weird relationship I'm in."

Hazel gasped. "You? In a weird relationship? Now, this I've got to hear. So, you're dating again, huh? I'm glad Mr. You're-Boring-in-Bed didn't ruin it for you, at least."

"Him and the loser from Starbucks, yeah. I've kind of been seeing two people, but it's super complicated right now. And, like, I'm kind of the mature one here? I don't know. It's messy."

"Sounds it. You're polyamorous?"

"I guess?" Jomari massaged his temples to ease the headache he felt coming on. At least he didn't have to explain all this to Hazel, from the sounds of it. "How do you even know a word like that?"

She huffed. "I'm twenty, not two. Besides, I took a Queer Studies class last semester. Also, a lot of my friends aren't doing the whole monogamy thing. I think for some of them, they're just like, 'Oh, yeah, I'm poly' but it's more like they're open to whatever because they're still with only one person at a time. For a few, they're like my friend Marco. He and his boyfriend hook up with other people, but they're a couple at the end of the day."

"Are—are you into that?"

"Nah. My girlfriend—Mee says you know about her—and I are totally monogamous. She says she's wired that way, and I figure I probably am too. It doesn't interest me much, at least not for now."

"Yeah, about your girlfriend. Does she have a name? And why didn't you tell me?"

"Her name's Raven, and she's awesome. I didn't tell you because, like, you do everything first. I didn't even know I was bi until Raven. I was freaked out, too. I told her I'd never been with a girl before, and she said it was okay because she hadn't either, even though she's known she was pansexual since she was in, like, middle school. But all her friends are super queer, so now I know all this stuff I didn't even think of before."

With a sigh, Jomari rolled over, taking the phone in his hand. He set it on his chest. "I didn't think of it either. Mr. Boring kept cheating on me. Hell, I was the guy he cheated on his ex-boyfriend with because *he* was allegedly boring. I thought it was because of something to do with me. I was a lot farther along in my transition, even though I'm younger. He wasn't out in high school like I was. So I figured it was that thing that sometimes happens where we kind of trigger each other. Not on purpose, and it's nobody's fault, but it's rough. Except I think he didn't want to admit he wasn't into monogamy."

"Maybe," Hazel agreed. "So what did you want to know? It kind of sounds like you're already deep in something. Raven says it's super important to talk about it, which is why she made it clear when we started going out that she does best with only one person."

"Oh my god. You're the fourth person to say exactly the same stupid, crappy advice." Jomari scowled at the phone as if Hazel could see him.

"Ooh, hit a nerve. Sorry-not-sorry! So basically, you're going out with two people, and you all haven't talked it through? Jeez. Didn't you say you were the mature one? I don't even know what that means, but clearly not, if you can't talk like grown-ups."

"Hazel!" Her name came out whiny. "Okay, fine. We need to talk. But, like, how? It's different with each of them. Amelia's—" He stopped short of saying *my soul mate*. He didn't believe in such a thing, but if anyone's heart spoke to his, it was Amelia's. "I love her. Mack doesn't do that kind of relationship. It's basically sex. But he's had this serious friendship with Amelia for something like fifteen years, including sex. I think they both sometimes hook up with other people, too. That's how she and I...and he and I...well, you get the idea."

"Oh, boy, do I. Yeah, you all need to get in the same room at the same time." She paused. "So is Mack aromantic?"

"I guess so. I don't think he likes to label it, but that's more or less what Amelia said. It's not going anywhere else between us."

"Fair enough. You know, Marco and his guy do this poly group. You could come to it."

"No way. Sit around with a bunch of college students?" Jomari cringed. "I'll pass."

"It was just an idea. You're not that much older than we are. You want me to ask them for ideas at least?"

"I..." Jomari thought about it. Hazel's idea made sense. "Sure."

"Okay. I'll get back to you with some stuff to open the door. But you'd better do it. What've you got to lose?"

Only my heart. "I know, I know."

"I take it things went bad when you tried to tell Mee and Da?" Her tone turned sympathetic.

"Mee was okay, but she doesn't understand. Da...you know how he is. He won't yell or get mad or throw you out, but it was like I could feel how much it disappointed him, y'know? Ugh." Jomari repeated his earlier sentiment; it hadn't changed.

"He'll be okay. Wait, you said I was the fourth person. Did you tell Grandad?"

"Yep." Jomari wasn't going to repeat Grandad's story for her. He had a feeling that was a private moment between the two of them, and if he'd wanted Hazel to know, he'd have told her.

"And he was okay?"

"Yeah. I dunno, sometimes he's better about that stuff. It's like when he gave me his old cap after I told him I was a boy."

"He's cool that way." Hazel paused. "I miss Grandma."

"Me too."

There was some muffled noise on the other end, and Hazel said something, probably to her roommate. "Gotta go. There's a dorm thing in, like, five minutes I have to be at. I promise, I'll ask Marco some stuff for you. Gonna be okay?"

"Sure, I will. Thanks, Hazel."

"Any time, JoJo. Love you, big brother."

"Love you too."

They ended the call, and Jomari lay there with the phone still in his hand. He didn't have a plan yet, but he felt much better with Hazel on the job. He smiled. She was turning out all right, even after her semi-goth-punk phase and her ill-advised not strictly legal body art and her habit of sneaking home well after curfew. Somehow, she'd grown up, and Jomari felt like it had been in a blink.

He turned onto his side and set the phone back on the bedside table before closing his eyes. A good night's sleep would clear his mind, and hopefully it wouldn't take long before Hazel got back to him with some ideas. He drifted off while having imaginary conversations with both Mack and Amelia.

Chapter Twenty-Four

There was still no phone call from Amelia even though she'd been back for a few days. Jomari wondered how her trip had gone, but he didn't want to push her to talk to him if she wasn't ready. Instead, he poured his energy into fixing Mack's guitar with Grandad's guidance.

When it was done, Jomari was about to call Mack when Grandad stopped him. "I already called this morning because I knew we'd be done today. He paid over the phone, and I said you would take it to him after we close up for the night."

"W-why?" Jomari stammered.

Grandad shrugged. "It sounded like you had unfinished business, and I don't mean the repairs."

"We already talked, Grandad. I went to see him, and he told me more about the guitar and its story." And other things, but Jomari couldn't reveal all those.

"Did you take my other advice?"

"Amelia hasn't called. I know we need to take care of it, but..."

"Then do it. Go see him, bring the guitar, and work it out." Grandad patted Jomari's arm on his way past into the workshop. Clearly the conversation was over.

Jomari threw himself into the rest of his work day and then took off as soon as he felt it reasonable to do so. Grandad had given him a mission of sorts, and he was going to carry it out. He took the guitar and headed for Mack's apartment, sending a quick text on the way to explain.

It was a longer walk from the commuter station than Jomari remembered. By the time he arrived, he was too warm in his winter coat, his fingers and toes were slightly numb, and his arm ached from lugging the guitar. It had started spitting cold rain, too. Inside the building's first set of doors, he shook the water out of his hair and pulled off his gloves.

Before he could press the buzzer for Mack's apartment, an older woman exited. She looked him up and down, and Jomari froze in place. He never knew what sort of reaction he was going to get anymore. The woman didn't seem entirely unfriendly, but it was hard to tell.

"Hm," she said. "You here to see the last of those nice young men upstairs?"

"Uh...what?"

She pointed at the guitar. "Musicians, all of 'em. I was guessing."

"I'm not sure. I'm here to see Mack Whitman."

The woman nodded. "The one with the tattoos all over." She leaned on her cane and pinned Jomari with her steely gaze. "He's hurting. Be good to him."

With that, she held open the inner door for Jomari and then stepped outside. He wondered where she was going in such awful weather. As he stared after her, she got into a waiting car. Once she was gone, he took off for the elevator.

Jomari rapped on Mack's apartment door. It took long enough for him to answer that Jomari began to fidget with nerves. Since he hadn't buzzed first, and he'd forgotten to text again when he arrived due to the odd exchange with the neighbor, he prayed he wasn't interrupting anything important.

At last the door swung open, and there Mack stood. It was at least thirty awkward seconds of staring before Jomari recovered enough to step inside. Mack looked incredible. He had his shirt off, so Jomari could see all the ink the old woman had been talking about. The tattoos covered his arms, his upper chest, and the backs of his shoulders. His hair was damp, and Jomari smelled his shampoo and whatever he put in it afterward. Mack's jeans were a little loose, riding low enough on his hips to reveal the waistband of his underwear. The sight of it made Jomari almost drool. He'd forgotten how attractive Mack was.

Jomari got hold of himself and stepped inside. He held up the guitar. "All fixed." He grimaced at how the words came out slightly squeaky, a function of his body going into overdrive in Mack's presence.

Mack accepted it and set it next to his couch. "Thanks for bringing it by."

Jomari licked his lips. He didn't know where to begin. They didn't have a plan like the last time. He was here, in Mack's apartment, with no idea what the next step was. All he knew was what he wanted, and that was Mack. There was nothing for it except to be assertive, since anything else could land both of them in trouble.

"Can I be honest with you?" he asked.

Mack gave him a puzzled frown. "Yeah, of course."

"I mostly did come here to give you the guitar because my grandfather suggested it, and it's probably a bad idea to bring him up right now because I would really like to be making out on your couch or your bed or your kitchen table. Basically the closest furniture. I'd rather not be thinking about Grandad while we do it. And I don't know if you feel the same or if that's a good idea—it's probably not—but—"

Mack stepped closer. "Dude. You talk way too much."

Jomari grinned, relieved Mack hadn't outright rejected him. "So you've said."

"Talk less. Kiss more." Mack stepped closer.

"Should we be doing this? With all the stuff you have going on, and what about Amelia—"

Mack was right in Jomari's personal space now. "I could use something to break all this tension."

Jomari laughed nervously. "Are you saying you're desperate?"

"Fuck, yes. I haven't had sex at all in weeks. And you walk in here looking like that?" Mack was now inches from Jomari, gently moving him so his back was against the door. He leaned in.

"Like wha-ha-ha...oh, god." Jomari inhaled sharply when Mack's lips brushed his neck. "A-are you allowed to be doing this right now?"

Mack sighed and backed off a little. "Because of my recovery?"
"Yeah."

"I shouldn't be starting anything new, and I'm not in a position to hook up with random strangers at Starbucks."

"What?" Jomari couldn't help the small, nervous laugh that escaped.

"Never mind. This is okay. You and I, this is familiar. It won't break me." He straightened up and put his hand on Jomari's cheek. "I'm learning to be honest with myself and people I care about. I'll tell you if something isn't all right."

Jomari closed his eyes and nodded. When he inhaled, he caught the scent of Mack's skin and hair again, and it made his knees weak. That's exactly what he was: weak. He couldn't stay away from the intense physical pleasure of being in Mack's arms if he tried.

"I want you. I've been wanting you."

It felt right when Mack kissed him. Dangerous, yes, but glorious and perfect. Mack trailed his lips down Jomari's jaw to the hollow under his chin, where he nibbled and licked until Jomari was reduced to incoherent sounds. Then he kissed his way up toward Jomari's ear.

"I'm sorry," Mack murmured. "If you wanted to fuck, I can't bottom. Not right now."

"It's okay. I didn't bring my other cock. We don't have to do anything you don't want to."

"Bedroom?"

"Yeah."

Mack took his hand, and it felt good, warm and gentle, calming to Jomari's galloping heart. They went to Mack's bedroom, and he closed the door. Not an old habit—Mack was willing to fuck in any room, on any surface, if it suited everyone involved. He was definitely a bit of an exhibitionist; he admitted he'd been walked in on multiple times, and he never said it with any shame. Now he lived alone, with no chance of a stray roommate showing up unannounced, and yet he opted for privacy. Jomari wondered what made tonight different.

He never asked, and Mack didn't offer a reason. Instead, once they were inside, Mack began undressing. He'd never stripped Jomari, maybe conscious of the fact that Jomari still had parts of his body about which his feelings were unclear. In any case, Mack provided a slow showing of his body, sliding off his jeans and then his underwear inch by beautiful inch with his back to Jomari.

Mack had ink on his ass and legs, too. A spider on the left cheek, spinning her web down his hip and thigh. The other side was music notes flying from the page and quill on his right leg. There were letters on his right ankle that Jomari assumed were someone's initials, or possibly multiple people.

Finally, he turned around slowly, and Jomari swooned at the

sight. Mack was only the second cisgender man Jomari had been with, and Jomari was endlessly fascinated by his body. He loved the way the tattoos curled around toward the front, teasingly close to his pubes, which were a wild, sexy bush. Mack was moderately hairy, and he didn't do anything to change or tame it.

The thought of putting his hands all over Mack made Jomari painfully aware of both how aroused he was and how much clothing was still in the way. He was faster than Mack had been, pulling off everything in a rush. When he yanked his pants down to his ankles, he finally looked up to see Mack grinning. Jomari rolled his eyes, but he smiled back—and nearly fell over trying to get out of his jeans.

He removed his binder and considered leaving his undershirt on like usual, but it wasn't comfortable, and this was Mack. He didn't need to be impressed. He'd never once done anything other than ask Jomari what he did or didn't like and if he wanted more or a different angle or to be touched in a certain way. So Jomari took the undershirt off just as Mack lay down on the bed.

Jomari joined him, pressing close in so they could get back to kissing. As hot and ready as Jomari was, he loved this part and wanted more. The way Mack kissed was sexy and powerful. Jomari probably couldn't have explained the difference, but it wasn't the same as with Amelia. He wondered briefly how it was for the two of them and whether Mack was like this with her. He growled in frustration, not wanting those thoughts to take over his brain.

Mack misinterpreted the sound, fortunately. He hovered over Jomari and said, "Tell me what you want."

"Kissing. More kissing."

Mack dived back in, and they rutted against each other. Mack slid down, keeping his lips in the center of Jomari's body and making a beeline straight past his navel. He stopped at the tightly trimmed pubes and looked up.

"Can I suck you off?"

Jomari panted out as much of a yes as he could manage, and then Mack was there, doing amazing things with his lips and tongue. Jomari lost focus on anything else. He rested his legs on Mack's shoulders to give both of them a better position. Every bit of Jomari's body was burning, his nerves alight and his muscles taut with anticipation.

He was close. Opening his eyes, he peered down at Mack, about to tell him he was going to come. When he looked, he saw

Mack had a hand between his own legs. The sight of him jerking himself while blowing him sent a hard spike of pleasure through Jomari. He put his hand in Mack's hair and tugged just as he came, lifting his ass off the bed and groaning.

Mack crawled up the bed and wiped his jaw before kissing Jomari again. Jomari tore his mouth away to say, "Inside. I need you in me."

Still half on top of him, Mack reached into the drawer to pull out a condom and rip it open with this teeth. He rolled it on, and Jomari angled so Mack could slide into his front hole. Jomari sighed with a combination of oversensitivity and relief. He loved the feeling of being filled right after coming.

It didn't take long before Mack gave in, thrusting through his own orgasm while Jomari gripped his ass. They stayed moulded together for a while after, Jomari rubbing Mack's back and Mack taking deep breaths against Jomari's shoulder.

Mack pulled out and sat up to shed the condom. He set a box of tissues between them and began cleaning himself. Jomari half watched him, lazily wiping off at the same time. It felt right, being there, but suddenly wrong too. They'd fallen back into a pattern they'd had before, though he had no agreement with Amelia that they were barred from it. Even so, it made Jomari uncomfortable that they still hadn't made a direct decision about what was and wasn't going to be part of their relationships.

"You done?" Mack asked tapping the tissue box.

"Yeah, I'm good."

Mack stuck it back on the bedside table. "We should probably talk."

"Probably. Maybe should've before we had wild monkey sex."

Mack chuckled. "You may be right."

He scooted closer, and Jomari rolled so he was tucked against his side. Mack curled an arm around him. Jomari put out a finger and traced the ink on Mack's right side where he could see it. There was a Celtic cross on his right pec, and his entire right arm was done to look like an electric guitar. Above the cross was a line of text. Jomari could only see part of it, but he knew what it said: *Seeking something yet unfound though I have diligently sought it.* He'd asked Mack about it the first time they'd been together, why he had that particular quote from Walt Whitman. Mack had been dismissive, saying they shared a last name. Jomari wondered if his answer would be different now they knew one another better.

Mack had ink on the other side, where Jomari couldn't

currently see it, though he knew what it was. Beneath where his cheek now rested, Mack had a heart made from the treble and bass clefs. In place of the dots on the bass clef symbol was a semicolon. The arm encircling Jomari's shoulders was covered in flames, and Mack had an androgynous angel on the back of that shoulder. His other shoulder blade had a second Whitman quote: *Every moment of light and dark is a miracle.* Jomari idly wondered now whether Mack planned to get any more or if he felt the canvas of his body was complete.

"You love her, don't you?" Mack's voice was a hesitant murmur.

Jomari contemplated pretending he had no idea what Mack was talking about, but that wouldn't solve anything. "Yeah."

"In love, not the way I love her."

"Yes."

"You tell her that?"

Jomari was caught by Mack, like every other person he'd spoken to about the subject. He sighed. "Not exactly. We had a date. I took her ice skating, and we—are you sure you're okay with me telling you this?"

"I am." Mack squeezed Jomari's shoulders. "Go on."

"We kissed, on the ice, right in front of everyone. After, I asked about going back to her place. I think she assumed I meant for sex, but I wanted to tell her in private how I feel about her. Instead, she told me she needed to slow things down. And then she left for England. She's back, but she hasn't called."

He settled back down and returned to contemplating Mack's tattoos. It was easier to focus on the letters and images than to allow himself to think about Amelia. Everything was so confusing. Before, he'd had the impression things were tense between Mack and Amelia because of him. Now Mack seemed to be trying to get them together.

Eventually, Mack pushed a little, and Jomari shifted off him. Mack turned over and propped himself on his elbow. He brushed Jomari's bangs off his forehead, and tiny worry lines appeared around Mack's eyes when he cupped Jomari's cheek.

"I hope this wasn't a bad idea."

Jomari sat up and hugged his knees. "I told you that from the beginning."

Mack sat up too. "You did. But I was thinking less with my brain and more with my dick at the time." He nudged Jomari's shoulder with his own.

"Same."

"We both have things to tell Amelia." Mack leaned his head on Jomari's shoulder. "The two of you can give each other something I can't."

"But—"

Mack lifted his head and turned slightly. He took Jomari's face between his palms. "That's not a bad thing. I see it now. I don't know how it all fits together, and I'm..." His shoulders rose and fell with a deep breath. "I'm scared of losing you both. But she deserves this happiness without worrying for me. So do you." He lowered Jomari's head to kiss the top of it. "Tell her."

They lay down again, pressed together shoulder to ankle. Mack was quiet, maybe drifting off to sleep. Jomari's brain was too full to rest. He wondered if he should go or if Mack wanted his company. It could go either way, and Jomari hadn't thought to ask ahead of time.

Mack's voice startled him. "You know what's weird?"

"Hm?"

"I haven't wanted to smoke in weeks."

"You smoke?"

"I quit in the fall for, like, the millionth time. Every time before this, I went back to it after a few months. I reached that point, went past it, and...it's not really that I don't still think about it. More like it's background noise. That's never happened before."

"Huh. I don't know a lot about it, but that sounds like a good thing."

"It is." Mack looked over and smiled. "It really is."

He kissed Jomari, and the light pressure turned more sensual. Mack flipped over to get a better angle, and Jomari opened his mouth to let Mack explore with his tongue. Their kissing veered toward the slight aggression Jomari loved, and he groaned against Mack's lips. Mack slid his hand down between Jomari's legs.

"This for me?" he asked, rubbing with his thumb.

"Yeah...ah, shit. Don't stop."

Mack didn't, and the heat between them temporarily drove Jomari's worry to the recesses of his mind.

CHAPTER TWENTY-FIVE

GRAND SLAM already looked gorgeous, the tables covered in rose gold table cloths with black napkins and vases of deep wine roses. It seemed like everyone Jomari knew—and a few he didn't—were there to help set up for Nate and Izzy's wedding. The bar wasn't normally open on Sundays until after four, but they'd unlocked it early to get ready. It would be closed to the public for the night as well.

They'd chosen to be married by Denver, one of the co-owners, instead of a rabbi. They'd already had a private ceremony earlier in the week with only their parents and a rabbi present; this was for their extended friends and family. Denver qualified on multiple counts—not only was she licensed to marry people, she was Jewish, so she understood what they wanted.

Jomari didn't know them well, aside through Amelia and Jamie, but he was there as part of the entertainment. They had a DJ for later in the evening, but they'd hired a number of people to perform during dinner. Cian and his company were among them, so there Jomari was too. He'd come in with Mack to lend a hand.

It didn't turn out to be as many people as Jomari first thought. Mack greeted Nate and Izzy, who were there until it was time to get themselves ready. Trevor and Jamie were directing the set-up, and Jomari caught them glaring at each other while straightening a table cloth. At first, he thought they really were mad at each other. He did a double take when he realized they were both trying not to smile. Apparently, they'd made up.

Denver was talking to Marlie and Nia, both of whom Jomari already knew from the Lighthouse clinic. Marlie had a pad of paper and a pen, and she was furiously scribbling something. Jomari didn't see Cian, which meant he either wasn't there yet or was somewhere in back. Amelia was nowhere in sight either. Since Jomari wasn't sure how he felt about seeing her, he was all right with that for now.

Mack made his way over to Trevor and Jamie, and Jomari followed, since he had nothing better to do. He set his violin down beside the table they'd just finished decorating. Jamie frowned at it, slightly adjusted a napkin, and gave Trevor a simmering look.

Trevor rolled his eyes, but he grinned and then turned to Mack and Jomari. "Hey, guys."

Mack snorted at Jamie. "I see you still have a thing for weddings."

"Shut up." But Jamie was smiling.

Jomari had no idea whatsoever what the joke was between them, and he didn't ask. He assumed it had something to do with the predatory look Jamie was now directing at Trevor.

"Get a room, guys," Mack said. "Mary Magdalene and the Seven Dwarves, you guys are awful."

"Mary who and the what?" Jamie asked. "Never mind. There's no time—we have to finish these tables, put out place cards, and find Jagathi to tell us what all these other things on the list are. We were only in charge of the decorating. She had everything else covered."

"You go talk to Jagathi," Mack said. "Trevor can fill us in on what to do with tables and place cards and whatever."

"Are you sure you can handle it? Maybe Trevor should—"

"Jay!" Trevor interrupted. "Seriously, it's fine. You can straighten the damn napkins later. Go."

Jamie sighed so deeply his shoulders rose and fell, and Jomari laughed at his theatrics. No one was angry, and they were all more relaxed than they were pretending to be. Jomari didn't know who Jagathi was—he assumed probably the wedding planner—but he guaranteed everything was under control. Nate and Izzy weren't the types to be stressed about whether or not the napkins formed a perfect angle with each other.

While Mack and Jomari began spreading another table cloth, Jamie bounced off toward the bar. It was good to see him so cheerful. Trevor pulled pre-folded napkins out of a box on one of the chairs and set them around the table. Because it was a bar, most of the tables were meant for two or four people. They'd left some of the four-seaters as they were, but they'd pushed a number of the others together to form larger ones. Jomari noticed for the first time that some of the chairs had been covered in the same rose gold fabric as the table cloths, tied with wine-colored ribbon. He glanced up from placing a napkin to see Marlie and Nia working on the rest. With a jolt, Jomari spotted Amelia alongside them.

She looked beautiful, even in casual jeans and a button-down blouse. Her hair was already done for the wedding, swept up with a few loose curls framing her face. She'd had highlights put in, maybe while they were away on vacation. The way the bar's soft overhead lighting hit her hair made it glow. She'd done her makeup already too, and it enhanced her natural beauty. Jomari lost himself staring at her.

Mack elbowed him, and he realized he was still holding onto the napkin, in danger of messing up the perfect fold. Jomari shook himself. He saw Mack gazing the same direction he had been and couldn't help looking over again. The women were laughing about something, and Jomari's chest tightened. He didn't want to intrude on her time with her friends, but he wished she were over at his table, having that same fun with him instead.

Right then, she looked up. Her gaze met Jomari's, and for a few seconds, he couldn't breathe. She smiled and gave him a tiny wave. He barely managed to wave back, so great was his relief. She wasn't angry with him; her face was warm and open. He had no idea what she was thinking about, but at least she didn't seem as if she would rather be away from him.

In fact, before Jomari could register it, she was setting down the ribbon in her hand and heading his way. He quickly set the napkin in place, noting out of the corner of his eye that Trevor adjusted it. Mack stepped away, following Trevor to the next table.

"Hi," Amelia said.

"Hi." Jomari wondered if her amused expression might have to do with the way his smile came out as more of a grimace. "Did you— um, was your trip good?"

"Oh, yeah. I can't wait to tell you about it." She fidgeted. "Maybe over dinner this week? We definitely have some catching up to do."

"I'd like that." He longed to reach out and wrap one of those luscious curls around his finger, then draw her close. He didn't, though. Instead, he shoved his hands into his pockets. "Um...your hair looks nice. Really pretty." *Wow, I sound like a dork.*

"Thanks. I had it done at this cute little salon when we were in England. I'll tell you about that too. The stylist..." Amelia blushed. "She was so sweet. And—I think I can say this without you being weirded out—she is freaking hot. But straight, sadly." She giggled.

Jomari laughed along with her. "Well, now I really need to know more."

Amelia smacked his arm playfully. "You've got no chance either, mister. She's married, has kids, and is also all the way on the other side of the ocean."

"That does sound like a problem. Or an excuse for me to—" He pulled up short before suggesting he could whisk Amelia away on another trip. Too much, too soon.

Fortunately, Amelia misread him. "Don't you dare!"

"Nah, I'd have to save up anyway." He relaxed, glad she hadn't made too much of his near-slip. Nodding at Mack, he said, "Maybe we should help finish this. I'd hate for Nate and Izzy to have to get married with the tables only half done."

Amelia's happiness seemed to fade a little. "Yeah, probably." She reached up and touched Jomari's cheek. "Save a dance for me, okay?"

"You bet."

He watched her return to her friends before he went back to helping Mack and Trevor with the table cloths. His hands were occupied with wedding preparations, but his mind was still on Amelia. She'd asked him to save her a dance, and he was determined not to waste that moment. Maybe he couldn't predict where it would go, but he had to tell her before the night was over, even if he risked rejection in the company of all their mutual friends.

Jomari had never attended a Jewish marriage ceremony before. He'd been to a number of weddings, almost all family on his mother's side. One of his mother's cousins had married another woman. Up until that point, Jomari hadn't had a whole lot of interest in weddings; he couldn't picture himself marrying a man or wearing all that lace. Watching two women exchange vows opened his eyes to new possibilities. Of course, that had been before he knew he was a man. Now, he had a vastly different perspective on the whole thing.

Jomari was seated with Cian, Jamie, and Mack at one of the

smaller tables. He made to slide into his seat, but Jamie said, "You have to go see Curtis first."

"Why?"

Jamie touched the small, round cap on his head. "This."

With a shrug, Jomari pushed his chair back in and headed for the main entrance. Curtis, usually Grand Slam's bouncer, was doing a different kind of door duty this time. He had a basket of kippot that he handed out to all the men in attendance as well as a few non-male people who chose to wear one. There were lace head coverings for the women and anyone else who chose one instead of a kippah.

Jomari peered into the basket. He had a choice of black, ivory, or burgundy; he chose the burgundy. The kippah was made of a soft fabric with brocade trim, and it had Hebrew lettering on it. Jomari had never worn one before, but he put it on and hoped he'd done it right. He returned to his table just in time for everything to begin.

Nate and Izzy's ceremony was as gorgeous and elegant as the decorations and color scheme suggested. Once all the guests were seated at their assigned tables, a string quartet began to play. Nate's family came in first—people who were clearly his parents, followed by another man and woman and two little girls. Izzy's mothers and his father were next, and then finally the grooms. Since neither of them was technically a bride, they'd chosen to walk together.

Izzy wore a traditional black tux, but Nate's was cream. They had matching wine-colored accessories. Both of them were impossibly handsome all dressed up, and Jomari enjoyed the beautiful view. It seemed everyone was having more or less the same reaction. Their families gathered under the chuppah, along with Denver.

She was dressed in a more subdued way than usual, and she matched the wedding colors in her burgundy suit and lace head covering. Fortunately for Jomari and every other non-Jewish guest there, she explained each part of their ceremony as it happened. They'd also hired an interpreter; whether for Cian alone or for multiple guests, Jomari thought it was good of them.

Although it was probably longer than other weddings he had attended, it didn't feel like it because Jomari was fascinated with the differences. Through most of it, both Nate and Izzy were emotional, wiping their eyes. Izzy's mothers were doing the same. His father kept patting them on the shoulders in a way that made Jomari have to stifle his amusement.

Before exchanging rings, Nate and Izzy addressed the assembled guests. Izzy said, "To seal our commitment, we will sing for you 'Au fond du temple saint' from Bizet's *The Pearl Fishers*. This is the first piece we ever sang together, when we hardly knew one another and only had fifteen minutes to practice."

They were accompanied by the string quartet, joined by Trevor on piano. It was a beautiful arrangement, though the lyrics were in French and Jomari couldn't understand what they were singing. It didn't seem to matter. Nate and Izzy had incredible voices, and they sang it with such tenderness that all around the room, people were dabbing their eyes by the time the song finished on a glorious note.

Once they had placed rings on one another's fingers, Denver said, "Nathaniel and Israel, along with both their families, have chosen to write their own seven blessings, based on the traditional *Sheva B'rachot*. They now invite you in as witnesses of their joy."

When they were through, Denver handed each of the grooms a wine-colored cloth bag. She said, "The tradition of breaking the glass has many meanings. For Nathaniel and Israel, they have been through many trials together. In marriage, there is sorrow as well as joy. May you both experience blessing even in times of distress."

Nate and Izzy set their bags down, looked at each other, and mouthed a count of three before stomping on them. Jomari almost missed it when the entire room shouted, "Mazel tov!" and erupted in cheers and whistles.

After everything was said and done, Nate and Izzy disappeared. Denver explained they were going for a time of quiet contemplation together, upstairs in the offices. Afterward, they would do all the traditional photographs and such. That was why they'd hired people to perform in between. Mercifully, they hadn't asked the Creepy Crullers to get back together and play. That wouldn't have ended well for anyone.

Mack leaned in and murmured, "Aren't you glad Trevor sold that song of his? I don't think we'll have to listen to it tonight."

Jamie snorted and then signed to Cian what Mack had said. "Nate threatened us with it if Trevor and I didn't get our shit together with the planning."

"You should've seen it," Cian told Jomari. "I happened to be there for it. I've never seen Trevor apologize so fast."

"Hey!" Jomari protested. "I like that song."

The others only laughed. They all turned their attention to the stage. Apparently, some of the drag queens from back when Izzy was still doing it had agreed to come, and they were the opening series of acts. Trevor would be on later with Andre and some friend of theirs who Jomari only vaguely recognized. In between numbers, Jamie, Jomari and Cian stood and made their way to the back to wait for their chance to perform.

Once again, there was Amelia. Now she was dressed for the wedding, in a stunning knee-length, dark blue dress with lace sleeves. Her curves—okay, Jomari had to be honest, her breasts—looked amazing. He knew he was blushing, and the minute Amelia caught his gaze, it was obvious she was aware of exactly where he was staring. She didn't even hide her smile, and he relaxed.

She stepped behind Cian to stand beside Jomari. "I'm only playing one song with the band," she said.

"I wondered. Cian didn't mention it." Jomari peered around Amelia; Cian shrugged and winked. Ah, payback. At least Cian's and Jamie's mutual misunderstandings about who they'd been set up with worked out for them. Cian was plain old meddling this time, but Jomari thought it might be a good thing, if it worked out.

"Well," Amelia said, "guess we'd better get ready. I can hear the quartet, and they're right before us."

They would have time later, he hoped, to talk. If not, then at least he sensed she'd be okay if he called. Relieved, Jomari set his violin on the counter and opened the case. The whole time he was putting rosin on his bow and tuning up, he kept Amelia in his peripheral vision. He internally crossed every finger and toe in hopes she would hear him out.

The reception was pretty much what Jomari expected: a party. There were a few things different from what Jomari remembered of other weddings he'd attended, but once all the more formal parts were over, it was mostly the same. Not only was this the first time Jomari had been to a Jewish wedding, it was also the first time he'd seen two men get married. He supposed he'd been imagining it would be nothing like what he'd experienced, but it was all pretty familiar territory, aside from the drag queens and maybe Cian.

Dinner was as incredible as everything else. Mack said the whole thing was catered by Cassie, formerly in the Crullers, and her girlfriend. They outdid themselves, and the food was amazing.

The DJ played a mix of Jewish traditional and contemporary pop music, and Jomari was glad to note Nate and Izzy had opted out of a lot of the more annoying party dances. He recalled being forced to do them at some cousin's wedding a few years ago and was happier avoiding all that.

Instead, they introduced all their friends from other backgrounds to some Jewish wedding dances. Jomari thought the Hora was easy…until it got faster. There were a few others as well, including one where everyone danced in a circle around Nate's and Izzy's parents. Jomari wondered how many of the customs the two of them had adapted for a same-gender wedding and how many were exactly as they'd be in a different-gender wedding. He would've known if it had been Catholic, but he knew very little about Jewish traditions.

After that, Jomari didn't do much dancing. Mack was more interested in messing around with the other guys, and Jomari had been avoiding Amelia while pretending not to. He didn't want to spoil Nate and Izzy's evening, although he couldn't have explained how sitting alone at his table was doing less damage than finding the one person he really wanted to see.

He sipped some fizzy non-alcoholic punch with a tiny straw and watched other couples moving onto the dance floor as a slower song played. It didn't matter how much he hated this song; he only wished he could be among them. The scrape of another chair at his table distracted him and he looked over. Jamie.

"You okay?"

"Sure." Jomari shrugged one shoulder.

"You seem really down. Maybe the others didn't notice, but I did."

"I feel like I should wait and not make a big deal about this at someone else's happy day."

Jamie looked around, and Jomari followed his gaze. Nate and Izzy were on the dance floor, first together and then breaking in to dance with other people. They looked like they were having the time of their lives.

"Do they seem like it would bother them if you dealt with your stuff?"

"They look like nothing would bother them right now."

"Uh-huh." Jamie nodded. "I've only known Nate for a couple years, but I can tell you he would be more upset that you thought you had to stay miserable for his sake than if you find Amelia and go somewhere private to talk."

Jomari gestured around. "Private?"

"I know a place, and I think Denver would be okay under the circumstances. Let me know."

Jamie left Jomari there with his drink, contemplating. The song ended, and the DJ played another slow one because Nate and Izzy were still taking turns with their guests. Jomari supposed if he asked Amelia to join him and dance with the grooms, maybe afterward she would agree to talking.

He scanned the room and finally spotted her, laughing with Marlie and Nia the way she had been earlier when they were all setting up. He rose slowly and made his way toward her. When he arrived at their table, they paused their conversation and looked up at him.

"Um." He rubbed the back of his neck. "Hi?"

"Hey, Jomari," Marlie said. She smiled. "Having fun?"

"Sure, yeah." His heart sped up, but he plowed ahead. "Amelia, um, I saved you that dance. Maybe we could go take our turns with the grooms?"

Amelia looked like she was considering it—or him. "All right." To her friends, she said, "I'll be back."

Jomari didn't know whether or not that meant right away. He didn't have a good read on the situation. He wanted very much to take Amelia's hand as they walked into the crowd of dancers, but he didn't. She made no attempt either, and he wondered if it was a bad sign.

She put her arms around his neck, and he rested his hands on her hips. They swayed to the music, and it felt...off. As if they were a fraction of a beat behind. It was only a minute before Nate and Izzy cut in. Izzy took Amelia, and Nate danced with Jomari. They made circles in the middle of the crowd, and other couples half watched them while they danced.

Jomari kept sneaking glances at Amelia, who looked entirely at ease. Nate picked up on it and looked over as well. He turned back to Jomari and grinned.

"Dude, you know I'm not into women, but she's pretty cool. Don't make the mistake I did."

"What mistake?" Jomari scoffed. "You got your man."

"Yeah, after I almost screwed it up thinking I wasn't good enough for him."

"I—"

The song ended, and Nate spun Jomari dramatically. They both laughed, and some of Jomari's tension eased. The DJ began another song, and Nate and Izzy continued working their way through the guests. Jomari stood there for a moment until he felt a tap on his shoulder.

"We didn't get to finish that one. Want to try again?"

Jomari nodded and took Amelia back in his arms. Was Nate right? Did he risk losing her because he wasn't sure he was good enough for her? He'd thought all along it was only about the complications between himself, Amelia and Mack. When she hadn't called him after her trip, he told himself it was her move. But he'd been avoiding her, and now he had to face his insecurities.

He drew her closer and let the music carry him. The awkwardness melted away, and soon all he thought about was holding Amelia and moving together in rhythm. He leaned in so he could murmur in her ear.

"I have to tell you something."

She pulled back a little to look at him. "Okay."

"Not here. After this dance."

Amelia nodded and then shifted so she could rest her head on his shoulder. If this was the last time he got to touch her, so be it. He would enjoy the moment before taking her somewhere they could talk. He closed his eyes and allowed everything else to fade temporarily.

The song ended, and with no one else to dance with the grooms, the DJ put on something more upbeat. Nate and Izzy joined hands and left the dance floor along with about half the couples. Everyone else stayed to keep dancing. Jomari led Amelia over to Jamie.

"Where did you say we could go for some privacy?"

Jamie tilted his head toward the bar. "Behind there is a set of stairs up to the offices. There's one they don't use."

"Are you sure it's okay?" Jomari said at the same time Amelia snickered and said "I wouldn't say it's unused."

Jomari arched an eyebrow at her. "Oh?"

"I don't kiss and tell." Amelia's cheeks were pink.

Jamie rolled his eyes. "Have that discussion later. C'mon, let's go."

He led them around the bar and held open the door to the stairs. Amelia went up first, and Jomari followed. He'd never been this way, even though he'd performed at Grand Slam many times. Amelia led him into a room with a desk and a few chairs and closed the door.

"This sounds important," she said.

"Are you sure you wouldn't rather be back down there at the party?"

"Yes, of course."

Now they were alone, Jomari felt his confidence drain away. Where to start? The minute he opened his mouth, though, words tumbled from it.

"I love you," he blurted. "I have for a while. You said you needed time, and that's okay, but I don't know how much longer I can wait. Everyone keeps telling me I have to talk to you and to Mack, and even my sister had some good advice. She got it from her gay friends because I guess they have an arrangement. Wait, that came out wrong. Her friends have one, not my sister and them. Anyway, I-"

Amelia stepped closer. "I knew what you meant." She sighed. "I did a lot of thinking while I was away. You're not the only one who got advice."

"Oh?"

"I thought I blew it after our date when I said I needed time. I meant it, but it's because I got scared. I love you too, and that freaked me out."

"What?" Jomari wasn't sure which part surprised him more.

"Yeah." Amelia pulled up a chair for each of them, and they sat. "I was happy having my agreement with Mack. He's no-strings, and we're not at risk of ruining our friendship. It's different with you. I've honestly never felt this way about anyone. Not because I couldn't have but because I've avoided it on purpose. I see that now."

Jomari held out his hand and she took it. "I know what I mean when I say I love you, and I know what I want. But I have to be sure you mean the same thing."

Amelia nodded. "Agreed. So what do you think of when you picture us together?"

He closed his eyes and took a deep breath. "I imagine us going places together and holding hands in public. Spending time with our friends, being a couple the way a lot of them are. I think about taking you to meet my family and creating a whole life together." He opened his eyes again and looked at Amelia.

"I can't take you to meet my family. I have no idea where my mother is—or even who she is. My father is in jail, hopefully for a very long time, and I don't want him to find me when he gets out. The rest? Yes. That's what I see too. But..."

"I know. Mack."

"Yeah."

Jomari squeezed Amelia's hand and let go. He angled so he

could face her directly. "That's what I meant about getting advice from my sister. She started dating a woman, and her girlfriend has a lot of queer friends. The guys I mentioned run a group for polyamorous students. They have sort of an open relationship, and we look a bit like that except our occasional partner is someone we both know."

"And Denver." Amelia looked guilty.

"Right. You mentioned that." He didn't have a problem with it, necessarily, but Amelia's relationship with Denver did complicate things a bit.

"I think..." Amelia bit her lip. "I have to talk to her. I think I might've been using her to avoid what I really wanted. Not when she and I first started—I didn't know you very well back then. I mean recently. Being with Mack, everyone assumed we were a couple. I could put them off and assert who I am, since we were never together. But with you, it's different."

"You don't want to look like a straight couple."

"I'm sorry," she said. "That's my issue, not yours, and I feel different now. I care about Denver, and I thought she and I would keep doing what we're doing. But I'm not sure it's what I want anymore."

That conversation didn't include Jomari, and he was okay with it. "We do have to tell Mack."

"I know."

There was a knock, and they both jumped. Amelia went to answer it, and her mouth fell open. Mack slid inside and shut the door. He turned to Jomari.

"You told her?"

"Yep."

Amelia looked between them. "Wait. Mack, you knew about Jomari and me?"

"He and I talked it through, yes. I let him know it's cool with me and that he should speak to you." Mack shooed the two of them back to their seats and pulled up a third chair. He turned it backwards and plunked down. To Jomari he said, "I didn't necessarily mean you should do it at our friends' wedding, but hey, romantic atmosphere and all. You two work it out?"

"Mostly," Jomari told him. "I guess the three of us should probably be adults and set some of what my sister calls 'boundaries.'"

Mack folded his arms on the chair back and rested his chin on them. "We should, and we will. There's probably something else I should tell you as well."

Amelia frowned. "Is everything okay?"

"Yes and no. I'm still really struggling with getting my addiction under control again. I talked a lot with Jamie about this, but I need to tell you too."

"Go on," Jomari said.

"I'm the reason Sage did what he did." He held up a hand when Amelia went to protest. "I didn't say I was at fault, only that I'm why he was such a warthog's anus. He was obsessed with me, not Jamie. None of you ever knew it. He used Jamie to get to me, and when that didn't work, he threatened all of us. I have to deal with the consequences of not being able to stop him."

"His behavior isn't on you," Amelia said. "I would know."

"You're right, but I still feel like I should've been able to prevent it. Part of being able to stay sober is facing that."

"Does Jamie blame you?" Jomari asked.

"Not at all. And I have to face that too because a big part of me thinks he should."

"If you'd given in to Sage's demands, he'd have done worse to you than he did to Jamie," Amelia said.

"I know."

"We all tried," Amelia told him. "Every last one of us, even you."

"We did. Jamie says if I'd said anything to him at the time, he wouldn't have believed me. I still can't shake the feeling I should've done it anyway."

"I hate to be that guy, but I'm not sure what that has to do with this." Jomari motioned between all of them.

"It means I've been unfair to you both. I do care about you. Maybe love is the right word for it. I don't know. I don't have those squishy, romantic feelings you both talk about, so I can't be sure. I do know that I'm not in a good place to keep hooking up with different people. That was fine when I was sober for a long time, but it isn't right now."

"Do you mean you want to stop being with us?" Jomari asked.

Mack shook his head. "Mm-mm. I hope part of taking care of myself includes time spent with both of you." He held out his hands to them.

Amelia took one of Mack's hands and one of Jomari's. "I like the sound of that."

"Me too." Jomari gave their fingers a squeeze.

"Good. I promise, we'll talk again as many times as we need. For now, why don't we go back down and enjoy what's left of Nate and Izzy's wedding? I'd originally come up here to tell you they said they're doing the cake at eight. It's about..." Mack looked at his phone. "Two minutes until then."

"Let's go," Jomari said. "I don't want to miss it. Their tiny cake for cutting is gorgeous, but did you see all those tiers of cupcakes? I seriously wanted to try them all when Jamie said what flavors they are."

"Same," Amelia said.

They put the chairs back and headed downstairs. Outside the door to the stairwell, both Amelia and Mack took Jomari's hands. He felt as if he were ten feet off the ground. There was nowhere he would rather be than right there, sandwiched between two of the people he cared about most in the world.

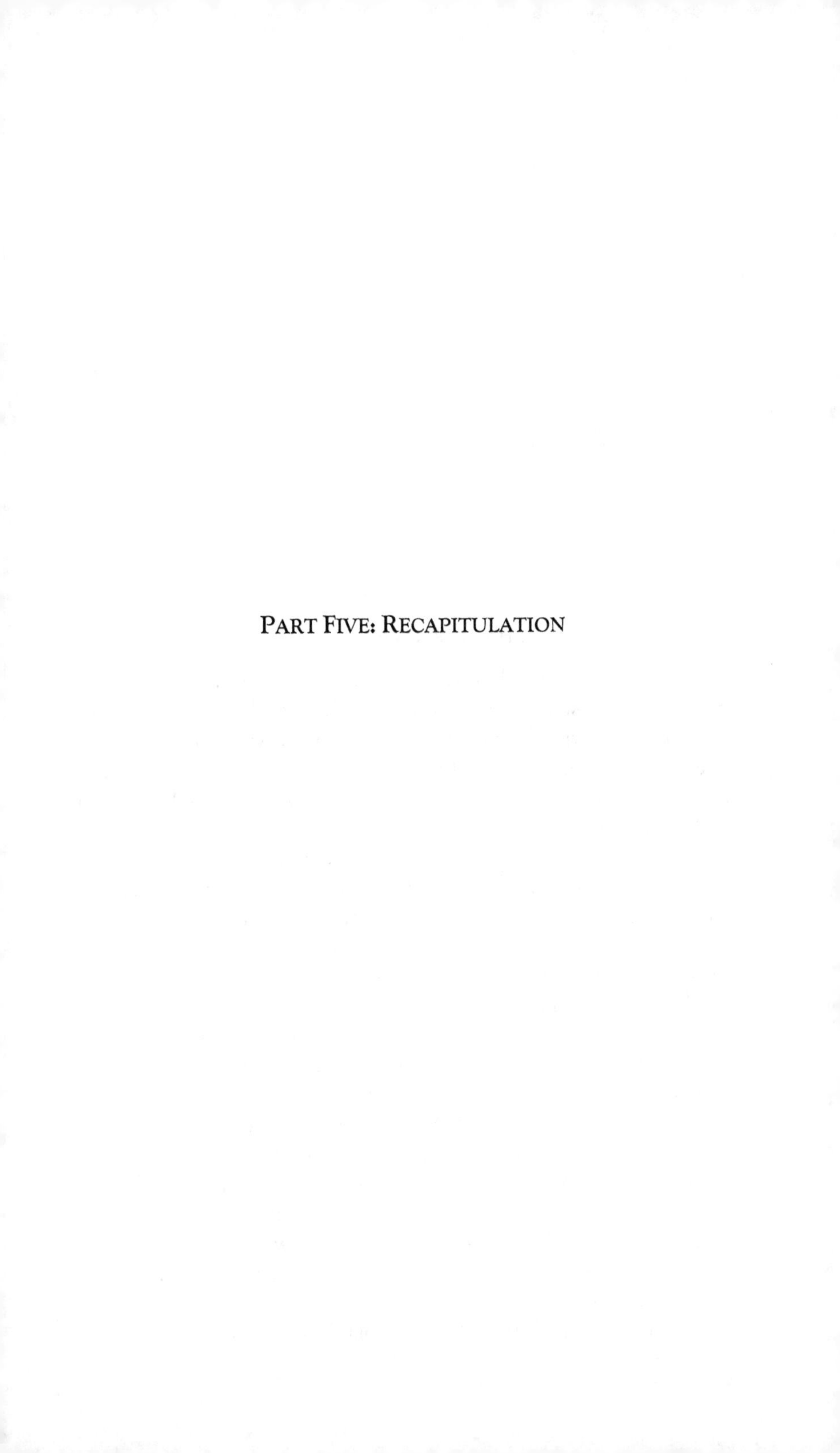

PART FIVE: RECAPITULATION

Chapter Twenty-Six

THE LATE May weather was gorgeous. Amelia found the perfect picnic spot, and she set everything up. She, Mack and Jomari had plans with their friends later, but for now, they were going to enjoy the feast Mack had prepared for them. He'd said he had news, and she was positively itching to know what it was. He wouldn't even give them a clue.

They'd been spending a lot of time together doing this sort of thing, the three of them. She had plenty of time with Jomari on their own as well—Mack did like his space. But it had been a while since their last group outing, and she had some news of her own. Technically, it was hers and Jomari's, and she was nervous about how Mack would take it.

She spread out the blanket and a few small cushions. Jomari set the two baskets on the grass. When Mack planned the menu, Jomari had asked if a picnic in the park was too close to the "hearts and flowers and shit" that Mack disliked. He'd laughed and dismissed Jomari with a comment about it only being food. He was avoiding an explanation, but Amelia understood. Mack might not have liked all the romantic, mushy stuff himself, but he loved how happy it made Amelia and Jomari. She'd known him long enough that she sensed his quiet joy in the love she shared with Jomari. And *that* made *her* happy.

She and Jomari lounged on the blanket, and Mack pulled out

containers. He explained—with probably more detail than strictly necessary—what each one was. Jomari's eyebrows rose higher with each new dish. It wasn't exactly traditional picnic food. Amelia couldn't wait to try everything. It had been a long time since she and Mack had cooked together, and she missed his bossy perfectionism.

They loaded their plates. Unable to wait even until she'd taken a bite, Amelia said, "So...news. You had something to tell us?"

"Maybe you should go first." Mack grinned at her in a way that suggested he knew perfectly well how desperate she was for him to tell them already.

"Don't you dare try to get out of it. You said whatever it was is big, so let's have it." She mock-glared at him.

"I'm going back to school."

Amelia dropped the fork she'd been holding. "Say what?"

"Yep. It's just a short program. Culinary arts. And I'm starting a new job. Cassie and Laura don't care about my tats or my record, so they hired me as a server for now. Eventually, I'll be working with the food."

"Holy crap!" Jomari exclaimed. "That's great!"

"Yep. In the meantime, I've also been practicing that guitar you and your grandfather fixed up. I did a couple open mics, and Denver's asked if I want to play at Grand Slam. Apparently, I'm not too shabby."

"Definitely not," Amelia assured him. "Wow. This is fantastic. I'm so excited for you."

"There's more." Mack cleared his throat. "I sent a poem for a collection. Well, technically, it was supposed to be a song, but obviously I'm not doing so much of that these days."

"And?" Amelia prompted.

"It got rejected."

"Aw, man. I'm sorry." Jomari reached out for Mack's hand, but Mack was still smiling.

"It's fine. The publisher said it didn't fit the theme, but she liked it so much she wanted to know if I had more. I have an entire drawer full of notebooks, so I said I did. And she asked me to send some samples."

"So did you?" Amelia probably didn't need to ask the question, but Mack wasn't telling them the whole story.

"Yeah, of course. And..." Mack paused for dramatic effect. "I now officially have a publisher. It's a super tiny press, but I don't care. Maybe no one will buy the book, even. But it's going to be out there. Official date is January of next year."

"Oh my god!" Jomari set his plate down and practically lunged at Mack, who hastily stuck his plate on top of one of the baskets just before Jomari tackled him.

Laughing, Amelia set her plate down too and joined the pile. Jomari kissed Mack, and then Mack leaned up to give Amelia a kiss. She put her heart into it, and when she pulled back, she caught sight of Jomari's parted lips and the flicker of interest in his eyes. She smiled and tilted her head toward Mack. Jomari leaned in again, and Amelia sighed at the vision of the two of them enjoying an open-mouthed kiss.

Jomari sat up, and Amelia leaned in to press her lips to his. She felt the smile, and they enjoyed their moment of connection before they separated and leaned back. The three of them were quiet, and Mack looked back and forth between Amelia and Jomari.

They'd never done that before. Always when they were together, it was out with friends or having dinner or taking in a concert. The physical was divided into their separate spheres. Amelia spent the most time with Jomari, but they were both open about when they planned to go individually to Mack's. Until now, anything else had seemed off-limits.

Mack broke the silence. "You said you had news too." He nudged Amelia with his toe.

"Right." She glanced at Jomari. "We've decided to move in together."

"Hey, that's great!" Mack said. He looked genuinely happy, so Amelia relaxed. "Where abouts?"

"We've looked at a bunch of places..." Jomari trailed off and looked at Amelia.

"The rent is kind of high..." she continued, prompting him.

"And the thing is..."

Amelia bit her lip. Only one way to do it. "The most affordable place is...your building."

Mack laughed. "Okay."

"You're not mad?"

"Why would I be?" Mack gave her a puzzled look. "It's great. We won't even have to drive to see each other, but I'll still have my own space. It's not like you're trying to move in with me, right?" He paused, a wary expression crossing his face. "You're not, are you?"

"Of course not!" Amelia giggled. "I get it. You like being alone.

I have no idea how you survived roommates for so long. We wouldn't dream of changing anything. I was only worried you'd still think it was too close."

"No, not at all."

Everything was out in the open, then. Amelia was relieved, but somehow, she still felt as if she was missing some vital piece of information. The guys didn't appear to notice anything, so she dismissed it as leftover worry from having to break her news to Mack. He was all right, and so were she and Jomari.

Amelia checked the time. "We should probably eat up all this food Mack brought. Then maybe we'll have time to enjoy the park before we go hear whatever it is Andre wanted to tell all of us."

"Ah, right, the village meeting," Mack joked. "It sounded important. We definitely don't want to listen on an empty stomach."

"Or be late and risk the wrath of Trevor," Jomari added.

Mack stabbed a cherry tomato half with his fork and offered it to Amelia. Then he did the same for Jomari. Whatever he'd marinated them in was delicious, and Amelia and Jomari sighed with pleasure at the same time. All three of them laughed, and they basked in the sun and fed one another bites of Mack's dishes. Afterward, they packed everything back into the van and hiked the park's trails, enjoying the fresh spring air.

Too soon, the sun began to set, and they had to head back. As the sky turned golden red, they emerged from the woods and followed the path out of the park. On the way to the van, Amelia walked between the two men. She looked from one to the other and then took one of each of their hands. Jomari and Mack glanced down to where their fingers were laced with hers and then back up. The three of them shared a smile.

The feeling she was missing something returned, but whatever it was, it remained just out of reach. Amelia turned it over and over, and with a start, she knew what it was. She had to talk to Jomari first—he might not be on the same page. But if he was, then they might be opening a whole new door. Calmer now, Amelia swung her hands between her two guys and hoped with all her heart she was right.

They were in the largest of the classrooms at the opera house, the entire collective of what Mack now thought of as his extended family. They'd considered meeting at Trevor, Marlie, and Andre's house, but Marlie had made it clear there was no way everyone would fit. Not only that, their house was currently a mess of boxes. They'd just bought a new, bigger house so Nia could join them, and they didn't close until June.

Instead, Cadence was babysitting at the old house so all the adults could be at the meeting. She'd wanted to come too, but Cian had assured her if she wrote down her ideas, he would bring them. Jamie had only been a little miffed at not being asked to watch their friend Julian's kids as well as Aidan. Cian had talked him down too, telling him he was needed at the meeting this time.

Pizza boxes sat open on the desks at one end of the room, and everyone lounged on the furniture and floor pillows, some dragged from other classrooms. The assembled group was comfortably full, and lazy conversations buzzed among them. Mack stretched his legs and yawned, half listening to Cian talking to Marlie about infant developmental milestones.

Andre cleared his throat, and everyone hushed. "We've all had side conversations for six months now, and I asked you here so we could put our thoughts together in one place. I'll bring the list back to Monty when we meet again. I think we're all together in thinking it hasn't been the same without Grams, but her work was important, and we need to find new ways to do it." Agreement went up around the room. Andre continued, "Everyone wants to reopen more than just the shelter, but we have to do it our way. We've got enough of us, and a couple people experienced in non-profits as well as Monty." He nodded at a few of their friends. "So tonight, we're going to get all our ideas out. Nothing is too weird or impossible right now. Maybe it won't happen, but let's start with our biggest dreams and whittle it down from there."

"A full healthcare team," Marlie said. "And ways to make testing and medication easily accessible." Her eyes briefly shifted toward Nate.

"Additional shelters for people who need a roof or a bed. A way to connect teens with a more permanent residence until they're at least eighteen." That was Nia.

Andre nodded. "A lot of what Grams did, but expanded? Okay. What else?"

"Referrals for more care, like mental health and stuff, but to people who won't mess with us for being queer." Jamie's answer made Mack wonder what he'd encountered, although he'd seemed to like his current therapist, so it probably wasn't her.

Jamie interpreted Cian's signed suggestion. "Cadence says she wants somewhere safe for teens to meet up. A cafe, maybe a bookstore. Not just for teens but available to them. Basically somewhere without alcohol."

"More arts," Nate said. "Expanded theater, music lessons, dance with access for people who can't pay."

"Political lobbying." That was Jomari's idea.

"Yeah," Amelia agreed, "but not like a lot of supposedly inclusive orgs that mostly just cater to 'gay' rights." She used air quotes, and then she looked around. "We've got a lot of different representation here. I want to make sure it stays that way."

"And not just, like, a bunch of white people." Nate's friend and co-director, Del, raised his eyebrows pointedly. "This group isn't totally like that, but yeah, there's a lot of pale people here."

"Right," Andre concurred. "Grams mostly served Black folks, with a few others who heard of her through friends. We probably need to think about how we can at the very least make sure this is safe space or that we have enough Black and other people of color on our board right from the start." He looked up from his laptop, where he'd been typing everyone's answers. "Anything else?"

Mack swallowed. "Recovery. For...addictions." Amelia put her arm around him, and Jomari squeezed his leg.

"Keeping families together or finding them again." Cian's idea, communicated through Jamie. "Programs and classes inclusive to people with disabilities."

Andre tapped the keyboard, adding those suggestions. "Okay. Doing all that is a tall order, but we can get a good start on some of it. Julian and I can put together a smaller, core team. Jagathi will work with Monty to start the process of getting it off the ground financially. It'll take all of us investing what precious little time we have into the project, but there are a lot of us to share the burden."

"Can we really do it?" Trevor asked.

Andre met his gaze, and Mack noticed the way his eyes softened. "None of this is too out there to make it work. We can't do it all in-house. It'll have to be referrals at first or maybe permanently. Something like a cafe or bookstore can't be fully our baby because that's not a non-profit. But yeah, I think we can do it." He swept his hand around. "Look at all of us who want it to happen. We're a community, a family. When we work together, we all bring our gifts to share."

They closed out the meeting. They would need to talk again

and again, but this was only meant for brainstorming. Mack didn't have the means or the connections to do much until they figured out what the next steps were. Andre did, though, and he was on top of it. He had the added bonus of his grandmother's extensive files.

Everyone drifted back into conversation. Some continued talking about the reinvented Project Lighthouse, most didn't. Mack listened to Amelia and Jomari speaking across him, but he didn't register what they were saying. Instead, he was lost in thought about what Andre said at the close of the meeting. *We all bring our gifts to share.*

Did that apply to something more intimate too? Something like Mack's relationship with Amelia and Jomari. He'd wondered lately if he was their third wheel, someone they didn't need intruding on their couplehood. They'd both continued to see Mack, and he indulged them. But he simply didn't have the same feelings with each of them that they obviously had together.

The rainbow rings they'd given each other flashed when they turned their hands in the light. One day, those would be replaced by gold bands, the same as the ones on Nate's and Izzy's hands. Would they still have room in their lives for Mack then? He closed his eyes, not wanting to look anymore. He'd thought this afternoon maybe things had shifted, but they slid right back into what was familiar as soon as they left the park and the warm sunshine behind. Now Mack wasn't sure if the spark was anything more than wishful thinking.

Amelia stopped talking, and Mack cracked one eye open. She smiled. "Jomari and I had an idea of our own. We wondered if you'd like to go back to your apartment and discuss it."

Mack's eyebrows rose. "Oh? What did you have in mind?"

"You'll see," Jomari said, and he exchanged a look with Amelia that Mack couldn't read.

They waited until a few of the others began getting up to leave before they stood. The three of them said goodnight to the others, and then they walked together out into the cool evening. The parking lot was empty, save for their friends' cars. Beside the van, Amelia stopped and put a hand on Mack's arm.

She looked at him, beautiful in the moonlight with her face tilted up. He leaned in, and she slipped her hand to the back of his neck to draw him closer. He kissed her, and then he looked over at Jomari. Mack was surprised when he licked his lips, his face open and interested. Mack shifted to kiss him too, and Jomari sighed against his mouth. When he pulled away, Amelia stepped in.

Watching them together sent a pleasurable shiver up Mack's spine. The spark returned, the unnamed thing he'd felt at the park. He had an idea what these two were up to, and he was definitely on board, as long as they kept their communication open. Not wanting to wait a moment longer, he opened the van door. If he was right, this was going to be a hell of a night.

Chapter Twenty-Seven

Jomari had his overnight bag in Mack's van because he'd thought he would be going back to Amelia's. Neither of them had to work the next morning, a rare treat of both having two days off in a row. They'd arranged it on purpose for the meeting and to spend time together beforehand, but it was still nice.

He set the bag down inside the door. He'd been entirely on board with Amelia's suggestion to go to Mack's instead, especially after what happened in the park. Now, he hesitated. It wasn't a matter of changing his mind. He still wanted to be here with both Mack and Amelia and see where it brought them. It was more that he felt awkward, like he didn't know where to begin.

Hazel's friends had passed along some excellent advice, primarily that the conversation among the three of them would never be finished. There wasn't a point in time when they could decide they didn't need to talk anymore. They collectively had four simultaneous relationships—one between each pair and one inclusive of all three. Any one of them could make choices that hurt the others. Right now, he was afraid they might all end up hurt.

Before he had time to start fixating on what could go wrong, Amelia stepped around him and into the kitchen. She plugged in Mack's tea kettle and grabbed four mugs. "Cocoa or tea?" she asked.

"Um...cocoa?" Jomari knew the instant kind wasn't anywhere

near as good as Mee's, but he didn't care for tea.

"You got it." Amelia pulled two canisters away from the set on the kitchen counter.

Jomari watched with interest as she spooned a rich, dark powder into his mug. "What is that?"

"Homemade cocoa mix. Mack can't stand the instant kind from the store. He does this up himself, and all you need to do is add water."

"You can do that?"

Mack sat down at the table and waved for Jomari to join him. "Yeah, of course. It's not that hard. I'll show you sometime."

Amelia plunked two tea bags into the other mugs and added the water. She brought everything to the table, and they sat quietly sipping their drinks. It all felt cozy and domestic. Jomari was still on edge, but the cocoa soothed him. He didn't know what he'd expected. Maybe that they'd get to Mack's apartment and it would all become some frenzy of ripping clothes off and pouncing on each other. Instead, here they sat, relaxing and enjoying the stillness after the boisterous meeting.

"So," Amelia said, "I made us tea and cocoa to have a chance to talk first. You know, you see it all the time, in books or on TV, where everyone just goes at it like they all know what they're doing and what they want. Not too much conversation. I can't do that. I've done this before, but..." She bit her lip and glanced sideways at Mack. "I haven't always enjoyed it that much. I'm sorry, but it's the truth. On the other hand, it's mostly been with people I didn't know, which matters to me."

Mack nodded. "I didn't know you felt that way. It's something I like, and I didn't realize you didn't. I should've asked."

"It's all right." Amelia took his hand and kissed it. "I agreed every time. I wanted to be with you and do what made you happy, and every time, I figured it would be okay. I didn't ever hate it or feel pressured, if that's what's worrying you. I just thought it was only so-so."

Jomari looked between them and swallowed. "Y-you've both done this before?"

"Yeah." Amelia smiled. "The first time, I was in college. My friend was so into this guy, and we'd gone out to a movie so she could hang out with him. Afterward, she blurted that she'd always wanted to try it. We were all so stupid." She laughed lightly. "It was...kind of terrible? But not? I'm not sure. The poor guy seemed so overwhelmed. Anyway, they did end up together, but we didn't do anything like that again."

Mack chuckled. "God, I remember you telling me about that. Probably one of the least sexy stories we ever shared."

"That and the dickhead from Starbucks," Amelia replied.

"Wait, what?" Jomari gaped at them. "What guy from Starbucks?"

"The skinny blond. Man, he was a massive tool," Mack said.

"Oh, crap." Jomari put his head down on his arms, unsure whether he should laugh or cry.

"I see he got to you too." Mack guffawed. "He's hot but an ass. I think I hooked up with him three or four times before I decided he wasn't worth the effort."

"He's terrible," Jomari agreed, finally looking up. "He's the one who texted his buddies right after. I can't believe you gave him another shot. I was done after the first one."

"I was kind of desperate at the time."

"Enough about that," Amelia said firmly. She took Jomari's hands. "It's okay if you change your mind. No one will be upset. We can spend our night together watching corny movies and cuddling on the couch instead. We could try again some other time, or we could take it off the table as an option. There's no right or wrong here."

Jomari met her gaze then looked to Mack, who gave a single nod. "Every bit of this is new. Before you, I only ever went out with one person at a time. I haven't been with many people at all, and now this. It's a lot." Before either of the others could jump in with more reassurances, he continued. "This is where I want to be. I'd like us to try."

Amelia stood and pushed her chair in. She gathered the empty mugs and washed them, giving everyone some time. When she was done, she turned around and faced the others.

"Go ahead and do what you need to get ready. Let me set some things up, okay?"

She disappeared into the bedroom, and Mack tilted his chin at the bathroom door. "You go first."

Jomari picked up his bag and went into the bathroom. He quickly brushed his teeth before changing. He had his pack'n'play prosthetic, the one he used sometimes when he and Amelia had sex. Jomari liked variety, so he sometimes didn't feel like using it. Mack still wouldn't let anyone top him, but Jomari figured Amelia might be interested tonight, or Mack might like to watch them, so he traded out his stand-to-pee. He pulled on the briefs that kept it in place then dragged loose pajama pants over everything.

Looking in the mirror, he eyed his binder. One of the things he'd done was schedule his surgery, but it wasn't for another couple of months. He didn't mind so much with Mack or Amelia now, knowing they were both conscientious about where and how to touch him. He removed the binder and put his T-shirt back on.

When he came out of the bathroom, the bedroom door was still shut, and Mack was on the couch, reading a book. He set it down when he spotted Jomari and stood, stretching. His shirt rode up and revealed his lean, lightly hair belly. Jomari smiled at the sight. He hoped there would never be a time when he didn't find Mack sexy.

Mack gave him a smug grin on the way past, as if he knew exactly what Jomari had been thinking about. Come to think of it, he probably did. Mack disappeared into the bathroom, and Jomari took his spot. He picked up the book Mack had been reading. Poetry, of course. By someone Jomari had never heard of. He opened to the middle, and the first poem he read made him flush within the first three lines. Hastily, he closed the book and set it on the coffee table.

He'd made up his mind to sneak another peek at it when both the doors opened at the same time. Jomari looked up, and the sight stole his breath. Mack was down to his boxer briefs, his chest bare so all his beautiful ink was revealed. Amelia wore a deep blue lace camisole and matching boy shorts. She'd taken her hair down, and it cascaded over her shoulders. Jomari didn't know where to look; the view was equally good.

The two of them came to stand beside the couch and offered Jomari their hands. He allowed himself to be pulled up, his mind already clouded by arousal. How lucky was he, to have these two wonderful, loving partners to tend to him? He thought he would follow them to the ends of the earth if they asked.

At the door to the bedroom, he gasped. Amelia had turned on electric candles everywhere, bathing the room in a soft, yellow glow. She'd already turned down the covers on the bed. The top of the nightstand was laid out with everything they would need—lube, condoms, toys, and soft cloths to clean up afterward. She'd thought of everything, and it all put Jomari's mind at ease.

He realized what he'd been worried about. With Amelia, this

was how she did things: soft, romantic, tender. She was playful and adventurous, yes, but when Jomari was with her, he felt cherished and nurtured. Mack was heat and electricity, spontaneous and powerful. With him, Jomari felt like he was on top of the world. But now, with them both, he realized the one thing they had in common. They both had a desire to please, but not at their own expense.

Jomari took a deep breath, held out his hands to them, and said, "I'm ready."

Amelia tugged a little, and they all stepped toward the bed. Judging from the look on Jomari's face, he liked what she'd done with the room. She'd seen how nervous he was, which was why she started their night with tea and cocoa. As exciting as it was for her to be all together like this, she also knew it was a risk.

They were so different in bed, she thought. As hot as it was with Jomari, underneath it was his way of making her feel beautiful. She loved sex with Mack, but he was definitely more focused on the getting naked and getting their hands on each other part. Jomari worshipped her body like she was a goddess, and she loved it.

On the other hand, Mack was quicker to get her hot. He treated sex like a good meal. In fact, she'd seen him on occasion eat something the same way he fucked. Which had led to actual fucking. There was no halfway with him, and he never bothered with wooing her. She loved that too.

There was no way to choose between them, which made her wonder how it was going to work tonight. And then it struck her, what they had in common: they both had a hunger for pleasing her, but not in an altruistic way. Jomari wanted her to feel adored, and Mack wanted her to be satisfied, but they expected the same in return. Her lips curled up in a naughty smile. Oh, this night was going to be incredible, and she couldn't wait to have her hands on them.

Jomari was now stretched out in the middle, and Mack flopped next to him, making the bed—and Jomari—bounce. They laughed, and then Mack leaned over and kissed Jomari. Amelia caught a flash of tongue as they both opened their mouths. Jomari groaned, and it was so hot Amelia fanned herself as she stood there watching them.

She'd wanted to for a while, but it had felt...not wrong, exactly, but as though she might be intruding on their privacy. She now understood what Marlie had meant and why it worked better for her to have Jamie there. Marlie wasn't attracted to Jamie in any more than an aesthetic way. Amelia had her two favorite men in the same place at the same time, making out and—

Oh, god. Mack's hand was inside Jomari's pajamas, and Jomari had his between Mack's legs. Amelia was torn on whether to keep watching them, as they were clearly not objecting, or join them. She opted for the second and slid onto the bed behind Jomari.

He moved his hand to reach behind himself and touch her hip before he returned to rubbing Mack through his boxer briefs. Mack pulled away from kissing Jomari to peer around him and smile at Amelia. Jomari let out a frustrated sigh that made Amelia giggle.

Jomari turned over and put his hand on Amelia's cheek. She rested her hand on his waist, and he leaned in to kiss her. She melted into the perfection of his lips on hers. She heard a slight rustle of the sheets as Mack slid closer. Amelia had her eyes closed, but Jomari inhaled sharply, and his kiss faltered, so she assumed Mack was touching him.

Amelia moaned when Jomari's lips traveled from hers down her neck as his hand slid up under her camisole. The pads of his fingers were soft on her breast. He gasped again, pushing his hips into hers, and Mack's answering growl sounded pleased. Jomari tore his lips from Amelia's neck.

"God, I don't even know which one of you to kiss," he complained.

Laughing now, Amelia pushed him gently until he rolled onto his back. She exchanged a glance with Mack, who was now propped on his elbow, reclining on his side.

"Oh, I think we can take care of that problem. Can't we, Mack?"

"Mm-hm. We definitely can."

Amelia slid down Jomari's body and tugged the waistband of his pajamas. "Can I take these off?"

"Yeah."

She pulled them down and took his prosthetic in hand. "Okay?"

"You know I love when you do that," Jomari replied.

Amelia did know. She took him in her mouth just as Mack kissed him. Angling herself so she could look up at his face, Amelia was delighted to see the look of bliss. He was gorgeous like this, and she committed everything to memory to hold onto for later.

She lost track of time as she licked and sucked Jomari and

listened to the men's soft groans of pleasure. She wanted to suck his natural cock too, but it could wait. He'd likely worn the artificial one so he could fuck her, and she needed to give him the chance. They had all night; there would be plenty of time for anything else they wanted to do.

It was never clear later how they orchestrated everything. Not smoothly at first; they had minor wrong notes as the three of them worked out positions and timing. But Amelia didn't mind. They had as long as they needed to figure it all out. All she knew was how much she desired them both.

In the end, they focused on her first. She rode Jomari, with Mack behind her, his arm around her waist, his fingers on her clit, and his hard cock against her back as she came in waves. Beneath her, Jomari's hips rose and fell with his thrusts. She toppled forward, kissing him. He was close too.

She shifted to murmur in his ear, "What do you need?"

He panted, trying to catch his breath so he could say, "I can come like this. Please."

Mack moved around to kiss him, and Amelia remained where she was. Jomari's prosthetic was designed for his pleasure as well as functionality, and she adjusted to let him find the right angle. It felt like hardly any time passed before his breathing sped up and his back arched as he came with Amelia still on top of him and Mack's mouth on his.

She slowly eased herself off him and lay on his right side. Mack was on his left. The two of them took turns kissing him and each other. Jomari looked so relaxed and content, his bronze skin flushed and glistening with sweat. Amelia brushed his bangs off his forehead then looked at Mack.

"Your turn," she said.

Mack licked his lips. Yes, he wanted whatever the two of them were cooking up. He saw the predatory gleam in Amelia's eyes when she told him it was his turn. Jomari's lashes fluttered as he opened his eyes and peered up at the two of them. He looked amused, but it passed quickly as he dragged first Amelia and then Mack into a heated kiss.

"You two are so hot," he said. "I feel like I've been missing out."

Amelia giggled. "You're not so bad yourself. I could happily watch you and Mack making out all night."

Mack leaned over to kiss her. "You'd give this up?"

"Hm," she said. "Maybe not." She reached down and touched Mack's dick, making him shiver. "We should take care of this."

She shifted away from Jomari and pushed on Mack's chest until he lay down. She didn't waste any time, taking him in her mouth and sucking him in the way she knew he liked. He groaned, and his legs were restless with want. When Jomari began fondling Mack's balls, he cried out and had to struggle to keep his ass firmly on the bed so he wouldn't choke Amelia.

The two of them made his whole body feel alive, and he knew what he wanted. A shiver of nerves raced up his spine. He needed it, though. It had been too long, and he wanted to replace painful, angry memories with new and better ones. He pushed on Amelia's shoulder.

"Hey," he said. "C'mere."

She crawled up the bed and kissed him. "Yeah?"

Mack looked at Jomari. "I need..." He took a deep breath. "I want one of you to fuck me."

Amelia nodded. "We can do that." She laid her arm across his chest and pressed in closer.

Jomari held him from the other side. "Which one of us?"

Mack closed his eyes, needing a moment to consider. At last he looked at Jomari and said, "You. Amelia was my first after what happened. I need you to be the one now." He glanced at Amelia. "You understand why?"

"I do, and I agree. I'll help you."

She knew what it was like, and Mack needed her in a way Jomari couldn't do. Not because he wasn't willing or because Mack didn't trust him but because he trusted each of them with different things. He saw on Jomari's face that he, too, understood why it had to be this way.

They both held him and cared for him as together they made him ready. He'd hoped he would be able to do this again, though only ever with either of them. No stranger would ever have that privilege. Mack put himself entirely in their care.

It was incredible, at last having Jomari behind him and Amelia in his arms, kissing him and touching him. He felt a freedom he hadn't in months. He let go of the rage and grief he'd been holding inside, and his body went taut in the suspended moment right before pleasure raced through him. He shook through his orgasm and continued to quiver afterward as he lay between the others.

His limbs were like jelly. Jomari eased out of him, and the two of them stretched him out. He let them move his body as if he were a doll, barely aware of what they were doing. When he'd recovered enough to open his eyes, he watched them cleaning themselves before they both ministered to him.

Amelia used one of the clean cloths to wipe Mack's forehead. "How are you doing? You feel okay?" Her eyes were full of tender concern.

"Y-yeah." Mack took a few slow breaths before he spoke again. "Saint Fiacre in a bottle, that was good."

"Who the hell is Saint Fiacre?" Amelia asked at the same time Jomari said, "Where do you get these weird sayings?"

"Patron saint of STDs," Jomari told Amelia.

"Jesus, I hope we don't need him," she remarked. "But also, how do you even know that?"

Jomari blushed. "Da's family is Irish. I know *all* the Irish saints. Mack, you didn't answer my question."

"I get them from the Big Book of Uncommon Exclamations," Mack replied right before he yawned.

The other two laughed. Amelia said, "There is no such thing."

Mack shrugged against the sheets. "There will be when I write it."

"Speaking of saints," Jomari said. "I have something for you. I'll bring it next time."

"Oh?" Mack raised his eyebrows.

"Yeah. It's a medallion. It's supposed to go on a rosary, but you don't have one, so you can do what you like with it. It's Saint Monica."

Mack pushed himself up on his elbows. "Who is she?"

"Patron saint of alcoholics. I hope that's okay."

Mack smiled, his fondness for Jomari warming his belly. "Yeah. I like that you got her for me."

Jomari bent down and kissed Mack then leaned around to kiss Amelia. She pressed her lips to Mack's, and he sighed. He'd wondered before how their night would go. Sex with them was different. When he and Amelia were together, it was all about trust—allowing each other into physical and emotional spaces no one else had access to. With Jomari, it was what he'd called "wild monkey sex." Goal-oriented, but full of humor and affection.

Mack watched them kiss again, and he understood what made it work between them. When they'd put him in the middle, encircling him and keeping him safe, he saw the way they were similar—focused on his pleasure but without denying themselves. The two of them were so tender and loving with each other that it spilled over into their care for Mack.

He would never love either—or both—of them in the same way they loved each other, and he wasn't sure whether someday he would no longer want or need to be exclusive with them. But here, in this room, he felt their love wash over him, protecting him from his ever-present demons. It was good.

Amelia and Jomari curled around Mack, and he yawned again. They lay naked and unashamed together, and he was glad Amelia had suggested this. There would always be room in their lives for each other, no matter the form that took. His last thought before the world faded away was how very lucky he was to share this time with them.

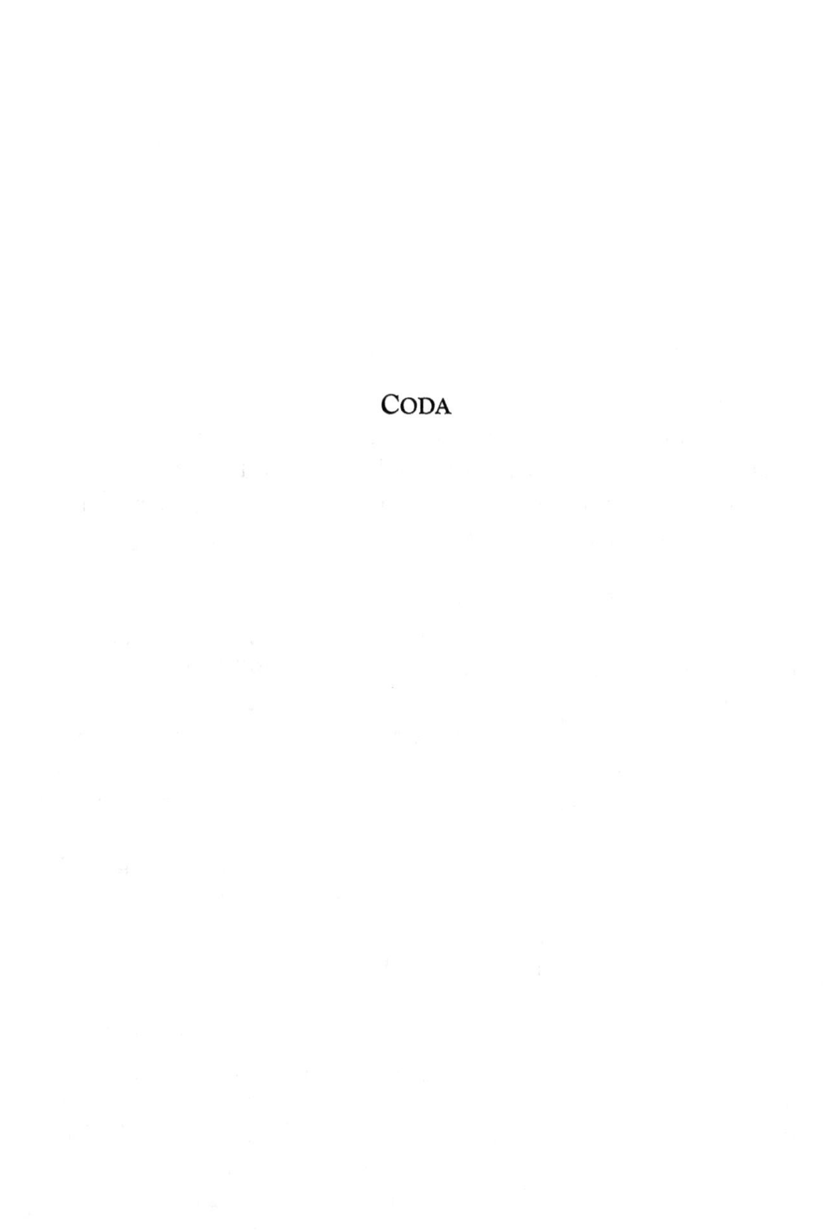

CODA

Four Years Later

A BLINDFOLD covered Mack's eyes, and Jomari and Amelia tugged on his hands. Mack stumbled, but the others made sure he remained upright. It seemed like an interminable trek, during which the ground under him changed from concrete to grass to gravel. At last they stopped.

Amelia yanked off the blindfold, snagging Mack's hair in the process and momentarily distracting him. When he recovered, he looked up and blinked. He was between two buildings. One was a cute little house in a cul-de-sac, surrounded by a generous lawn. The other looked like a couple of those tiny houses pushed together into a single building with a little gravel walkway leading up to it.

Mack turned to the others. "It's nice. So this is your new house?"

Jomari and Amelia exchanged grins. She bounced a little as she replied, "Yes, it's *ours*." She emphasized the word as she made a sweeping motion with her finger to encompass all three of them.

"I don't understand."

"Then let us show you," Jomari said.

He unlocked the smaller house and led them inside. Mack looked around in awe. It was roughly the same size as the apartment Mack had once shared with the guys. The main part of the house had an open layout and was fully furnished. There was a little living room with a couch, a television, and three book shelves, already mostly full. The other half was an eat-in kitchen with a little round table and chairs.

"Follow me," Amelia said, taking Mack's hand again.

He let her lead him into the short hallway, glancing back at the main area to see Jomari still grinning. To Mack's right was a bathroom. No tub, but there was a nice shower and several built-in shelves. To his left were two more rooms. Amelia pushed open the door to the first.

A bedroom, also fully furnished with a dresser, a writing desk, and a king-sized bed, all in neutral colors. Mack was tempted to test out the bed, but his curiosity about the other room won out. He followed Amelia into the hallway, still too surprised to say anything.

That is, until Amelia opened the door to the second room. Mack couldn't hold back the "Holy shit!" that escaped his mouth when he saw it.

His guitars, the ones he'd had in storage, were all lined up on one wall. There were music stands and shelves full of music books and Mack's three-ring binders of his songs. There was a keyboard in the corner, and another desk against the wall opposite the guitars. This one had a computer and minimal sound recording equipment.

Mack faced Amelia and Jomari. "I don't know what to say." He swallowed around the sudden lump in his throat.

Amelia pulled Mack in for a long hug. When she let go, she said again, "This is *our* home. JoJo and I will live in the big house, and you get the in-law apartment. We knew you'd need your space. We're here as long as you want us. Technically, you're listed as renting." She grinned. "So I guess now you're our 'tenant with benefits.'" She made air quotes.

Mack snorted. He turned in a slow circle, thinking about everything he could do here. He'd begun writing songs again, and he'd published a number of them. The same local band who'd bought Trevor's song, the Undertones, had commissioned him. They were fantastic, and Mack loved working with them. It still amused him, and annoyed Trevor, that they'd continued to play "You Draw Me In," but now Mack also enjoyed hearing his own songs performed again.

He returned his attention to Jomari and Amelia. "I can't wait to bring Dad and Louisa for a visit."

"He's doing okay these days?" Jomari asked.

"Yeah. It's always a worry that the cancer will come back, but so far, he's all right." Mack smiled. "If anyone deserves a happy ending, it's him."

Dad had finally put an end to his self-imposed misery. Mom was in a long-term care facility, and Louisa had helped Dad file for divorce. He was financially and physically free, although Mack didn't believe he would ever let go emotionally. He visited Mom regularly. Mack thought Louisa was beyond patient, but she never seemed troubled by any of it. She made Dad happy, and that was all Mack cared about.

"You ready to go over to the other house?" Amelia asked.

"Wait till you see it." Jomari flashed another wide grin.

The gravel path went directly to the larger house, and they made their way back across it. Mack imagined one day, they'd fill their home with visiting friends and neighbors. Maybe Amelia and Jomari would decide to have kids; or maybe they wouldn't. Either way, they'd made it clear—they were a family, and Mack was part of it even if that didn't look the same as most of their friends.

Inside, the larger house looked like a bigger version of Mack's apartment. The layout was similar, except there was a dining room separate from the kitchen and two additional bedrooms and a bathroom upstairs. There was a finished basement, and when they led Mack down into it, he was hit again with delighted surprise.

This, too, was a music room. Jomari's primary violin and his two back-ups were there, as well as Amelia's flute. There was a second keyboard, one of Mack's guitars, three music stands, and shelving for their books and loose pages. The other half of the basement had comfortable old furniture and a small refrigerator.

Something occurred to Mack, and his heart sank. "You did all this for us. But what about Jomari's work? And yours?"

Amelia laughed, startling Mack. "What do you think is on our second floor? I've got a bunch of physio stuff up there. I'll show you in a minute. Besides, I just got a promotion at work, so I probably won't do any consulting for a while."

"But..." Mack turned to Jomari. "I thought you wanted to have your own wood shop."

He shook his head. "I was going to, but I'm taking over for Grandad now that he's semi-retired. He'll still work there, but I am now the proud owner of O'Brien's."

Mack grabbed him in a fierce embrace. He couldn't have been more proud of both of them. Even if the love he had for them was different from what they had together, he was glad to be part of it all.

"When do we all move in?" he asked.

"Any time," Amelia said. "We've started bringing our personal stuff over from the apartment, now the house is set up."

"I figure we should do it soon," Jomari added. "The ribbon cutting on the brand new Lighthouse is coming up, and I'd like us all to be settled by then."

"Good plan," Mack said. "I know our schedules haven't been lining up recently, what with all the time I'm working with Cassie and Laura. I can't believe how busy we are."

"Well, it is wedding season," Amelia said. "I have some time free over the next couple weeks, so maybe we can give each other a hand."

"Sounds good to me."

"Hey," Jomari said. "I'm starving. You want to go grab some food and get started on clearing out the apartments?"

Mack and Amelia agreed, and they stepped out of the house. The others got in Amelia's car, but Mack stood there for another minute, looking around the neighborhood. There were a couple of kids on bikes and an older man clipping his hedges. A woman stopped and waved at him, and he waved back. Mack breathed in the scents of freshly cut grass, spring flowers, and cooking food. He could definitely get used to this.

A light tap on Amelia's car horn brought Mack back to his senses. He grinned and slid into the back seat. Amelia pulled out of the driveway, and they headed up the tree-lined street toward the main road. Mack only looked back once.

Mack was actually wearing a tie. True, he'd paired it with a slightly rumpled button-down shirt and black jeans. Also true, the tie had a skull print. Mack wasn't about to show up to the ribbon cutting dressed like Andre, in a full suit. He did want to look nice for the cameras, though, so he'd gone to a bit of extra trouble. He'd even pulled back his hair and tied it with a black and silver ribbon.

The four former roommates had spent the night together like they had before Nate and Izzy's wedding. This time, they'd all camped out at Mack's place. He was proud to show off his new home. Trevor's voice drifted down the hallway from the kitchen, and Nate answered. Mack stepped into the hallway and pulled the door to his bedroom shut just as Jamie emerged from the bathroom.

Mack had to work not to let his jaw drop. Jamie had always liked to be a bit of a fashion plate, but this was stunning even for them. They had on a pale pink sleeveless dress shirt with several buttons left undone. Their black pants were tight, and they wore black suede sneakers. When Mack finally brought his gaze back to Jamie's face, he was enthralled by the expertly applied smoky eyes and the lip gloss. Jamie had replaced several of their facial jewelry with pink gems that caught the light and sparkled. They'd grown their hair out a little more, and it hung almost to their shoulders in a straight, dark curtain. They scooped it back with their hand and smiled.

"What?"

Mack swallowed any response that might seem inappropriate between friends and simply said, "You look good."

The smile expanded. "Thanks. But I think there might be more you wanted to say."

After opening and closing his mouth a few times, Mack nodded. "This"—he gestured to Jamie's outfit—"is different."

"Mm-hm." Jamie's cheeks reddened.

"Damn." Mack couldn't even come up with a creative swear this time. He cleared his throat.

Jamie laughed. "I've made you speechless. That's got to be a first."

They were doing well. The road was long, but it was paved with more good days than bad. Jamie and Cian had gotten married the previous year, though nothing as elaborate as Nate and Izzy's wedding had been. The two of them had opted for a Justice of the Peace at town hall with only their nearest and dearest present. Mack had been pleased to be among those. He was equally pleased to see Jamie's evolution. They were much more comfortable and confident with themself, and Mack was happy for them.

Trevor came out of the kitchen, wiping his hands on a dish towel. "Everything's cleaned up." He eyed Jamie up and down. "Nice." He drew out the word and leaned in to kiss them.

Jamie stopped him with a hand. "Uh-uh. Don't smear my lip gloss."

Nate was still in his bathrobe, his sandy hair damp and tousled. "Crap. I gotta get moving." He tossed Trevor the other dish towel.

Mack, Trevor, and Jamie tidied up the rest of the house while they waited for Nate, putting everything back where it belonged. So much had changed in the last few years, but Mack was grateful their friendship wasn't one of them.

He was long finished with his two-year degree program, but he wasn't the only one to go back to school. Trevor was working on his degree in education, and Marlie had gotten her license as a nurse practitioner. Jamie hadn't gone full-time, but they'd taken a few classes in media because they were now working behind the camera. Even Amelia had continued her education. Through all of that, they'd learned to lean on each other instead of isolating themselves. It had made their bonds stronger.

Nate must've sped through his morning routine because it seemed like only five minutes later when he emerged, dressed and ready. "All right, let's go!" he hollered.

Trevor emerged from the spare room and shut the door, saying, "I'm coming, I'm coming."

"That's what he said," Nate and Jamie chorused, producing fits of laughter from the four of them. It brought Mack into the past, to the day they all moved in together.

The four of them met Amelia and Jomari outside, and the six of them piled in Mack's van—a brand new lease—and headed into the city toward the Dyer Theatre. The Lighthouse team, with the help of Joyce's endowment, had purchased the adjacent building and turned it into a clinic, shelter, and staff office space.

Fortunately, they were early, but the news stations and a small crowd had already gathered outside. Most of Mack's friends had come ahead to set things up, so the four of them entered the building next to the theater. There would be the ribbon cutting for the public followed by a private party for friends and family at the theatre. Even with only those folks, the number of people was overwhelming.

Inside, Andre was already there, along with Marlie, Nia, and their kids. Aidan, who had remained a sweet, gentle child, was now five and a half. He was sitting on the floor, stacking blocks with Nia's two-year-old. Both Marlie and Nia were pregnant again, and they got a kick out of doing it at the same time. Marlie was due sooner, and she was already worried this baby would arrive early the way Aidan had. Nia was expecting twins. Mack definitely did not envy them the volume of diapers and baby drool in their future.

Izzy wheeled over to them. He didn't always use his chair, but for times like this, he did in order to be guaranteed not to have to stay on his feet too long. Nate bent down to give him a peck on the cheek. They weren't likely to add to their family. Neither of them particularly liked or wanted children, and they had enough on their plates, dealing with Izzy's health issues in particular.

Cian showed up about five minutes later with all three of his siblings in tow. Cadence was home from college for the summer. She was excited to see Amelia and talk about her freshman year in an athletic trainer program. Mack figured after the ribbon cutting, he probably wouldn't see either of them for a while—they could talk each other's ears off. The younger siblings went to help out with the little kids while Cadence stayed with Cian.

Mack and Jamie met up with Cian, who signed something to Jamie. Mack caught about fifty percent of it; his ASL had improved, but he still struggled a bit. From what he got, Cian was asking something about the night before.

Jamie turned to Mack. "He wanted to know if I told you our news last night."

Mack managed to form the sign for *parents*, and Cian replied with a yes. "Jay, what's the sign for 'congratulations'?"

Jamie showed him, and Mack signed it to Cian, who grinned. According to Jamie, one of Cian's partners was willing to carry a baby for the two of them. It sounded more complicated than that, and Mack wasn't sure of all the details. But he did know how excited Jamie was to be able to have their own children. They'd continued to care for the kids in Trevor's family, but it meant so much to Jamie to become a parent. Mack remembered how everyone had once told Jamie that babies don't stay little, and he'd wondered then if Jamie would feel the same about Aidan as he grew. Jamie, maybe to no one's surprise, still adored Aidan.

Amelia and Jomari stuck by Mack, presumably to prevent him escaping to the other building. Cassie and Laura were over there with the catering team. They would pop out to watch the ceremony, but otherwise, they were busy. Mack would join them after the formalities. Initially, Andre had wanted him among the guests for his part in reopening the Lighthouse, but Mack refused. He'd said he was far more comfortable being on the catering team instead, and it would be his contribution to the event. He reminded Andre that he'd said everyone brings their own gifts. Andre was still reluctant, so Mack, Cassie, and Laura let him sample the menu. After that, Andre was fully on board with Mack's role.

Mack gave each of his partners—he felt okay using that word; it didn't feel overly romantic to him—a kiss on the cheek and watched them step away to mingle. He still loved seeing them together; their joy hadn't faded over time. He slid his hand into his pocket to touch the medallion of Saint Monica Jomari had given him when he reached five months sober. He'd now made it to four and a half years, and instead of a token for time passed, he only kept the medallion. He saw every day as a choice, and instead of looking back at how many years had gone by, he preferred to think of it as being watched over and guided to make good decisions—by Saint Monica or the Universe or something else, he didn't really know or care.

All of them became absorbed in making the new building ready for the ribbon cutting and the press tour. The Lighthouse was unofficially already open and operating, to avoid an influx they couldn't handle the minute they became official. However, that was all behind the scenes. Today was a celebration of the hard work it had taken to make it happen.

The Lighthouse didn't have all the programs they'd wanted four years earlier when they were dreaming big. But it had most of what Andre's grandmother had put in place when she opened her clinic and shelter so many decades ago. They'd chosen to have their ceremony on the fiftieth anniversary of the original Lighthouse opening, and it felt exactly right.

The door opened again, letting in a flood of sunshine and making the entry bell tinkle. Mack looked up, as did most of the others. The noise in the room died down. Mack's hands automatically curled into fists.

"What are you doing here?" he asked Sage.

"I came to tell you congratulations." His voice was subdued, so unlike him. Mack didn't trust it.

"Who let you in?" Trevor stepped up next to Mack. "This is for the trustees and volunteers only."

Sage shrugged. "It's not like you have tight security."

"There's a police line you're not supposed to cross." Nate stood on Trevor's other side, his arms folded. He could be menacing when he wanted, with his height and build.

"Well, I crossed it. You might want to think about that." Ah, there was the familiar attitude.

"Which brings me to why you're really here," Mack said.

Sage huffed. "Fine. I told them I was with you. I wanted to see if this was really what you did with your life."

He would never, ever understand. Of course he'd have known about the grand reopening; it had been in the news for weeks. Mack and the others had their names splashed across the media for the work they'd done in getting the Lighthouse up and running again, especially given its history and the anniversary. Sage didn't care about anything except that the people he'd attached himself to in order to ride their wave had moved on. They'd made a name for themselves in a different way than they'd expected, and none of it included Sage.

Jamie stepped forward. Mack reached for them to hold them back, but Trevor put up a hand. Swallowing back what he wanted to say, Mack nodded and let Jamie pass.

"You need to go." Jamie's voice didn't waver.

"But..." Sage protested. He put out his hands, palms up. "People can change, right?"

Jamie acknowledged him with a tilt of their chin. "They can. But sometimes that change has to happen far away from anyone they've hurt."

Sage's expression twisted into the same old cross between a sneer and a pout. "We can't work this out?"

"No."

The word hung in the air, everything else silent. No one moved. Even the children were still, Aidan's hand poised over the block tower. Jamie and Sage faced off, neither backing down.

Mack saw it first, the tiniest tremble in Jamie's fingers where they rested against their pants. Before anything else happened, Mack stepped up next to them. He kept his eyes on Sage, aware of the others shifting only when he heard the faint rustle of their movement. In seconds, Jamie and Mack were flanked by Nate and Trevor, with all the other adults gathered behind the four of them.

And that was it. Without another word, Sage turned around and stormed out. He hadn't won, and he never would. Mack breathed easy knowing neither he nor Jamie were alone. This encounter with Sage wouldn't break either of them.

Slowly, they returned to talking and mingling. Mack stood off to the side, taking a couple of much-needed minutes semi-alone before the big moment. He glanced around at all his assembled friends and family. A few years ago, he wouldn't have pictured this. Yet here he was, among the people he loved most in the world. It wasn't as if they hadn't had difficult times; Sage barging in on them reminded him joy wasn't a bubble to live in forever. But here, in this moment, he thought it was okay to lay it all aside and bask in the present happiness. He could feel all around him that the others were doing the same.

Andre checked his phone and tapped something. He looked

up and yelled, "Monty says five minutes till the ribbon cutting!"

Everyone gathered themselves, and Marlie and Nia scooped up their kids. Cian's siblings helped them clean up the toys and stayed nearby to lend a hand if needed. At last they were all finished, and they gathered by the door just in time. Andre put his hand on it then looked back at the group.

"Let's go make Grams proud," he said, and then he pushed open the door and led them all out into the bright sunshine.

Fine.

ABOUT THE AUTHOR

A.M. Leibowitz is a queer spouse, parent, feminist, and book-lover falling somewhere on the Geek-Nerd Spectrum. They keep warm through the long, cold western New York winters by writing about life, relationships, hope, and happy-for-now endings. Their published fiction includes several novels as well as a number of short works, and their stories have been included in multiple anthologies. They are an occasional host for The BiCast, a podcast for the bi+ community, as well as doing bi+ advocacy work and curating the best-of bi list on the QueerBooksForTeens website. They are a social media contributor for Supposed Crimes, LLC, and they post about news, reviews, and updates. In between, they blog coffee-fueled, quirky commentary on faith, culture, books, chronic illness, and their family.

www.ingramcontent.com/pod-product-compliance
Lightning Source LLC
Chambersburg PA
CBHW070619170726
48291CB00003B/798